Pivotal Shift

A Novel

Don Ellison

This is a work of fiction. All of the characters, names, incidents, organizations, and dialogue in this novel are either the products of the author's imagination or are used fictitiously.

Balboa Press books may be ordered through booksellers or by contacting:

Balboa Press
A Division of Hay House
1663 Liberty Drive
Bloomington, IN 47403
www.balboapress.com
1 (877) 407-4847

Print information available on the last page.

ISBN: 978-1-9822-1003-8 (sc)
ISBN: 978-1-9822-1004-5 (e)

Library of Congress Control Number: 2018910615

Balboa Press rev. date: 11/21/2018

Contents

Acknowledgements

I give thanks to Ed Tillotson for his prompting to write this novel; and his financial backing, for which, this publication would not come to fruition. To my spiritual sister whom I'm ideated for her continued friendship and spiritual experiences that would not have taken place if we had not merged our consciousness; and to her sister who, I hope, has received a small reprieve from a monumental injustice done to her sovereignty. And finally to all others seen and unseen for their help crafting this publication to last for generations to come.

In Light and Love

Preface

This story concerns the deciphering energetic manipulation of individual consciousness, on the wings of Grace. This has been a lifelong pursuit for Ben as his life unfolds before his eyes. He continues to learn that he can rely on the messages he receives from spirit, guides and angels.

"There is more in heaven and earth than in your philosophy"

-Shakespeare

"When you change the way you look at things, the things you look at change"

"Attention to radiance must first be an intense feeling and that, in its turn, must depend on a clear experience. Man cannot love something he does not know. Hence, the belief spoken of implies knowledge."

Chapter One

The Long Journey

Ben Chavez did not feel well. Driving up the San Francisco Peninsula on his commute back from his job as a substitute teacher in development centers and secondary schools, he felt exhausted and dizzy. Back in the city, Ben began to feel truly terrible and retreated to his bedroom. Waking the next afternoon, he found he had slept for 24-hours straight, yet he felt even worse and began to throw up. He decided he had no choice but to go to the emergency room over the hill at San Francisco General Hospital. Slowly, he got up, got dressed, walked to the elevator and descended to the garage to retrieve his car.

San Francisco General was a dismal, turn-of-the-century brick building in the Mission district, but the emergency room was Ben's only option on a substitute teacher's salary, since he didn't have health insurance. As he walked through the doorway, Ben found the right desk and approached the nurse on duty. She saw right away that he was feeling terrible and had him sit down in the lobby area to fill out the necessary forms. Returning the forms to the nurse, Ben waited for about a half an hour before he was seen by a doctor.

The doctor walked in and greeted him, "Hi. Mr. Chavez. My name is Dr. Dicicco. How are you today?"

Ben described the events of the last day. "Actually, I've been feeling terrible for a few days now," he added.

"Let me take some blood and check your blood pressure and temperature, then I'll run some other tests." The doctor said.

Ben agreed. As the doctor took his vitals, Ben began to feel more and more miserable. As he waited for the doctor to return, he closed his eyes and nearly fell asleep in his chair.

The door swung open a short time later, and Dr. Dicicco returned looking puzzled and alarmed. "Your blood pressure is 174 over 174, and you're showing a fever of 105 degrees, but I'm not sure what it is you have at this point – the tests were inconclusive. If you're in agreement, I'm going to admit you to the hospital overnight to bring your blood pressure down and run a few more tests."

Ben frowned. "Well, I don't have insurance. I work part time and I'm currently drawing unemployment."

"That's OK, the state will cover you if you're low income," the doctor explained.

Relieved, Ben agreed.

The hospital was in atrocious condition and it was understaffed because the nurses were on strike for higher wages. Ben found waking up in a hospital with limited staff to be bewildering to say the least. There was no one on duty to answer his questions and he was left in his bed virtually unattended until noon the next day when the doctor came in to look at him. Doctor Dicicco was somber as he explained his diagnosis.

"Mr. Chavez, my findings show that you have childhood dysentery-shigella. You'll need to stay in the hospital for at least three days on a diphtheria diet."

"OK," Ben said dryly, "you have my attention now. But what is shigella and how did I contract it?"

"It's a virus associated with young children. You could have contracted it by being around kids. You're not contagious, but you should stay here for at least three days, so we can monitor you," said the doctor.

He really didn't answer my question, Ben thought. *I'll have to get more information at a later date.*

"I really don't feel well," Ben said and lay back down in the hospital bed. As he tried to fall asleep, he thought to himself, *my karma has caught up with me yet again.*

Ben was soon visited by a social services insurance worker who informed him that that he would have to pay a lot of money for this stay in the hospital. He found this news shocking since the doctor had told him he would not have to pay anything. Then, listening to KGO radio in his hospital bed, he heard about a hotline that could help low income individuals to get state funds. He called and tried to get someone to help him to hold the hospital accountable for their program guidelines. After explaining his situation, which was a daunting task at the time, he convinced them to take on the issue. They called a few days later, saying that the state had miscategorized his stay in the hospital and he would be able stay at no cost. Ben was deeply relieved to hear this news as he had no extra money to spend on hospitals; his rent took priority.

Ben served his time in the hospital and was released in three days' time. He looked forward to taking a shower after the horrendous ordeal in what was called a "hospital." He was still very much under the weather and his energy level had not returned to 100 percent. Looking in the mirror, he thought the weight loss was not a pretty sight, but it would still take a few more days to wean himself off the diphtheria diet. In the hospital, he could only take in chicken broth and Jell-O, but soon he would resume eating solid foods and, hopefully, return to normal. Ben drove slowly back over the hill to his apartment, parked and went inside. After gathering three-day's mail from his mailbox, he decided to walk up the stairs to start his recovery back to normal health and life. As he walked up the stairs, he was struck by the magnificent view of downtown San Francisco, and his mind flashed back to knowledge the city had taught him ten years earlier. The city was a magical place. It had a stong intuitive feeling manifesting unforeseen certcenstances that would change your life in sutle ways.

The Potrero Hill neighborhood of San Francisco was an interesting place to live in the 1970's and 80's. It was a somewhat sleepy little district just south east of downtown San Francisco. Locals called it "Goat Hill," a nickname rooted in its pastoral history of rolling green hills and sheep herds. In Ben's day, the area was still a quiet refuge from the hustle and bustle of commerce down the hill near the Design Center and further down in the Financial District. Ben's apartment was three quarters of the way up the hill on Carolina Street just down from the Russian Orthodox Church. It was quite a place to live. The hillside, across the street was chiseled out to accommodate the apartment sitting at the top of asmall rock cliff. Long stairs, painted stark white, made their way up the side of the small cliff adjoining the apartments above. It was a rustic scene worthy of an old oil painting from an earlier time in history.

Down the hill and around the corner, there was a small lesbian-run deli that served sandwiches named after famous women in history, such as the Roosevelt, the Rosa Parks, and the Imogene Cunningham. Down on 18th Street, there were many small, intimate restaurants and local coffee shops with extensive magazine racks and the work of city artisan on the walls. The local bar was a lively place with a killer view of downtown San Francisco and the Bay Bridge, which had just recently been strung with its famous twinkling lights like a pearl necklace stretched the across the vista on a clear fogless night. The gay community considered this a fabulous tribute to the city. At the other end of 18th, new artists' lofts were cropping up, adding even more color to the area. Around the hill, there was also a small park, a community garden and the second crookedness street in San Francisco; a fact little-known to any but the locals.

Finally home in his apartment, Ben appreciated the view from his window. He was so high up, he felt like he was perched in an eagle's nest overlooking the backyards of the Russian sauna huts down the hill. In the distance, he could see the city's skyline and the magnificent bay. Ben's picture postcard view brought to his mind the Barbara Streisand song "On a Clear Day You Can See Forever." Hecould see from the Golden Gate Bridge to the East Bay, and on days like this one, the clear bluesky and puffy white cloudsmade him appreciate that he was living somewhere truly special. Still weak from the illness, he closed the curtains, sat down in his sofa and fell fast asleep.

Ben had a fighter's spirit. In fact, he was a wrestler in high school and college. He had been a top competitor, winning the nationals several times as well as many state meets. He had done very well in Olympic competition as well. His determination and skill may have stemmed from being a warrior in many cultures in the past as he would find out in future psychic readings and communications with his guides. This determination would serve him well as he faced trials and tribulations in his life. Little did he know what would manifest in the coming year of his life. Little did he know, even at San Francisco State University, in the early days, that he would be directed to lose his identity, values and rearing paradigms. He set out to fulfill this prophecy by joining various groups on campus. This was of course divine intervention as he had gotten telepathic communication about this as a senior in high school on the way to a wrestling match that he would come to San Francisco and experience these changes.

In fact, Ben led a double life: in one, he was a struggling substitute teacher; in the other, he concentrated on his true passion — Metaphysics. His childhood and young adulthood were experiences of a psychic nature that has always motivated him to seek knowledge in organizations that motivated his passion and transmute life challenges and continuing his learning curve expressed by his destiny. His spiritual quest lead Ben into experiences with consciousness studies, holistic food preparation, alterative drugs, martial arts, Tai Chi and creative movement, fine arts, christen mysticism, sociology, psychology and philosophy. One of his eastern religious experiences was practicing Mahayana Buddhist for over four years. Chanting Dimoko reciting the Lotus Sutras every morning and evening with fresh smells of pure incenses was an exzilerating experience. The Gohonzon,the personification of the Buddha,would light up with a golden light as he chanted.

In the 1980's, in his late 20's, Ben pursued an advanced degree at JFC University in San Francisco. He saw this as more of a committed approach to extending his notion of knowledge related to metaphysics. Of course, this would be a pursuit of honing his knowledge into more of a scientific perspective to receive a master's degree. Parapsychology education and art seemed very appealing at the time, to extend his knowledge in the program. Ben was recruited into the program by his undergraduate art professor. Francisco was a brilliant and interesting man, an artist and sculptor from the East Coast. Though he was the head of the art department at SFSU at one time, he had recently been let go as a result of his antiwar activities. Ben met Francisco at the time when anti-Vietnam War protests were happening at most major universities in the country. Francisco was a strong proponent of the anti-war movement and could often be seen on the picket lines confronting the tactical squad, the military component of the police department, making V-lines through the large groups of protesters on campus. When he moved to JFC, he created a master's program and Ben was one of his first recruits. One of his previous students was the now famous contemporary artists – Wiley.

Ben studied for five years, commuting most days across the Golden Gate Bridge to Mill Valley, where he performed work-study, working around Francisco's place doing odd jobs, to supplement his scholarship. He worked diligently to complete a book/thesis for the master degree. There, he also participated in life drawing get-togethers with other students in the program. He especially enjoyed this time drawing and modeling with his classmates.

Many of the members of his program were very interesting "alternative" people who impressed Ben. Renée, for example, was a beautiful former model who had lived in Greenwich Village and modeled for major agencies. When Ben first saw her, she was decked out to the nines in the wildest fashion and on the arm of her African-American boyfriend, an impressive sight for the times. She once invited him to go to a recital with the rock group, Credence Clearwater Revival in Marin County, but Ben was busy and had to decline. That was last time he saw Renée, and he often wondered what happened to her and what she had made of herself.

By the time of his bout with shigella, Ben had been out of school for a number of years and was working as a substitute teacher at a prominent child development center. As a specialist in early childhood development, he took his responsibilities as an educator seriously. He accepted the work as a substitute partially to maneuver himself into full-time position by learning different educational approaches for a variety of young learner populations. He was no stranger to educating older students either; he also substitute taught in secondary schools in San Francisco and other communities. He mostly taught art and physical education, his major and minor as an undergrad. This all came about in advanced studies in education, art and physical education becoming a credentialed teacher, initially.

It was Sunday afternoon, and Ben wasn't totally recovered from his hospital stay yet, but he knew he had to get the shopping done since he would have to get up at the crack of dawn on Monday morning and head down the peninsula again to teach. His roommate was due to walk through the door around three o'clock. Of course, Mark was aware of Ben's three-day hospital stay with shigella. He had commented on how emaciated Ben looked when he had been released from the hospital, worrying that his sunken eyes sockets weight loss that made Ben look like a different person.

Mark walked through the door, flashing a hand to acknowledge he was back.

"Listen," Ben said, "we need to get going to Joe's Market so I can get back to cooking dinner and preparing for the work week."

"So, you're feeling strong enough to shop? Great!" said Mark, "Let's go."

While out shopping at one of the best organic markets in the area, Mark told Ben he'd soon be going on a trip to Europe for three weeks, paid for by his well-to-do parents. Mark had grown up in an affluent upper-middleclass family in Hillsboro, California. He'd attended two of the best schools in the state, Stanford and UCLA, to round out his privileged lifestyle. After graduating in the '60s, Mark had worked on a political campaign for prominent senator Adam 11, managed rock bands, and become an up-and-comer at Channels 4 and 9 along the way. He had a high-strung personality, and with the combination of snorting cocaine after a long day working as a producer-director, his body couldn't handle the stress. His karma eventually caught up with him and he had a stroke at the age of 25. But Ben had to hand it to Mark — he'd had persevered and come back with only a bum hand and foot after learning to talk again. Ben wondered if Mark, being a 22 super master vibration, with its maximum endurance levels, made it possible for him to recover faster than most other vibrations. Learning and practicing numerology for so many years had given Ben some insights into aspects of human nature that Benefited him his entire life. Ben drove Mark to the San Francisco airport the following week, they said their goodbyes, and Mark boarded the plane to Europe.

On the drive back, Ben began to feel feverish and dizzy, and he worried that his had pushed his fragile immune system too hard after leaving the hospital. He tried to rest, but when he woke up in the middle of the night with a fever of one hundred three, he decided to return to the emergency room at San Francisco General. He got there after two o'clock in the morning and was relieved to see there were only a couple of people ahead of him. Surveying the cold and sterile space, he though how stark emergency rooms always are. Looking down at his feet, he noticed drops of blood on the floor, a sign that the nurses' strike was still on. *They could do was a feng shui redecoration program*, Ben thought as he began to doze in his chair.

Soon a young orderly, noticing how weak Ben looked, helped him onto a gurney and wheeled him into a curtained stall. After taking Ben's temperature and blood pressure, the orderly determined Ben needed an IV immediately. The young man repeatedly attempted to put the IV needle in Ben's arm but couldn't find the vein. Ben, delirious and in pain found this funny. "Missed again!" You've been doing this long?" he joked as the flustered orderly stabbed his arm harder each time. For some reason, this made him laugh even harder.

The pain reminded Ben of a James Bond movie he'd seen where the spy was tortured with blows from a knotted rope. After each blow, Bond would laugh and taunt his adversary with a big grin. Delirious and weak, Ben suddenly felt the presence of a pink auric field approaching, and he realized without looking that a seasoned doctor, a woman, had entered the stall. Looking up at her and confirming he was right, Ben wondered how he had known this.

"What's going on here!" she demanded? The embarrassed intern handed her the IV needle and she inserted in Ben's vein as slick as silk.

"How are you feeling?" she asked Ben while softly caressing his arm.

"Could be better."

The doctor explained to Ben that she had checked his records and determined that shigella was not what Ben had contracted earlier.

Incredulous, Ben asked, "What did you say? What do I have then?"

"I don't know," she said, with a disdainful look in her eyes as she stared off into the distance.

Ben spent about an hour in the emergency room recovering and contemplating what the doctor had said to him. *If I had more of my wits to me*, he thought, *I would have asked her name.* He continued to contemplate the misdiagnosis and came to a possible satisfactory answer or conclusion by going deep inside himself and interfacing with his ascended self. *This is one type of situation that smells of psychic manipulation*, he thought. *Did someone try to take me out by giving me a disease; is that even possible?* Ben wondered.

After the incident in the emergency room, Ben felt that his life had entered a new level of awareness; that the proverbial light bulb had gone off in his head. His senses became more attuned to his environment around him and he felt every situation he encountered with new eyes and new awareness. Years later, Ben would think back to this period and it would dawn on him that this was one of the first encroachments on his individual solvency that he could remember — this was when his life had taken a devious turn.

Ben always attributed his compatibility his roommate Mark to the fact that they were both naturally intuitive. Three weeks had passed, and Ben was relieved that Mark would be returning today. Ben's condition hadn't improved, and he could use a friend.

As Mark walked into their apartment he came face-to-face with Ben and stopped in his tracks.

"What happened to you?" he shouted.

In a low tone Ben explained everything that had happened while Mark was away in Europe.

As Ben spoke he could see Mark's eyes worriedly take in his haggard appearance. Ben had lost a considerable amount of weight since Mark left, and he was a shadow of his former self, with sunken eyes, hollow cheekbones and a fragile frame. He looked emaciated and his immune system was not even close to its optimum level.

After hearing Ben's story, Mark told him he was sorry for Ben having to go through all that again. After a while the conversation turned to Mark's trip, and he recounted various details. He told Ben about his positive impression of Scandinavia and described the strange energy he felt in the communist Eastern Bloc countries he visited. The trains there were so boring, tedious, and repressive, he explained, that he slept the whole time he was on them; the energy was that repressive.

"I guess It wasn't the Orient Express," Ben grinning.

Mark arched his eyebrows upward, a smirk on his face.

Ben continued to recuperate from his illness over a period of a month. While at home one morning, he and Mark were having coffee and enjoying the beautiful San Francisco skyline when they heard a buzz on the intercom, letting them know there was someone was at the front door of the apartment. Mark answered, and the voice said, "Hey Ben! It's Karen!" A look of surprise came over Ben's face. *So, Karen was back from Hawaii!*

"Let her in," Ben said to Mark, and soon, Karen, his ex-girlfriend, was standing at the front door. She still looked the same as the last time she appeared to him. She was a strong Italian woman with a curvaceous body and the sort of long, oval-shaped face that most super-masters exhibited. The last time Ben had seen her, she was on her way to the Sheraton Palace Hotel in Waikiki, Honolulu to begin a new job as assistant food and beverage controller. Later, he heard she'd moved to a branch in Oregon.

Ben had been introduced to her by his friend Tom who was personnel director at the Sheraton Palace

San Francisco. Tom once wrote for the Stars & Stripes newspaper for the Army, and he was a very smart man in a down home sort of way. Ben found Karen to be a very interesting, intelligent, and capable person with all the characteristics of a super-master vibration. For example, she got the job in Hawaii on the strength of her charisma and superior speaking skills despite having little relevant experience. In fact, she told Ben she had the ability to role-play with herself before important meetings, imagining her interviewers before meeting them and anticipating their questions and responses, essentially constructing the interview in advance. In this way, she would know what to say in response to each of the employer's questions.

"God!" Ben said, "I couldn't do that."

"Oh, sure you could," she said."It's easy!"

Ben rolled his eyes. "Right."

At one point in their relationship, she fumed to him that her boss had taught her the skills for her new position all wrong and she'd have to learn them all over again. But Ben knew it wouldn't be hard for her; she was brilliant.

Ben had fond memories of the Sheraton. He remembered that the first time he saw it, he thought it was a magical place the Garden Court room. French mirrored doors opened on a huge area with high arched stained-glass ceilings and pink marble Greek columns rotating around a rotunda. It had a feeling of space like no other room in the city. It felt like being back in the 1900s, prominent men, top hats, white gloves and canes. This was back in the day when the hotel's chef was on front cover of Time magazine.

It was also the time when Ben asked Karen if she wanted to have a baby. Ben had experienced a powerful psychic episode wherein a little black-haired girl appeared to him vividly that he was overwhelmed by her intense desire to be born. He thought the experience must have been similar to what women feel like when they want to have a baby, an irresistible feeling coming from a disincarnated being. Ben firmly believed there was a lot more consciousness then we know or believe or understand as human beings, and he took the episode very seriously. Karen, however, would have no part of it, recoiling in horror at the thought. They broke up shortly after that, and the baby was never born.

"Karen, how did you find me?" Ben asked her.

"I looked up Tom when I got back to the city, and he was able to help me find your address." She appraised at him worriedly. "You look like you've been sick," she said.

"Yes, something called shigella — a kind of dysentery, "maybe," Ben replied.

"I'm so sorry" said Karen."Are you all right?"

"Oh yeah," Ben replied, "I'm pretty much over it now."

They had coffee on the balcony and Karen talked about her experiences in Hawaii and at the Oregon Sheraton Palace. She said she hated Hawaii after a while because there was discrimination against mainlanders taking over the island and local jobs. She found the Oregon Sheraton to be much friendlier.

"I took some courses in creative writing at the university to continue my poetry," she said, looking at Ben meaningfully.

Ben remembered that when he and Karen were together, she told him that a psychic had predicted she would publish a small book of poetry in the future. It made sense to him; she loved words.

During their chat, Ben felt Karen moving an energy wave into his auric fields — a love vibration. He started shaking so strongly he could hardly control himself. Karen smiled and stopped her barrage, and Ben settled down again. She indicated she understood what had passed between them with an impish smile. Ben wished he understood her intentions. *I think*, Ben thought, *maybe she's trying to see if I still love her and might try to get me back. Of course that wasn't possible, too much water under the bridge, sort to speak.* His thoughts must have projected, because Karen suddenly stood up.

"Alright guys. I think I'll be on my way. You have a beautiful apartment here and what a view!" And out the door she went. Ben never saw her again.

Shortly after that day, Ben got a call from his friend Gary who told him he'd just moved to the Haight Ashbury neighborhood of San Francisco. In fact, just down the street from Haight Street and Ashbury, the famous center of the hippie movement in the '60s. Gary was, of course, himself a hippie. He had long blonde hair and piercing blue eyes and still wore tie-dyed clothes; Ben was sure he wore a flower in his long hair at some time during the 60s movement. He was also into all things spiritual and metaphysical. After all, he was a double of 11+11 making number 22 vibration. One 11 was a spiritual master but two 11's was a very high master spiritual vibration. As a 22 vibration, he had a scientific perspective and was master of the Earth plane. Gary a very interesting conservationist on a wide range of new age topics such as spiritual politics, new energy devices, UFOs and new healing modalities.

Radionics and Psychotronics as well as various spiritual groups became a part of their discussions. Ben had known Gary since his Buddhist days in Nichren Shoshu, a Japanese Buddhist group. He had used Buddhism to get out of the draft for the Vietnam War. Ben first met Gary on the street one day as he was proselytizing on a corner; termed *shakuku* in Buddhism. He would engage people and invite them to Buddhist meetings, and that's how the two found each other. They became good friends immediately because of their shared interesting metaphysics and the New Age movement.

Gary invited Ben over to his new flat and showed him around. Then he presented him with his latest discovery.

"I want to turn you on to algae water, Ben. It's created by a special process I used to grow ethic white algae."

Ben inspected the jar in Gary's window. It contained white algae and there was a piece of red glass behind it, so the sun could filter through it, in the afternoon.

"Here, Take a swig of this water," Gary said, opening the jar.

After just one sip, Ben's eyes lit up like a powerful drug had just interfaced with his brain cells. Ben stepped back and exclaimed, "What is this stuff!"

Gary laughed and said, "It's just algae water, man."

"Wow! Is this stuff safe to drink?" Ben asked, feeling a clear high that was nothing at all like his drug of choice, marijuana. Having come up through hippie and antiwar culture, neither Ben nor and Gary were strangers to drugs like LSD, marijuana, or ecstasy.

"Oh, it's fine. I've taken it for a long time, said Gary. He explained that he knew a woman down the peninsula that had created a similar version the algae water using cement cubes developed by her chemist father. He called them "David cubes.""

Crystallized sunlight is the way of the future, he explained. "There are a lot of amino acids and B complex in the algae water."

Ben asked to take some home and Gary gave him a small jar of the stuff.

"By the way," Gary said, "I also wanted to turn you on to Cosolargy. It's my sun looking group run by an archaeologist named Gene Canvoy. He created a system of looking at the sun with different colored filters and your biorhythm chart. I've been doing it for a short while and it's amazing. It irradiates the spiritual, physical, mental and emotional bodies with sunlight to raise your vibration and consciousness levels and your life force. Gene's having an introductory meeting at the California Hotel downtown. Do you want to go with me next week?

Ben thought, *I wondered, where he got those globes for eyes. They were big and deep with splendid color. I wonder if he is hiding an extraterrestrial inside.*

"Sure," Ben replied, "it sounds like an interesting idea." Ben was all for raising his consciousness anyway that he could.

"It's on Tuesday. You want to meet at my place or yours?"

"My place at seven," Ben replied.

"OK, but right now I want to tell you about something that happened to me last week. I heard a knock on my door and a guy introduced himself as an ex- CIA agent and asked if he could come in."

Ben was intrigued.

"Well," Gary continued, "I sized the guy up for a moment and decided to see what he was about and let him in."

Ben listened in wonder as Gary told his story. The man identified himself only as "Larry" and told Gary he had learned his name when a colleague in a special PSYOPs program gave him a folder outlining Gary's history. It seems they had been keeping tabs on Gary since his antiwar activities and continued tracking him because of his high psychic spiritual abilities and the special level of consciousness that he exhibited.

"The guy told me I'm off the charts" Gary said.

It seemed they tracked everyone whose abilities showed up on their psychotronic equipment and in some cases remote viewing prospects. Remote viewing is an advanced psychic development process used by the military and the CIA too originally find MIA's anywhere around the planet developed by SRI at Sanford. Gary said the man told him that the CIA had information and technologies almost beyond the imagination. He said they had built on information gathered from the Soviets during the Cold War and discovered in ancient texts they had in their possession.

"The guy told me that they have the ability to suck your life force out of your auric field and hold it in a glass container," Gary said, looking worried.

"What?" Ben asked, shocked.

"Yeah. But here's the scary part. This guy Larry told me that the CIA has psychics trying to tune into my brain waves and auric field to disrupt my consciousness, including my emotions," Gary said in a low voice.

"Wow," was all Ben could say.

"I know," Gary replied. "The agent told me to stop what I was doing and move to another location immediately, and that's why I moved here. I'm on the run. If they know my location, they can tune into my individual frequency and disrupt my mind or draw off my life force. And you don't want to have them drawing off your life force."

"What would happen?" Ben asked.

"Well, it would age you in short time and your body would go into survival mode, drastically reducing your energy levels," Gray explained. This would create a situation where your immune system would be compromised, and you'd be vulnerable to any pathogens in the air."

"What happened to the guy? Larry?" Ben asked.

"Well, Gary said, "my mind was spinning after I heard what he had to say. Almost as soon as I could thank him for the information, he moved towards the door and was gone in a flash. I never saw him again. But I believed him enough to move to a new place."

"Don't worry," Ben said, "I won't tell anyone where you are. But what else are you doing to keep them from tuning into your individual frequency?"

Gary told Ben that he had started researching every alternative he could find to protect himself, even lining his kitchen with tin foil.

Ben and Gary discussed the implications of the man's story and Gary's predicament for a good while. Ben felt bad for his friend. As he left, he slapped Gary on the back and promised again not to breathe a word about the story to anyone. As he was leaving, Gary grabbed him by the arm and said, "Next time we meet, I want to turn you onto the Order of Melchezedeck."

"Sure," Ben replied. He had a lot to think about as drove to his flat while the solar orb was going down.

Chapter Two

Higher Consciousness Reveals It's Self

In those days, San Francisco was in full swing with the New Age movement. One of the touchstones of this interest in the development of personal consciousness was the Samadhi Tank. This was an apparatus created by John Riley, the Famous biologist and dolphin communication linguist. It was the result of cutting-edge consciousness research into the question of what would happen if you cut off all your senses to the world around you. The prevailing view was that, in such a condition, the subject would die, but through the Samadhi Tank, Lily proved that this was not the case. It was basically a closed tank filled with body-temperature salt water in which a subject would float. No light could get into the tank and headphone blocked all sound. The water was the same temperature as the human body, so there was little to feel, nor was there much to smell or taste.

Lilly tested it on himself first and found that the experience did not harm him in any way; instead, it created an environment that heightened focus and facilitated meditation. When Ben first read about the Samadhi Tank he was excited about the possibilities it could afford him to develop his consciousness further. One day, Ben was reading through the Sunday paper and ran across an advertisement for Samadhi Tank sessions at a spa on Van Ness Avenue in San Francisco. He was surprised but overjoyed to run across information on Samadhi Tanks in the local newspaper. He immediately called to make an appointment to try out the tank.

Saturday came fast, and Ben was very excited to try out this famous tank and to experience the possibilities to raise his consciousness. He jumped into his car and headed down to Van Ness Avenue. It was an area that Ben knew well because he often attended the Amron metaphysical center on the same street. It was in an affluent neighborhood with a turn-of-the-century Catholic Church and interesting shops, stores and restaurants. Ben pulled into the parking lot of the Samadhi Center and went inside. He was impressed by the center's well-ordered level of feng shui. It felt like a sanctuary with candles and the scent of incense piercing the air and his nostrils.

Soft sofas and couches created a soft compatible environment, and diffused designer lighting gave a relaxing ambience. The young woman at the desk greeted Ben with a big smile.

"Hello, come on in."

"Hi." said Ben. My name's Ben Chavez. I read about the Samadhi Tank and wanted to experience it for myself."

"Yes, I remember. You made an appointment," she replied pleasantly.

She led him to the dressing room, handed him a towel, and instructed him to take off all of his clothes. Ben got undressed and pushed the com to let the attendant know he was ready. She led him to the tank room and Ben began to feel wary. Peering into the dark steel structure, he thought, *maybe I should rethink this.*

Sensing his nervousness, the attendant attempted to put him at ease. "It's OK. You'll be all right. It's really not as bad as you might think. It's a pleasant trip."

She explained that after he got into the tank, she would close the door and all he had to do was float on the salt water.

"If you have any problems with anything, just talk into the com and I'll come and get you out," she promised.

"OK," said Ben. "I don't think I'll have a problem."

Then he stepped into the warm water and felt the granulation of the salt. The space was small, but big enough for one person. Then he lay back into the water and relaxed, floating on top of the salt.

"OK, I'm closing the door now," the attendant said.

"OK, I'm ready, if I'm not here when you come back to get me I was beamed up onto the ship," he joked.

The attendant chuckled. "OK, I'll be back in an hour."

Ben settled in and tried to go into a deep meditation to wipe out the idea of being in a metal box. *Boy this water is hard... I've never realized water could be so hard*, he thought. It wasn't like lying in a comfortable bed. Ben tried to relax as much as he could and finally got into a somewhat comfortable position. Suddenly, he felt a negative thought arrive. *If I get anything out of this experience I'll be surprised.* He couldn't keep it out — the negative thought plundered through his mind. Suddenly, a waveform shot through his body and disrupted his whole structure with a jerk, creating a small wave in the tank. It was like an automatic response to the negative thought. *God, one negative thought created an energy wave that disrupted my whole system. Now I understand how important it was to keep your thoughts positive.* Ben made sure to keep his thoughts positive for the rest of his time in the tank.

As he floated, Ben thought, *Well, I'm not dead yet. I'll try a meditation/visualization.* He decided he would try and contact the eighth chakra, the Christ center, to see what effects it would have, since he had done this visualization many times before. He used consciousness like a flashlight to locate the Christ center and bring down the atomic energy. Seeing the sun orb, it released its plasma, once again instantaneously through the top of his head on through his body and through his feet. The charge was really powerful this time. It reverberated in every corner of his body and consciousness, and he experienced a powerful mental energy in the tank. He continued his involvement in the Samadhi experience. *If I could afford it, I would come here every chance I got*, Ben thought.

As the heavy metal door opened, Ben felt the cool breeze waft past him. *Back to three-dimensional life*, he thought as he lifted himself out of the tank.

"I see you're still here. Did you get a chance to go up on the ship?" the attendant asked with a grin.

"Oh, not this time," Ben replied with a big smile.

"Here's your towel. Be careful to get your footing. Some people aren't grounded when they come out of the tank," the attendant said.

"I'm fine, Ben replied."I've meditated for a number of years and taken acid. I've learned to ground myself when I need to. I also looked at the sun, and I have a pretty balanced consciousness.

"Good. How did you like the tank?" she asked as they walked to the changing room.

"It was very interesting. He replied. "I had an experience of having a negative thought in the tank and I didn't do that again."

"I know what you mean," the attendant said. "I've had that experience myself."

"But the meditation I did in there was powerful," said Ben.

"Yes, it can be very powerful." She replied and left Ben to get dressed.

Ben later thought about what he had read in a book by U.S. Anderson where he described Lilly taking acid and going into the Samadhi Tank and returning with his mind intact. He said that his guide told him that it was a risky and dangerous way to raise his consciousness. *He must've had nerves of steel*, Ben thought,and out the door he went.

Ben arriving home got a call from Gary and said he would over in a couple of hours. He had something important he wanted to talk to Ben about.

Ben buzzed Gary in and opened the front door, to let him in when he got off the elevator.

They went to the balcony and sat down. Ben could see Gary had something important on his mind leaned forward in the lounge chair.

"So, Ben, I wanted to turn you on to Cosolargy because it is a great way to raise your consciousness," Gary began.

"Yeah, I know, you mentioned a few details over the phone.

OK, what's the practice, Ben through into the conversation.

Gary hesitated and said, "Let's get going to the lecture and Ill fill you in on more of the details on the way."

"Okay," said Ben, "I'm game."

By that time it was evening, and Ben and Gary drove to the Cosolargy meeting together. As Ben drove, Gary filled him in on a few of the sign-up procedures. He explained that new members had to be sponsored by someone in the group. There would also be a questionnaire to fill out, and the different levels of Ben's aura and chakras would be read to determine where his consciousness fell on their levels chart.

The lobby of the California Hotel was a spacious, with art deco décor from the 1930s and heavy, dark stylish hardwood furniture of the period. Ben thought it was the kind of lobby he would feel comfortable sitting in and reading the paper nestled among the fichus trees that stood comfortably beside the ornately upholstered chairs and couches. They made their way across the lobby and followed the signs to the conference were Gene Canvoy was lecturing. Taking their seats in folding chairs near the front, Ben observed Canvoy. He was a small Latino man dressed in slacks, a sports jacket and a well-tailored plaid shirt. Ben considered himself a keen judge of character and noted that Canvoy was quite low key. *He doesn't carry himself like a man who is world-renowned in his field*, Ben thought to himself. In particular, his personality didn't express the dynamic personality of a master vibration or someone with an enlightened presence. He had no light expression emanating from his auric field as most enlightened charismatic individuals of power have. On the other hand, Ben thought, he was a warm and personable speaker.

Cosolargy had a multifaceted history. They were very progressive and dealt with theological issues expressing some concepts of Christ consciousness and the truths of the Bible. Canvoy was an archeologist whose team had found ancient texts and artifacts in Peruvian ruins that he believed pertained to the Garden of Eden as referenced in the Book of Revelations. After submitting the documents to a scholar for authentication, the Cosarlogists published a revised version of that part of the Bible. Ben bought a copy later on when he became a member. He found it to be very interesting reading.

Canvoy also investigated specific information pertaining to the ancient sun worshiping practices of a Peruvian tribe he studied. He had taken the tribe's practices and integrated it into a biorhythm chart, and developed different colored filters expressing specific nanometer frequencies for observing the sun in the morning, midday, and afternoon. According to Canvoy you irradiated your emotional body in the morning, your mental body at high noon and the physical body in the afternoon. This meant you could raise your levels of consciousness to a high balance plateau reaching a spiritual balance and feed more energy to your light body, and your IM present, or Mererba self — whatever term you related to in your practice.

After the lecture ended, they spoke for a while. Ben told Gary that he thought this practice sounded interesting, but he questioned whether it really worked.

"Well, it works for me," replied Gary. "I can now look at the sun for an hour without filters, and it has raised my physical and emotional bodies off the charts. My psychic abilities too. Right now, I can hear what your thoughts are. In fact, I almost always know when someone is talking about me anywhere. Plus, my precognitive dreams come true most of the time."

"This is from looking at the sun?" Ben asked.

"I believe so. I get information by communicating with the solar orb," Gary replied confidently.

Ben was always open to new practices that could open and expand reality, so Gary's testimony was music to his ears. "It sounds really good to me. I want to try it. What do I have to do to sign up?"

Gary made his way to the front of the small group of about 20 or 30 people, with Ben in tow. Gary walked up Canvoy, introduced Ben, and told him he was interested in joining the group. Canvoy looked at Ben with a big smile and said, "OK!" Then he gave Ben a huge hug, an aspect of compassion Ben had not seen in the course of the lecture. He handed Ben an application form and told him to fill it out and send it in so that Ben could be evaluated.

"What are you evaluating?" asked Ben.

Canvoy replied, "We do an in-depth reading of your chakras and auric energy field levels to determine what spiritual levels we need to help you with and set you on the path to developing your consciousness. We also have a numeral breakdown to determine what energetic level your chakras are functioning at. I use colored gems from the ancient **Vedic** system to determine your frequency levels."

Impressed, Ben thanked him, and he and Gary and left the conference room.

In hindsight, Ben wished he had talked with Canvoy a bit longer as he would never have the chance to speak with him again.

A couple weeks passed, and Ben received an envelope in the mail. He opened it and looked at the information inside. The letter from Canvoy said: "Thank you for your inquiry. Enclosed you will find a frequency colors/ reading of your force centers and an application for consideration. I have nominated you out of a large number response. You can find out more about me by looking up my name in *Who's Who in America* or *Who's in the World*."

There was other information included with the letter, such as incidents of color and energy in each of the eight force centers and the seven chakras and the Christ consciousness centers above the head.

Well, I guess I made in an impression on him at the lecture, Ben mused.

Later he received several small books about their research program – Project X: the search for immortality. The first books summarized Canvoy's experience exploring the Peruvian ruins, and the knowledge he found there. There was also a book that covered the creation of Jamilian University and one on Canvoy's spiritual quests around the world.

Ben had received the materials to start the practice of looking at the sun a month after the Canvoy's letter. *Let's see, the first thing I need to do is create a biorhythm chart*, Ben thought to himself as he looked over the materials. The manual laid out a complex method for constructing a chart. *God, this is hard*, Ben thought. *How do I begin? How am I supposed to start off the chart from my birthday?* He reread the material several times and still couldn't figure it out. Finally, he called Gary in frustration.

"Don't worry," Gary said. "I had the same problem when I went to make my chart. What you need to do is start the chart with a positive upward movement of the sang wave. This is because we all start out life on a positive upward footing when we are first born."

"I see now," Ben said, relieved. "OK, Gary, thanks for your help. Your super master vibration always figures out the logic and solution to problems easily."

Ben went ahead and started his biorhythm chart on with ascending swing on the sang wave. Ascending emotional, physical or mental rhythms meant that you needed to look at the sun with a particular color filter at that time of day. You looked at the sun for the physical body, in the afternoon with the violet filter and the mental body, at high noon with the yellow filter. This day Ben had to look at the sun in the morning with the blue filter to irradiate the emotional body according to his biorhythm chart. It was still morning, so Ben went out to the balcony, lay on his back, as described in the manuals, and used the blue filter to look at the sun for 60 seconds, the recommended length of time to look in the beginning. He really didn't feel much of anything after looking at the sun, but he continued looking at the morning sun every other day until the sang wave moved upward, signifying a swing into a more positive biorhythm. After a while, he could always tell he'd had enough sun a he would begin to see spots before his eyes or he would feel that he couldn't bring in any more sunlight into his body. He was full, so to speak. He also had to remember to massage the back part of his head when he got a headache because sunlight tended to crystallize at the back of the skull, though this was a minor and rare occurrence.

According the Canvoy's theories, Ben was actually feeding himself the power of the solar orb and it would take a digestion period of about a year and a half before he would feel any lasting effects. As it turned out, Ben felt some effects after a short while. For example, he started feeling rushes of energy up and down his frame and the sunlight radiating the cells of his body had the effect of a warm soothing vibration that mimicked eating chocolate. Ben thought of the feeling as "solar love." He continued the practice for the recommended year and a half, and it led to much more unusual experiences than solar love. In fact, he began to undergo channeled experiences wherein an extraterrestrial being, or ET, was dropping into his body.

One day, Ben was looking out his picture window enjoying the blue sky and the puffy white clouds when all of a sudden, he saw a flash of penlight intersect his eyes. For some reason, he felt strongly that it could be an extraterrestrial, or ET, craft. He focused intently on the cloud and tried to communicate with the spacecraft he suspected was camouflaged there. Then he felt it — a powerful energy dropped into his body. As his eyes grew as large as saucers, he felt a powerful energy anchor itself to his frame.

"I'm commander Aton of the Astara fleet," the energy communicated to Ben.

"My name's Ben," Ben replied through thought.

"We know who you are," was the reply. "We are here to monitor the mind control and manipulation of humanity that is occurring on your planet. We intend to periodically enter your body to conduct our surveillance."

Then Ben felt a dropping in Plumb Bob sensation and also a snuggle in sensation.

"We will use these techniques to enter your physical body," the being continued.

There were other processes that were not clear to Ben.

"Please continue serving the needs of the Astara Command. Your government now has the technology to control the emotional body level on your planet. This is the continuing process of the suppression of human beings consciousnesses on Gaia. We have seen it on other planets and wish to help your planet rid itself of this evil influence, for the total expansion of the consciousness of human kind. We will continue to communicate with you from time to time. Love be with you always, Astara Command – commander Aton."

Then he was gone as quickly as he had arrived, and Ben came back to his own consciousness.

Needless to say, Ben was stunned. Though he did not feel violated, he still thought to himself, *What right does this being have to drop into my body and control me, or even communicate with me?* However, shortly afterwards, Ben had a dream where he willingly signed a contract with Astara Command to let them use his body for surveillance purposes. He eventually accepted that he was helping humanity by serving as a host to the beings, and he would grow used to the experience.

In fact, at no time was he ever afraid of the beings dropping into his body. Though he didn't understand the mechanics, he understood implicitly that it was a noninvasive form of channeling.

The Astara Command was a group of extraterrestrials called Arterians that were part of the Galactic Federation. One of this group's goals was the liberation of planet Earth, or Gaia as they called it-Ascension. They were known throughout the universe as master healers that have created light chambers where we will be rejuvenated, transforming into our full consciousness, according to Sheldon Neidl, a spiritual communicator... when the light forces land on the planet. You see we have a reprieve from God for these beings to help us to reconstitute back into our full consciousness. Little did Ben know at the time that these alterative experiences would raise his consciousness to a higher level. Ben remembered a small pamphlet he had picked once written by a woman named Tuwella about her channeled information from Astara Command that gave more information about their group. Other sources' have also mentioned Astara command before in the literature.

Ben certainly was well read in this field having other experiences with this phenomenon as well. UFO's and extratessrestrail are well documented in alterative sources as a cultural phenomenon with a large part of the sociality believing in the possibility that this manifestation is real.

Channeling is well documented with the advent of John Climo's book of the same name.

Ben would continue to have other experience with ET's in the future.

I shouldn't have any problem convincing my friends of my experience, thought Ben.
The Astara Command would become involved in Ben's life going forward, but not long after their first contact with him, he was invited to meet another group that would become important in his life. Gary called and invited him to attend the Order of Melchezedeck's Sunday service. Ben agreed, and they made an appointment to meet at Gary's apartment in the Haight on Sunday morning.

During their ride to the California Hotel, Ben told Gary about the member of Astara Command that channeled into him.

Uncharacteristically expressionless, Gary replied flatly, "I've heard of that group," leaving Ben wondering what he knew.

They took their seats in the hotel's conference room around 11 am along with about 20 other people. The façade flower design around the room created a comfortable, homely feeling. Soft music was playing that added to the ambience of the environment. Shortly, a small white-haired woman came walking down the aisle towards the podium, and the Sunday service of the order of Melchezedeck began.

As Dr. Grace Petticot's sermon intensified, her voice grew to a boom, and Ben began to perceive this tiny lady expanding – puffing up like an inflated doll. This wasn't like a spirit possession; rather, it seemed to Ben that a divine energy had entered her body. *God works in strange ways, he thought to himself.* Dr. Petticot's voice was like wild storms carrying the message of truth personified into a powerful omnipresence. She interpreted current events through a spiritual perspective that Ben had never heard before. She had an uncanny way of dropping her personal experiences into her message as she spoke. Ben remembered her saying that she was sitting, looking out her open window in England and seeing Billy Graham walking by the window just below her. She pitched her voice out the window and said, "Billy, why haven't you told the people the truth about themselves – that we are all God."

He replied, "The people are not ready to hear this message of truth."

With a disgruntled expression on her face, she told the audience, "He has something to hide. An alternative agenda, that the people cannot be free until they know God fully and develop more faith." Naming several orthodox religious groups, she asked, "Where have I heard this before?"

Ben was impressed.

When the service was over, Gary introduced Ben to Dr. Petticot. She looked above Ben's head and spoke, not to him, but to the being she seemed to perceive ascended over him. "Hello," she said enthusiastically, nice to meet you!"

She shook Ben's hand but continued looking above his head.

I wish I knew who she was talking to, Ben thought.

"I see from your bulletin that you're conducting a numerology class soon," Ben said, knowing through Gary she'd written a book on the subject.

"Well yes, would you like to attend?" She asked.

"Very much so."

"Great! See my assistant at the table over there. She has all the information you'll need," she told Ben, or whoever was above him.

Grace, as Ben would later know her, was an international lecturer and a religious scholar of the Christian faith, especially Christ consciousness. The other books she had written — on color theory, astrology, the Tarot and various treaties on Christ consciousness – were bestsellers in the religious community. The Order of Melchezedeck was an expression of her interpretation of the Christian faith. Melchezedeck came before Jesus Christ to lay the way for his coming. He is referenced in the first part of the Old Testament. In addition to the Order of Melchezedeck, Grace was connected with Grace Cathedral and the Lutheran lineage of religious persuasion. These were very progressive groups and Ben had walked the Labyrinth on many occasions at the church at the top of Nob Hill. Ben soon began attending Grace's classes and the Order's Sunday services. This was a life-changing group for Ben, as he met some people who would forward his spiritual development and become lifelong friends. They would also fill in for him some of the puzzle pieces surrounding the suppression of human consciousness and spiritual processes of awaking the spiritual human spirit.

For example, Dan met Len and Tom through the Order, and in many ways and for many reasons, they both became like brothers to Ben. Tom was a San Francisco sheriff and Len was a retired FBI agent. Little did he know in those early days of their relationship how important they would be in revealing to him the how deeply he was being deceived and the extent to which his mind was being controlled.

Others in the Melchezedeck Order family included Robbie, Diane, Eric, Bill and Lance. Although they were all very well-known in Bay Area alternative spiritual circles for their complete dedication to Christ consciousness, they had other New Age and spiritual interests as well. Robbie and Diana, for instance, were a couple with a strong belief in the spiritual practices described in the movie and novel *Dune*, practicing the Bene Gesserit style of metaphysical arts of the ancient female religious group depicted in them. Steve was reared Catholic who would attend orthodox religious groups when Grace asked him to; he was her eyes and ears at these meetings. He was also very involved in the study of the Uranita book and facilitated study groups for years expressing his super master vibration number 22. And, of course, there was Carlos, a very well-known choreographer for a dance troupe named Spectrum. They would compete with alternative Ad-Vanguard dance groups in the city. Ben saw them perform the dance of Shiva at Stern Grove, and he thought they were fantastic. The whole group would drop in for Sunday service most of the time. There were also spectacular people that would rotate through the service that were internationally known as well; grace had a reputation.

For a time, a young French painter attended the group, and she had painted Grace's portrait. Ben was later given a copy of the painting, and this became a prized memento after Grace's death. Ben Spent two more years with the group before moving on after Grace passed away from natural causes. He felt privileged to have met this great spiritual personality in this life time.

Ben continued his practice of looking at the sun off and on for about 10 years. One of the most impressive experiences he had while interfacing with the sun was when he met a Mayan in the 80's.Gene Canvoy was an expert in Peruvian culture and spiritual practices, and Ben decided to research them as well. He acquired as many Mayan and Aztec references as he could at the library and learned as much as he could. One day, he checked his biorhythm chart, selected his violet filters and reclined on the living room floor as the sun was coming through the West window. He opened the window knowing that glass cut some of the solar orb's wavelengths, exposed himself to the full effects of the solar winds all of the waveforms — the long and short.

Closing his eyes to let them acclimate to the warm sun, he opened them to take in the full force of the light. At that moment, his mind registered an Aztec warrior with a full feathered headdress, leather loincloths, magnificent jewelry on his wrists and ankles, a chest of gold and a special tooled colored gem necklace. This being was standing with his arms and legs pressed against the walls and floor of a square tube-like structure. He seemed to be looking at the sun and then Ben realized that he was trying to take in the solar winds to astral project his light body self – his Merkiba, out of his body to shoot his consciousness through the Gateway of the Sun.

The Gateway of the Sun is an ancient Andean structure, part of which survived to modern times. Ben had read about it during his research and had seen a television documentary on it at one point. He recalled that archeologists believed it may have been part of a much large structure surrounding a square tunnel. Ben didn't know that much about the gateway, but he perceived that both he and this Aztec being were related to it in some way. This image of the Aztec and the tunnel seemed to him like an ancient memory coming up from the depths of his subconscious mind.

He always had a fondness for Aztec culture but didn't understand why. Maybe this was an inkling of a past incarnation's relationship to it. Mel Gibson had recently made a movie depicting Aztec culture and the different classes that were structured into the Aztec hierarchy. Ben really related to the warrior classes depicted in the movie. He had a strong feeling that he was in that culture at one time in world history; and who knows, maybe he was.

Chapter Three

Tools For Transformation

In the late 80's Ben became part of a crystal healing group. He had been a part of the group for about a year when he got talking to his friends Liz and Ann about his personal experiences with scanners and being in the hospital with shigella. He told them what the doctor said about the disease he supposedly had.

Liz looked him in the eyes and said, "That wasn't shigella, "they have been irradiating your head for about four years now."

Confused, Ben stammered, "OK... How do you know that?" said Ben. He'd heard Liz had some psychic abilities, but this was something different.

She said nothing in reply.

Later, a mutual friend explained that Liz was a very powerful psychic who had participated in a program that experimented with projecting noxious energies through psychic subjects' bodies then projecting and directing the energy towards others to disrupt their emotional and physical levels. She explained that Liz's internal organs had begun to malfunction as a result of the experiment, putting her in the hospital. Liz later recovered, and they were able to resolve that problem with her and other subjects that were affected by the noxious energies coming into their bodies.

This corresponded with what Ben had intuitively sensed for a while now; namely, that something or someone was interfering with his consciousness. The information about the experiments Liz had participated in was a confirmation that something might really be happening to him. If his suspicions were correct, he had to wonder how long and how often he was being interfered with and who was behind it. As he started paying more attention to what was going on around him, the pieces of the puzzle started falling into place. He wondered if it was really possible that the proverbial "they" were really trying to stop him from pursuing his spiritual and psychic quest. Was there other evidence that pointed to the manipulation of his life lurking in his memory banks? Looking at the sun had made him very sensitive to feeling subtle energies – ELF frequencies in the radionics and psychotronics sense – and even subtler vibrations.

His mind raced through other memories in search of clues. Was the incident in a café one day on 16th St. and Mission an example of a puzzle piece? Standing in line waiting to get a coffee, Ben felt his head go numb. Then he felt someone clearly tugging at the new purple sweater he had strung through his backpack strap. He felt frozen and blank as he felt the sweater give way, yet he couldn't respond or check to see if the sweater was still with him. It wasn't until he collected his coffee and sat at a table that he was finally able to confirm that his sweater was long gone. Ben was confused. What had caused him to freeze both physically and mentally? Why did no one else in line intervene? It seemed that he had been psychically manipulated somehow, but he did not have enough information at the time to guess how,

Another memory flashed into Ben's conscious mind. There was another, similar event. He was standing on the 22 Fillmore bus holding the rail bar. Ben again became aware that his head was becoming numb, and he lost all memory of where he was going; he went blank. This was an upsetting feeling, forgetting where he was and not knowing where he was going. He later thought it must have been similar to what Alzheimer's patients feel when they lose their memory. He thought, *I'm being psychically manipulated. How am I going to get out of this?* Just then, Ben's rational mind kicked in and he decided to get off at the next stop. As he pulled the stop-line and got off the bus, his memory returned, and he remembered where he was and where he was going. He got on the next bus and continued to his destination. Looking back on it, he wondered why this experience hadn't filled him with fear. Instead, he had almost forgotten about it. Now he wondered: *Are they really that advanced? Can they manipulate me that easily?* Studying parapsychology was becoming more and more important to Ben all the time.

One more memory came to him. As Ben was driving to the store in the Castro, he stopped at a streetlight on 17th and Mission. As he waited, he saw the light turn from red to green and he started into the intersection. Suddenly a voice said to him, "stop" and he slammed on his brake as another car blasted through the intersection from his left and disappearing into the distance to his right. Ben realized his light was not green but red. He looked in his rearview mirror and tuned into the driver behind him. Yes, energy was coming from this car. Ben mentally projected a spinning conic wave form around the car and the noxious energy collided as it had done many times before.

At that point in the development of his intuitive and psychic abilities, he could tune into a person and feel psychotronic bombardment coming from any location. After continued practice of looking at the sun, he had the ability to affect the person, sometimes projecting a laser beam at their middle eye, taught to him by a yogi at UCLA and sometimes at the energy coming through the radio in their car. Sometimes this would work to disrupt their energy barrage and sometimes it wouldn't. Ben continued to prefect his craft of visualization through trial and error and had reached a professional level that fit almost every situation with the help of his guides.

At that point Ben would make a game of the scanners manipulation while he was driving. He would feel the energy as a car was coming up behind him at a stop light or sign and deliberately focus on going right or left. Every time, he would watch them signal a turn in that direction, but he'd go the other way. After doing this manipulation a few times, they stopped following him around and trying to disrupt him in this way. The pieces of the puzzle were starting to form a rational picture now.

It was at the end of the year and a half time digestion period for looking at the sun. Ben didn't know how it happened but one day after looking at the sun he went through a total transformation physiologically, psychologically and spiritually. Ben's physical senses opened up, for lack of better terminology –his hearing was acute, his smell was more dynamic and his sight was perfect – 20/20; in watch he had naturally already. Virtually, all his psychic senses were also open; his clairvoyance, clairsentience and clairaudience were giving additional information to his senses, allowing him to perceive subtle energies.

As he met different individuals, he could see their spiritual light energy emanating off their being that was reflecting in his consciousness. That subtle perception helped him develop his dowsing skills. Later in Ben's life he would become very involved in the Dowsing/ Devining field. Ben's intuitive-PSI sense was also highly developed. Ben continued his reflection, he even started taking a shower in the morning before work. *This was weird,* Ben thought. He had a compulsion to be clean. I wonder if the saying "cleanliness is close to godliness" applied here. It was as if Ben had come out of the fog into the light. Everything was crystal clear and clean as perceived from Ben's consciousness. And most importantly, Ben's energy level was much higher. *I love transformation*, thought Ben. Ben's empathic senses were in full bloom now and would further help him defeat the forces railing against him, trying to remove him from the planet.

Ben picked Gary up at his place and they headed down to the California Hotel in downtown San Francisco for Grace's Tuesday evening numerological class. Because Ben went to college in San Francisco he knew just about every street in the area. They dropped out on Market Street parallel to the cable car tracks, went down Market for few blocks then crossed 8th Street towards the Nob Hill district. On the way, Gary told Ben about recent interaction he'd had with Gene Canvoy.

He said, "I want to go to Gene's Cosolargy retreat in Hawaii, but I don't have the money. Could you lend me the money, Ben?"

Ben had recently received four thousand dollars from his great grandmother, Nanny, after she passed at the age of 89. Ben thought for a minute about Gary's request and replied, "How much do you need?"

Gary said, "Two thousand would make it comfortable for me to stay for about eight to ten days." At the time, that was a lot of money for Ben, but he thought about how Gary had helped him by introducing him to Cosolargy, the Order of Melchezedeck and other spiritual ideas and practices. He also knew Gary had landed a good job in sales and was good at it, being an excellent communicator. Being a super master vibration gave Gary the endurance to spend long grueling hours working, Ben thought. But in the end, he just trusted Gary.

"OK, I'll write you a check, but you have to pay me back as soon as you can after you get back from your trip," Ben said.

"OK, Gary promised, "I won't let you down." He had to leave at the end of the week, so they agreed to meet so Ben could give him the check.

They pulled into parking space across from the California hotel and walked quickly inside, as Grace didn't like people to be late to her classes. She was from the old school, and considered this a character flaw. Grace started with a short meditation to bring in the Christ consciousness energy. It was a common process in this Christian spiritual organization. Their focus on the seven chakras was an Eastern meditation process with the exception of the eighth chakra, the Christ consciousness center where they brought down the atomic energy of the Christ into the ethic chakras through the body. Ben had experiences in energy coming down to the chakras, and he'd also experienced kundalini energy coming up the spine when he looked at the sun. But he hadn't known that the atomic energy of the Christ was a meditation that the mystics of the early Christian church practiced.

Then Grace started lecturing about numbers starting with the number one, the monad. She continued with the spiritual and practical implications of the numbers straight through to number 10. Then the Master numbers were covered. They learned a lot about numbers that night and Ben bought a copy of Grace's book. It was out-of-print, and Ben had one of the only precious copies of the best basic book on numerology ever printed, he found out later in his practice. It was a really interesting night with Grace. She had a powerful spiritual presence on the planet at the time. Ben and Gary met other interesting people that night, as well, Margie being one such person.

She had been spiritual for a long time, and Ben recognized a psychic ability in her.

She introduced herself: "Hi, my name is Margie. I've been in the order of Melchezedeck for more years than I can count," continuing, "We in the order have a different way of having sex. Would you like me to show you?"

Ben thought to himself, *that was a strange request. I must have a sign in my auric field that expresses I'm an overly sexual person* although he didn't think he was. Ben played along just because he wanted to find out what she was up to.

"Put your hands up so we can touch palms," she instructed.

As Ben followed her directions, he started feeling warmth on his palms and sweat started to form on his forehead. Unfortunately, Grace came running over and said in a schoolmarm authoritarian voice, "What's going on here! We don't do that here!"

They both recoiled like schoolchildren doing something that they were not supposed to be doing.

"Oh, it's nothing," Margie said, as she sheepishly retreated to another part of the room.

Ben looked on, saying nothing.

As Grace returned to the person she had been speaking with, she gave Ben a look of disapproval, and he knew she understood exactly what they had started to do.

As everyone was leaving, Margie came over to Ben and said, "Sorry, Grace gets perturbed with us if we give away the secrets of the Order."

Ben reflected, this was a spiritual secret, that's interesting.

"That's OK, it was an interesting experience," Ben said. "Do you want to meet me later in the day and teach me more?"

"No! I can't do that," said Margie.

Ben was perplexed but accepted her answer. But he was taken aback by what she had to say next. "I wanted to tell you if you ever get in trouble with negative entities, you can call on the Archangel Michael to dismember the entity's parts and have the other archangels take them away using large nets."

This Margie is a very strange person, Ben thought. *Why is she telling me this? Do I also have tell-tale signs in my auric field of possible future trouble? Is she a good psychic or is it something else?*

Margie said, "I need to get going now," excusing herself as she moved towards the door.

"Nice to talk to you," said Ben, with a confused look on his face.

Margie was strange, but interesting. Ben sometimes wondered what would have happened with Margie and him if Grace hadn't interrupted them.

As they were driving home, Gary said to Ben, "I want to tell you what happened to me a little while back before I got my job. I had to go through garbage cans looking for food, because I didn't have enough money that month."

This caused Ben to raise his eyebrows, but he knew enough about numbers to understand that Gary, being an 11-11 had a vibration that made it difficult for him to stay grounded and focused on the Earth plane. Often times people like Gary needed someone to take care of them because some days, mundane things could escape them.

"A police car pulled up and checked me out," Gary continued, "they told me to get into the squad car."

"I'm sorry" said Ben, "I didn't realize you were in such dire straits. You should have called me."

"Don't worry about it, Gary said. "We drove down to the lock-up and I was processed. It got surreal as they processed me as a 5150 and took me for a psychiatric evaluation. I protested, that I was sane and didn't need a shrink, but that fell on deaf ears."

He said he was locked up overnight, and the next day they gave him shock treatments. When he was released, he realized in horror that he had trouble remembering things. "I'm now trying to reconstruct the memories I lost from the shock treatments."

"Oh God! I'm sorry Gary, that's terrible!" Ben said.

He had heard this often happens to individuals who received shock treatments.

"Did they think you were a vagrant? Is that why they picked you up?"

"Frankly, I think I was targeted by people that didn't want me to remember the things I learned about the spiritual metaphysical sciences and higher stages of beingness and consciousness. Remember the CIA agent that showed up on my door step," Gary replied.

Ben was thoughtful for a while. "What are you going to do now?" he finally inquired.

"I've decided to go back East after the retreat with Gene to see my wife and son."

"Well, that sounds like a good plan," said Ben.

Ben considered how little money seemed to mean to Gary. Not long before, he had allowed himself to get so broke he had to scrounge for food in the trash. Then, when he finally had a good job, he spent money so quickly that he had to borrow from Ben to attend the Cosolargy retreat. Still, when the two friends met a few weeks later, Gary had the money he owed Ben. He also had shared his views about the retreat.

"Hawaii's a wonderful and beautiful place!" said Gary."We had a workshop everyday talked about many things that related to the process and the spiritual aspects of the organization that Gene was trying to develop in those early days." Basically, they wanted to recruit people to proselytize and develop the organization, but I wasn't really interested in that — it kind of turned me off, to be honest."

Ben often thought about all that Gary had done for him. He'd opened many doors for Ben, introducing him to figures and practices that had changed his perspective on life. But Ben was also becoming more aware of the dark forces on the planet, and he could see them manifesting in every walk of life. When Ben considered the difficult times Gary had recently endured, he began to realize the scope of the dark forces' infiltration.

It was around this time that Ben started delving into dowsing and the dowsing community. At one point he attended Golden Gate Dowsing Society meetings at the University of San Francisco. One day, he attended a dowsing meeting carrying his finished manuscript from the JFC University master's program. There were many big hitters from the dowsing community in attendance that day. The meeting came to order, and they all sat around a solid oak table typical of the decor of the university. It was a Jesuit college, but it had started accepted women some time before. The school was steeped in theology, with a functioning church on campus and a theological and spiritual library.

One time, Ben had found a copy of Arthur Conan Doyle's little-known collection, *The History of Spiritualism*. Doyle had worked with psychics and mediums to communicate with spirits and ask them spiritual questions. Ben remembered one of his descriptions of the aura – a pliable net-like energy, like docile dough.

Ben's friend Ken was the coordinator for the dowsing community in their area and was liaison with headquarters in Lakemont, Geogia.

He called the meeting to order. "Come to order please, I'll read the minutes from the last meeting. Please go around the table and add any relevant information about yourselves and your history."

Ben went first. "My name is Ben Chavez. Some of you know me from the dowsing conference in Santa Cruz. I would like to introduce my new book, *The Acts of the looming Creation* that I just completed for a master's degree at JFC University. It's a curriculum book for children, young adults and adults to teach them how to develop intuitive, psychic and spiritual scientific skills. My chapter on pendulums, I feel, is excellent, and I have had fun teaching individual children to use them."

Bill Plate was sitting across from Ben, and as he was speaking, Bill became very agitated. So much so that Ben could feel Bill's energy impinging on his auric field and consciousness. Ben suddenly found that he couldn't think. Finally, he lowered his head and stopped speaking. He didn't know what else to do. He realized this was a powerful energy coming from Bill.

The room was completely quiet now, so much so, that it caused an uncomfortable silence in the entire room. At that point Bill realized his thought forms had disrupted Ben's thought patterns. With a surprised look on his face, he ceased his barrage of disdain, and Ben's thoughts immediately returned, and he could speak again.

"S-so you see," he continued, "I feel my publication will be a great instrument to teach individual children to develop their dowsing skills."

Everyone at the table came back from their thoughts and realized what had just transpired; they were all high energy and knowledgeable consciousness people. For some reason, Ben had gained some respect from the group with this display. After the meeting broke up, they all wanted to look at his book.

Bill Plate was one of the big hitters in the group because he dowsed for the California Department of Highways and Transportation. His knowledge and experience in the field was monumental, and there had even been several articles written on his skills as a dowser. Bill took his turn at keeping up to date with what was going on with dowsing individually and through the transportation department.

Bill Plate introduced himself last since he had a lot to say. "Well, we use L-rods and pendulums in the department to find underground power lines and railroad ties, in addition to charts. The department has used dowsers for a long time, and a lot of the guys on my team have abilities like mine. I also do my own dowsing to find water for wells, and I have a 95% accuracy rate."

Ben thought, *this guy is a superstar.*

After the introductions, another heavy hitter, Gary Hackett, came up to Ben and put his hand on the cover of Ben's book, which portrayed a blue sunflower. "Well, this flower has a lot of energy!" he said as his eyes sparkled.

"Yes," Ben replied. I took the photo myself. It was a real find. It was just sticking its lone head over a fence on Potrero Hill."

Guy was the presenter for the day and went on to teach the group how to dowse their personal apartments or house environments. Finding ley lines was a specialty of his. After he had finished the tutorial, Ben, for some reason, laid out for Guy an energetic problem he was experiencing.

"I'm having a little trouble with what I call "scanners" in my apartment. Could you give me some indication that my empassive abilities are accrete. Ben created this term, Scanners to describe individuals that were determined to disrupt his life and consciousness.

Guy went into a deep meditation for a minute and said, "It is an energy something like X-rays. There must be someone nearby projecting a disruptive energy field at your apartment." He also said that there could be an arcing energy coming into Ben's apartment like radio waves.

Ben thanked Guy. "That helps me clarify my intuitive feelings." Ben had suspected that the people in the apartment above him were tuning into his apartment using psychotronics devices.

"Good," said Guy."I always like helping my fellow practitioners. I hoped that helped."

Guy's background was pretty impressive. He was a B- 52 bomber pilot turned school administrator, and he had dowsed thousands of water wells. He was not into a scientific approach but rather a religious and practical approach. He put his faith in the Lord's energies and a personal connection with God. In fact, a Bible was never far from his grasp.

Guy had a connection with a local drilling company called HAMA. They had said of him that he has worked for them on many occasions to find water in the areas where water was scarce or historically only where there was never water before. He has been accurate nine times out of ten, they replied.

It was an interesting and monumental meeting for Ben. He learned a lot and made more friends in the community. Guy's analysis of his problems was especially useful. The puzzle pieces seemed to be falling into place rapidly now as Ben continued to gather more information on the forces that continued to rail against him.

Chapter Four

Intuitive Truth Comes To The Forefront

Ben went down to the California dowsing conference held every year at the University of California at Santa Cruz. The conference happened over three days. This year, Ben wanted to meet Marcel Vogel. He was famous in the dowsing community and a world renowned crystalologist.

Ben made plans to attend the conference with a friend he had recently made. Her name was Michelle, and she was from England. He had prayed to meet more spiritual people to develop more of a spiritual growth focus in the community, and Michelle came into his life. She was an interesting person. She came to the US from England with little money but a determination to follow her spiritual destiny. He stayed with friends and made a little money doing readings and healings. Michelle was an independent and revolutionary spirit, living life as it came to her. It seemed at times like she had no fear or reservations. Ben's intuition was always accessing others' consciousnesses to ascertain where they were coming from, and he could tell Michelle was truly a spiritual person.

Ben liked the UCSC campus. It was canopied in pines and redwood trees and had a resort-type feeling to it. They parked near the administration building to get a map to the campus and workshops, and they saw other conference goers getting maps as well. It was a pleasant walk to the conference building. In the forested areas, small pathways and globe lights lined the walkways every five feet creating a serene and meditative feel. The forest then opened onto a wide grassy area adjacent to stylish buildings with conference attendees milling around. Arrived just in time for Marcel Vogel's workshop, they sat down in folding chairs in front of a small stage. Soft spiritual music was playing in the background, setting the mood for the workshop. As they sat quietly waiting for Vogel, Michelle said out of the blue, "Let's go up on stage. I want to tune up your chakras."

Ben consider this for a moment with a faint smile. This was characteristic of Michelle –

you never knew what would happen next.

"OK, let's go. I'm game."

They ascended the stairs, and in front of probably 50 people, Michelle started putting her head on Ben's solar plexus chakra, tuning the spiritual center from the back with her hand, listening for a particular frequency. They had suddenly become the entertainment for the workshop. Ben knew Michelle lived outside the box, but was a new experience for him. He wasn't used to being the center of attention even though he was a Leo.

"Can you feel that?" Michelle asked.

As she worked, Ben tried to overcome a feeling of embarrassment by focusing on the energy changes in his body that Michelle was trying to affect. He could only imagine what the audience was thinking. They probably had little understanding of what Michelle was doing, and in truth, Ben didn't really understand either.

Soon Vogel emerged from behind the stage, with a little snicker and smile, as if he knew what they were doing and said, "I'm going to be starting the workshop now, thanks for coming up." He was a very cordial man.

They smiled and descended the stage, taking their seats. Vogel was a senior scientist at IBM and a world-renowned crystalologist. During the workshop,Marcel proved to Ben how knowledgeable he was about crystals both spiritually and scientifically.In fact, Vogel also tracked information in the fields of radionics and psychotronics. He was an experienced radionics practitioner, and part of the work he did at his research facility in Menlo Park involved using radionic devices to tool special crystals for doctors that were cut into shapes with 10, 15 and 18 facets with a pyramid on each end. Ben was deep into radionics at the time and was consuming everything on the subject he could get his hands on. Upon learning of Vogel's expertise, he looked at Michelle and said, "Now I have to buy his audiotapes." Ben's interest in Radionics would prove fruitful in the future when it became a foundation for his later work with psychotronic manipulation.

After the workshop, Ben went up to Vogel to introduce himself, and as he was about to shake his hand, he felt a psychic flash of a dream he'd recently had about a golden hand related to his self and its expansion. Marcel seemed to recognize a light within Ben. Smiling, he said, "Hello," not so much to Ben but to the being he perceived.

"I really enjoyed your workshop, Ben said. I especially liked your story about the Mach 2 camera from De La Warr in England." De La Warr was an electrical engineer and the president of the United States dowsing association. The Mach 2 camera was a device that De La Warr could use to take pictures of past and the future. It was illegal to ship the devices across borders, so Vogel had smuggled one into the country for his research, making him the only person in the U.S. who could work the machine. Through his experiments, he had been able to prove that thought forms were real.

Later, as Ben and Michele left the workshop, they stopped by the campus bookstore to buy some tapes. Outside, there were vendors selling their wares and Ben noticed a young woman selling Purolator water filters. Ben looked at her intently for a moment, then he suddenly approached her.

"I can tell you have an ET inside of you," he said.

The woman raised her eyebrows a bit, but replied casually, "Oh, really? I didn't know that." Thinking, *I like this person, I want to get to know him better.*

"Hi, I'm Ben and this is Michelle."

"Hi, I'm Janette."

"Michele and I were just going to have something to eat at the café. Would you like to join us?"

"Well, yes. I guess I can leave my booth for a little while." Turning to a coworker she said, "Bill take my place, would you? I'll be back soon." Michele took the opportunity to learn more about Ben's psychic perception of her.

Sitting the café near the bookstore, Ben was eager to learn about who she was, what was going on in her life?

She told Ben and Michelle that she had just bought a new warehouse loft in Oakland and was halfway through fixing it up with a friend. She said she wanted to create her living quarters inside an art museum.

"Wow! Great idea," Ben said.

Eventually Janette addressed what Ben had told her earlier. "How do you know I have an ET inside of me?" She asked.

"It's a psychic sixth sense I have. I also communicate with ETs myself."

"Do you think you'd like to meet me at my loft sometime learn more about this ET using a Ouija board?"

"Sure. That would be perfect," Ben said, nodding to Michelle, who was just as intrigued as Ben.

They exchanged numbers and Ben promised to call in a few days. With that, Ben and Michelle headed to another workshop and Janette returned to her booth.

The next workshop was led by an acquaintance of Ben's called Louise. She was another interesting presenter because of her knowledge of the local Mt.Diablo area. Ben had met Louise before at a women's group where she had talked about dowsing. She was a staunch no-nonsense person, with a strong character, as most super master vibrations were. She looked like an ordinary person you would meet on the street, but her knowledge of the Mt.Diablo area was very interesting. In her workshop, she described a place where she could tune into specific energies that would make her laugh. She called it a Laughing Spot and she could sit in the spot and laugh for 5 minutes straight.

She went on to say she had developed a theory of energy memory. She believed that the energy of ancient indigenous peoples remained in particular areas, locked into the land by rock formations. Dowsers and other sensory people could walk into the area and pick up thought forms created by the energy of the indigenous people in that area.

Experienced dowsers use pendulums or L-rods to amplify the energy signature of the same energy. Louise always had pamphlets of her outings to special spots along with pictures of power rocks. She shared with the attendees a power place observation record form she had designed that dowsers could use to record their discoveries. In it, one could log names, dates, times, places visited, directions, weather, ground conditions, how does the place make you felt.

Afterwards, Ben complimented Louise on her presentation and handouts, then he introduced Michelle.

"I also enjoyed myself," Michelle said. "Your workshop was very informative. In England we have a lot of famous sacred locations that I have visited and received healing energy from, over the years like crop circles, Stonehenge, Avery Hill, and various Stonewall formations and monoliths."

"Yes, I've been to some of those locations myself. Please send me your observations and I'll add them into my pamphlet with the pictures and articles," Louise responded.

"OK. Great!" Michelle replied, smiling.

After that, Ben and Michelle split up. He attended an advanced dowsing workshop and Michelle headed to a different workshop. Waving to Michelle, Ben told her to meet him at the bookstore later.

Will Bracey was a master dowser with his own tapes and forms to show you how to dowse water, oil, minerals, and do mapped dowsing. The advanced dowsing workshop was part lecturer and part practicum.

Will said, "We're going to have an exercise in dowsing for water. We are going to map dowse first and then you will try and locate the water outside the building in containers." Will's assistant Genie gave the attendees paper and pencil.

Ben immediately got out his pendulum and started dowsing the area that he had recorded on a piece of paper of the outside of the grassy area. After a few minutes, Will called the group together and they all went outside to see how they did.

Looking at his drawing, Ben noticed that the location he dowsed was opposite most of the water containers; his hits had been reversed. Ben mentioned this to Genie and she remarked, that she had once had the same problem of reversing her locations.

"OK," Ben said, "how did you deal with that?"

For some reason, she wouldn't answer him. Had she solved her problem or not, Ben wondered. He mentioned the exchange to Will later, but he just recommended that Ben sign up for his classes. Since he taught in the southern part of the state, Ben decided to check out his tapes instead.

The dowsing conference was an interesting place but strange. The agenda listed workshops and book sales, as usual, but there were also book signings and talent show where various members could sing, dance, tell jokes and do magic. There were even parties with dancing and cocktails. Ben arched his eyebrows as he made mention to Michele of the strange goings on – strange for people in an advanced consciousness group. But, there were also some very interesting and knowledgeable people there. Big hitters in the dowsing field – real spiritual scientists. Michelle and Ben met at the bookstore and decided they would come back another day and attend more workshops. They made the long trek back to San Francisco.

The next week Ben called Janette to see if he could see her loft. Agreeing, she told him she had read something she wanted to talk to him about. She lived in a low-rent part of Oakland close to the freeway. The city had been trying for some time to build up that area with artist lofts and small businesses. The buildings were rustic 50s-style rectangles with the traditional façades of the times. The entrance was encased in steel with several buzzers next to the door. When Ben rang the doorbell, he heard a sweet voice saying, "Is that you Ben?"

"Yes, it's me."

"Come on up!" and the buzzer buzzed to release the door mechanism with a click.

Ben walked down the dusty hallway and pushed the button for the elevator to the first floor. He raised the gate, stepped in and the automatic steel doors closed in front of him. When he got off at the fifth floor, he saw Janette standing in her doorway down the hallway.

"You got here in record time," she said.

"Yes, I know my way around the Bay Area pretty well."

"Come on in and I'll fix you some tea," she said.

Ben was impressed with Janette's living environment inside an art gallery.

"This is really great," he said as he perused the kitchen, living room, dining room and the ascended to the bedroom up a staircase. "How long have you lived here?"

"About a year now," Janette replied. "I love it! It inspires my creativity to do my artwork living in an art gallery."

"I would think so," he replied. "Is all the art on the wall yours?"

"No, it's a combination of my artwork and a few of my friends," said Jeanette. "I have gatherings – art parties — and I have an average of about 50 people that attend. I'm pretty well-known in the community."

She got to the purpose of Ben's visit. "I have a friend coming over in a little bit, and she's bringing her Ouija board with her to learn about the ET persona you saw in me at the dowsing conference. That's what I wanted to talk to about."

"OK, that'd be very interesting," Ben replied. "I actually have my own board that I've used to ascertain the names of the beings I've seen. Does your friend know how to use a Ouija board?"

"Yes, Tina's an expert. She's a clear channel."

As they were waiting for Tina to arrive they walked around and looked at the artwork in Janette's loft. Janette's artwork was a combination of various ultra-colors encased in black graphics creating a very interesting abstract quality. It reminded Ben of futuristic landscapes and building structures. She had incorporated some of the qualities of Picasso, De Kooning, De Staebler and other famous artists. The intercom buzzed, and Janette went to answer it. Ben continued enjoying the art.

A few minutes passed, and Tina was at the door greeting Janette. Then they both came around the corner to greet Ben. Tina was a very beautiful Asian female with large coal black colored eyes. She seemed to read Ben's every detail in his body language, expressions and emotion. She took his persona in immediately. She seemed to She was obviously an empath. She floated as she approached. Her dress was a traditional and modern Asian design, metallic green. Ben picked up a hidden geisha as she moved.

"Hi, I'm Tina," she said, as she extended her metallic green finger nailed hand.

Ben took it like a delicate flower and kissed it.

She pulled her hand back with a little giggle.

Ben couldn't fathom why he had reacted that way, it was something out of a European movie, Ben thought. She seemed as if she needed a long white silken glove to accommodate that long elegant arm.

Janette said, "now that you're acquainted, why don't we go into the living room and talk about the Ouija board?"

As they sat down on the multicolored modern couch, Lisa said, "so you saw an ET inside of Janette?"

"Yes," Ben replied, "I can recognize ET in people because I have one myself and I have personal experiences with different ET groups."

"Well, do you see an ET in me," said Tina? "No, but that doesn't mean you don't communicate with them. I don't see them right now," replied Ben.

Janette got out the Ouija board and Tina and Ben placed their fingers on the diviner. Tina did a short affirmation to protect them from any negative spirits.

"Who is the ET persona inside Janette that Ben recognized at the dowsing conference?" Tina asked.

Within a minute their fingers started moving across the Ouija board, spelling out words, as Janet recorded.

"You have contacted me," the words said."I am Emeria, an android from your future. I'm a partial persona personality for Janette to learn discernment of what is true and what is not in your trying times. Your planet has been co-opted for around eleven centuries by the dark cabal forces that have manipulated you into thinking you have no power and you should give your power away to them. They are overlords who manipulate humans as slaves for their sinister plots and perversions. That is all for now," and the pointer stopped moving.

"Well that was interesting," said Ben. "Janette do you feel that Emeria is a personality aspect to you?"

"Well, I guess so, I mean, I'm not sure, this is a new experience for me," she replied.

"Well, research into Multiple Personality Disorder, especially the work done in channeling by Dr. Joan Climo, has shed light on normal personalities coming forth into our consciousness," Ben said.

Tina jumped in saying, "You may have something there, Ben. At times, I feel like I'm someone else."

"I have experience with channeling, and this perspective is not foreign to me either," said Ben.

This was all very interesting to Janette.

Ben said, "I hope you got some relevant information out of the Ouija board this time. We should do this again to see if we can get more information, when I have more time."

Nice to meet you Tina, I hope to see you again, you are a special person. We should do this again sometime that would be fun.

"Absolutely," said Tina. "I would like that." She clasped her hands together, bowed and said, "Namaste."

Ben knew it is an ancient custom in the Eastern religions to point out that you have recognized the soul light essence of the person you are communicating with.

"I'll communicate with you later if I think we may have a future destiny together. Bye for now," she added.

That's interesting thought Ben, *I wonder what she meant by that.*

"Ok, Janette," Ben said, giving her a hug, "it's been an interesting evening."

Driving home that night back to San Francisco he briefly experienced an interesting anomaly, a soft supple long fingered hand over his. It was the softest vibration he had ever felt. Ben thought to himself, *Is that Emeria's hand on mine? Fantastic! "Bye, Emeria. I enjoyed the short talk on the Ouija board."*

"Bye Ben," came back the response in Ben's mind.

We should try and get more information next time...this is fascinating, Ben thought. *Is it possible for a being to come back from the future and inundate a person's body?* He wondered. What we don't know about consciousness boggles the mind.

Little did Ben know that these experiences were feeding his knowledge of the tremendous beings we are, and we are not aware of the state of consciousness we find ourselves in these trying times.

Ben attended another of Dr. Peticot Sunday services to hear her personal experiences and current affairs going on in society and treaties on Christ consciousness. After the service he met with people at the service and had coffee. Ben got into an interesting conversation with Robbie. Grace had been trying to start a church called the Living Light Christ Church for about two years. She had been waiting for the right people to show up to start the church. Ben assumed this would be a denomination of the Lutheran Church at Grace Cathedral in San Francisco. A few more people walked up to the small group and Ben was introduced to the "Family."

Robbie introduced Ben to Diana, Eric, Bill, and Lance and suggested they go to a restaurant called Sean's. The group seemed very aware of everything around them and had a balanced cohesiveness to them that made them flow together as one. Sean's Bar and Grill had an old provincial flavor to it. There was a sense of class and elegance to the decor but not overly stated. It was like a fine aged cognac, soft warm and smooth as it filtered through the eyes and other senses. It seemed that everyone was there from the church, and they waved to the others, including Grace, as they entered the door. There was a table available, so they all sat down. They ate and talked like old friends. Ben learned that Eric was a premed student, Robbie and Diana were a couple and Bill and Lance individuals with backgrounds from new age metaphysical groups to organized religion and of course, hippies from a communal era.

They all lived together in a large flat in Haight Ashbury. They organized their group around spiritual principles even down to the last piece of furniture. Sacred geometry played a large part in the organization of the environment. They would meet every morning and evening to pray and meditate as a group. It seemed that everybody in the group would shift their eyes as they looked at you, reading your auric fields. Robbie and Diana were probably the best at this. On a very subtle level, they tuned into your intuitive and psychic information and the emotional and physiological details about you. The family was well known in spiritual groups in the Bay Area because they had visited most of them at least once.

Eric said, "We are going to go and see Warner Earhart next week. Would you like to go with us?"

"Yes! That would be great," said Ben. Werner Erhard was the biggest thing since sliced bread when it came to contemporary alternative consciousness groups in the Bay Area. Ben had a lot of friends that attended Earhart seminars in those days. But Ben couldn't bring himself to take a seminar because of the personal testimonies from some of his friends.

He couldn't see himself being called an asshole or being denied going to the bathroom. Some of it was brutal, he'd heard.

In Los Angeles, there were the Life Spring seminars, which were patterned after the Erhard seminars but used a softer approach, impressing Ben as more dignified. Eric must have learned a little bit about Ben from Grace, but Ben didn't know anything about him at the time.

Was it his uncanny psychic sense that led him to the belief that Ben had some spiritual credentials; or maybe he heard it from Gary.

Robbie was becoming somewhat of a brother to Ben as he always kept in contact with him. The next week he called Ben to let him know where to meet them and go to the Werner Erhard seminar.

Standing on Robbie's doorstep facing a traditional Victorian apartment house with a beautiful ornate facade delighted Ben. He had always liked Victorians in the Haight. The Family lived just down the street from the famous multicolored flat with its red, green, purple and yellow colors with a green alligator crawling up the outside wall, owned by the Jefferson Airplane rock band.

Ben pushed the buzzer on the front door.

Robbie came to the front door, and he bent over slightly and waved him in like a butler. He had an interesting sense of humor. As Ben ascended the stairs to the living room it, started to reveal itself in the details of sacred geometry. The spiral plastic and glass lit chandelier first showed itself cascading downwards like a waterfall into the center of the large couches arranged around an imaginary circle ending up on a glass circular table with wooden trim. There were a couple of breaks in the couches to allow entrance to the sacred circle. The walls were a soft pink. The living room looked into the yellow and soft green kitchen. Off the other side of the circle, were two hallways that led to the bathroom and bedrooms. Looking down the hallway towards the bedrooms, Ben could see a stained-glass window with Jesus and his light coming down with multiple colors. So, this was the Family that everyone was talking about.

Eric came out from the direction of the bedroom raising his hand as he approached Ben. He greeted Ben and offered him some coffee. Then Lance, Bill and Diana joined the group.

"We want to welcome you to the family and our humble home, Ben," said Eric.

"Well, thank you. I feel really balanced here and can see the sacred geometry and the spiritual influence you have created for yourselves," Ben said.

Robbie and Diana both popped into the conversation at the same time and smiled to acknowledge their two minds being in sync together. Diana said, "We have worked hard to create a God/Christ environment in our home."

At that moment Ben felt that he was under scrutiny by everyone, especially Diana and Robbie. Diana squinted her eyes as the others did, tuning into Ben's auric field psychically, to read as much intuitive information as she could while sitting in that pristine environment. Ben imagined that this must have been how the Bene Gesserits of the *Great Dune Trilogy* would perform their sacred duties of trying to interrogate another soul's consciousness. He didn't feel uncomfortable with the process, as he somehow knew that it was what he also did on a subconscious level; they were just doing it on a conscious level. He also had his abilities to tune information. Ben thought maybe he should acknowledge what he was perceiving from them, but for some reason he didn't. *I'll leave that for another time.*

They finished their conversation and Eric, being the spokesman for the group, said, "We must get going to meet Werner Erhard, I told him we would be there by 2:30 PM."

They all piled into one car and drove through San Francisco to the Moscone Center on Third Street. The Center was a huge city-block sized area with a waterfall, a grassy park, shops, restaurants, a theater, an art museum and a convention center. Ben and the family descended the escalator down to the main hall. Seeing signs to the Erhard seminars, they entered the hall to see hundreds of folding chairs lined in neat rows with a sizable amount of people sitting waiting for Werner, and ushered close by to help people with any questions they might have. There were tables of information lining the walls, with details about Werner Erhard seminars.

Eric said, "Let's go backstage. I'm meeting Werner in his dressing room."

An attendant answered the door and Eric explained who they were. "Go right in, he's expecting you," he said.

As they crossed the threshold of the doorway, they saw Erhard sitting at a mirrored table after just having finished a seminar. He rose from his chair and greeted the group with a big enthusiastic smile and hugs all around.

The family surrounded Erhard, and in style of the Bene Gesserit, they narrowed their eyes and tuned into his auric fields, reading him psychically.

"Hello, Eric," he said, "I've heard of the Family and the good spiritual work you are doing in the San Francisco Area."

"And we have heard of the good work you are doing changing people's consciousness," Eric replied. "As you know, we live together as a family because we're interested in communal living for spiritual focus and personal growth. But we also try to connect with the other spiritual groups in the Bay Area to get an idea of their different approaches to spiritual development. You have a huge following, so we wanted to meet you."

Erhard replied that he was also interested in individual communal growth, but his focus was on individual growth first; hence, his personal growth seminars. "We're about to start the next seminar, so I need you to go, but we can talk more when it is over if you'd like."

"Well, we won't have time after the seminar, but maybe we can chat some other time," Eric said.

"Of course," Erhard replied.

They all proceeded to the seminar. Knowing these events lasted for four hours with no breaks, Ben used the restroom first, and on the way back to the conference hall, he noticed a balcony on a higher floor and decided to clear his head a bit before heading inside. He climbed the steep stairs and until he stood looking over the railing at the front row of the balcony. As he hovered over the center seat, he indulged in an urge to lower himself very slowly into the chair, standing on just one foot, with the other raised and his arms outstretched. This was the first and only time that Ben had perceived himself as having giant wings. Time suddenly slowed, and he perceived his form to be that of an angel– he was no longer sitting down, he was floating down. But as soon as he landed, two Erhard attendants rushed over to him and tried to sign him up for the seminars. He explained he was there as an observer at Erhard's invitation, and they quickly moved away and disappeared out of sight.

He met up with the Family about 15 or 20 minutes after he left them. The seminar got underway and continued long into the night. The seminar consisted, in part, of groups gathering together to roll play and learn more about each other. There was also a metaphysical aspect that used creative visualization to asquint the participants with soul aspect of themselves. It was quite late when they made it back to the Family's flat. Ben thanked them for inviting him and told them it had been an interesting experience.

"We have you in mind," said Eric with a glint in his eye. "Goodbye for now."

It was late, so Ben said his goodbyes and headed down the street towards his car.

CHAPTER FIVE

Other Dimensional Realities Manifest

Rising early, Ben had coffee on the balcony and had an intuition that he should meditate soon, a daily ritual for him to center and balance himself. First, though, he would look at the sun because the ultraviolet energy in the morning was perfect for the emotional biorhythm, and his emotional biorhythm was down – he could feel it in his energy field. He pulled out his blue filters for that biorhythm, acclimated his eyes to the sun and opened them to a full-on pulsation of solar energy. He felt the energy go into his optic nerve and then down to all the cells in the body. As it pulsated through his body, he felt that familiar warm feeling and a rush of bioplasmatic energy reverberating up and down his body; he did love it so.

Then he began the process for getting into a deep meditation. He used altar candles, Buddhist bells and incenses. He still used an incense container that he'd made years before in a ceramics class. It was full of incense residue from long use, especially the years Ben practiced Buddhism. He started having that familiar feeling of ascending into an alternative consciousness. Ben chooses a particular subject to focus on this time.

He was in meditation for about ten minutes, trying to determine the difference between a node point and a non-node point. The node point came from Ben's studies in radionics and psychotronics in which energy center vortexes around the frame of a person's auric field were considered in relation to the magnetic field nodes around the Earth.

All of a sudden, in Ben's mind's eye, the picture of a doorway opened up and an ethic planet appeared. The energy was loving and balancing that Ben started stepping through the doorway to partake of the energy field, but at the same instant, the door slammed shut and he nearly fell backwards out of his chair. He focused for a minute, wondering that had all been about. It would be another 20 years before he would understand what that vision was and what it meant.

Mark came through the door later as Ben was the preparing dinner.

"Ben, I have something I want to talk to you about," he said with a serious look on his face.

Ben looked up at Mark, concerned. "Sure, what is it?"

Mark thought for minute and said, "I've decided to move. I have a friend that just bought a house and wants to rent me a room in Pacific Heights. I'd like to move by the end of the month. You've been a great roommate, and I enjoyed this apartment immensely."

"OK Mark," Ben replied."I feel the same way. You've been a good roommate these past five years, I'm sorry to see you go."

"Thanks." Mark said."Now that I'm studying real estate, the new neighborhood will put me in a better position to work. I'll leave the dishwasher with you if you want it – I don't want to lug it around."

"Sure, that'd be great. Thanks Mark. You're a good person."

Then Mark went into his room, and that was that. Mark never did have the spiritual focus that Ben had in his life, and Ben hoped this would be an opportunity to get someone into the apartment with interests and practices more in line with his own.

The following week, Ben put an ad in the local roommate service that he had used in the past. It wasn't very long before Ben started receiving calls for the room in his two-bedroom apartment on the Hill. He started interviewing people right away. He had gotten a handy questionnaire from the rental agency that he used with the prospective roommates. In San Francisco, there was no problem interviewing six people a month in a good area. But Ben's area really required a car because of the steep hill, and not a lot applicant had one.

One day, after interviewing several candidates, Ben got a call on phone from a man name Robert. He wanted to come right over and see the apartment. Ben agreed, and Robert arrived within a few minutes.

"Wow, you've got a killer view here," he said after the two had said their greetings.

"Yes, isn't it?" Ben replied. "This is one of the great things about the apartment. It has a panoramic view on a clear day."

Robert was a tall slender man in good shape with a prismatic personality. He was a graduate of UCLA in biology, so he had no trouble with the questionnaire, and after he was done, they talked for a long time. Ben soon became convinced he was the right person to ask to move in. He showed Robert around the apartment and told him it would take a couple of days to check his references and credit score. "Where did you say you work Robert?" Ben said.

"I'm a caterer and bartender."

"OK, good. I'll call you in a couple of days."

Though he was a little concerned about Robert's income as an on-call caterer, Ben accepted him as a roommate. He moved in the next week and turned out to be quite reliable. They ended up living together for nine years.

Ben met a lot of interesting people that year. One day while drinking coffee and looking at the paper in his kitchen, he saw drops of fresh paint dripping down the fire escape. One of the upstairs tenants suddenly came quickly down the fire escape, mopping up as he went.

"Oh, hi! I'm so sorry! I knocked over a can of copper paint out the fire escape window." He apologized over and over, to the point where Ben found it peculiar.

"It's OK," Ben replied, "Don't worry about it."

The neighbor disappeared back up the stairs after cleaning up as best he could. Ben thought about what had happened, and his intuition kicked in as it did when something unusual happened in his life. He flashed on how, when he and his roommate were making their own PC boards for electronics, they needed to paint the masionary mother boards with copper paint before putting the electronic components on. *Were the neighbors making electronic devices upstairs?* Ben wondered. *If so, for what purpose?* He thought Guy Hackett from the dowsing group and Liz from his healing group may have been correct about his neighbors projecting psychotronics and other forms waves through his apartment.

This incident caused Ben to start paying more attention to potential disruptive frequencies in his home environment. He also paid more attention to the muffled conversations he could hear, somewhat, coming from the flats above and below him, trying to catch any relevant bits of information. *I'm keeping my ears open from now on*, thought Ben.

After looking at the sun for some time, Ben would feel very subtle frequencies of all kinds. One night he felt a waveform coming from the apartment above that made him feel uneasy and queasy to his stomach. This energy also affected his concentration and memory. He decided right then he was not going to be a guinea pig for these psychopaths. He started focusing on that frequency vibration and picturing pushing the energy wave back to its source. All of a sudden, he heard an alarmed voice upstairs shout, "Oh my god!" He had tuned into their psychotronics device – clairvoyantly. Ben moved the needle on their radionics device gradually back to zero, and the noxious wave stopped. It was over. Ben didn't hear or feel anything from the flat above for the rest of the night. The ordeal was over, and he felt a lot better and had a renewed sense of power.

Ben continued monitoring his apartment over the weeks to come. He derived a sense of accomplishment from overcoming the noxious energy wave, and he was coming to the conclusion that he could get the upper hand and overcome physical disruptions just by using his mind in creative ways.

One day, Ben ran into the guys upstairs coming through the front door of the apartment building. Overhearing their conversation, he heard one comment, "They didn't believe our research even though we were precise and methodical."

At first, Ben paid no attention, but at that specific moment, his intuition kicked in and he suddenly knew what they were talking about –him. They were researching Ben and the experience in his apartment the night before. They had presented their research on Ben to some group or scientific organization, but these others found the reports unconvincing. Of whom they were, Ben was unsure, but he knew that they were connected with the police department. This incident got Ben thinking about what he could do to protect himself further from psychotronic and psychic bombardment.

He thought back to his research putting together the radionics and psychotronics chapters for his book. He got out all of his old papers and research references and came up with a headband that he could wear to protect himself from the bombardment; it was a stroke of genius. He had adapted the design from Wilhelm Reich's orgone blanket. He found the materials he needed, and being an art major, he knew how to work with tools and materials. Sculpture was his area of concentration in college and it wasn't long before he had come up with a workable prototype. De La Warr and

Jerry Gilimore were a big influence on Ben as well as others in the radionics and psychotronics field. Crystals, too, became useful at times as he determined different uses in different situation.

Ben started wearing the headband on his head and as he had surmised, it worked wonderfully. He used it in different situations as well as an orgone blanket he made. It cut out a lot of the noxious-ELF energies wave forms that he experienced. *I'm sure I had help from others unseen forces to bring this product to fruition*, Ben thought to himself.

His consciousness was functioning at a high level now, thanks to his practice of looking at the sun, and the next experience Ben had confirmed to him that he had extraterrestrial connections. One evening, when the space shuttle was orbiting Earth, he went into meditation. All of a sudden, he felt himself pulled up above the planet in his light body. There, he saw two hovercrafts maneuvering around in space. The crafts were very large and had four-sided, triangular pyramid cabins with the tops of the pyramids missing. Two long tubular shapes protruded from the front with a cross tubular shape across the front portion. There were two large circular portals in the front and the sides like looked like windows except larger. There were ornate shapes covering the outside of the crafts. He watched for a moment and his attention was drawn to a portal in a compartment area of one of the ships. There he saw an alien in a black spacesuit beckoning him to enter the round portal into the ship.

Ben floated over to the ship and went through the glass, as far as he knew. Using a focusing technique he had learned in transgressional hypnosis to feel entities' frequency vibrations, he managed to get a short glimpse of this being's face as he entered the craft. He brought the alien face front and center and saw a being with human features, big humble black eyes, and white opalescent skin with a bluish tinge. He could see into the surface of the skin about half an inch. Ben's gaze seemed to startle this being as Ben focused on his face. He looked at Ben with those large black eyes and gestured, acknowledging his presence. He exuded an extremely high vibration.

As Ben had moved through the portal into the console area, everything became clear as a bell. It was much clearer than being in a third or fourth dimensional space. Later, Ben was to learn he had passed into the fifth dimension where no past or future exists, manifestation of thought is instantaneous, and all lower dimensions are visible, making it possible to time travel.

The being sitting in the console chair moved to escort Ben down a hallway to a room with a pearl-white staircase, and they ascended into a lit room. Ben had the intuition that the pyramid shape at the top of the craft that he originally perceived to be invisible existed only in the fifth dimension. The next thing he saw was a crosshatch skylight of stars in the night sky as they came into view. He found himself on a metal platform, where there were many consoles lined with dials, switches and something like a radar screen. Other alien like beings, were manipulating their equipment and paid no attention to their presence. Ben's alien friend said, "You can expand your consciousness by standing on the screen on one of the consoles."

Ben wasn't sure where this was going, but he decided to comply with his alien friend's request; there was a screen angled at about 45 degrees. Ben stepped onto it, and it started spinning down a time tunnel. He flew with its momentum for a moment but became afraid and he suddenly found himself back in the console room. Just as suddenly, he was back in his room in his physical body. He later learned that fear in this situation triggers a failsafe system that will automatically return the person to their body. This seemed to be a universal law that astro-projectors had experienced many times before.

That was the first-time Ben had met his "space brother," as ETs prefer to be called. This is because modern humans share past life and DNA connections with Aliens. Through the years, Ben continued to have other telepathic encounters with his ET friends. This encounter was a jumping off point for the next time his space brother returned to the planet.

The second time Ben was pulled up was shortly after the first, he was shown six or seven of what he thought were guides. Each of these beings were stretched out across the planet – Gaia, and morphed back into Ben. There was an extraterrestrial in a black spacesuit, a Persian magician, an American Indian with a full headdress to the ground, Vishnu the blue Indian god, a Hebrew Sage, and a prehistoric blue being. Ben didn't know what to make of this last dimensional shift. *Why are they showing me these images?* He wondered.

After this vision, Ben consulted a trance channel named Kevin who was very well known in the area. He said that they were well-balanced aspects of Ben's selves that came back into him unlike multiple personality disorder; that split the personality persona because of some trauma in their lives. It would be another 20 years before Ben would realize the true significance of having this experience with these beings. It was a memorable experience that would stimulate him to have other experiences with these beings that would stay with him for years to come.

Ben sought out a local crystal master teacher named Dale because he loved quartz crystal for their healing properties and wanted to know more about these historical stones. He had heard about Dale from other people in the Healing and UFO community. He read about Dale putting on a crystal workshop the following week and he decided he would attend.

As Ben showed up for the crystal workshops, he categorized the peaceful environment in the sleepy town of Walnut Creek. Oak, fir, and pine trees nestled next to a fertile growth of redwood trees. It was a picturesque suburban community with wide paved streets. The next house was an acre away. When he arrived in the evening, he found that the others had arrived only shortly before he had. He knocked on the door and a young woman opened it with an enthusiastic smile saying, "Come in we're in the living room."

Ben entered a step-down sunken living room with upholstered leather chairs and couches. He sat and perused the wide variety of people men and women in attendance. Of course, Ben could tell that these were affluent guests by their fashionable clothes of bright and expensive fabrics. They gave off an air of being unique free-thinkers; Ben felt right at home with them.

Dale walked out from another part of the house and announced, "I'm ready to start now."

He was an unassuming plain person and with a working-class persona. Ben had read that he was a Wiccan, and he wondered if all Wiccans dressed as he did. He had the feeling of being almost Amish but different.

"I hope you have brought your favorite crystal tonight," Dale said, "we have lots of work to do."

"I brought my favorite crystal," Ben said, holding it up. One of the clearest Arkansas crystals, it was like holding up a piece of glass. Ben could hear faint sighs and compliments.

"Great!" Dale exclaimed.

Dale led them into a crystal meditation after they learned that holding the crystal in their hands for a few minutes would release piezo-electric energy and facilitate healing energy, leading to a more concentrated meditation.

"Now, go into your crystal," Dale instructed, "and feel the walls, then smell, taste, and listen for any sound you might hear. Now, see an elevator, and as the doors open, step in and ride it down to your crystal healing room. As you get off the elevator, see your guides sitting in chairs. Remember to record the type of chair your guide is sitting in."

As Ben followed Dale's directions, he perceived a line of about four guides but was drawn to the fourth one wearing the black spacesuit he had seen in the hovercraft the night he was pulled up around the planet. Ben, this time, asked him his name.

He told him – Zaln, and he spelled it.

Ben asked him why he wore a black spacesuit instead of his light body for traveling.

He replied that his race had found the secret to immortality, but once they had changed, they could not reverse the process and their space suits were their only life support systems. They had thousands of years to discover how to travel through different dimensions wearing their suits. They could also rearrange their molecules to change their composition. He demonstrated this ability by stretching his body to infinity, creating an effect similar to looking through the other end of a telescope. He drew Ben's consciousness up with him, creating a great rushing sensation, as if Ben were being sucked up in a giant vacuum cleaner.

Ben had to recoil from Zaln a bit in order to remain conscious.

Ben asked Zaln another question: "What is my relationship to you as one of my guides?"

"I'm specifically qualified to keep an eye on the electronic, ELF frequency-psychotronics consciousness surveillance and manipulation movement going on in your world," he explained. "Moreover, you were once a member of our race at the beginning of our diverse cultural history. You are a Pleiadian."

Just then, Dale interrupted, saying, "You can come back up into your elevator to your waking consciousness."

Unfortunately, Ben had to break off communication with Zaln, but Zaln interjected one last comment: "Understand this, Ben. I am not merely a guide, but one of your personas. We will discuss this concept further at another time."

Still reeling from the encounter with Zaln, Ben focused on Dale as he began to lead the group in some healing techniques.

"I want to show you how to connect with another person's auric field through their nervous system," He said. "Stand behind the person with your crystal pointed between their shoulder blades. Rotate your crystal 360° one way and then 360° the other way, then do it again slowly, feeling for a glitch or some other anomaly to occur. It will feel like a key fitting in a lock. This means you have successfully tuned into your partner's nervous system, and you can begin sending healing energy through this portal." Ben tried this technique with his partner and felt a russ of energy reverberate through his body.

Dale went on to show them other healing techniques, ending the workshop about nine in the evening. Ben chatted with Dale at the end of the workshop, and they hit it off.

"I'm going to meet with my mentor, Nick Noririno, tomorrow," Dale said. "We're going to a rock specimen shop. Would you like to go with us?"

"Yes, I would," Ben replied."I'm always looking for another crystal to add to my collection and other resources."

Dale told Ben that Nick had been in the military police during World War II and went through different European countries looking for crystal skulls. He would also follow individuals in a car and triangulate their location to tune into them and know where they were going at all times. This was a highly developed psychic skill that he naturally was attuned to in his field work. He was also in various New Age groups, participating in anything to do with crystals, parapsychology and psychic events.

Dale told Ben that Nick used Wiccan knowledge, explaining that its history was inundated with philosophy and the practice of magic. Nick put on a workshop about metaphysical and scientific approaches to opening the secrets of crystal skulls using various lasers, EFL frequencies, thought forms, and a metallic blue color that was one of the keys. Nick had told Dale that, among other things, there were people watching other people watching other people in the crystal skull. *Whatever that means*, Ben thought. But Ben also noted that the military was much farther along in the psychic ability arena than he had previously thought.

Bill picked Ben up at 10:30 am the next morning and Ben met Nick. They drove out to Vacaville and parked in front of a rock shop. The building was pretty basic and aesthetically uninspiring. Going inside they saw triple rows of bins with rocks of all kinds. There were a lot of raw materials available. Looking through the bins, Ben stumbled across what he thought was a real find, a piece of lavender Jasper. Tumbling it through his fingers to feel the energy of the stone, a man came up from behind Ben and slapped him on the shoulder, releasing a sound that you could hear clear across the warehouse. The owner of the warehouse let out a yell, shaking his hand and recoiling from Ben with a glare. Ben just looked back in confusion, without responding."

"Hi," the man said. "I'm Phil the proprietor here." Shaking Ben's hand, he continued, "I see you found lavender Jasper. Why, I didn't even know we had any of that stone of that color in the store."

"Well, I'm glad you have this color. It's supposed to be a high energy vibration," Ben replied. In fact, Nick and Dale had coincidentally explained on the ride over that lavender Jasper is a much more powerful stone than even quartz crystal. Ben wasn't sure he believed that, but they were the experts.

Looking at the vast array specimens in the warehouse, Ben commented, "It sure seems like you guys know a lot about stones and crystals."

"Well we have a few things," Phil said with a smile. "Have a look around and let me know if anything else interests you."

Then he headed over to talk with Nick and Dale. They laughed as he approached, shaking his hand.

He wondered, *Did they set me up to try and make a point*? It didn't work. *Oh well, boys will be boys.*

Ben continued around the shop and picked out a few other stones of the same kind, but these were polished spheres, one green and one red-jasper. He also found some nice quartz crystals.

He walked up to the register where Nick and Dale were checking out after buying several crystals specimens. He could see they were envious of his finds.

"Good eye," Dale said.

They all jumped in the car and headed to a restaurant where Dale and Nick had made reservations. It was an upscale Thai restaurant with white tablecloths. Ben was surprised to see others waiting at their table. As they got closer Ben recognized Margie, whom he had met through the Order of Melchezedeck. He flashed on his strange experience exchanging energy with her at Grace's numerological workshop.

"Well, Hi Margie," Ben said as he set down the table. "What are you doing here!"

"Oh, Ben!" Margie said, as she looked up from her menu with a surprised look on her face. "I'm an old friend of Dale's from years past," she replied.

As it turned out, Dale knew people in the order, including Grace.

It's funny how high spiritual beings flock together and run in the same circles, Ben thought.

"I didn't know you knew Dale," she said with a smile.

"I met Dale at his last crystal workshop. We have similar destinies," he replied.

Dale was only one of two individuals he knew who had the ability to impress or transfer the divine spark to another person. This was an effect talked about in various religious groups, and the first time Ben felt it was years ago when he was a Buddhist. George, the second in command to the Buddhist president, Ikida, had the same effect on Ben as Dale. The divine spark George transferred to Ben was similar to the energy effect he experienced at Dale's workshop.

Ben had not discussed the divine spark with anyone yet, not even Dale. It was basically a spark of divine energy that awakened one's consciousness to the spiritual work of another enlightened individual. One who receives this spark is stimulated to follow the giver; doing so leads to the expansion of spiritual gifts. When the student is ready, the teacher will appear, it has been said.

Dale rang his glass with a spoon and said, "Let's do a short meditation and blessing before dinner." They all went into a meditation in their own way.

"Please God, great spirit, transform this food that we are taking in," Dale said, "send love and healing to the planet and all its people. Also bring back the life force to our food."

At that moment Ben found himself, in consciousness, as he sat next to Dale, starting to ascend just a little higher above his head, wavering from side to side, as if he was a balloon on the end of the string. It started to make Ben uncomfortable and it was all he could do to stay conscious without passing out. The energy was so intense he almost didn't come back. This is something that happens energetically when you are in the presence of a high spiritual being. Dale ended the meditation and he found himself coming back to Earth to his body. Then they all opened their eyes and held their hands over their food to inundate it with life force. Ben felt a spark of energy as he focused on the thought of the food. Everyone continued their conversations over dinner and shortly afterwards they finished their meal and headed home.

Arriving home after a long night talking about spiritual and metaphysical topics, Ben walked through the door and went straight to bed. The next day, he awoke to hear his roommate Robert talking to someone in the living room. Ben rolled out of bed and shuffled into the living room.

Offering Ben a cup of coffee, Robert said, "You stayed out quite late last night with your friends, didn't you?"

He's just like a mother hen sometimes, Ben thought in amusement.

Robert then introduced Ben to his guest Stan, explaining they'd been friends for years. As he greeted Stan, Ben realized he was still wearing his headband. A bit embarrassed, he explained what the headband was.

"This headband attracts orgone in the atmosphere. I made it by modifying an orgone blanket designed by a researcher named Wilhelm Reich whose work I ran across while researching my book. He was a biochemist and psychologist who studied with Freud. He wrote a number of books in the 1950s on the study of orgone energy in therapy, weather and chemistry. He developed tools to use to accumulate orgone energy, a few being, the orgone box for patients, the orgone tubes for cloud busting and a tube with a wire mesh so you could see orgone in the air. He grew single celled animals- bison, in nutrient soil, so you could see the animal with an electron microscope. In fact, when you hit your head, for instance, people say they see stars. In fact, they are seeing orgone energy in the atmosphere."

"He wears that all the time," Robert said.

"Wilhelm also suggested that orgone energy in the atmosphere emulated the sexual dance we all go through in sex. The undulation during the climax mimics the rise and fall of the physical body and energy."

"Interesting," said Stan, "how does the headband accumulate orgone energy?"

"Well, that's a Trade Secret," he said laughing and winking at Stan. "You'd have to research this question yourself to really understand."

Ben was not prepared to reveal that the real reason he developed the headband was to help deflect noxious energies coming into his environment and his body. Nor did he tell which materials he used to make it. This is because Ben perceived Stan as CIA.

Robert looked perplexed at Ben's reluctance and Stan recoiled like someone that had just revealed a hidden secret. Robert moved towards his room and a few beats after, his telephone rang.

Stan and Ben stood in silence, staring at the view out the picture window.

Robert came back shortly and made some comment about an obscure something and Stan said, "Yes, it's used to block energy coming into it."

As Stan spoke, Ben felt his ascended self drop into his body. His eyes grew larger as they often did when his ascended self moved into his structure. He became fully aware of what they were talking about was, his orgone headband, as if he had a telepathic connection to their thoughts. Ben jumped in at that point and said, that's interesting I don't remember bringing up that subject.

Robert cursed, "Damn!" and Stan looked surprised that Ben knew what they were talking about. Then Robert moved towards his room again and the phone rang again as before.

What is going on here! Ben thought to himself.

Robert moved towards his phone because he was getting a telepathic signal from his source to pick up the phone before it rang. This was a technique for training an individual to execute a simple telepathic command sequence.

It became clear as a bell to Ben what was going on. *Well*, he thought, *this is interesting. My own roommate was laying the groundwork to be a psychic informant.*

It was not that Robert had this psychic ability; rather, every aspect of his life would be under the spotlight and communicated back to Stan's people, and they could create protocol to control his life and maybe even worse.

Ben did not drop into a fear space upon learning this information. He had long since overcome fear in his consciousness. He had lost his fear in his college days, when he would work extra night jobs. More than once, he was held up by gunpoint or knifepoint by low lives on the street, looking to get money for their habit. It was a good thing that Ben was a Buddhist at that time as it was the only thing that helped him keep his sanity and balance. He would preach to the thieves that they could change their lives if they gave up the life of crime and came to a Buddhist meeting. This was the practice of Shakabuku, the art of introducing Buddhism to the lost souls of the underworld. But it never really work, and he lost his money anyway. He almost succeeded in persuading an assailant to attend a meeting on one occasion, but it never really worked, and he lost his money anyway. Nonetheless, it helped him to keep his balance and overcome his fears. He also learned to keep most of his money in his shoe.

Considering Robert's betrayal, Ben thought, *Robert is a great guy on many levels, but the lure of power is irresistible to some people. I myself would never be tempted by power in that way.*

"Well Robert, I'll see you at the yacht club tomorrow, we need to talk about the big race to the Hawaiian Islands coming up in a couple of weeks," said Stan. "Nice to meet you Ben."

Ben reluctantly shook his hand and gave him a weird look, thinking, *the hypocrisy in this room is so deep I need to lift my feet.*

"That's what I wanted to mention to you, Ben. My trip to the islands," Robert said, as sweet as pie, trying to mask that their cover was blown. "The owner of the sailing boat has just gotten a new boat and wants my amateur crew to sail the boat to Hawaii to break it in before the big race. I'll be gone for about two weeks. I'll let you know the dates later."

Then Robert headed to his room again and Stan went out the door.

"Great! I'll have the apartment to myself for two weeks," said Ben, to mask his resentment at these two people's manipulations. From then on, he tried to think of ways he could replace his roommate with another. *God help me with this one* he worried to himself.

That Sunday, Grace was her usual self, sharing the latest scoop about current affairs from a spiritual perspective. The world was becoming a different place with the ascension process in full swing. The Comet Kohoutek was passing over the skies, bringing a new spiritual vibration to the planet. Grace also had the ability to inform different individuals of special abilities, as she spoke. As it turned out, she gave Ben a telepathic message, "*You can never be deceived by anyone because you can look behind the façades most people present in ordinary conversation; you are a strong clairvoyance and clairesence.*"

Ben was talking to his friends Robbie and Eric when their friends Len and Tom walked over, greeting everybody in the group.

Robbie introduced Ben and Tom and Len asked him if he'd been coming to Grace's for long.

"No, I just started recently, but I've been taking her workshop in numerology."

"I've been coming to see Grace for about two years," said Tom. "We heard about her through Grace Cathedral. She is the most progressive religious speaker in the area. We have seen a lot of religious speakers over the years and Graces a real gem; we heard about her in Arizona. Len got skin cancer last year and we went to the Philippine's to see a faith healer who might had heal his cancer," said Tom. "I have a feeling that I was targeted by possibly the FBI with psychotronics devices. I was not in their good graces with them when I left the agency."

Ben said, "I have heard something about a man named Dr. Bear along these lines. It was a good thing he was a medical doctor because they – the proverbial they – gave him cancer along with a couple of his friends.

Ben explained that a man name Gallimore was reported to be able to tune into a person's thoughts using a calibrated radionics device that he built, also being the author of "The History of Psychotronics". He added that he was also president of the Radionic Congress back in the day.

"I've heard of that before," said Len. "We have some very talented people in the FBI who are advanced psychics, and they've dabbled in that area as well."

As it turned out, the healing didn't work. Perusing the videos, Len noted it was clear the healer had palmed a chicken liver that he faked pulling out of Len's body. "At any rate," he said, "we use different medicines and alternative healing processes to heal the sarcoma. Chemo and God's elixir was effective in removing the cancer."

"Oh, great. I hope you're feeling better now. What is the God's elixir anyway?" Ben asked.

Len explained: "We ran into a special water, D-cube water to be exact, to apply to the wound. It worked like a charm. It's a solar energy process to make the algae for the D-cubes."

"D-Cube water, that sounds familiar," said Ben. "My friend Gary used to grow a white ethic alga in his bedroom window. I got a hell of a rush when I drank some, one time; I drink it myself on occasion. I contacted the woman down the peninsula to inquire about the DQ water and she hasn't gotten back to me yet."

"Oh," said Len, "that's interesting, we'd like to hear more about that at some point."

They then explained they needed to leave for a meeting. They were both 33rd degree Masons. and had taken a job redesigning a hair salon using sacred geometry and spiritual principles.

"You have to come and see us Ben, we have a new place in Antioch."

"Sure thing. Nice to meet you both," Ben replied as they headed for the door.

Watching them go, Robbie leaned in to Ben and said, "Let's gets something to eat, and I'll fill you in on Len and Tom."

Accompanied by Eric and Diane, Ben and Robbie found a cushy booth at Sears diner and sat down. After the waitress took their order, Robbie launched into Len and Tom's history. He explained that Len was a retired FBI agent and Tom worked for the San Francisco Police Department. They were very spiritual people that also happened to work for law enforcement. They were also gay and were part of the leather crowd that hung out with the "biker daddies" at the Eagle Bar. He said that Tom lived for a time in Mexico and had recently over come cancer. His doctors had removed a large chunk of the side of his neck, and that was the reason his face looked a little lopsided. *That's too bad*, Ben thought. *He's a good-looking man otherwise.*

They continued chatting as they ate, and when the conversation dwindled to trivial small talk, Ben took his leave.

Arriving home in the afternoon, Ben smoked a small amount of marijuana and decided to look at the sun because his physical biorhythm was particularly low. He felt the familiar energy move up and down his body as he looked at the solar orb. This time, Ben used his meditation crystal, a single terminated quartz that he had bought at the Hyatt Regency a few years earlier. It was a really nice specimen – as clear as a bell. It was one of those rare finds from a mine in Arkansas that produced many of the clearest crystals. This particular one had a violet aura surrounding it. He had another clear crystal from Madagascar that was also really nice and clear. Clear crystals are very powerful and relate to the brow chakra.

Ben opened his eyes to let in the powerful force of the sun so it could irradiate his optic nerve, and a shiver of energy moved up and down his spine. The combination of looking at the sun and marijuana seemed to create an especially intense experience. Eventually, Ben perceived a man standing above him; he knew it was his light body, and it bathed him in a column of descending golden light. Then a mental hologram resonated in his physical body and throughout his entire physiology. He fine-tuned the image until he perceived a light beam. It was being projected through a hole in the bottom of a golden saucer-shaped craft above. Then Ben started receiving a communication from Zaln.

"You should meditate each day," he said. "Your destiny awaits you."

It was an urgent and strong message accompanied by a gradually intensifying ray that impinged upon him as he sat in meditation. Then the energy field of this being surrounded him, and Ben's body was pulled up into the ship. Once again, he was greeted by Zaln in his familiar black spacesuit. The image of Zaln and the ship were faint and bathed in golden light, and Zaln was accompanied by other beings who seemed happy to see Ben. He shook their hands and hugged them.

The episode only lasted about a minute or so, but it had a strong impact on Ben and helped strengthen future communications from Zaln. He recalled a book he'd read by the physicist Itzhak Bentov called *Stalking the Wild Pendulum*. Bentov described the difference between subjective and objective time, pointing out that LSD research that showed humans could experience much more information in subjective time than in objective time. Though only a couple of minute had passed, Ben felt positive and rejuvenated and came away with another expanded experience. *I always enjoy being up on Zaln's ship*, Ben thought. *The energy of the other light beings has a healing aspect on him.*

Chapter Six

Pieces of The Puzzle Continue To Manifest

Ben had a crystal healing group meeting at seven o'clock, as he had every Tuesday night for the last three years. Though he didn't realize it at the time, the group was connected with the church of Tilzelli in Arizona as well as other crystal groups in the Bay Area. Ben's good friend Andrea greeted him at the door, and Ben was happy to see her.

Andrea and Ben were very close during this period in his life. She was a mother of two and an excellent psychic and intuitive. Her ex-partner, Steve, was an independent businessman who had moved to Oregon to make ends meet. Andrea didn't follow him, and she and Ben became intimate. In fact, Ben wondered for a time if Stefan, the youngest of her children, was actually his.

"No, he isn't," she replied. He had the choice to be born to you or Steve, but he chose the latter."

Still, Ben wondered. He had a number 33 in his name, which was one of the master numbers and though it has little to do with the three-dimensional world. Jesus's number was also 33, and little Stefan had two 33s in his name. He would be very spiritual being when he grew up.

Ben and Andrea headed inside, and the meeting got started. Lynelle, a number 11 master spiritual universal vibration,led the group, as usual."

"Close your eyes, "she instructed, "take in a few deep breaths and relax. Tonight, we are going to use an Alantian chant from Frank Blper's channeling. He's the director of the church of Tizelli in Arizona, and he'll be visiting our group next week."

They all chanted, "Ta- bay- ohooo" as if they were on top of a mountain and were sending a message to the next mountain range. They chanted for five minutes and felt exhilarated as they finished. Then they settled down with their crystals and followed Lynelle's guided visualization to enter their crystals and talk to their guides.

"Go inside your crystal and take the elevator down to your healing room. See your guides sitting in chairs," she said. This reminded Ben of Dale Walker's workshops, and he wondered if she'd attended one too.

This turned out to be a special session for Ben. In meditation, Ben saw a hand come out of a lake with a faceted diamond in it. He had seen this image for the past few weeks. As he focused on the diamonds in the hand, it suddenly changed into a being composed of thousands of diamonds. It was moving through a fog, and light was reflecting and refracting in all directions, flashing over the being's body. As Ben tuned into the image, he was suddenly caught in a light ray and felt a rushing sensation from the pit of his stomach as he ascended to a higher dimension. The being spoke: "I want to be called the Over Soul." Ben maintained his connection with the full force of the Over Soul, riding a surge of new, clear energy upward and outward. His consciousness was expanding, and elation coursed through his body as he let his spirit soar upwards to infinity.

The intensity of the experience finally pulled Ben out of meditation and he perceived that his eyes were wide open like saucers, but so was his pineal gland and brow chakra, creating a sparkling light sensation around his body. By that time, everyone had come out of meditation and were looking at him because they knew something was amiss. The voice inside Ben bellowed, "I'm Ben's Over Soul. If you want more energy, call upon your Over Soul to lift you up. Consult your Over Soul to ask any questions you wish to ask. Take your lead from Ben to facilitate this process."

The light seemed to subside after a while as some people peered closely at Ben's face, and others contemplated what had just transpired. No one spoke.

"OK," said Lynelle, breaking the silence. "That was exhilarating. "How long have you been channeling your Over Soul, Ben?"

"Well, I've been seeing a faceted diamond for a couple of weeks now, but this was the first time I've seen a faceted being moving through fog. It carried me to infinity and I felt compelled to speak," he replied.

"Can you do what your Over Soul said?" Lynelle asked. "Can you teach us to get in touch with our Over Souls?"

Ben thought for a moment. "Let me figure out the details. I'll teach you when I understand the process better."

"That sounds fine," she replied, and led the group in the closing.

As they were leaving, Lynelle announced that she had a commitment the following week, so Andrea offered to host the group at her place instead.

Ben felt mesmerized by the experience of raising his Over Soul. He had way too much energy for that hour, and spent the night reading one of his spiritual books. He also recorded the episode in his journal so he could refer to it at a later date.

Ben woke early Saturday morning because he was going to a street fair in the Castro. As he arrived, he appreciated the familiar locations of an alternative community such as the cafés where the locals met to discuss community issues. He headed for one of his favorites, the Shenandoah Café, to get a cup of coffee. Passing through the archway towards the wooden steps of the rustic front door, he scanned the outdoor seating area for a spot to sit. *There's one*, he thought, as he went to place his order. Waiting for his coffee, Ben appreciated the colorful poster touting an Arabian Prince in full regalia behind the bar. Several of the café's patrons announced their revolutionary views through attire accessorized with colored scarfs and political buttons. A great deal of leather was on display being an important symbol of gay culture. Others wore herring bone scarves from Israel and Palestine around their necks with Nike caps firmly on their heads.

"That'll be a $1.85," the service person said with a wink and a nod; Ben guessed he liked what he saw.

"OK, here's two dollars keep the change."

Ben grabbed the seat on the patio and sipped his coffee while focusing on the various conversations buzzing around him. The discussion ranged from gossip to activist rallies and marches. Across the street he could see the Fried Green Tomatoes Café – naming local venues after indie movies was a trend in the neighborhood. Ben finished his coffee and walked towards the street fair, dropping into alternative shops as he went. He picked up some safe soap, soap with a condom in it, as a novelty gift for his friend Allison, a backup singer for Paul Simon. She had a special device she could record music and transmitted to studios around the world with no loss of clarity. Ben was at her house one time, and they sang a familiar song and sent it to a studio in England using this device. Allison said that they had done a pretty good job, seeming pleased.

Looking at the various booths displaying creative arts and crafts or community organizations, Ben came upon his friends Len and Tom manning a booth advertising jobs for the city sheriff's department.

Ben took a step back, "Hi guys, doing some recruiting?"

"Yes," Tom said, "interested in working for the department?"

Ben smiled, "I'm afraid not. I'm a teacher at heart."

"Sure." Tom replied, "If you change your mind give me a call."

Then Len pulled Ben close. "Listen," he said, I should tell you about an experience Tom and I had recently."

His tone caused Ben to raise his eyebrows.

"The FBI flew Tom and me to Washington DC. When we got there, they asked us to roll over on all the people in Grace's group –The Order of Melchezedeck. They wanted a complete list of members."

Concerned, Ben asked, "What did you tell them?"

"Of course, we just were not going to do that," he replied. "Things got pretty tense – they called us fags and told us they knew our sexual history and all of that. But we have nothing to hide, and we were not going along with the program no matter what they used for persuasion. In the end, they just flew us back to San Francisco."

Now Ben had another confirmation that he was being targeted by at least an alternative group in the FBI. It seemed like all his friends were too, from the way it sounded. *This is just another way to control the populace*, Ben thought, *getting as much intelligence as they can gather to set up sting operations thwarting the development of any kind of real knowledge to determine what was truth and what was not truth.* This was a real crux of the issue.

"Thanks for telling me this, I think. "he said with a grim smile. "But why did you tell me?"

"You need to get out of the psychic spiritual fields," replied Len. "They're coming down on everyone."

Ben shook his head. "For me, that would be like ripping off one of my arms. I could no more stop my spiritual quest then ask an artist to stop doing his artwork," he said as he met Len's eyes.

Len and Tom exchanged glances of concern. "Well it's up to you." Len said, "We're just giving you a heads up."

"And I appreciate it." Ben replied. "We'll talk more at Grace's." Then he took his leave and continued down the street, letting the colors and buzz of the fair envelop him.

Later that week Len called Ben asking to buy a copy of his book. *The pieces of the puzzle are falling into place*, Ben thought.

The next week, Ben went to Andrea's flat for their crystal healing group. Andrea grabbed Ben's hand and led him over to an unfamiliar participant.

"We have a special person here tonight, Ben. This is Lidia. She owns a care facility in Hillsboro. I met her at another spiritual group."

"Hi, Lidia, I'm Ben. Is that your car outside?" He had noticed a Gold Rolls Royce sitting on the street in front of the flat.

"Yes, it is," she replied. "My husband is in the oil business. He's a Saudi and likes to show off his success."

"Have you been doing meditation long?" Ben continued.

"Yes, it's been years for me. I communicate with the tree diva among other beings."

Andrea jumped in and said, "Lidia wants to lead the group tonight. Let's get started."

Ben greeted a few of the others as everyone settled in for meditation. Then Lidia started the session.

"Take a couple of deep breaths and let go slowly," she began."Go inside your Crystal, and focus your energy there with your own process. I'm going to my healing room to try contacting the tree diva." After a time, she continued. "I made contact, it is in the Black Forest in England. All divas have a kingdom that they keep track of. They, are ascended Masters with metaphysical abilities, working in multiple dimensions."

Suddenly her posture and facial expression changed subtlety but in manner that made her seem like a different being. "Good evening beings of crystal consciousness," the tree diva spoke through Lidia. "The trees all over the world are in jeopardy because of rampant deforestation. You should honor the trees as you honor the mother Earth, because they provide you with an ecosystem that breathes oxygen into the world. Tree forests provide habitats for all types of animal species and medicine and food for humans to consume. The trees love you humans, but they wish you would be more respectful to them and the role they play on mother Earth. May the prime creator be with you."

As Lidia returned to herself, she told the group that kingdom had a diva, minerals, animals, plants, and insects. These divas guide them and watch over them because they do not have free will. Ben later learned that some animal kingdoms have extraterrestrials as their representatives; for instance, the Insectoid kingdom.

"Mankind is the only species that doesn't have a Diva because we all have free will as decreed by the prime creator," she continued. "That is the reason you are protected by the law of one – you are unique in all the world."

At the end of the session, Lidia led the group out of their crystals into waking consciousness. "Ground yourself if you are out of balance," she said.

"Thank you, Lidia," Ben said, speaking to her and the group. "That was a very interesting and a special message. You have given us a new perspective about trees as sentient beings on mother Earth – Gaia. This has given me a different perspective on trees. We should give them ample respect. Ben felt his consciousness expanding in leaps and bounds.

"I would like to take over now and lead everyone in some crystal healing," he said.

"Oh yes," Lidia spoke up enthusiastically.

Opening the chakras was a special focus for Ben, and he proceeded to lead each member of group in the healing process of bringing down the atomic energy from the Christ center, on high, and opening up the chakras.

Before the session ended, Andrea announced that, Lynelle, the group's usual host, was arranging for the group to travel to Mount Shasta soon. She also told them they would have a special guest at the next session.

The next week, Ben arrived at Lynelle's early and found that she had invited Frank Blper to their healing group. Frank directed an Institute in Arizona for the church of Tazelli.

Ben introduced himself. "Hi Frank," said Ben, I'm Ben. "I've been a crystal healer for a few years. Can you tell me something about yourself and your spiritual group?"

"Well," he replied, "I channel Adamis, a thirteenth-century philosopher. I have written books on Atlantis 1, 2,3, Moses and the Bible and universal life and spiritual laws. I am a conscious channel. I am no longer part of the fire of life. I don't intend to return next lifetime – this is my last incarnation."

Ben thought he was referring to the wheel of life talked about by Yoga and Buddhist traditions and reincarnation in the Western world.

Frank continued, "Our church conducts master trainings in carousel out grows all over the world, we also sell healing crystals and tapes of channeling sessions, and we publish the newsletter The Spiritual Connection."

Frank led the group that evening channeling the thirteenth-century ascended master Adamis. "Good evening," said Adamis. "I want to speak to you tonight about universal law, the law of attraction and Christ consciousness as well as the individual readings for each of you here tonight. One aspect of the universe is the law of attraction. This is basically reading your aura field for the information to the deepest aspect of self, setting up conditions without fear, and picturing what you want as the end product. You must really focus on the end product – see it, feel it, create it. This will help manifest it in the 3-D world. You also have to work for your cause in the conscious world by being – give of yourself and give thanks – be grateful for everything you receive."

As he went into a deep reflection on the subject, Ben noticed his words resonating with his deepest self, his Over Soul self.

"The Christ self, "The Christos," inside of you the light body, the "I am" present, or the super conscious self, is an aspect of yourself that is responsible for your entire organism and spiritual development," Frank continued."It also can be raised to interface with the highest aspect of yourself to ask any questions you might have in your life. It can stretch from the Over Soul Christed self on high at the eights chakra above your head, the inter Sun Orb, or even further. After all, Jesus said, you have to go through me to reach the father. Interface with your Over Soul often to receive the answers you want to receive for your own life. When Adamis had finished with his presentation, he started reading each member, delivering information that they were unaware of at the time.

"Ben, I see you in another lifetime as an extraterrestrial called Orix. Your ship was called Roltar, part of the Jupiter 12 Fleet. You spent a whole lifetime on the ship and were instrumental in tracing mental manipulation and control of the emotional body by organized groups, similar to the CIA on this planet. You will have a visitation by the Jupiter 12 in the near future with a group conducting a ceremony in the woods. You will have a further communication from them after this outing."

This was the first time that he had heard this of this group. *It seems I'm destined to have a lot of experiences with ETs*, Ben thought.

During coffee after the meeting, Ben mentioned to Frank him he was interested in a crystal expert name Marcel Vogel he had met at a dowsing conference.

"Yes," said Frank, "I tried to communicate with him about working together and coordinating our efforts. He told me he was only interested in researching crystals from a scientific perspective not a spiritual perspective."

The group discussed consciousness with Frank long into the evening before finally saying goodnight.

Chapter Seven

Ben' Destiny Becomes Real

Ben woke early the next morning for work and drove to the school where he was teaching.

As he punched the clock, he thought how much he resented it the machine – it showed he wasn't considered a professional even though he was a credentialed teacher. Teachers at most jobs didn't have to punch a time clock.

Judy, the administrator, stopped Ben in the hallway and said she wanted to talk with him after school.

After teaching his classes, Ben headed to Judy's office. Sitting in her waiting room, he considered the possible reasons she wanted to meet him and recalled a conflict with a coworker earlier in the week He couldn't afford to lose the position, and he was sweating by the time he was called into Judy's office.

She glared at him as he took a seat. "Ben, I'm really upset about the way you are not getting along with your teammates in your room," she said. Ben could feel her anger towards him creeping out from her auric fields, and he pushed it back with his mental intention.

She looked down at her paper, recording the feeling she had in her mind's eye. It was at that point that Ben saw, with his physical eyes, a dark dirty brown furrowing energy of anger coming from Judy's auric field. His aura suddenly expanded to the ultimate egg shape that signified his soul's self boundary, and Ben felt his dynamic energy expand in all directions at once, creating a bubble around and through his body, fortifying his field and at the same time stressing his perceptions to their maximum. His hands were sweating heavily.

Judy continued, "We need to have a talk about whether you can remain on the team in the future." She rose and shook his hand. "Let's talk tomorrow. I have another meeting to go to right now."

Ben thought it was strange that the meeting was over as soon as it started.

Driving back to San Francisco in an expanded daze, Ben went over what happened in this meeting with Judy in a detached state. He was on autopilot, letting his memory take him back to the meeting. *What was going on in that meeting with Judy?* he thought. He tried to integrate this experience into his cognitive structures, rationalizing the details and feelings he received from Judy. He thought, why did we have a meeting where we didn't really get anything done or discuss anything? He was in a high stress mode – adrenaline was flowing through his body like water. The feeling he had in the meeting was similar to life-threatening incidents he had encountered in his life in the city.

He remembered being approached by a gunman once in a laundromat. At that time, his basic aura also expanded to the edge of his egg shape. The reaction was similar to the flight- fright syndrome described in psychology textbooks. Ben feared for his life when this person pulled out his gun. Could fear of losing his job cause the same effect? He really didn't think so – there must have been something else at work. As Ben thought over the energetic dynamics of the meeting, he felt that on an energetic level, it had been a complete manipulation of his physiology. He really thought Judy was psychically manipulating him energetically. This was very disheartening, having this thrust upon him from a professional that he respected. Was she really fooling around with mental manipulation?

The conflict at work was eventually smoothed over but he never forgot the feeling of psychic manipulation in his meeting with Judy. Later, he was talking to the assistant principal when she mentioned to him – out of the blue – that he could earn money using his psychic abilities. "How much would you charge?" she asked.

Ben was taken aback with the ramifications of this question. But he played along. "I would need about $50,000 a year," he said.

She laughed with a surprised look on her face. "OK, you're expensive," as she walked away smiling.

How did she know I was psychic? Ben wondered. *Was she talking to Judy earlier?* He worried that he was being targeted at work also. That would mean the surveillance was much more widespread than he had thought. Ben drove home still thinking about these issues. He was wondering how far he wanted to go down this rabbit hole. *Are they watching me everywhere I go? Do I have a choice to make?*

After work, he went to a bookstore to clear his head. He thumbed through the latest *Psychology Today* and *Sociology Today* as well as other references magazines, but he didn't run across any interesting articles. Finally, he picked up a copy of *OMNI*, the science and sci-fi magazine. Synchronistically, he ran across an article called "Zapped."

The article described a couple of women with unique and personal experiences that related to mind control. It was the '80s and synchronistic expressions of this type of thing were happening all around Ben. According to the article, Dorsey B. was having sex with her husband and began channeling a demonic voice that spoke though her. She had never had such an uncontrolled outburst in her husband's arms, and the words she spoke were not anything she would have known about. She talked with her husband and his advice was to see a psychiatrist. But psychiatry didn't stop the thoughts coming into her mind. She sought the advice of her brother, an MIT scientist who had worked on military projects for the government. He told her information about a secret government long-distance mind control program.

This did not surprise Ben. He had researched psychotronics and was familiar with the government's track record of doing research on its own citizens. In one case, a unknown chemical was sprinkled in the New York subways. In another case, a member of the Canadian Parliament was zapped with an exotic weapon, and she was able to use her computer to discover minute impressions in her brain similar to Morse code. This person went on to construct an apparatus to wear on her clothing to ward off being zapped energetically. Ben wondered if the government had used scaler wave technologies on the woman. There was also another article in Omni magazine talking about new research proving that the subconscious mind signals in the brain, a microsecond before we make a decision about any action we take.

Ben wondered if that's what happened to him when he had the experience with being manipulated in his car as he stopped at a stop light. At that point he was wondering where he fit into this picture that was developing before his eyes. He never had so many synchronistic experiences in his life.

As Ben was puttering around the apartment, he picked up a flyer from a group called Hike and Bike. They were putting together a trip to the Northern California area, kind of a spiritual retreat and Native American ritual. It would be a spiritual group ceremony with about 150 people. Ben made a call and found out when the ceremony was going to take place and the time and place to meet. The day came quickly, and Ben headed for the big trees in Northern California.

Arriving in the parking lot in the late afternoon, he saw a large group of people gathered listening to a speaker outlining the day's itinerary. Ben made his way to the circle and followed the large group of people as they moved up the hill hand-in-hand towards the ceremonial circle of the moon. Ben looked up into the darkening sky and saw a craft moving past with red, green and orange lights. He gazed at this slow-moving craft thinking it was an airplane, but then it started jumping around – it jumped so fast it looked like flashing lights in a checkerboard pattern. Then, just as suddenly, it disappeared. *That wasn't a plane, that was a spacecraft*, Ben thought. *Fantastic, I just had a sighting.*

I wonder if anyone else saw it? Then Ben recalled the prediction Frank Blper made at the crystal channeling session. *I wonder if this is the day he was referring to,* he thought.

As they topped the hill and descended the other side, they made their way to the circle of the moon. The participants all made a circle and were led in an Indian chant. A naked man with a red cape came running past the group as a naked woman in a red cape came running by from the other direction. Ben thought to himself, *What have I gotten myself into?* When the chanting finished, the spokeswoman gave praise to the moon and the feminine expression of power.

She and others spoke for about ten minutes, then members of the circle offered personal reflections. Then they were instructed to form smaller groups to experience nature and make further spiritual offerings to the goddess. Ben felt the energy of the male and female group members and decided he resonated with the feminine energy better than the masculine energy. He joined a group mostly women and they started dancing around the fire singing and chanting. Ben noticed another male in the group with a very interesting charisma who stood out from the rest of the males in the group.

"Hi, my name is Ben," he said to the man. "I enjoy the feminine energy. It is not as gross as masculine energy." Ben really didn't know why he said this.

"I'm Jason. Have you been to these rituals before?"

"No, I haven't, but it seemed interesting reading about it, so I decided to come out. Did you see the UFO in the sky?"

"Yes! I did. I was wondering what that was bouncing around in the sky. I've never seen colors do that before. It didn't occur to me that it was a UFO, though."

He had a feeling about Jason. There was something interesting under his demeanor that he couldn't put his finger on.

When the group ended, Jason and Ben went out for coffee even though it was one in the morning. They found a coffee shop in the town and talked for a couple of hours about healing modalities and spiritual issues.

Jason told Ben, "I'm a whistler and I'm writing book on holistic health."

"A whistler?" Ben asked.

"I do professional whistling. I have a bird sounds CD and have been in national contests. I was even on the Johnny Carson show whistling different songs and bird impressions."

"What an interesting occupation," Ben said. What training do you need to be good at whistling?"

"Well it's all about breath control and having a keen ear for differences in sound. I do a lot of yoga and meditation to prepare myself for competition."

Eventually, they made plans to connect again and said their goodbyes.

The next day, Ben was reflecting on the checkerboard UFO pattern he had seen in the long progression over the hill the night of the ceremony. His intuition was telling him that this checkerboard pattern was a symbol or a word of a language; he believed each pattern was a different word. Ben thought back to something he had read on the Pythagorean mathematical theorems and patterns. The three mathematical triangles, one small, one medium and one large,fit together corner to corner making a grid with a triangle in the center. *Could that be more than a geometric relationship? Perhaps a coded language for the inhabitants of Jupiter 12*, Ben wondered?

Ben received a communication stream from Orix. Orix is a being that Ben is not really aquanted with but he considered it interesting that Adamis's channeling information showed up on the door step of his mind to communicate with him.He told Ben that the movie *Tron* was a visualization he could use to protect himself from scanners. Ben wasn't interested in watching the movie again, but he was interested in seeing what Orix might be talking about."The lights on the suit can be used to protect you from psychotronics bombardment energies from, as you say, 'scanners,'" Orix explained. Your intuition about language structured in geometric mathematical colored shapes and patterns was correct. In fact, we were in communication with the ancient mathematician Pythagoras during his lifetime. We considered his mathematical theorems to be a perfect structure for a language. Of course, our culture has known Pythagoras for many many millennia and he was instrumental in our language development."

The light suit consisted of bands of light on the arms, legs and chest as well as the helmet. Ben practiced visualizing the light patterns as best he could. He used the patterns for a while but ultimately put them aside as he had new experiences that revealed new ways of protecting himself. He wasn't contactedby Orix again, but he knew he could call on him whenever he needed him.

The next Tuesday evening, Ben attended his healing group again. This particular night, he met a woman named Anya. She had a three-year-old child with Down syndrome.

Ben asked her if she had attended similar groups before.

"Well, somewhat," she replied. "I have gone to Dale Falker's crystal classes. That's where I met Andrea. I've also been to other spiritual groups in the area. I used to live in Albuquerque and Sedona. These areas have high psychic energy vortex's and individuals working on their spiritual development."

"Well, you seem like an interesting person, I would like to get to know you better, I'll talk with you later then," said Ben.

Lynelle got the group started with an opening affirmation chant and visualization. Thinking about Lynelle, he appreciated what an interesting person she was. Ben did a short reading of her numbers one time, as he did with all members in the group, and she had an 11 universal master number in her name. That vibration had gone through all the lower vibrations, lifetime after lifetime, to arrive at her master status. The number 11 showed an advanced spiritual wisdom, structural technical abilities and excellent oration and leadership skills to guide large groups of people in a spiritual direction. She laughed a lot and was very personable with a light and joyful heart. She was also clairsentient and clairaudience, but not very clairvoyant, if at all. Ben often wondered how she led visualizations because she felt the energy vibration without seeing the imagery she was expressing. Of course, Ben was very clairvoyant and could see what he led people towards as a visualization progress. Ben asked her about this once, and she said, "I feel the energy. That's how I lead group."

Lynelle took her place in the group circle and said, "OK, we are going to bring in the gold energy tonight through our communication with our guides. I hope everyone brought their crystals for meditation tonight because I want to lead you into your crystals. I have an extra crystal if you don't have one." Everyone had brought a crystal.

She continued. "Take a few deep breaths and visualize a gold energy going clock-wise around the outside of a circle and a gold energy going counter-clock-wise, around the inside of the circle. Only the highest vibrations may enter the circles of light, we call upon the angelic forms and healing masters to come into the circles of light."

It's important to do a prayer invocation at the beginning of a guided visualization to protect yourself from the lower astral energies and spirits, Ben thought.

"Now," Lynelle continued, "go inside your crystal, feel the sides, smell the smells and hear the sounds. See an elevator opening, step inside it, push the button and move down to your healing room. When the doors open, greet your guides by saying 'Hello,' and give them a hug. See the chairs they are sitting in. Then ask the question you want them to answer. When you have gotten your answer, get back on the elevator and ascend to the top floor again. When you're comfortable, come back into the room and open your eyes, but don't forget to ground yourself when you come out of the meditation, so you won't feel flighty or off-balanced. You can reach up and pull your spirit back into your body if you are out; only you know if you are out of your body. You will feel it when it comes back in."

Ben knew several different grounding exercises but this one was a new experience for him that he had practiced on only a few occasions. He found it very effective and fast. It was funny, he thought, you could actually feel the spirit coming back in your body with the energy fortification to your whole system.

When all of the members had returned to their bodies, Lynelle asked them to share the answers they received from their guides. One person in the group said her guide told her that her energy was getting stronger and she should be experiencing a change in her consciousness that would facilitate a faster manifestation of her thoughts in the world-look for the changes.

Later, she asked group members to describe the chairs that their guides were sitting in.

Ben thought about it for a minute and said, "I think my guide's chair was a French provincial style."

Others mentioned a stone chair, a heavy Baroque chair and something like an Art Nouveau chair. It was interesting to hear the variety of chairs everyone had in the group. *I wonder what that means? At minimum it demonstrates variety in the creative process*, thought Ben.

After the group healing ended, Ben spoke some more with Anya. She told him about her son and his many health problems. "We're in and out of the hospital all the time," she confided.

As Ben sat next to Anya, he started feeling energy attached to his auric field and all of a sudden, he felt his light body move upward just above his head. It was an experience of elation he had never felt before. He was feeling no pain, only bliss. The feeling lasted for a few minutes and then he was pulled down as quickly as he had risen, into a normal consciousness.

Ben looked over at Anya and said, "Did you do that?"

"Yes," she said with a mischievous smile.

"Can you teach me the technique? I would love to learn that," said Ben.

"Well, maybe," she said, "if we become closer friends."

"I'm your buddy from now on," said Ben, smiling.

Jason, Ben's whistling writer friend, called a couple of days later and they met at Baker Beach for a walk. Baker Beach is a great San Francisco beach because the parking lot is right on the water in a nice neighborhood in the Presidio, just down the street from the Golden Gate Bridge. From there, it's a nice walk down the beach towards the rocks past the nudist area of the beach where people playing volleyball. The walk in the other direction was also nice, with families relaxing and views of affluent homes. Ben found the energy of the beach quite serene. As the tide came in, the riptide riffled over the rocks, creating a musical cadence. As they walked down the beach, Jason told Ben more about himself.

"I'm almost finished writing my second book and will be taking it to my publisher pretty soon,"

"Oh? What's it about?"

"It's about healing and holistic health. I do yoga, Ti-Chi and I'm a vegetation to keep myself in perfect health," said Jason.

As they walked and talked, Ben saw a young man down the beach. Ben intuitively picked up a vibe from him, that he had something on his mind. As they passed him the man said under his breath, "You know you we will never let you go." Ben could hear what he said, and he started to respond, but a voice in his head told him to hold his tongue. As they passed the man, he looked at Ben with an expectant expression that turned to confusion when Ben showed no reaction. *This man is trying to initiate an interesting dialogue process*, Ben thought to himself, *I've used it myself.* Ben knew that If you said something to someone under your breath which has meaning to them, they will hear and understand what you have said. If it does not concern them, they will not understand what you said.

I think my higher self didn't want me to respond to this person's query for some reason, thought Ben. Ben didn't bother to speculate on the reason; he trusted his higher self to make the best decision for him, especially when it came to covert surveillance and manipulation.

Jason heard something, and asked Ben, "What did that guy say to you?"

Ben replied, "They would never let me go".

"What did he mean by that?"

"I don't really know," Ben said.

Of course, Ben knew exactly what the man had meant by. He got the inference. They – the proverbial they – were now keeping track of him on a regular basis and it they would continue to do so for a long time. But Ben chose not to worry – it was what it was. He had no intention of getting out of the psychic field, and he just had to resign himself to the back lash that was going to lead to. He knew how they thought; after all, he had set up everything that was happening in his life on a karmic level before he incarnated into the planet to ascend his consciousness and help Gaia with her Ascension as well. Ben and Jason continued down the beach and went to a café to get something to eat after the long walk.

Lunch with Jason was pleasant with no further incidents, but on the way home, Ben thought more about it. The man on the beach reminded him of a similar incident he had experienced earlier. He was sitting in his favorite café on Church Street writing feedback on his students' artwork. Pretty soon a stranger came and said down at the table next to him.

"Chavez. we need to talk," he barked.

Ben looked at him for what must have been a full minute before going back to grading his student's artwork. He thought to himself, *This guy's no good. Anyone who speaks that disrespectfully isn't going to have your best interests in mind.*

Ben knew this was a tactic they used to get you interested when they wanted something from you with little or no effort. Instead of introducing themselves, they approached with a derogatory tone. It was a way to avoid exposing themselves and who they really were. If you said anything to anyone, you would have few details of your interaction, not even a name. They used vagueness as a tool.

In the end, the tactic worked. Reluctantly, Ben asked the man, "Who are you?"

"That's not important right now."

Ben sighed. "What do you want from me?"

"We've been following your work for some time now. My friends and I want to know if you'd be interested in joining a special task force. We have groups of talented psychics all over the country. There's a group in Haight Ashbury. We want you to instruct them in developing their psychic abilities further."

"So, you want to recruit me," Ben said.

"Yes! Your connections with extraterrestrials and spirit beings alone would be a great asset to our team. And your headband and orgone tools are of particular interest to us."

"What's in it for me?"

"Well, you'd be volunteering at the beginning until we get funded. We've petitioned the CIA for funds under the Remote Viewing Project."

As Ben sat thinking about the possibilities of working for this group, he recalled a party he'd attended in the upper Haight at the invitation of his friends Robbie and Diane. Ben remembered watching them dance happily to beat music in the living room then heading into the kitchen to sample some hors d'oeuvres. There was a good looking, buff young man preparing food who handed Ben a devilish crab and an anchovy spread on rice.

Ben took a bite then exclaimed, "Oh, I don't like anchovies!"

Suddenly, the man's energy turned dark and violent. He pulled a butcher knife from the block and flashed it at Ben in a quiet anger. Then he registered the shock on Ben's face and caught himself, quickly putting the knife down on the counter and returning to his preparation of the hors d'oeuvres.

Ben moved backwards out of the kitchen, thinking to himself, *What kind of party is this? This guy has some major problems! I wonder if he would have cut me if no one was around.* Ben wondered what the other people at the party were like. Scanning the low-lit dance floor, he noticed a dancer with psychic blue balls of light free floating around his head connected to energetic light lines going from one ball to another. *A knife and now psychic balls. This isn't an ordinary party. What else am I going to encounter?* he thought.

Focusing on the blue balls spinning around the dancing man's head, Ben wondered how and why this person had produced such a psychic projection. It seemed like a mental projection that would take hours to create to protect him from psychic bombardment. He wondered if he could accomplish the same thing through mental concentration if he tried. Ben's intuition was kicking in once again, and he began to consider how it was done. He knew the auric field was connected to the mind as he had detected the outer levels of the aura using his aura meter in dowsing workshops and in his crystal healing groups.

As he was thinking, Ben started picking up a noxious energy vibration as he had done many times with his clairsentience ability. He did his tuning process to determine the direction of the bombardment. *Yep, it's coming from the guy with the blue balls around his head*, Ben thought. Focusing more deeply, he also sensed noxious energy vibrations coming from almost everyone else dancing at the party. *This is a den of snakes!* He thought. He realized there was no way to protect himself, and decided to leave.

"We're sorry you can't stay for the festivities," Robbie and Diana and said.

"Yeah," Ben responded with a disgruntled face.

In the café, considering the stranger's offer, Ben connected the dots and realized the party in the Haight was probably full of agents working for the man sitting across from him. *If that's the kind of thing in I have store, I want no part of this guy's group*, he thought. Ben looked straight into the stranger's eyes, said, "No thanks," and went back to his grading.

The guy waved to the other side of the café and said, "We're out of here. Let's go!" Then he and two men Ben hadn't noticed hustled out of the café.

The next day Andrea called Ben and said Anya's son Devon was in the hospital and he may not recover. She asked Ben if he could come over to the hospital and see if he could do some crystal healing on him.

"Of course. I'll do whatever I can" Ben said. The he grabbed his crystal and drove to the hospital as quickly as he could.

Arriving at the emergency room at San Francisco General, he spotted Andrea. "How's he doing? He asked.

"He's not getting better," she said sadly.

Anya approached and said, "Hi Ben. Do you think you could go in try to do a healing on Devon? I put crystals all around his bed already. It's all right with the nurses."

"Of course," said Ben, "anything to help you and Devon."

Ben walked into the room and saw Devon's face, smiling even in the face of death.

Though Devon always had a satisfied and happy demeanor, Anya had known for some time that he was living on borrowed time as children with Down syndrome often are.

Ben reached out and took the child's hand. "Hi, Devon," he said, trying to do some type of spiritual healing on him. He stayed and worked with the boy for about five minutes when a thought came to him: *Tell him you'll give him some your life force if he wants it.* Then he said just that to Devon. As soon as Ben spoke the words, his life force was instantaneously drawn from him and he fell a fatigue come over him that he hadn't felt before. Gasping, Ben stumbled out the door of the room muttering, "He took my life force," as people looked on in puzzlement. Ben continued, "I asked if he wanted my life force, and he took it." Ben had been with individuals before who had passed, but this was the first time that he had experienced anything like this.

He sat in a chair and composed himself. *I don't begrudge him taking my life force*, he thought. *I gave him permission, and I'm glad I could help in some way.* Sitting up straight, he asked himself the important question: *Would I do it again?* And the answer was yes, he would.

In fact, Ben's life force eventually came back into him. At the time he offered it, he had been under the impression that if he parted with his life force, he would never get it back, that we all have a finite level of energy to sustain ourselves through life. His experience of sharing life force with Devon had taught him that this belief was untrue. Ben derived a certain amount of pleasure knowing that we have access to an abundance of energy and we can replenish it when needed.

Unfortunately, the infusion of Ben's life force could not help Devon. He was already too far gone, and he passed later that night with Anya watching over him. All of them there that night went into Devon's room and did a group healing, calling upon the ascended Masters and angels to guide Devon's progress as he ascended into the afterlife. They consoled Anya and did a healing on her as well, and then they left her alone with her son and departed.

Later, Ben thought how strange life is. This three-year-old child had understood what life force was and how to access it. He thought Devon must have been an ascended Master that he'd had the privilege of interacting with in his short lifespan, and he hoped he would hear from him at a later date. Thanks to this experience and others, energy and consciousness were taking on different meanings for Ben.

Chapter Eight

The light In The Illusionary World

Ben woke that Saturday morning anticipating the trip to Mount Shasta with his crystal group. He continued packing for the three-day weekend and made it out the door by 8 o'clock. Arriving at Andrea's he noticed everyone was there loading up cars.

"Ben, can you take Liz and Ann in your car?" Andrea asked.

"Oh sure, no problem," Ben replied. Liz and Ann loaded up their gear and all eight members of the group were on the road heading for the Golden Gate Bridge out of San Francisco northward. This was Ben's first visit to Mount Shasta, and he had heard it was a remarkable place. The mountain was revered for its magical occurrences and UFOs sightings. It was rumored that the extraterrestrials there were remnants of the beings from the continent of Mu, the ancient Lemnian Island spoken about by Homer and Plato in the same sentence as Atlantis. Ben understood that the occupants of Mu were spiritual beings who floated rather than walked.

Liz was excited. "This should be a great trip," she said. "I haven't been up to Mount Shasta in a couple of years, but I wanted to get back up on the mountain again; it's magical. I also want to go to Stewart Hot Springs this time. There's a town nearby with a large crystal store and a community bookstore where we can find out about the spiritual sites in the area. They also have hot tubs and mineral baths and massage areas in abundance there."

Ann jumped in, "I want to go back up to Panther Meadows again and Pluto Caves. Cloud formations on the mountain are some of the best anywhere in the world. Some clouds look like large spaceships sitting atop the summit." She said she'd read somewhere about there was an entrance to Middle Earth there and ET ships came and went all the time.

It was afternoon when they pulled into the parking lot of the Holiday Inn. After checking in, they all gathered in the lobby.

"Let's get something to eat and visit the crystal shop downtown," Ben said.

They decided to have lunch at a restaurant with large UFO model outside.

Waiting for their food, Joan said, "One of the first things we need to do is go to Panther Meadows and deposit our personal crystals in the sacred ground of Mount Shasta."

Joan was a very special person because she was about to relocate to Hawaii with her French boyfriend to start a business taking people out to swim with the dolphins. They also had grandiose ideas about creating a modern aquatic structure that would be a hub for dolphin research and mammal research on the ocean. The design was ultramodern and would let the dolphins swim in and out of the complex. It was huge, with an accessible sun pool.

After their late lunch, they all headed to Panther Meadows. It took about 30 minutes to get to the sacred Indian grounds. They parked and walked a short distance to the meadow. As the group stood in a circle, Joan took a shovel and dug a hole for the crystals. Each of member dropped a personal crystal in the hole.

Ben thought, I'm going to drop a twin crystal, growing together, into the hole; it was one of Ben's favorite clear single terminated crystals at the time.

In a clear voice, Joan said, "We offer these crystals to the mountain to cement our personal crystal vibrations into mother Earth and to make it possible for us to visit Mount Shasta in meditation when we choose to communicate with this sacred place and when we need to regenerate ourselves under this sacred mountain."

Joan covered the hole and they rolled a huge rock over the spot. Then, with their hands outstretched, they irradiated the crystals with their group energy. As they finished, it was getting close to dark, so they made their way downtown to the crystal store before dinner. Shasta was a sleepy little town that rolled up streets at dusk. They made it into the crystal store before it closed, and they were flabbergasted seeing how many crystals were on display. There were six rooms of crystal magic and consciousness. Some rooms were dedicated to one particular color, including Ben's favorite – clear quartz crystals that resonated with the brow charka. This crystal enhanced the visual center of the pineal gland which helped with Ben's clairvoyance. Crystals could have their own names and personality structures. Ben was especially interested in finding a crystal with a seventh facet and one with a diamond facet to round out his collection. He found the diamond crystal in the shop, but the seven-faceted crystal was still elusive. Of course, the Lamanian Crystals were very common in Mount Shasta; after all, the mountain was the connection to both the Lamanian spirit and the continent of Mu.They were all very satisfied with the shop – Lynelle got a nice Lamanian crystal and Andrea found a huge amethyst clustered geo she intended to make a centerpiece.

Turning to Ben, Andrea said, "I found your birthday gift – a clear generator crystal." Generator crystals were for meditation and visualization with groups of people. Perhaps she thought it was time he consider leading groups.

"Thanks, Andrea. It's such a clear crystal." Grimacing, he added, "I'm afraid I can't get anything for you right now. My funds are a little low."

"Don't worry — it won't be my birthday for a while," she replied with a smile. "I'll put the crystal on layaway and have them send it to me later," she added.

That's a really great gift. I'll have to get her something nice for her birthday, thought Ben. The crystal was about 8 inches tall, 5 inches round and hexagonal – it was very clear with few inclusions. Andrea and Ben had been friends for some time. They'd had a tryst together at one point, but it just evolved into a good friendship. Romantically, she actually liked his roommate Mark better – Ben had never seen a woman shiver when they were in the company of a particular male energy before.

After shopping they all met at the restaurant again and headed for the inn to sleep the night away. Whoever booked the rooms could only get two with two beds and a cot in each, so two members would have to sleep on the floor in a sleeping bag. Ben had been given the task of organizing the sleeping arrangements, and he was having a hard time dealing with Ann and Andréa, who were bickering over who was going to sleep with Liz, who hadn't arrived yet. Liz had powerful psychic abilities and was known to scan people with noxious vibrations at times. Ben sensed her aura was ripe with toxic vibrations which was not good for a roomful of sensitives. "Listen," Ben said, trying to lighten the mood, "if it will make you feel better, I'll sleep with Liz!" Getting down on one knee with one hand outstretched and the other on his heart, he recited a bit of Shakespeare: "It is a far, far better thing that I do, than I have ever done."

Everyone broke out into a laughing fit. "Your sense of humor is too much, Ben!" Ann shouted.

Having lightened the mood, Ben took that moment to recommend that they all draw straws for who would sleep in the two beds.

"I have a handful of straws cut into different sizes. Each size has a male and female pair. The four people who get the first two pairs will share the two beds. Fair?"

They all agreed and chose their straws.

Ben discovered that he and Ann had gotten matching straws, meaning they'd share a bed. He couldn't help but feel secretly pleased. She was nice-looking, and he was hoping they would be compatible. He didn't know at the time that his intuition would prove correct that night. Meanwhile, the others accepted their sleeping assignments with no further disagreements. By the time Liz arrived, she had no choice but to accept use a sleeping bag that night.

The next morning, they rose early, dropped into the spaceship restaurant for breakfast and were off to hike on the mountain. They parked about midway up the mountain then gathered in a circle so Andrea could outline the hiking parameters.

"OK, so if you move away from the group, make sure you bring your whistle and water with you, because voices are hard to hear on the mountain and you might need to hydrate. Listen for the whistle in about an hour or so to regroup," she instructed.

Ben headed to Panther Meadows with a few others. The Meadows was a very serene and spiritual place revered by the Native Americans for centuries. The springtime view of the mountain's summit was especially spectacular. From their perspective, it looked to be right in front of their faces, even though it was ten miles away. Deer, squirrels and even bears were frequent visitors to the area. Ben was enchanted by a small brook running through the meadow that, to his mind, was so perfect, it seemed to be the prototype of a "babbling brook." Reviewing his photos of this place later, he saw multicolored orbs floating in the meadow reflecting the sunlight.

Ben thought, *It feels like a time warp up here. Maybe that's why you can't hear voices and you have to use a whistle to hear someone.*

"I'm going further up the mountain to see what's there," Ben told his friends. He blissfully wound his way up the mountain for a while until he looked back and realized how easily he could get lost if he didn't mark his trail. Remembering his Boy Scout training, he gathered up a group of rocks and made a totem. About every 50 or 100 feet he would build another one to make sure he could get back to the others. As Ben was walking, he could see red shale rock up ahead of him, which was his landmark to move towards as he headed up the mountain.

As he reached the rocks, a strong wind blew his hat off. The wind came up again out of nowhere, but he didn't think much about it at the time. Putting his hat back on, another wind came up, blowing it off again, and this time, he heard a craft reverberate within the mountain. *Oh,* he thought, *there are ships coming toward me reverberating inside the mountain.* Outstanding! he felt no fear or concern; instead, he thought projected towards the ships, *"Hi guys! Nice to meet you,* "Ben heard a voice say to him, telepathically, nice to interact with you Ben. We can read your auric field and consciousness signaling us that you are an ascended being well on your way in your ascension process. You are a master being and star seed here to uplift humanity and Gaia's energy expression towards transmutation of lower energies on her way to create the 5th dimensional density. Your auric colors are very dynamic and express your consciousness reflected in fuchsia, blue and metallic purple.

Just then, Ben heard a whistle off in the distance – Andrea's signal to regroup. He turned and walked briskly down the hill, waving a hand to his new friends saying, "nice to interact with you."

Ben followed his totems and listening for the whistle sound until he reunited with his friends at Panther Meadows.

Ben said, "You won't believe what happened to me."

"What?" said Lynelle inquisitively?

Ben recounted the story of the wind and the ships reverberating inside the mountain.

"Well," said Lynelle, "you have all the luck."

"Yeah," Ben said, "being an American Indian, I like to commune with nature – it sometimes turns out to be very special."

"I'd like to experience that myself," said Lynelle.

"Sorry Lynelle. Maybe next time," Ben said.

After Panther Meadows, they headed back to town to check out Joe's bookstore and find out about local spiritual locations and possible functions going on that weekend. Thumbing through a spiritual pamphlet, Andrea said to the group, "This has a couple of ideas for places we can visit while we're here. Stewart Hot Springs, for example. I heard that place is really great."

Ann chimed in, "We were talking about Stewart's on the way up."

"Oh yeah," said Ben, "I heard that Pluto Caves and the Three Falls are also spiritual places."

"Well, we have time to visit some of these places this weekend," continued Andrea.

While they were there, Ben bought a copy of the Crystal Bible, not having a current copy at the time. It was one of the best books on crystals from a spiritual and scientific point of view. He also found a book on dowsing that he was interested in. They all shopped on their own and reconvened at the UFO craft restaurant. *I don't know what it is about that restaurant, but it has an elusive energy draw*, Ben thought. They had dinner, headed back to the rooms and worked out that night's sleeping arrangements. Luckily, Ben was paired with Ann again, and they ended up having a little fun while the others slept. *Divorced women know all the right places to touch*, Ben thought.

As he was falling asleep, Ben suddenly felt an excruciating pain energy coming into his head. Just as quickly as the pain came on, an image came into his mind of a metallic purple spoon moving across a metallic purple grid that tipped and poured this metallic purple energy substance all over him. As he felt the flow of the energy, it completely dissipated the pain in his head. Ben had never seen a purple that dark with a metallic sheen before. He pondered for a long time what this energy was. It wasn't until later that he found out that it was spiritual energy from one of his guides whom he had yet to meet.

Ben would be pulled up around the planet a second time, and this time, he would meet Zamacodod, a Persian magician. The seemingly impossible shade of purple was the color ray that Zamacodod worked with. It was part of his consciousness that related to his own individual hue, just as it is with all beings. Some may have more than one color. Colors are an energy vibration/frequency, and as such, they have a consciousness and life force. This particular color energy communicated to Ben that it was a higher vibration even than St. Germain's violet flame, though Ben didn't know what to make of this information – he wouldn't understand it until much later.

Ben wondered what had caused the pain energy. He assumed it was a toxic energy coming from a psychotronics frequency projection somewhere in the Shasta area. Shortly after Ben woke up from sleeping, he told his experience to the others, and they were flabbergasted at the possibility of something like this happening to him in such a serene place. *Consciousness is something we really don't understand much about,* Ben thought. *Of course, if you are locked into the third dimension that makes sense too.*

When he got back to San Francisco, there would be interesting synchronistic events related to the experience he had in Shasta that night, but the next day, Ben's focus was on Stewart Hot Springs, just north of the town. Following the frontage road, Ben watched the majestic mountain loom full ahead as they drove –a treat in itself. The snowcapped mountain looked like a picture postcard. The wooden fences that held back the dry grasses lining the asphalt road painted a picture of a different, long ago time. They turned off onto a dirt road that wound through tall grasses and ended at a rustic wooden structure next to a pristine clear stream of mountain snow water. This was the massage and hot tub center. They all got out of the cars and walked into the building. Inside, there was a stillness that cut through the incensed airways that titillated your senses to its maximum capacity. Beautiful rugs helped to soften the spaces. A bookstore stood off to one side, with the latest poster of a UFO cloud surrounding the Mount Shasta summit and books on meditation and New Age practices.

Healing tools and exotic soaps and UFO cards abounded on display shelves and tables. *Don't forget the card racks*, a thought said to Ben. *OK thanks,* said Ben, to himself. Tubs full of mineral spring water and mud baths were allotted to the smaller rooms on both sides of the hallway. Massage was an important part of this environment and additional rooms were provided for this purpose.

"I'm going to book a room in the mineral baths," Andrea said.

"I'm going to buy a book and head for the room for a mud bath," said Lynelle.

"Let's get a room with two baths so we can talk about the trip." Andrea suggested.

"Ok." said Lynelle, "that's a good idea."

Andrea said, "do you want to do the mud bath or the mineral baths first," Lynelle.

Lynelle replied, "the mud bath."

Ben said, "I'm going to book an hour massage."

And Bill replied, "that sounds good to me too."

The others moved down the hallway to a wooden deck area overlooking the stream and towards the books.

After his massage, Ben grabbed his clothes walked down the hall towards the outside balcony. As he stepped out through the double doors onto the outside deck, he felt the warmth and stillness. Ben leaned over the rail musing over the crystal-clear water with his bum hanging out. He was no stranger to being naked. In college he modeled for life drawing classes to make extra money to go to school. He was proud of his body, having been a high-level wrestler in his younger days. He had that quintessentially athletic body that was depicted in Michelangelo's David.

A couple of patrons ran out of the double doors and down the stairs and jumped into the icy water. Yells of "Eeooo!" could be heard as they hit the water. They were people from the mud baths that needed to cool themselves off. However, it wasn't long before they came out of the water. It originated in glaciers and Ben assumed it was extremely cold. Ben thought to himself, *I think I'm going to try the water myself.* He walked down the steps and tested the water was his big toe exclaiming, "Yeoooo," as he recoiled his foot from the water, this would be harder than he thought. He didn't mind being naked in the open air but stepping into this ice water was going to be a challenge. He took a deep breath and waded into the pool of icy water. He felt the cold in his gonads first as they shrank to half their size. Then the cold moved up his torso, sending a shiver up and down his body. Every muscle tensed in his frame making him feel like he was the tin man in the *Wizard of Oz*. He slowly waded across the stream to the other side and stepped out onto the rocks with lightning speed, all the while grunting "Au,oo,au,oo" as he moved across the rocks. Fortunately, there was a chair on the other side for sunbathing or meditating. Relaxing into the chair, Ben thought, *You could get frostbite in that water if you stayed in too long.*

As soon as he started to warm up, he went into a meditation. The smells of nature came wafting through his nostrils and the babbling brook stimulated his ears as he settled into the serenity of nature. He wished he had his crystal that would cement the experience. He had been meditating for years and knew that meditating with a crystal led to a clearer and stronger meditation by far; a clear quartz crystal was preferable. Nonetheless, his feeling of peace was at its peak. He decided to bring down the atomic energy of the Christ in his meditation in this place of serenity.

Ben visualized the chakras. He started with the root chakra, the red center, then the sacral center, orange, solarplex's, yellow center, heart center, green and pink center, throat chakra, blue center, brow chakra, indigo recess, and the crown charka where the violet colored vortex resides. Then he used his consciousness like a flashlight to search, four to eight feet above his head for the Christ center. Finding the solar orb, the atomic gold energy ran automatically down to the crown chakra; stimulating the brow chakra, moving to the throat center. He finds that this chakra blocks the energy and doesn't run to the lower chakras.

He visualizes blue lotus flower opening, feeling the atomic flow again moving through the chakra heading for the heart center. As it flows through the other chakras Ben grounds the Chi into Gaia's center. He at this point, feels the euphoria that comes upon him as the force integrates through the body. He is feeling peace.

Ben heard a faint voice call his name. He opened his eyes and saw Lynelle waving to him across the brook.

"It's time to come back, Ben. We need to get going to Pluto caves."

Finishing the chakra meditation naked, Ben felt free, alive and especially balanced now. He looked down at his little friend. Shrunken in the cold, he looked like a puppy nesting in his lap. Ben had a fond feeling for it; after all, they had been together their whole lives. Ben lifted off from the chair and waded across the stream shivering, blue and free of embarrassment.

Lynelle said, "Get dressed. We're off to Pluto caves. Nice birthday suit, by the way. I haven't seen it before."

"I know," said Ben, jokingly. "The question is would you like to see more."

"I may," she replied with a wink and a hip throw. She had a tall slender shape that made a perfect silhouette against the background. She, too, was nude and looked to Ben like a gazelle walking across a meadow; she was very poetic and erotic.

"See you up front in about 5 minutes," said Ben.

Chapter Nine

Spirit Becomes manifest In 3-D time

They pulled into the Pluto Caves parking in the early afternoon. They couldn't see anything of the cave from the parking lot. The caves were the location of a Native American settlement. Located in a desert region of Northern California, there were no hills or mounds nearby that would signify a normal cave system. Ben walked across the parking lot looking for a trail to the caves. As he moved across the paved terrain, a very angry Indian spirit came flying towards him out of nowhere, plowing into his left shoulder feet first and almost knocking him down. Ben immediately let out a yell and called in the Christ consciousness from on high as he had done many times in similar situations. As the dynamic atomic energy came down, he felt the release of any fear from his body as his spirit rebalanced itself. That was all it took to block any more aggression from the negative spirit.

Andrea called across the parking lot, "Are you all right Ben?" Being an excellent psychic, she had seen the whole episodes transpire.

"Yes. The Christ consciousness did the trick. I'm safe."

The others asked what was going on, and ben and Andrea filled them in.

Lynelle jumped in and said, "Let's make a circle and do a prayer of protection before we go into the caves." She led them as they projected a golden light that moved counterclockwise around the outside of the circle and then another around the group going the opposite direction. They were all familiar with this process because they always did such an invocation before the crystal healing group started. She called upon the healing masters and angelic forms and personal guides to protect them while they were in the caves. "It is done. It is finished in light," she said.

In later years, Ben would occasionally think about the incident at Pluto Caves. The sheer amount of negative force it must have taken for the spirit to have penetrated the veil between the dimensions and impact both Ben's auric field and physical body was both remarkable and terribly sad.

They all headed down the path towards the caves. As they traversed the arid terrain, they started to see a large opening in the Earth among the green scrub brush. Suddenly they came upon a large, open entrance that passed down underground. They walked a short distance down, running their hands across the fine grasses that signified the Indian birthing area, according to the little sign protruding out of the ground. The energy there was very nice. After the nursery, there was a cooking area that had a feeling of utility and work environment. He could see in his mind's eye some Indian women grinding raw plants into fine powder and manipulating them into tortillas to be grilled on a flat rock heated over a fire.

Off to the left was the largest area with a huge concave ceiling scorched with black soot from many campfires. Ben felt incredibly noxious energy in that area and decided it would be better for him to avoid this space. He didn't think he could transmute the energy there.

Lynelle said, "We are going to look into that big cave over there."

Ben interjected, "Are you sure you want to venture into that toxic environment?"

Lynelle replied, "Are you kidding? I don't fear evil. I'm protected by the higher forces."

"I hope you're right," said Ben. "If you come back with a weird look in your eyes, I'm going to a local shaman so we can get the negative spirit out of your body."

Lynelle and Andrea laughed and took off for the big cave.

Ben sat down to meditate in the birthing area. In about 10 or 15 min. Lynelle and Andrea came back in a somber mood with a strange look in their eyes, as if they were in a trance state.

Ben thought, *Oh God, this is going to be a strange ride back to town.*

"What was that local shaman's name?" said Lynelle.

Lynelle and Andrea started laughing. "We got you! You thought we'd been possessed, didn't you? We gotcha!"

Then Andrea became more serious. "We did feel some powerful negative energies in the cave, but after calling in the light of the Christ energy, we protected ourselves."

"There were a whole group of negative Indian spirits huddled around their campfire, but they didn't bother us," Lynelle added.

The other people in the group had more normal experiences, and they all headed back to town in early evening. At the inn, they made a circle of protection, did an affirmation and said their goodbyes so they could rise early to head back to San Francisco at a leisurely pace. Packing for the trip back to San Francisco Ben discussed the ride back with his passengers, Ann and Liz. Ben wanted to stop off at the home of a friend of his, a local crystal practitioner and artist named Jed. The women agreed.

As they pulled up to Jed's place, Ben could see him waiting in the driveway. Jed greeted them with a wave. After introductions, they headed inside to see Jed's art. His home was full of painting after painting of MT. Shasta and those famous clouds at the summit. A realistic spaceship came flying in from space in pink and blue and yellow. There was a photograph of a white mountain and a purple swatch, and Ben asked what it was.

Jed replied, "It's the Himalayas. It's not a photograph – it's one of my paintings."

On closer inspection, Ben saw that it was indeed a painting. He could tell by the color swatch in purple flying by on the lower part of the mountain.

"Wow, Jed. I thought it was a photograph at first, you really did a good job. I like that purple swatch at the bottom and the old man face at the highest peak of the mountain. The face at the top of the mountain was an optical illusion Jed had incorporated into painting. It was not immediately apparent to the eye, but it revealed itself when the brain was switched to the left or right hemispheres.

Ben had a unit in his art curriculum that showed how to look at an optical illusion one way and then the other. Most artists, even great artists, switch from the left brain to the right brain because it accesses the holistic creative side of the brain. More than likely, they are not aware that they are making the switch. Ben taught kids how to make their own optical illusions themselves. In fact, while subbing for a middle school in Marin County, he discovered the kids in the art class were far ahead of the game, creating their own optical illusions before he even got there. These kids were producing optical illusions all over the place. They really understood the concept.

Ben offered to buy the Himalaya painting and one with an ET craft coming in towards Mount Shasta from space, and Jed agreed to just forty dollars for both. Then Ben spied a large shivalina stone in the corner with the smooth egg shape and beautiful colors of rust browns and purple stripes running through it that distinguished it from other stones. The stones were typically found in the streams of India and came in all sizes. Ben picked it up and tuned into its energy; he immediately saw a crystal-clear image of where the stone was found. Ben remarked to Jed and the others that he could see the location of the stone in a desert scene with tall cactuses at the end of a road.

Jed's eyebrows arched upward in surprise as Ben described the scene. "You're right Ben. I found that shivalina stone not far from the Mount Shasta foothills. Your sight is really clear."

"My second sight has never been this clear before. It must be the energy of this area," replied Ben.

"Maybe," Jed said. "This type of thing happens a lot up here."

"You have some really clear quartz crystals here," said Ben, "I wish I could afford them."

"Well, maybe next time you come to visit me, you can pick up some others."

"I look forward to it." Turning to the others, Ben said,"OK, let's push off. We have a long drive back to San Francisco."

As they left Mt. Shasta, they took one last look at the majestic view. An hour into the drive, Ben heard Liz and Ann in the backseat trying to connect their consciousness together and experimenting with techniques for sending colors, shapes, textures and numbers telepathically. After a while, they tuned in on Ben's nervous system. He felt them trying to enter his auric field to entrain him in some manner. Unhappy with this intrusion, Ben felt he needed to protect himself. He had several methods of doing this and spent the next two hours defending himself.

The mental concentration needed to protect himself was monumental, but coming into San Francisco, his mind was ablaze. He had reached a level of consciousness and mental clarity, that he had not reached before. He had won out on this test of wills and still retained control of his cognitive faculties, emotional willpower and life force. They could not penetrate his auric field.

The primary technique he used was holding his breath, which locks out unwanted energies coming into one's field and body. This was only one technique that he used to divert their toxic, controlling energy. Ben learned the other methods over the years from experiments, trial and error, sacred texts and higher forces. Ben made a mental note to keep a close eye on those two in the future.

The incident reminded Ben of a woman he had met at his sun gazing workshop. Nellie was dynamic and had an effervescent personality and expressed a lot of light through her auric field as Ben perceived it. You could see the light shining off her from a long way off. Ben was talking over in the corner with someone and excused himself to say hello.

"Hi Nellie. I haven't seen you since the time you attended my workshop a couple years ago."

"Hi Ben," she said in a low, unconfident manner. "I didn't know you were coming to our meditation group."

"Yes. Lidia comes up to our group in San Francisco from time to time. We thought we would try and see what her group was like tonight."

Ben mused to himself, *She is totally different than the first time I met her. She's no longer the effervescent person she was at my Solar lecture.* Her lack of energy was disturbing. The three people flanking her took an interest in Ben's energy level as they conversed.

"Are you all right? You seem very off," Ben said, in a questioning sincere tone.

"Oh, I'm going through a rebirth in my consciousness right now," replied Nellie.

Ben thought to himself, *I don't believe a word she said. She is exhibiting characteristics of a person going through a mental breakdown*. It was at that time that Ben intuitively realized those three women around her were connected to her auric field and drawing off her life force.

Ben tried to get Nellie's attention to communicate that her sacred space was being violated and she needed help to recover from this, but she wasn't listening or couldn't listen.

Ben tried again. "Let's go to the other room, I have something I want to say to you."

Her friends seemed upset by this request, but Ben and Nellie went into the other room anyway. Ben told her what he was feeling.

Nellie protested, "No I'm having a consciousness rebirth."

"No," replied Ben. "You're having a nervous breakdown. Search yourself. It will tell you the truth."

Nellie thought for a moment and started crying.

"It's all right," said Ben, "I can help you recover back to your vibrant self."

Nellie stopped crying and a big smile spread across her face. "OK, how can you help me?"

"First you should get away from the three friends that are around you tonight. They're sucking off your life force energy; they're psychic vampires. I can give you a ride home if you need my help," said Ben. "Next, you should call me next week, and I can start you back on a program of looking at the sun. This will bring back your energy level and connect you with your true self again. Let's go back to the group now."

"OK," said Nellie, "I could use a ride home and I'll call you next week, I really appreciate your help… you are a Godsend."

"Ok,I look forward to it," said Ben and they rejoined the group.

Lidia led the group and started with her favorite opening affirmation. It was an interesting, but it wasn't at all like Lynelle's visualization. Ben notice Joan Scean was there from the sister group in Belmont. After the meditation, Ben approached Joan.

"Hi Joan," said Ben.

"Oh, hi Ben, What have you been up to?"

"We have just come back from Mount Shasta. I had an ET craft experience on the mountain, among other things."

"That sounds exciting, I'd like to hear about it sometime, but right now I have to get home because I'm flying out tomorrow to meet my boyfriend Pierre. We are going to start our dolphin connection business, and we need to firm up a deal on the boat. We're pursuing our idea of building an aquatic structure for dolphins that swim in and out, with a special research center. We have been swimming with the dolphins for a long time now and I have a special connection with dolphin communication – sonic wave forms."

"Good luck, Joan," Ben said. Joan and her boyfriend Pierre had envisioned this business and dolphin center for a long time. They had been speaking around the Bay Area for a number of years about their idea.

Back at his apartment the next day, Ben engaged in his usual early morning practice of looking at the sun then meditating, but a bothersome housefly was interrupting his meditation process. Annoyed, Ben wondered how he could get the fly to leave or settle down. *If we are all one, we all have the same consciousness on certain levels,* he thought. *If I can find this fly's level, I should be able to communicate with it.* Then he chuckled to himself, *this sounds like a Buddhist parable.* Determined to try, Ben began the creative and intuitive process of seeking the fly's consciousness when he started receiving a communication from Zaln, his ET guide.

"Experiencing with your Over Soul is important in communication with other life forms. Focusing on the sound of the fly's energy pattern and perceiving the fly's flight pattern will enable you to impart a simple message to it. Of course, you will first need to access your Over Soul to do this," Zaln advised.

Ben contacted his Over Soul by raising it upwards through his being. Eventually, he began to perceive the spirit of the fly's energy and flight patterns until he was able to form a connection with the insect. Through their connected consciousnesses, Ben told the fly to land and remain quiet for a while, and it followed his request. *That was easy,* Ben thought.

Zaln, still present, communicated with Ben again. "This is a process you can use to communicate not only with insects but all other life forms as well. In fact, it is not even limited animate life forms; you can contact any form or level of life. This marks a new stage in your spiritual development," Zaln continued. "Your thoughts are real, your fantasies are real, the thoughts in your super consciousness are real, they are a reality; a different dimensional/density reality. You are creating force fields all the time that move out from your being, reading energy patterns that create the images you see in your mind's eye. In terms of energy, you are no different than what you see in front of you in the physical reality at any given time. You are not separate from the reality you perceive. You are energetically connected through your ectoplasm field."

I understand, Ben thought.

"But there is more to understand," Zaln went on. "There are even greater implications. If you are able to perceive a physical object on an energetic level – if you can perceive its true essence – you can put your hand right through it. This is because, in such a state, you are perceiving that you are not different from the object you are perceiving. You're actually one and the same in consciousness. It is a question of the level at which you perceive the object, as with the fly. Perceiving an object at the right level of consciousness allows you to merge or integrate with it, but it requires a shift to a super level of consciousness, an expansion of consciousness to the outer reaches of your auric field or the depths of your eternal light or self or soul; the faceted diamond that contains your consciousness that you first received in your crystal meditation group so many years ago."

Ben had a lot to think about. "Thank you, Zaln," he said. "You have given me a lot to think about. I appreciate you sharing special consciousness with me on a soul level."

"I'm here to serve," Zaln replied. Then he bowed and extended his arms to his sides in acknowledgement.

Coming out of this state of consciousness, Ben felt very peaceful and balanced. He stood up and walked to the deck, focusing on the view. It was a beautiful day, and the Bay Bridge was as majestic as always. Taking out the journal where he recorded all his spiritual experiences, he flipped to the page that contained a poem he had recently written. He had read a poem by Margret Atwood in the Sunday World section of the paper and was inspired to write one of his own about psychotronics bombardment:

> There is a sickly sweetness around the parameters of his body, as he contemplates the ramifications of a thought, he became aware of the minute pulses of energy hitting his stomach area;
>
> There is a rain of intangible energy coming down upon his head, as he listened to the sweet music of Vivaldi;
>
> He put the crown of inference patterns upon his head to counteract the bizarre encroachment of his freedom of thoughts, mind controllers are here to stay;
>
> His auric field cries out for the expansion of light, that is its birth right, that expresses his soul's aspirations;
>
> Here is little piece from the mind suppressors as they weave their disruptive web of control, but at last he breaks through the barrier with the help of sound vibrations and poetry;
>
> The creative spirit is upon him again, as he enters the column waveform, the

old familiar feeling that floods his auric fields, Kataro now rushes through his head, and he flies on the wings of his sound, like the winged gods of old;

He can express himself again, moving through the sound as in a dream expressed long ago, once upon a time, in another land and another time.

Ben Chavez

Reading this poem gave Ben peace again.

For some reason he had the desire to pull out his Ouija board, which he could sometimes use, with help, to communicate with higher spiritual beings and not drop into the lower astral level of consciousness. He was not afraid of this divining instrument as he had always had a good result from using it. He thought he would communicate with Ariel the archangel as he had designated letter A to him, but he realized as he started to communicate with him that he felt a different energy coming into his consciousness. With that energy he left the Ouija board behind and started receiving a direct communication from what turned out to be Commander Aton from the Astara. Aton's energy, by now, had become very familiar to Ben.

"You must continue serving the needs of the Astara Command," Aton said.

"What are your needs?" asked Ben.

"You must continue to monitor the communications of the evil forces on your planet. As you well know, your government has a tactical knowledge now to control the emotional body level of beings on your planet. Understand: this may be the beginning of the suppression of mankind on your globe through the control of free will. We have seen it happen on other planets and wish to help your planet rid itself of evil influence, for the total expansion of humankind. We will continue to communicate with you from time to time, Love be with you always, Aton, Astara Command."

Chapter Ten

The Puzzle Continues To Reveal It's Self

Coming out of the communication from Aton, Ben heard the phone ringing. Lucid again, he picked it up. It was Sean. Sean was an old friend from Ben's past at one of the many jobs that he had worked at for the last couple of years.

"I haven't heard from to you for a long time," said Ben.

"Yes, I'm going with a friend of mine to the Russian River this weekend. Would you like to go with us? We can catch up on our way up to the river."

"Sure, said Ben, I haven't been back to the Russian River for a long time and I would like to hear what you have been up to for the last few of years.

"OK, I'll pick you up Saturday at nine in the morning," said Sean. "You'll really like my friend he's an ex-CIA agent."

Ben hung up the phone and started packing for an overnight get-together with his friend for the weekend. He thought about what Sean had said about his CIA friend and wondered what that was all about. *This could be an interesting trip*, he thought.

Nine o'clock Saturday morning rolled around sooner than Ben had anticipated. When Ben got down to the ground floor of the apartment Sean and another man were waiting in the car. As Ben got in, Sean said, "This is my friend Larry."

"Hi, Ben," said Larry, "Sean was telling me that you're interested in metaphysics and parapsychology. He said you have your own psychic abilities."

"Yes, I have a Master's degree in parapsychology education and art. It was a mixed major at an alternative college."

Larry continued, "The CIA had a few programs over the years in this area." Larry was a typical agent giving you a carrot stick of information without really giving you much information at all.

"Yes," Ben said, "I have heard of some of these programs."

Ben told Larry he knew full well about MK Ultra, the research with Ingo Swann, and the more recent research into directing toxic energy through one person's body and into anyone they wanted to disrupt to throw them emotionally off balance. And of course, Remote Viewing was a big subject area with the CIA.

Larry raised an eyebrow over the last subject, Ben noticed.

Ben thought, *I got his attention with that mention.* They talked very little after that as they drove the hour and a half to the Russian River.

They pulled into the cottage parking lot area around 3 o'clock. The Russian River was a somewhat interesting area in the northern part of California. It was known for its alternative lifestyles – gay, straight and others – that drew different groups to the area for a fun weekend. Ben thought about the girlfriend he had taken up to the river on a horseback riding excursion at a pretty little blue and white lodge nestled among the Ponderosa Pine forest. Some gays had a disco dancing and swimming retreat nestled into the trees down the street. There were several small, rural communities quietly situated on the river. Of course, the famous political retreat for high rollers and politicians and statesmen from all over the world was there – the Bohemian Grove. Ben had heard of the demonic rituals that went on there and had even seen a documentary by people who had snuck into the Grove to film of the proceedings. A huge stone owl acted as a backdrop for the demonic ritual that was its main focal point. The statute seemed to be an ancient symbol for demonic groups in the historical past.

They checked into their rooms and then had dinner at the hotel restaurant. After dinner they went out to the lawn area just off the River, to talk and have a drink. Ben learned that Larry was applying for a supervisor job at Blue Shield. Eventually, of course, he launched into a story of his work at the CIA, where he was a spy in Russia.

"I was in Red Square waiting for a Russian courier to hand off a microchip, but instead, he shot a cap into my knee," Larry said. "As I went down, I positioned my gun at just the right angle to get off one shot between his eyes, and he fell like so much dead weight sprawling on the ground. I picked myself up and retreated as quickly as possible, hailing a cab back to a safe house where I was staying. That was one shot in a lifetime, and it saved my life," Larry continued.

Sean and Ben were captivated by Larry's stories well into the night. At last, they retreated to their rooms to sleep, leaving Larry as he headed to the bar to tell his stories of the Russian cold war to a new audience.

The next morning, they rose early to have some breakfast. Afterwards, Sean said, "I want to go on a run before we head back to the city."

Larry suggested Ben take a walk with him while Larry ran.

"Sure." said Ben, wanting to get out in nature as much as possible. This appealed to his long-standing history of being an American Indian not only in this lifetime but others as well.

They made their way to a dirt trail through the woods. In a few minutes, Sean came running past with a big grin on face and continued down the path. This struck Ben as peculiar for some reason. His intuition was on high alert in this particular environment.

Larry started talking and said, "Is there anything you want to know about the CIA, Ben?"

This was a strange request, Ben thought. "Oh," replied Ben, "I haven't really thought about it."

"Go ahead, "prompted Larry. "I'll answer anything you want to know."

Ben shrugged his shoulders and thought, *I should ask him something about the CIA mind control programs*, but Ben didn't go there for some reason.

Ben's evasive responses seemed to create an angry reaction in Larry who suddenly blurted out, "Maybe I should just teach you how to spell!"

This stuck Ben as strange. How did Larry know he was a bad speller? Then he realized Larry had just blown his cover. Larry was still CIA, and he was trying to pump Ben for information on what he knew about psychical mind control. *I wonder if this was the reason Sean wanted me to go on this trip in the first place?* Ben thought.

They walked silently back to the cottage, had an early dinner with little conversation and started the long drive back to San Francisco.

As he said his goodbyes, Ben turned to Larry with a big smile and said, "See you, Larry. Hope you learned something educational."

Larry just brooded and said nothing.

Then Ben said, "Bye Sean. It's been nice knowing you."

Checking his messages, he found one from Michael Bennelli, a old friend, who wanted to know about going on a day trip to Inverness on the northern coast of California. It was late, so Ben put off calling Michael until the next day after work.

Ben told Michael he would like to take a trip up north and enjoying the fantastic scenic views. They made plans to leave the following Saturday morning.

Ben checked for other messages on this machine. David called and wanted to get together for a movie. Ben gave him a call. "I'm busy on Saturday. I'm going up the coast on a day trip with Michael, who I met at my favorite pastry café in the Castro."

"Yes," David replied, "I know where you are talking about. I love their chocolate blackberry Tart."

"That's my favorite," Ben said.

"How about Sunday or next weekend? There's a new Star Trek movie I'd like to see," said David. "I was also thinking about the new Jesus Christ movie. It is very controversial, and a lot of the local religious groups are protesting the film. I like to see what all the hubbub is about."

"OK, that sounds like a good movie to see," said Ben, being somewhat of a revolutionary himself. "Give me a call next week David."

David was an old friend of Ben's from his Buddhist days. He hit it off right away with him and his girlfriend who had just graduated from Arizona State University. One of the many funny stories David had told Ben was about his nickname – The Biggest Soft Man in the World. He had gotten it from a construction crew while working his way out to California from Arizona. That was a fitting name for him as he was a big meaty lumberjack type of man who had a considerable amount of baby fat. When you gave David a hug, his aura was really soft and cuddly. He was also a hairy man -- Bigfoot had nothing over David. They had many fun and interesting experiences over the years. Ben knew him when he married his wife and had a son. He was a creative and avant-garde type of person who was always on the front lines of any social issues. He even dyed his hair white one time to keep up with local styles. At that time, it was known as "campy."

The end of the week came quickly, and Ben rose early and prepared the things he would need for the day trip with Michael. Ben heard the doorbell ring, and Michael's voice came over the intercom. "It's me Michael."

Ben loaded his stuff in the car and they headed north. On the drive, Ben got to know Michael little better. "As you know, I'm an artist – a painter – and I own an advertising company. In fact, I have a deal pending with Hallmark to revitalize their card line," said Michael. "I'm moving to San Diego because the rental prices are so much lower there."

"What's the deal you have with Hallmark?"

"It has to do with adding an object to the card related to the message you are reading. I'm in confidential negotiations with them to give this line to my company exclusively."

"Do you think they will go for it," Ben inquired.

"I'm not sure right now, but they would be stupid to pass this idea up. I think it's a matter of having to retool their product line to move in that direction. But It would cost them a considerable amount of money, so I have my fingers crossed," Michael said.

They drove on in silence for a short while when Michael started revealing to Ben more of what his life was like. "I also have a few paintings in a prestigious art gallery in Paris. And I also have a full-size photograph of myself in a tuxedo and a straw hat in that gallery."

Ben laughed heartily at the thought of such a photo in a gallery, but Michael said it wasn't supposed to be funny.

"But you have two contrasting cultures," said Ben. "That's funny."

"Well, maybe. But you see, my families on one side were farmers while my families on the other side were aristocrats from royalty. I'm the last remaining prince of Italy."

"Oh really?" said Ben, "Wow!"

Michael went on to say that when the time came, he would find a woman to have a baby with to keep the line going.

"I can find a couple of lesbians that will have my baby, if necessary."

"So, you're gay," Ben asked?

"Yes," said Michael. "You didn't know that?"

"No," replied Ben. "Well, It's OK I'm not going to bother you. You're a cute guy and I found something interesting in your demeanor and personality that I liked. Gay's just a relative term. I'm more universal than that – I'm European. That's why I want to get to know you better. I sensed something more in you. I planned for us to stay overnight at an inn at Point Rays. Is that OK? We can sleep in separate beds."

Ben fumbled with his thoughts and feelings. *I don't discriminate against any group or person, h*e thought, *so why should I be fearful? We are all God's children.*

"OK," said Ben. "No problem. It will be a nice trip." He also felt something more in Michael. "But I'm not gay,' he added, though he thought Michael understood that already.

They arrived at the inn in early evening and checked into the room; there were two beds.

Michael said, "I know a small restaurant not far from here that has good seafood. Let's get a bite to eat."

"OK," Ben said, nodding his head.

As they sat down at the table, Michael said to the waiter, I know what I want but you can bring a menu for my friend. The waiter nodded and disappeared into the back of the restaurant.

"They have a great lobster here. That's what I'm having, How about you?"

The waiter returned with a menu. Looking over the entrées Ben said, "I'll have the lobster too. It looks pretty good."

The restaurant was nestled into the pine trees with a rustic wood siding with outside boards that still had the bark of the trees still on them. Inside, it was quiet and comfortable with small tables with decorative red and white checkered tablecloths. Small copper candleholders reflected the candlelight creating metallic reddish colors. It added to the softness of the surroundings.

Michael started telling Ben about his youth in Italy. He was born with an extra rib and had to have it removed. He described the horrific ordeal having the rib removed without any anesthesia.

Michael said, "I know my pain threshold now."

"Why are you telling me this Michael?"

"Oh, no reason it's just part of my story."

Somehow Ben felt there was more to his comment than he was letting on. "What is your artwork like? asked Ben. "I'm an art teacher, myself."

"It's hard to describe," replied Michael, "There are figures moving through a dense fog that morphs in and out of the background."

"That sounds really interesting," said Ben. "It sounds like you are creating a dream state with these figures."

"Yes, maybe you're right. That's an interesting perspective." Michael changed the subject and spoke no more of his artwork for the rest of the trip.

"You are an art teacher. What is your preferred medium?" Michael asked.

"Well, I gravitated towards sculpture and design in college but evolved into photography later on in my life. I developed my own photos in my darkroom for my book."

"I'd like to see your photographs sometime," said Michael. "What is your book about?"

"It concerns teaching children and young adults psychic, intuitive and spiritual skills. It also contains new information for adults also. I published it through an indie publisher; it's also an e-book."

"Great. That sounds like an interesting book. Was it a lot of work putting it together?"

"Yes, it was, but I had a lot of support from people in my Master's program and later on, when it was updated," said Ben. "It was a combined major – art, education and parapsychology. I created my own program. It took my two and half years to write the manuscript."

"I can relate," said Michael, "I have a PhD in international finance. I travel back and forth to Europe for my company. It all started when I had to get out of Italy and couldn't bring my parents' money because of the communist. My parents were in the Roads and Highway Department for the state of Morales. I went to New York and locked myself into my hotel for two weeks and mass-produced artwork. I took it down to the local fabric design studios and they liked my work so much that I was able to start my own fabric printing company in France. I had seventeen employees at one time. Eventually I sold the business and went into creating designs for prospective clients. I developed my own design firm and moved to the United States."

This person is brilliant, Ben thought. "Are you part of the CIA?" Ben asked off the cuff. Ben felt intuitively that something else was going on with Michael.

"Well," Michael replied, "the CIA was checking my credentials for a long time, and I had a problem with them trying to get my personal identification, so they could entrap me in some scheme of theirs, I'm sure."

Ben let it go at that. After dinner they headed for the cottage and turned in for the evening. It turned out to be a very quiet evening. They woke early that morning and went over for breakfast and discussed the next stop on their trip. They decided to stop by Muir Woods on the way back to San Francisco. They wound their way down to Muir Woods and arrived at a lush forest paradise of old redwood trees and other old-growth trees and flowering plants. They walked a short distance along the wooden walkways reading individual placards for each tree and shrub. It was a photographer's paradise as they saw the most incredible 100-year-old trees. They stopped at the United Nations memorial plaque commemorating Pres. Franklin D Roosevelt's redwood tree. He made many trips to the woods during his tenure as president.

From there, they started their ascent back up Mount Tamaulipas, heading to the main road back to San Francisco. It was always slow going on the winding roads up and down, Ben thought. Rounding a corner, Ben started feeling and noxious energy coming from Michael. It was making him sick.

"Michael," Ben said. "Is that noxious energy coming from you? It's making me sick."

Michael replied, "It's making me sick too. Let's pull over."

Ben got out the car and took some deep breaths to clear his energy and head; Michael did the same. It wasn't long before the energy dissipated. *Is Michael trying to disrupt my energy field?* Ben thought. *Was that deliberate? What is he trying to do?*

Are you trying to scan me?" asked Ben."We had a woman in our crystal healing group that was involved in the first research along these lines," Ben said.

"Oh, no." said Michael. "They try to download energy through me from a satellite, but I try and cut it off as much as I can."

"Well, I hope you can counteract the energy. I don't want to deal with this vibration all the way back to San Francisco."

"Yes, I think I can divert it," said Michael. "You can help me with a spinning waveform round my body. That will help somewhat. The satellite will be out of range pretty soon."

"How long have you been feeling this energy and trying to divert it from your body? asked Ben.

"I began noticing it a couple of years ago. I believed I have a strong psychic ability."

"I do to," said Ben.

"I noticed it coming from the satellites recently. And I also have done my own research on what is going on here. I have a couple of friends in the Italian Parliament's that have mentioned to me that the Americans have been doing this research since the 1950s. The Montauk Project comes to mind right now."

Ben didn't know if he believed Michael, but he had heard of the Montauk Project himself. They had done mind control projects using LSD where they pulled people's light bodies out of their bodies. There was also some talk about creating dimensional portals into the past and the future.

Ben thought, *God this is incredible. Now we have to contend with satellites disrupting our consciousness.*"I have heard that satellites can photograph a person on the ground from a foot away," said Ben.

"Yes, I've heard that too," Michael replied. "Let's get going. It's getting late."

Continuing up the mountain, Ben said to Michael, "You seem sad right now."

"Yes," he replied, "It's not being bombarded, but I was thinking about finding a woman to have my child. After all, I'm the last remaining heir of Italy."

Ben replied, "You were a prince and now you're a queen, nothing wrong with that."

Michael burst out laughing. "That's a good one." They laughed all the way back to San Francisco without further incident.

Ben mused to himself; *a queen was a flamboyant gay man usually in a female drag costume; high heels, glamorous dress and make-up.*

Chapter Eleven

There Is More In Heaven & Earth …

Ben had a full day of teaching children and got back at his apartment around 6:30. He was puttering around his space fixing dinner when the phone rang. It was David, Ben's best friend.

"I want to see that new movie we talked about last week this weekend if you're up for it."

"Sure," said Ben. "I'll order tickets because with this hullabaloo going on we will need them ahead of time. I'll swing around your place on Saturday at 4:30."

"OK, see you then."

Saturday rolled around, and Ben made his way to Hayes Valley, one of the districts in San Francisco. David lived in a Victorian flat across from a black Pentecostal church. He had the good fortune to hear gospel music every Sunday. He had a huge window papered out with crazy graffiti that his son had done for him instead doing graffiti on city property. David was a very creative and hip person, and he knew his teenage son and his friends well. In fact, they had laid out a long white piece of paper and had everyone over for a graffiti party at his flat. They hung it in an arching Japanese-style from the 19-foot ceiling. David also lived catty corner from the San Francisco Zen center. You could feel the harmony blocks away. It took up almost the whole block– a huge place.

Ben pulled up in front of David's place – there was actually a parking space. He made his way up the long two-story stairs and knocked on David's door.

The door swung open, and David greeted him. Ben thought the place felt as comfortable as always. There was a huge poster on the wall of the physician's cadaver body with each organ and muscle labeled in detail. David was a pre-med student.

David said, "Come on back to my porch. I have something I want show you."

As they walked outside ben saw a huge metal sculpture of a simulated man with a planter on the top of his head.

Ben took a step back and exclaimed, "That's one of Garren's sculptures isn't it."

"Yes." he said. "I always liked it and he saved it for me when he left San Francisco."

Garren was a Japanese artist that they met at one of the Hans – Buddhist groups meetings. It looked to Ben like David was growing marijuana in this sculpture's head. David was a fine horticulturist. He also had several large pots full of plants in the yard. David worked downtown selling plants from one of those little booths on the street just outside of Saks Fifth Avenue. It was a good job.

"How's the harvest going?" Ben asked.

David replied, "It's almost ready to harvest, they are about six feet tall now and the buds are maturing. I still have a little from the last crop, do you want some?"

"Oh," Ben said. "Yes, I'm just about out." He and Dave went inside and smoked a doobie.

"Let's hit the road," said Ben. "We want to get to the theater on time."

David was one of the few people that could drive on weed or any drug, for that matter. In the 60s, he had dropped acid,magic mushrooms and peyote buttons many times and went to concerts featuring such names as the Grateful Dead, Jimi Hendrix and Janis Joplin to name a few. *You wouldn't catch me driving high*, thought Ben. *I couldn't handle that much energy input while driving.*

They pulled into the theater garage with 15 minutes to spare. As they went up into the lobby on the elevator, protesters were canvassing back and forth on the sidewalk outside the theater. They got their tickets and went inside and sat down about halfway from the front of the theater screen. During the film, they sat transfixed on the incredible, violent images of Jesus crucifixion. Ben wasn't really into the gore and blood and tried to concentrate on the storyline. The movie got to Palm Sunday, when Jesus was riding on the back of a donkey into Jerusalem, when a wave form suddenly hit Ben straight in the heart. He recoiled a little and wondered what had just happened to him. He had been through a lot of interesting things in his life but nothing like this.

After the movie was over, Ben asked David if he felt energy from the image of Jesus on the back of the donkey on Palm Sunday.

David replied, "Yes, I did. The energy hit me in the head."

"That's interesting," Ben replied. "It hit me in the heart." I wonder what that's all about, he mused. He wondered if it was the marijuana they had smoked back at the apartment. He knew that marijuana made people sensitive in some ways. He had, in the past, noticed it made him extra sensitive to subtle vibrations. He liked to go to museums the day after smoking, so he could feel the subtle energy emanating from the ancient objects.

They both considered this phenomenon in silence for about 10 or 15 minutes, mulling it over in their minds. It was very rewarding being an empath. There was a certain feeling of Zen and serenity experiencing energy at subtle levels.

Ben wondered what it meant to connect with an image from a movie so strongly that he felt a physical energetic response. Could it be that he had actually been there in a past life when Jesus was riding into Jerusalem? Was David there as well? Ben didn't really know but it was an interesting thought. It was just another metaphysical experience that Ben perceived on a deep level. This would be the norm for the rest of his life.

After the movie, Ben remembered how he learned of his special connection to Jesus at the Amron metaphysical center in San Francisco in the 1980s. Amron was an interesting place at that time. Ben's friend Norma had opened it with a university professor partner, and they named it using Norma's name spelled backwards. Norma and her partner were into magic and ritual and Ben would attend the center's Sunday services. He would always run into some interesting people there; for example, one Sunday, he met a man who went to Calcutta every summer to help mother Theresa attend to the indigent and sick.

One time, Ben got to celebrate the Leo birthdays and his own at the center by setting up a medicine circle ceremony. The medicine circle is a very special Native American event that celebrates their culture and its spiritual elements; it's metaphysical. They cornered off the four cardinal directions of the Amron center using colored yarn – yellow, red, black and white. He played an Indian shaman dance CD and read each individual sign breakdown and used a talking stick that someone gave him from an Indian powwow in Lake Tahoe. It was a very interesting extension of an Indian medicine circle that one of the center's members had put on earlier in Saratoga Park.

Ben had attended that circle too. Each member had to select a name out of a hat that was a totem animal or cardinal direction and or Indian deity. There were 25 to 30 people in attendance. It was very interesting because Ben drew a cougar the first round to portray on the black side, which signified the universe. He remembered being able to synthesize his consciousness with this totem animal. He was able to represent the cougar perfectly with its sounds and body movements. He felt like he was a cougar, it was so real. After the circle, people remarked how real Ben's portrayal was.

Ben learned about his connection to Jesus during one of Norma's famous séances. Once or twice a year, Norma would hold séances at the center. She would arrange the participants in concentric circles, and then she would contact the spirits and receive a chronicle of the major past life events of a person in the inner circle. Most of the time Ben would just sit on the outer circle and listen to the others' stories, but one year, he decided to participate in the inner circle and got a reading. He couldn't recall all of the details, but a couple of things stuck in his mind. It turned out, for example, that he invented the first battery in history. More importantly, he was also present at the tomb of Jesus when he was resurrected. There was a prominent blue light that permeated the whole cave, and he and two Indians participated in the healing of Jesus. From this, he learned he had a closer connection with Jesus that he had thought.

His Amron days were also interesting for Ben in that he had begun to teach workshops in numerology. He had a few students interested in a more in-depth understanding of numbers, and he found Gace Petticot's book to be a perfect reference for these workshops. Grace provided a practical but deep understanding of the numbers. She gave ample detail for each number and double number, and she had created a whole chapter for the number 10. There was no book Ben knew of in the numerological field that had this type of in depth information about the numbers. Gan,a personal friend of Norma's, was Ben's main numerology student. She was very dedicated to developing her craft, and teaching her helped Ben solidify his own knowledge of the numbers.

Many years later, Ben would become involved in a UFO group in Berkeley. Ben was at home on Potrero Hill when a call came in from Dr. Jim Harder, the retired Berkeley engineering professor and UFO and ET expert who ran the abduction group.

"Ben, I wanted to invite you to speak to my group and share your personal story of being pulled out of your body and entering into a spaceship."

"Wow! Thanks Jim, I would be honored to speak in front of the group," replied Ben.

"Great I'll see you then."

When Sunday came around, Ben was ready and raring to talk about his personal experiences of his contact with extraterrestrials. Dr. Harder's house had an unusual setup and location. It was nestled in the Berkeley hills just above UC Berkeley campus. His house was on the side of a hill as many homes are up in that area. Jim had built a lift to take people to the top of the hill right under his balcony. The ride up the small tram provided s a moving picture postcard of the San Francisco Bay directly across from downtown San Francisco. Ben was reminded of why people called San Francisco "Baghdad by the sea." He could see Sausalito, Richmond and Oakland at the same time. He had spent a number of Fourth of Julys in the Berkeley Hills watching simultaneous fireworks displays from four counties. The sunsets were amazing from that vantage point too. *San Francisco has some of the best sunsets in the world, rivaling even Hawaii*, thought Ben.

Ben started the group shortly after three o'clock. "Those of you who have read my book know my story of being pulled up around the planet and going inside a spaceship. There were two hovercrafts sitting above the planet watching the space shuttle launches. I was in meditation and found myself pulled up above the planet. As I focused on one of the crafts, I maneuvered over to one of them, after being beckoned to join a space being peering out of a large portal in the craft. Going through the large round porthole into the seating area, I was met by space being whose name was Zaln. The clarity was perfect when I went through the veil into what was the fifth dimension. Zaln had an alabaster skin tone and human features that were perfect. The contrast of his black spacesuit without a helmet provided a good view of his face and his bluest aura. Telepathically, Zaln told me to go down the hallway and ascend the spiral pearlzed staircase up into the main navigation area where other light beings were working. He followed and prompted me to step up on a 45-degree screen to change my consciousness. As I did, I flew down a spiraling time tunnel for what seemed like seconds. I became afraid and ended up back in my body. It seemed like only a few seconds had passed. In the days to follow,Zaln continued to communicate with me."

Ben seemed to come back to Earth and continue with the group saying, "I was also pulled up a second time. I would like to go into this second encounter in more detail. I saw nine beings stretched out over the planet – my spiritual guides. I found out later that some were my personas from previous lifetimes. I'll go into what I mean by that shortly. I later found out their names using the Ouija board. The first was Rodney, a working-class figure, the second was Rose, a psychologist and ET, the third was a healer named Damien, the fourth was Zaln, the fifth was Great Bear, a Sioux tribal chief, sixth was Yasses, a Hebrew scholar that helps me with numerology, the seventh was Zamacodod a Persian magician, and the eighth and ninth were the blue Hindu God Vishnu, and another blue being, Mazda. They stretched back into, and later were described to me by a famous channeler that some of these guides were my personas that reintegrated back into my being in a balanced fashion."

Ben continued: "I later realized their significance to me on the wheel of reincarnation lifetime expressions. These beings go on to become sentient beings and reincarnate as their own personalities evolving their own lives through time. We are all co-creators with God. I'm in communication with some of them, if I need them, on a regular basis. Zaln is the persona that pulled me up the first time. He is a Pleiadian being. He protects me when I'm being scanned and facilitates a healing center aboard his ship which I have used on a number of occasions." Ben later learned that Creation had decreed the healing center on Zaln's ship.

Great Bear was the persona that Ben checked out in American Indian history. The department of Indian affairs was very helpful in pointing out a figure in Indian history that lived in 1871 and was counsel to chief Red Cloud. They communicated with each other, but Great Bear was not listed as one of the people who were there. Ben surmised that he was Red Clouds' spirit guide.

Zamacodod was the being Ben had experienced at Mount Shasta with the metallic purple energy. The rest of the beings I work with on a periodic basis when needed.

"I hope this has been informative for you today, please ask me any questions at this time.

One man there, a scientist working in nanotechnology, said, "Yes. How do the extraterrestrials feel about group consciousness in creating one conscious mind?"

Ben replied, "They feel that the individual consciousness is the most important focus for all conscious beings. The law of one is the focus for any sentient being. We all have our individual personalities, and individual sovereignty that is personal for each being. You have your skills and personal frequencies that are unique to yourself and no other in the universe; you're a perfect creation of God. Your individual energy frequency is developed by lifetimes of experience that has your own unique signature. No one can co-opt your energy frequency unless you give them your permission. Unfortunately, there are negative forces in the universe that have manipulated us into giving up our sovereignty through coercion and false advertising techniques. Other techniques by the shadow government have been used for eleven centuries to create the illusion, our-so called reality."

For some reason, the person who asked the question became angry and marched out of the meeting, leaving everyone to ponder this person's disgruntlement. Ben never did find out what that was all about.

"OK then, "Jim said. "If there are no more questions, let's adjourn for some coffee or tea."

Safely back at home that night, Ben settled down into a meditation to communicate with Zaln. "Zaln," Ben said, "one of the things I would like to know is where I would have gone if I had not become afraid in my spinning time consciousness experience aboard the ship."

Zaln replied, "You would have gone to a way station, a jumping off point, a space between time, were you could have chosen the timeline you wanted to experience."

"Like choosing a wormhole to travel through?"

"Wormholes are three-dimensional concepts, not fourth dimensional time," replied Zaln. "You're given a choice from a higher source consciousness to choose a time period to experience."

"Are these energy beings, gatekeepers?" asked Ben.

"In a manner of speaking. You can think of them as gatekeepers, but they are higher beings with more expanded consciousnesses; they don't have physical bodies," replied Zaln.

"How does one choose a time?" Ben inquired.

"You ask yourself what you want to learn," said Zaln.

"Is this a better way of learning then, say, communication with your guides or reading a book?"

"You get the actual experience, which works on your psyche on many different levels. Hearing a guide tell you about a consciousness experience means it is run through their filters – not your filters – so it is a different experience," he replied.

"Why did you pull me up out of my body above the planet?" asked Ben.

"You were ready to experience consciousness on a different level," said Zaln.

"What does that mean, I was ready?" asked Ben.

"Your consciousness was fast enough to move into the higher fourth and fifth dimensions," Zaln explained. "You came into the fourth density when you were pulled up above the planet and went through the veil, you came into the fifth density as you entered the ship's porthole. Time expanded for you (subjective time) making it possible for you to experience spinning through a time tunnel and moving through time."

"When I became afraid," said Ben, "I was pulled back into my body."

"Your life-support system consciousness pulled you back in your body," said Zaln.

"What is my support system?"

"Your organism (biological system) has a failsafe system – a fright-flight system response that kicks in when you are in danger. It pulls you back into your body using your silver cord," said Zaln.

"What is my silver cord?"

"The silver cord is a concept in the old hermetic thought forms. If you had been schooled in that philosophy, you would have experienced that reality's thought form. You didn't see a silver cord because you were schooled in a different philosophy."

"Could it be I didn't really project my consciousness to the ship," asked Ben?

Zaln replied, "You passed through the veil into the fifth dimension. It is not possible that you were not out of your body. Your consciousness was on the ship, not in your physical structure. You didn't have conscious awareness of your body at the time."

In the following months, Ben attended more meetings and found out more about Jim. On occasion, he still gave testimony to Congress on extraterrestrials, and he would sometimes lecture to the engineering department and alumni group about extraterrestrials at UC Berkeley.

At one of the meetings, Ben told Jim he had healed a horse's hoof through laying on hands and telepathic communication. He was rubbing the horse's face and projecting healing energy telepathically at his friend's stallion's hoof, and all of a sudden, it shot Ben an image of itself as a colt. Ben entered that image and did the healing from that level of consciousness. A week later the owner called Ben and said the horses hoof was healed. In one sense, you could say that Ben entered a past memory to heal the horse.

Jim told Ben he knew a professor who worked with language communication who told him that animals communicate clairvoyantly. She was doing research in that area of her study. Then Jim asked Ben if he wanted to be hypnotized – regressed. Jim assumed that Ben would want to reexperience his extraterrestrial extraction and other experiences.

Ben said, "Sure, I've been meaning to see if I can recall more information about Zaln and his ship."

Jim was the first person to regress Travis Walton, the famous abductee in Arizona who made the movie, Fire in the Sky. He took Ben to his regression room, and they began.

"Lay down over the here, Ben," Jim instructed. "Now, when you are hypnotized, I'll ask you questions, and you just raise your first finger for "yes" and your little finger for "no."

After hypnotizing Ben, Jim began his questions. "When was the first time you were abducted by extraterrestrials? Was it six years old?"

Ben raised his first finger for "yes."

"Were you abducted at age eight?

"No," Ben signaled.

"Nine?"

"No."

"Ten?"

"No."

"Eleven?"

"Yes. OK, Ben, which age would you like to go into for more information?"

"The eleven-year-old time," Ben muttered.

"Think back to when you were eleven years old and were abducted. What do you see?"

"I see a paved country road on a warm day with lots of pine trees all around us," said Ben. "I see two aliens holding me under each arm, elevating me into the sky."

"What else do you see," asked Jim."Can you see a craft?"

"No," Ben signaled.

"Ok, let's go back a little. Can you describe the beings?"

Ben stirred slightly and signaled, "Yes." Then he said, "Each being was little like green spun glass, sort of, with tiny tubular arms and legs that were transparent. They had large transparent heads with large eyes."

"Did they say anything to you?"

Ben indicated with his little finger – "No."

"Can you recall anything else?"

"No."

"OK, at the count of ten you will be wide awake and back in the room," said Jim.

Ben came back to waking consciousness and shook his head.

"That was intense and fascinating at the same time," said Jim."But we couldn't access your memories of their ship for some reason."

Ben said, "I wonder if the ET's had put a memory block on me so he couldn't remember any more details." He said Dolores Fanon described this phenomenon in one of her books. She was a highly developed counselor and psychologist who had developed her own regression process and published books on Jesus, Nostradamus, extraterrestrials and other topics; she was a spiritual historian.

"Yes," said Jim, "I have read of that recently. We really don't know how that works. How they can they manipulate us to block an experiential memory."

"They also change shapes and identity to make you think they are someone else," remarked Ben.

It wasn't until the next month that Ben agreed to try the regression again. This time he wanted to pursue more information about the glass beings.

"OK Ben, you're going deeper and deeper now. Try seeing the glass beings again like before."

"OK" Ben replied, raising his first finger for "yes."

"Can you see them?" asked Jim.

"Oh, no! Stop it. I don't want to go!" said Ben in a distressed voice.

"What are you seeing right now Ben?"

"There are two small Sasquatches holding me under each arm taking me to a big Sasquatch." Ben could feel that Jim didn't understand what he meant.

After a long pause Jim finally said, "Who?"

"Sasquatch, Sasquatch," Ben said, squirming on the couch and becoming more agitated as time went by.

"Ah! Let me go! I don't want to go! Leave me alone!" Ben shouted. Ben was almost in a frantic state of mind now, moving his head from side to side in a jerky fashion. Ben wondered why Jim was letting him feel this negative emotion when he could cut it off by giving a hypnotic suggestion.

Jim cut in that moment and replied, “Bigfoot. You mean Bigfoot.”

“Yes,” said Ben.

“I’m sorry,” said Jim. “I don’t have a tape to tape this session.”

Ben remembered that as he was presented to the big Sasquatch, it grabbed his head in both hands and looked into his brain.

What was he looking for? Ben wondered.

By now, eleven-year-old Ben was frantic in his memories. Jim tried to calm him down, and he came out of the regression by himself through his fright-flight response.

Jim caught him by the arm and gave him a suggestion, “Calm down, you are relaxing. Calm down, you are feeling safe now.”

This seemed to work as Ben slipped into a relaxed state.

Jim counted Ben down, “You will awaken totally balanced and alert.”

“That was frightening,” said Ben as he came back out of the regression.

“Yes, it was,” said Jim, “but a very interesting experience. Where were you when you were eleven years old to have this type experience?”

"From the terrain, it seems that it might have been when I was a Boy Scout away at summer camp in the Sierras," Ben replied."We went there every year for four years. I would like to go into that experience again sometime to get more information," said Ben.

"Me too," replied Jim.

Ben thought to himself, *each person does the regression process differently*. Helen Wombat, a famous regressor, had a process where she would have you see yourself up on a cloud and descend down to a particular timeline/lifetime. This was a process used by Dolores Fanon as well, and her special in-depth regressions that also included the process of connecting with the higher self. It seemed to be a process that worked to get to deeper levels of regression meaning.

Ben thanked Jim for the regression and Jim invited Ben to his Fourth of July party. Descending down the hill on Jim's tram, Ben mulled over the Sasquatch information. He remembered a blog he had read that described a telepathic communication with Bigfoot by a scientist in British Columbia. According to the article, once you make telepathic contact with Sasquatch, you will always be in contact through consciousness. Leaving Berkeley, Ben headed for the East Bay.

Chapter Twelve

Ufo's And Higher Consciousness

As he drove, Ben started thinking about his trip to Crestone Colorado for the ISETI retreat. Dr. Steven Bear a well-known emergency room doctor with connections with the UFO community and his personal ET experiences. He was at one time part of a Washington insider group that briefed the head of the CIA and the Joint Chiefs of Staff. Steven had his own ET experience while backpacking in the wilderness. Every year he would organize a group to go to hotspots for UFO activity in different parts of the country and a few other countries as well. A few locations that Ben was aware of was the Mount Shasta area, Joshua tree and Crestone Colorado.

Ben wanted to go to Mount Shasta but that location this year was not available, so he decided to sign up for Crestone Colorado. Dr. Bear also created the disclosure project and the scientific part of ISETI. The disclosure project brought together high-level military and civilian witnesses to UFO's and ET's at a press conference in Washington DC. The Science wing of the ISETI was involved in studying and tracking down free energy devices and tracing the guided missile system satellites that guarded the Earth from extraterrestrial craft moving into our space.

Ben caught his flight at the San Francisco international Airport early in the morning and arrived in Colorado three hours later. He drove a rental to Crestone and checked into the very nice rustic sandstone structure in the desert; a remote location for sure. Cacti and other yucca plants were in the foreground and the majestic Mount Blanca was visible in the distance.

In the main conference area, he met the others in the group that had arrived before him. The first daily meeting was to commence in a few minutes, and it seemed Ben had made it on time. The Conference room was pretty traditional as rustic hotels go, but he enjoyed the soft pastel colors of the Midwest. The artwork on the walls was by local artists, and during the talk, one piece of art caught Ben's eye. It jumped out at him from the wall and reminded him of a spaceship coming down through the trees, if you were underneath it. He ended up buying the collage and having it shipped back to San Francisco.

Dr. Bear came into the room and went to the podium and started speaking about the itinerary for the days and evenings for that week. During the day they would, after lunch, meet to discuss the previous night's activities. They then had free time until meeting later that night about an hour before sunset. They would meet on the open plane of Crestone's desert to coordinate their chairs in a circle for the night's activities. Dr. Bear would lecture on all subjects to do with extraterrestrials and techniques for reviewing crafts. Most of the nights were pretty much the same and involved watching for satellites over the night sky. But one night was special.

It started as he and a Larry, a new friend Ben had just made, drove out to the site one night. Larry was a very sincere person and with a worldly intelligence that attracted Ben to him. He was an interesting older gentleman with white and gray streaks in his hair. He exhibited the quality and look of an old soul – that super master vibration that Ben had become so for familiar with over the years. They had been driving into the desert for ten or fifteen minutes when they drove through a thick energy anomaly, and Ben noticed a force field energy glitch. *It was the strangest energy feeling he had ever felt,* Ben thought. Going through a force field, where the energy moved through every space in his body, at the microscopic level, was an experience Ben hadn't encountered before. The field puzzled Ben, and he couldn't determine if it was a positive energy field or not. He was able to determine that it was a positive energy field after passing through it a few times and noticing no ill effects. It occurred to him that there was a protective transparent dome over the whole area that became apparent to him from his clairvoyant sense.

They parked and walked towards the circle of chairs with a backdrop of Mt. Blanca. The stars were like Xircom plumbs, as Shirley MacLaine would say. They were far enough away from town that they could see millions of stars, including shooting stars. The velvet blackness of the sky expanded in all directions. They set up their chairs in a circle and sat down as Dr. Bear made his way to the center. "Thank you for coming out again," said Dr. Bear. "I feel we are going to have an interesting night tonight. Let's start by using the coherent thought sequencing process that you all have in your binders. I have left this process until tonight to let people acclimate themselves to the energies of the location. So, as it is outlined in your packet, thought sequencing is a process that we at ISETI have created to project our intent out into the universe, to alert various ET groups that we are here to communicate with them."

He continued, "As you remember from the tape – I hope you listened to it – you will first project your consciousness out into the universe and look at the Milky Way at the furthest edge while picturing each planet in our solar system. Go to the last planet, and use your intent to lead any ETs to follow you back to our home planet Earth. Put yourself in a place to see Pluto, then Neptune, Uranus, Saturn, Jupiter, Mars, the Moon and finally the Earth. Continue envisioning the way back to our planet. Then focus on the continent we live on in the northern hemisphere, and see the state of Colorado down to the area of Crestone and envision our group sitting in a circle on the planes. Keep picturing this and we may pull in an ET craft."

As they finished the exercise, Dr. Bear drew their attention to two metallic spheres moving across the sky, one above the other. As they moved across the sky, one of the slow walkers abruptly took a right turn and headed out to deep space. "That was not a satellite you just witnessed," said Dr. Bear, "it was an ET craft, obviously. They do a good job of masking their crafts to mimic ours. The military have special computers for the recording the slow and fast walkers' – satellites. I wonder what they thought of this one," he added with a snicker.

He went on to point out a semi cloud shape out in the field, a couple of feet off the ground, not far from the group. Ben thought the mist look like a McDonald's sign with two arches. "It looks like a domed craft partially materialized from the crossing point of light where speed and time move faster than the speed of light," said Dr. Bear.

Ben thought to himself, *I should be scanning the area for any clairvoyant images I can see in the other dimension – the fourth dimension.* As Ben did this, he picked up a group of five aliens in green spacesuits with transparent green domes over their green heads and sunken faces. Aware that Ben could see them in his mind, they looked back at him with startled expressions. Ben tried to make the connection clearer so he could have a dialogue with them, but their image was frozen in time and faded out quickly. *There really are little green men*, Ben thought. *I wonder what they will think when I tell the group this story at tomorrow's discussion.*

Dr. Bear continued, "As you can see, the mist never moved, even when the wind came up. This is another telltale sign that it was a craft, partially materialized. If you will tune into it, you will perceive that the ship has relocated around the group now. Take a minute to meditate."

Ben could sense a subtle energy around the group now to the extent that he couldn't meditate effectively with the ELF residual energy field that permeated the entire circle. Then suddenly, there was strong activity from all three of the magnetometers, the devices that calibrated the movement in the air in a particular vicinity. They started going off in different parts of the circle, signifying that something was inside of the group, upsetting the magnetic fields flux with its motion.

Dr. Bear spoke about threats to the planet, and as he did, the magnetometers would acknowledge what he was saying, seeming to indicate that what he was saying was true. It seemed to Ben that the air was so still he could hear a pin drop. Not even the mosquitoes buzzed around, as they usually did. Except for the magnetometers and the movement of the textured clouds above their heads, everything was still and silent. "There are many different groups of extraterrestrials visiting us tonight both within our circle and without," said Dr. Bear.

Eventually, things settled down and Ben and the others took a break. He walked out into the field, looking for any signs of ETs or other crafts among the sagebrush. At one point, Ben thought he saw a small ET that ducked behind a bush as he looked down, but he never told anyone about this experience. Ben had his camera with him and he took about four shots, shooting up into the night sky as his guides had prompted him to do. He used his 35-millimeter camera and would have to wait to get the shots developed before he could see what was on the film.

It was getting late but. Dr. Bear and some and others used lasers, infrared scopes and visualization to try and communicate with the ETs in the night sky. This process was developed by ISETI and was called "SE –5," or "close encounters of the fifth kind. Contacting ETs using this method and getting a response from them in some way was hoped-for outcome. One of the women in the group said, "I'm sending a picture of the IETI logo out into the night sky," and she pointed to a triangular cloud formation that looked like the logo. They all took a picture to capture the moment.

Dr. Bear said, "OK, let's head back to the hotel. Tomorrow night, I have a special treat for you – we're going to the top of Mount Blanca." Everyone's was very enthusiastic about the prospect of visiting this great mountain to look for ET crafts. In English, the mountain was part of the Blood of Christ mountain range. The next day, they had their midmorning meeting. Everyone gave their testimonies of what had happened the night before. Ben related his experience of the little green men. He also recounted his sighting of a white circle he'd seen around sunset. It had appeared near the meeting place and hovered 5 feet off the ground. "I don't know if anyone saw this shape but me," said Ben. "It ran life force through my body for a few seconds and disappeared. I felt a hundred percent better afterwards. It was exhilarating." Dr. Bear seemed genuinely intrigued.

They broke up for the day and Ben decided to go to a hot tub place he had seen when he drove into the area. It was on the edge of the rainy season, and Ben didn't know how he would respond to the cool weather in the hot tub, but it turned out fine. The hot tubs all had blue nylon canopies over them for just this type of weather. He could see the muted sky come through the fabric. A nice-looking young woman greeted him at the front desk.

"Good afternoon," she said, "welcome to the Bungalow. Are you from the ISETI group?"

"Yes." *Word sure gets around fast*, he thought.

"Would you like a hot tub for one?"

"I would, but I also wouldn't mind company."

"OK. A couple of people just came in from your group."

She led him to a small outdoor room with a very nice square hot tub; its tiles had a blue Arabic motif.

Ben greeted the couple in the tub. "Hi, I'm Ben from the group. I remember seeing you both there."

"Hi," said the attractive young woman."My name is Sally, and this is Rod my friend and cameraman."

"Hey," said Rod.

"What are you both doing at the retreat?" asked Ben, curiously.

"We're here to document Dr. Bear's retreats and create a documentary on the real stories of the participants and UFOs. We plan to approach PBS and community stations with the film to raise awareness of what's going on in the UFO community. After this, we're going to Washington State to document UFO events at Wililand Ranch."

"Cool," said Ben. "So, you're filmmakers."

"Yes," she continued. "Actually, Rod does the filming, and I write the copy. I also write cookbooks about Arizona cuisine."

"Well, all right," said Ben, "you guys are on a mission. I'm an artist and a physical education and child development teacher. I have a book of my own on spiritual education for kids that I wrote as part of my Master's degree."

"Well, said Sally, "you're busy too. You should come and visit us if you ever get to Arizona."

"Thanks," said Ben, "I may take you up on that."

It started sprinkling, but the cover cut out most of the moisture and created a warm cozy environment in the hot tub. He spent the next couple of hours talking about metaphysical things with Sally and Ron until it was time to meet the group on the planes of Crestone.

Mount Blanca was cloudy as they watched the thunder and lightning move across the valley floor. Ben admired the spectacular display of light and shadow as they drove up the mountain side. On the way, they passed the microwave radar tower which would turn out to be a detriment to Ben shortly after setting up the circle of chairs, he experienced a pain in the back of his head. Ben retreated to the car to get some Advil, but this didn't work to stop the pain. Dr. Bear and another doctor came over and diagnosed him as having altitude sickness. Ben lay down in the car unable to balance himself out and stop the pain at the back of his head; it was excruciating. Dr. Bear decided that someone would need to take Ben to a hospital, but a healer in the group convinced him to let her try a healing first. In just about five minutes, she balanced out Ben's energy system and the pain went away like it had never existed. Ben thanked the woman, and after a bit of recovery, he was able to rejoin the group in time for meditation. However, a little while later, he felt a major pain in his leg. *Now what?* thought Ben. He had felt this kind of disruption many times before. It was a sign of nearby psychotronics energy bursts. He felt like a live electrified wire had been attached to his leg; so much so, he could no longer meditate, and he moved to another seat in the group. This seemed to work as the twitching leg stopped jumping. He was convinced this incident wasn't altitude sickness but psychotronics energy bombardment. Possibly, the whole area had a discordant ELF energy grid to disrupt the bio fields of not only human physiology but extraterrestrials as well. Ben wondered why the doctors were not aware of this possibility. Dr. Bear was a well-known emergency room doctor – funny he thought.

After about ten minutes in the circle, it started raining and they all quickly retreated to their cars so that they would not be struck by lightning. The circle area was perched like a bird's nest on the side of the mountain. As they sat in their cars waiting for the rain to stop, the people in the car next to Ben started yelling and jumping around. Turning around in their seats, Ben and his companions saw a spacecraft shoot past from the top of Mount Blanca from a secret location. Going over the incident with the fifty or so eyewitnesses, they pieced the details together to come up with a composite picture.

The craft was oval-shaped and just about the size of a dime. Him was ultra blue with white lights all around its exterior. They continued to see slow and fast walkers throughout the evening. The next day's meeting was very interesting.

"What did you think of last night's episode?" asked Dr. Bear. "That blue craft that came shooting out from the top of Mount Blanca was the highlight of the conference. If it had stayed around longer, we could have used the SC-5 techniques to communicate with the beings."

"What type of ship do you think it was?" someone in the group asked.

Dr.Bear ventured to guess it was a Syrian or Evian blue being ship. "They have been seen in this area," he told them. He also mentioned that black military helicopters regularly surveilled the area.

Dr. Bear continued, "We're taking a special trip to a Buddhist ashram on Mount Blanca later this afternoon. Get some lunch, and meet me back here 3 o'clock." Everyone was excited at the prospect of going to the ashram.

The caravan moved up Mount Blanca again, this time in the daylight, so its panoramic views were visible. It was raining slightly, but the gray clouds over the sagebrush plain made the incredible view look like a black-and-white photograph. After about thirty minutes, they stopped at a modern Asian structure made of hardwood. A Japanese garden stream filled with different colored coy circled the structure. They stepped through the doorway and Ben noticed the solid teak beams arcing across the ceiling of the building. There were chairs on the main floor and seats on the balcony. They took their seats on the main floor. Dr. Bear related a short history of UFO sightings, but he really interested in guiding the group on a trip to Creation. He talked about his own experiences interacting with Creation. He said was of the Baha'i faith and had studied the philosophy and history and many of the meditations in the Hindu tradition. He went on to say when he could interface with Creation he would be shown the face and location of the person he was looking for. This was only one situation I'm sure, that related to Creation.

Dr. Bear next led them all in a guided meditation. Their consciousness lifted off, moving, as usual, through the top of their head. The Earth became a blue white ball below them as they moved towards the moon and passed it quickly towards Mars. See the red planet loom by, with its red desert scenes, and his trajectory took them towards Jupiter, the biggest planet in the solar system. Recognize the giant orange storm swirling around inside the surface of the planet as we whizz by at breakneck speed towards Saturn and its rainbow rings. Soon, you will spy the blue-green planet Uranus followed by a hint of Neptune, the indigo planet with so much Greek history. Focus on Pluto, silver–white small planet next, with its icy mountain ranges and pockmarked terrain, and then there is deep space, with the indigo-black matter that enveloped it.

Suddenly a fissure opened in space exposing a large ethic white planet that expressed its energy in all directions as if a magnificent sun of energy was rising above it, he suggested. As you moved closer to the giant ethic planet, feel its energy and immediately experience the shiver of love emanation reverberate through your body, healing any noxious energy you have brought with you. Just float in space just experiencing the bioplasmic energy from the planet. Now move into the center of creation and ask any questions that might come to you. As soon as you here my voice, you will be instantly there.

Ben was in the seer presence of metallic white plasma that enveloped him with fluid loving arms. He felt like a child that that was being rocked by his mother's arms experiencing tranquility that he had rarely felt.

Now Pose a question to Creation, "What do I need to focus at this time," and heard a voice say in response.

Ben heard "Continue what you are doing in your life and your experiences. You will come to recognize your destiny in this lifetime. I have sent your persona self, the Pleadian revealed to as Zaln, to assist in your healing when you have need of it. You possess the image of this process in your subconscious. The light beings on the ship have created the crystal healing table for you."

"Come back out of the planet," Dr. Bear coaxed. "We need to start the journey back to your bodies." They followed the planets back to the Earth and back into their bodies at a speed that felt supersonic. "Come back into the room and open your eyes, said Dr. Bear. Would anyone like to describe your experience?" A few people said how much they enjoyed the experience while others said they had gotten answers to their questions. Ben told about his feeling of tremendous love energy.

As Ben was listening to the others talk about their experiences, he realized he had experienced this planet before. It was fifteen years earlier, and he was living on Potrero Hill in San Francisco. He was meditating on the node points around the human body when, all of a sudden, a door opened in his mind's eye, exposing an ethic white planet. He felt a loving energy and moved to step through the door to experience this wonderful feeling when the door slammed shut in front of his face. That was Ben's first experience with Creation. The energy he felt then was the same loving energy he had just felt in the ashram. The realization surprised him. *What is this connection I'm having with this planet's energy?* Ben wondered. He didn't know he would have more experiences with this planet in the future. He did realize, that he could return to the planet when he wished to communicate with her.

When Dr. Bear finished the meditation, they moved to their cars and headed down the mountain with a renewed sense of balanced awareness. Back at the hotel, Ben went out to the back veranda to enjoy the view when he noticed Valerie, the healer that healed him from the psychotronics bombardment earlier.

"How are you feeling now?" she asked.

"I feel much better since you realigned my auric field. The pain was definitely caused by psychotronics energy. I've felt it before but not to that extent," Ben said.

"Psychotronics?"

"Yes," replied Ben."I've been dealing with this energy for many years now. Did you see the array towers on our way up Mount Blanca? Are you familiar was psychotronics and ELF frequency?"

"I may have read something about them. But I didn't notice the array towers you're talking about. You mean to say this caused you that tremendous headache?"

"Yes," said Ben, "there's no doubt in my mind. Anyway, I really appreciate what you did for me. In fact, I wanted to repay you by guiding you onto a Pleiadean ship so you can experience their crystal healing tables."

Taken aback, Valerie smiled and said, "OK. I'm game."

Ben asked her to sit, and instructed her to follow his visualizations. "We are going to ascend our light bodies through the top of our heads towards the sky and into the stratosphere. Look up and you will see a ship. Pierce the bottom of the ship then move through the open bay into the platform area. Go to the healing room where you will see two giant slabs of crystal six feet long, four feet wide and 6 inches deep. One is suspended from the ceiling and the other is floating just beneath it a few feet off the floor. Can you see them?"

"Yes, I'm there," said Valerie.

"Good," Ben continued. "Crawl up between the two suspended beds and lie still. You will feel metallic color energies – blue, green and purple – start pulsating through one slab of crystal, then they will rotate around the ends, and move through the other slab of crystal. Can you feel it, Valerie?"

"Yes," she replied.

"This color motion will continue as you lie between the slabs, generating healing energy throughout your body. The pure energy will dissipate all noxious energy in your body and rejuvenating energy will inundate your whole being." Ben let her bask in the energy for a while before instructing her to crawl out from between the crystal slabs and move out of the ship and back to her body.

"That was the short version. How do you feel?" asked Ben.

Valerie lit up like a Christmas bulb. "That was great! Just fantastic! Thank you so much for turning me on to this visualization! I'll work with it when I do my healings."

"Well, I wanted to give you something for coming to my aid when you did. You really saved my bacon," said Ben.

"No problem at all. That's what I do in my practice. I'm glad I was there to save your bacon," she said with a chuckle.

The next day, after meeting the others in the hotel to go over that night's itinerary, Ben looked for a partner to drive with him back up Mount Blanca to the Baha'i ashram, so he could check out their bookstore. Finding no takers, he decided to go it alone. He was especially interested in finding a picture of Vishnu, the blue Indian God he had seen when he was pulled up around the planet the second time. Winding up the mountain in his rented RV Ben at last found the sign he was looking for: Baha'i Bookstore and Retreat. After looking through stacks of cards, he finally found a picture that represented the blue being he had seen in his vision above the planet.

It was a striking picture of Vishnu wearing a golden headdress and breastplate with various jewels that adorned the headdress. It seemed to have an androgynous face, both female and male, at the same time. The powerful blue eyes seemed to be studying the viewer. Ben asked the girl behind the desk what she could tell him about Vishnu.

She told him that Vishnu had many incarnations and was represented by a different color each time. He was usually represented as black, blue, and white. He was a warrior but fought for positive aspects of man. He destroyed at times and created at other times. He was said to be an aspect of Krishna, the supreme God of the Indian culture.

Ben bought the card.

He rejoined the group on the plain about thirty minutes before dark. Ben sat in one of the chairs in the circle, waiting for the group to get started when a being suddenly dropped into his body. At first, he assumed it was an extraterrestrial, but its discordant energy tipped him off that it was another type of entity. Ben was accustomed to beings dropping into his body, and he knew how to protect himself from unwanted energy invasions. He flexed his solar plexus muscles and catapulted the entity out of his body with a fast compression. It worked. Ben felt a lot better after expelling this less positive energy. He mentioned what had just happened to some of the people nearby, and they were interested in the phenomenon of beings entering a human body. It was something they had not heard of before. Ben explained that it was just another aspect of channeling. Later, he would explain the phenomena in some detail to Valerie the healer, who had asked him about it after hearing about the incident from others.

Soon, the meditation started, and they used their thought sequencing process to call in ETs in the area. To see some ET crafts, night vision goggles were necessary. Others could be identified by flashes of light that came and went. People in the circle would signal these with laser pen lights, and some would light up, expanding their light in all directions to create a large multicolored circular light energy. Some of the group tried and communicate with ET crafts telepathically, including Dr. Bear. And of course, they saw slow and fast walkers move often across the night sky. About one o'clock in the morning, they headed back to the hotel. This night had not been as dynamic as the previous night, which was fine with Ben – it was all part of the experience.

The next day, after discussing the sightings of the previous night, Dr. Bear began his closing talk. "I just want to say that I appreciate all of you who attended the retreat and I hope you will return. Don't forget, you have your binders with all the information you need to start your own ET sighting groups in your hometowns. To reiterate, you have the protocols for contacting extraterrestrial species, protocols for introductions in the event of an ET landing and protocols for categorizing close encounters of the first, second, third, fourth or fifth kind. You also have a description forms to record the incidents. Remember, you are ambassadors of the Earth now, and I hope you take this responsibility seriously."

The meeting broke up, and Ben said goodbye to his friends and promised to stay in touch. He was eager to get back to San Francisco. Driving to the airport, Ben reflected on the retreat and the week's events. He also considered a few complaints about some misleading things Dr. Bear had told the group. One person in particular, James Williland, was outraged when Bear said not to be afraid to let any energy or entity into your consciousness. That didn't sit well with Ben either, with his experience fielding scanners and with entities inundating his body. Ben agreed it was an irresponsible comment, especially considering all the experience Bear had with extraterrestrial consciousnesses.

After Ben got back to San Francisco, he got the film from his trip developed. When he picked the photos up a few days later, he noticed something interesting. He had taken four shots of the night sky and those four pictures showed colored energy formations that resembled vivid neon shapes moving in space. Some of the shapes were almost three-dimensional; the reds, greens, yellows, blues and purples were so brilliant. Ben was very surprised at capturing these images on film. He had captured other psychic images on film before but nothing like this. Were they intelligent beings or anomalies of nature?

Later, he was thumbing through a Dolores Fannon book, the last in the series on the Convoluted Universe, and was stunned to find a section on the very energy images he had captured in his photographs of the night sky. Cannon described this colored energy as beings of light who worked with Gaia to uplift the planet's evolutionary process. According to the book, they impacted all energy structures of Gaia down to the basic DNA of the planet, and they were involved in raising the consciousness of Gaia to a higher evolutionary level. *They are part of the source energy, the prime creator*, Ben thought, appreciating the wonders of Creation as it expanded his consciousness.

Back home after a week in nature, Ben needed to reacclimatize himself to an everyday life schedule. Being summertime, he was off work and had plenty of time to do anything he wanted. Looking at a website for free activities in the Bay Area, he noticed a crafts fair being held that weekend in Los Altos.

Ben rose early on Saturday and headed down the 280 freeway towards San Jose. He was moving down the freeway just below San Mateo at the Crystal Springs area, admiring the clear view of the hills when he suddenly saw a silver UFO materialize. The cigar-shaped was about a mile away over the hills. *Close-up, this would be a huge ship*, Ben thought. He got the feeling that the craft was actually longer than it appeared because it looked as if a portion of the ship was not materialized in the front. The metallic silver color reflected the sun like a mirror, and from Ben's perspective, he could see the back end of the circular opening of the craft. It was a brilliant luminescent white light with textured cells inside. The light was brighter than the sun reflecting off the outside of the ship, but it didn't hurt his eyes like the sun would if you stared at it directly.

Ben tried to communicate telepathically with the beings inside, but he felt a disgruntled attitude from the occupants that he didn't understand. A handful of seconds later, the craft disappeared without a trace. Ben looked around in all directions to see if he could locate the craft again, but it had disappeared as fast as it had appeared. When he got to the fair, he sat down on the grass and made a drawing of the craft. He labeled everything and wrote a few notes that were fresh in his mind.

The craft fair was great. Los Altos was a town partially tucked away under redwood trees, and the fair booths were laid out in well-defined rows of stylish cloth structures that followed the street and walkways around and through the park where it was held. Ben left shortly after viewing the arts and crafts, and was satisfied with their quality. He liked the local street fairs much better than state fairs; they seemed more personable with better crafts. Ben hadn't forgotten about the UFO he saw, and when he got back to his apartment, he went online and looked up the Northern California MUFON group.

MUFON was the reporting agency that catalogued local sightings of UFOs and other Ariel phenomena. Ben requested a reporting form from Ruben, the head of the Northern California chapter. He had met Ruben at the New Life Expo one year. He was a friend of a friend of his and had set up the Expo. Shortly, Ben received a packet with the reporting form, and he filled it out as thoroughly as he could, including a detailed drawing. Ben saw Ruben at the Expo the next year they discussed Ben's report.

"I remember your report. It was terrifically precise and detailed, especially the drawing of the craft," Ruben said.

Ben replied, "I'm an art teacher, so drawing is easy for me."

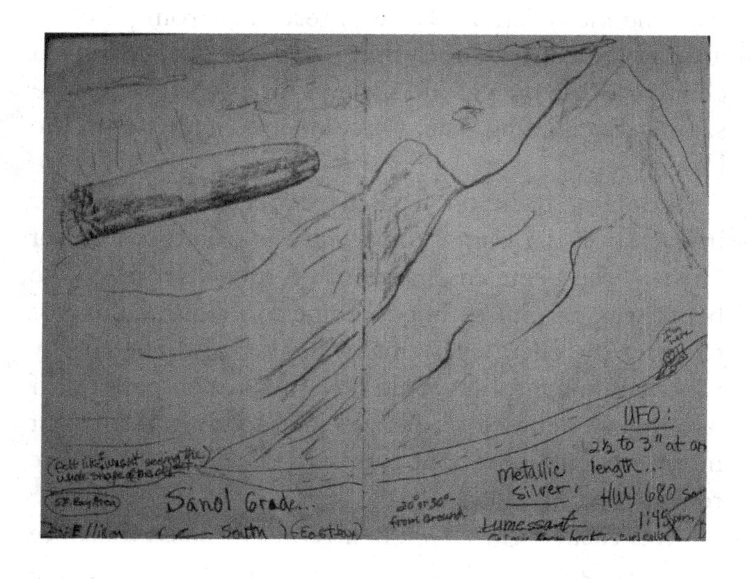

After their discussion, Ben recalled a spiritual incident that had happened to him while he was driving to the supermarket in the Castro District. While he was stopped at a stoplight, a spirit entered his consciousness forcefully enough to push him into his steering wheel.

"Why are you feeling down?" it asked, and suddenly an incredible feeling of elation and effervescence came over him as if he was in the presence of God itself.

He felt, at the time, that from that day on, he would be continually happy and never have a negative thought again. Of course, that didn't turn out to be true, but he had a great deal of newly acquired fortune around that time. He landed a new job at a secondary school teaching art, and he was in a very comfortable living situation at the time, which hadn't always been the case. And the many letters Ben was receiving from psychics around the country everything was laid out for him to change his life on a grand scale. A lot of what they were saying was coming true. Of course, he hadn't won the lottery yet.

Looking back on it, Ben realized the telepathic information the visitor conveyed was from the Lord of Hosts – the being in charge of all angelic forces. The being was careful to not to come too close, so as not to upset the energy systems in Ben's body. The energy was dynamic, and it would have made Ben pass out if it had gotten too close. Ben decided to try and find out more information about the Lord of Hosts for future reference.

Just then, at the Expo, Ben's consciousness was once again contacted by the being. This time, it informed Ben of an unavoidable medical problem in his future. "You will have a heart attack. This will take you out of your normal life, so that your ET friends can work on your body."

The host didn't go into detail about the changes, but Ben hoped he would receive more longevity on the planet, and, perhaps, a DNA upgrade too. Coming back to his conscious awareness, Ben considered what the being had said. Just then, Ben recognized Steve Went at *The Urantia Book* booth nearby.

"Hi, Steven. How are you?"

Steven looked up an acknowledged Ben with a nod, "I'm fine."

Ben met Steven in the Order of Melchezedeck years ago. He had been leading focus groups on *The Urantia Book* for 30 years. This book was channeled by a group of ascended beings that have remained anonymous for many decades. Ben remembered that he had, in the past, perceived Steven to be a scanner, so he made sure not to let Steven access his thoughts. Still, he was an expert on *The Urantia Book*, so Ben revealed that he had been visited by the Lord of Hosts and asked if there was a reference to the being in the book.

Steven told Ben that Lord of Hosts was referenced in the early Bible as the overseer of all of the Angels.

Ben replied, "I know that much because the Lord of hosts conveyed it to me." Looking surprised, Steven handed Ben his business card and asked him to keep in touch.

After leaving Steven's booth, Ben found his friends Alexandra and Ed, whom he had driven to the Expo with. Alexandra said she was going to get a reading by a good psychic, and Ben and Ed decided to attend a lecture by Dr.Fred Bell. Dr. Bell was connected with the CIA, and his company did work for them researching scalar waves in connection with exotic weapons. These were technological weapons that dealt with mind control, remote viewing, time travel, UFO propulsion cutting edge devices with military applications. Dr. Bell also researched pyramid energy and manufactured gold wire pyramids and devices to block ELF frequencies. At one point in the discussion, Ben asked Dr.Bell if he could talk about ELF frequencies. This didn't appear to sit well with Dr.Bell, who totally ignored Ben's question. He must not have realized how sensitive his microphone was, however, and Ben could hear him mutter, "That's what we use to tune into people."

Ben thought to himself, *I guess I hit upon some kind of secret*. After that, the lecture didn't seem as interesting to Ben even though Bell said he was in communication with Semjase, a Pleiadean extraterrestrial. At any rate, Bell's gaffe added to Ben's accumulating knowledge of the scope of the surveillance manipulation taking place on the planet.

CHAPTER THIRTEEN

Continuing To Wake Up From The Illusion

One night, Ben came home and felt a familiar psychotronics bombardment in his apartment. He decided he would try out his new device, the Trifield Natural Meter. It had been pricey, but it was very sensitive and had all the features that Ben needed to tune into ELF and other frequencies. A handheld device that could be set on the coffee table, its sensitivity could be set to fire off on magnetic, electromagnetic, electric, and radio and microwave frequencies at as little as .5% of the strength of the Earth's magnetic field. It could sense a human's energy field through a wall or measure fluctuations in the atmosphere and the sky's magnetic frequencies to spot UFOs or airplanes, even behind a hill. It also cut out all high tower frequencies, Wi-Fi, and radio and television signals.

He turned the device to the electromagnetic field and the sound meter started going off intermittently, forwards and backwards, from 1 Hz to 100 Hz. It continued to rise and fall for a good 10 minutes, when Ben got tired of the grueling alarm sound. The alarm signified a specific waveform coming into his apartment. He put his headband on and started a few visualizations to redirect the energy field, producing a spinning conic waveform for this purpose. It didn't take long to collide the energy field in the direction it was coming from; his only regret was he didn't turn on the device again to check the levels in the apartment. Over time, he used various visualizations to disrupt the psychotronics field, and at one time, Astara Command had communicated to him to use tuning forks to disrupt the energy fields; it worked for a while but then it stopped.

Ben often wondered if his meeting with Robbie, his friend from the Order of Melchezedeck, had anything to do with the psychotronics bombardment. Ben remembered Robbie calling him on the phone and inviting him to a small restaurant in Haight Ashbury in San Francisco one day.

"Hi, Robbie," Ben said while giving him a hug, "Nice to see you again. How's the spiritual family doing?"

"Hi, Ben, The family is doing fine. Eric has moved on in his pre-med program so we don't see him very much anymore. Diane and I are moving out soon – we want our own place."

Ben always knew when Robbie was scanning his auric field, because his eyes would go squinty as he went into soft focus.

"How am I doing?" Ben asked Robbie.

"You're good. I don't see any problems looking at your auric field. Your chakras seem to be functioning at a high level right now."

Ben moved into the restaurant with Robbie not far behind and picked up the energy of a person sitting on a covered stool at the bar. Ben and Robbie sat down at the bar and Ben leaned over a little to Robbie and whispered, "I'm shutting the door on this one," as he motioned with his hands to the person sitting next to him. He knew this individual was a psychic spy.

Robbie laughed at the visual picture.

Ben noticed another person sitting at a table across from them listening to their conversation intently.

"You said you are using tuning forks to disrupt psychic energy fields," Robbie said. "What frequencies work the best for you?"

"The one in the 550 range works best," Ben responded.

Robbie eyed the person at the table across from them. He had a very distinct hostile look on his face and seemed very interested in their conversation. *I would hate to be around him on a bad day,* thought Ben. Ben didn't signal Robbie that he was most likely a scanner also. The presence of these scanners gave Ben all the information he needed to conclude that Robbie was working for the other side now and could no longer be trusted. Though it saddened him, his intuition was working clearly now. He thought about a photograph he had of Robbie dressed as an Esence from biblical times that he had taken at the World's Fair rotunda building near the Exploratorium. He really liked that picture. Robbie's betrayal made him feel sad and sick at heart. Ben had always considered him to be somewhat of a brother, perhaps from a past lifetime.

Still, the pieces of evidence all fell into place in Ben's mind, and now, here he was, a short time later, experiencing a new wave of invasive psychotronics bombardment in his own apartment.

Chapter Fourteen

Spiritual Insights Continue To Manifest

Ben was fixing himself some lunch when a call came into his apartment. It was another of his spiritual friends. Steve was an internet stock trader who worked out of his home.

"Hi, Steve! I haven't heard from you for a long time."

"How've you been, Ben?"

"I'm doing well. I just came back from Steven Bears retreat in Colorado."

"Oh, really?"

"I had an interesting trip, and it was an eye-opener on many levels. I'll tell you about it next time I see you."

"OK. Listen, I wanted to talk to you about another trip," said Steve. "I'm setting up a trip to Williland Ranch in Washington State at the end of the month with some other Shift members." The Shift Group was our friends who pursued spiritual and paranormal interests. "Would you like to go along with us?"

"Well!" said Ben, "I just came back from Colorado. But I think I have enough money to swing one more trip, and I don't go back to work for another month. Yes, I'd like to come."

"OK, great," Steve said. "I'll e-mail you the dates. We're flying into the Portland airport."

"Thanks for the invite, Steve. I've always wanted to go up to Williland Ranch"

The Ranch, run by James Williland, was a center for religious, philosophical and paranormal studies and investigations and was located near Mount Hood and Mount Adams, where ET craft sightings were a common occurrence. Ben got to work setting up the trip to Oregon – booking a flight, getting on James Williland's email list, and packing. Rising early on Friday morning, he drove to Oakland Airport and checked in for his afternoon flight. It was a fast and easy trip – just over an hour. *No snacks on this flight* Ben thought. In Portland, Ben collected his luggage and waited for the team from the Shift Group to arrive. It wasn't long before he spotted Steven.

"Hi, Steve, he said, "you're looking good."

"Thanks, Ben. Have the others arrived?"

"No, I haven't seen them."

"Oh, there they are," Steve said, waving at his John, Gary and Tilly.

After introductions, they all lugged their bags over to the rental car place, and soon they were crammed into a rented truck, headed toward north Trout Lake in Washington. During the two-hour drive, Ben got to know his traveling companions and found they had a lot in common, especially their interest in UFOs and extraterrestrial contact."We live near each other in San Mateo, and we've attended many UFO conferences together," Tilly explained.

It was a very scenic drive with a great arcing stone bridge in the distance visible in the Columbia Gorge area just past the town of Trout Lake. The low-lying trees were reminiscent of Lake Tahoe. When they finally pulled into the driveway of ASETI, they spied a carved painted wooden sign that said, "Satti," that meant something in the Eastern Indian language, maybe Nirvana. They saw in the distance Mount Hood, snowcapped and majestic. James would later tell them that there were a lot of ET dogfights on the mountain. In the other direction stood Mount Adams where the Native Americans had lived. It looked serene and peaceful, but they would later learn it hid a portal from which extraterrestrial crafts would fly.

At the front door, James came out to greet them with open arms. "Hi, guys! Come on in and let me show you to the cottage. I know you want to get settled in since it's getting late. The lady gets the private room and you guys will have to work out sleeping arrangements for yourself. You all get the large room. Here's the communal kitchen and the bathroom. I guess that's it for the night, I'll meet you tomorrow morning on the deck for coffee around nine o'clock." That night, the guys thought they could hear what seemed like animals and people walking around the property at night. It was a strange perception at the time.

When Ben made it out to the deck the next morning, he found that everyone was already there having coffee.

"Have a seat and a cup coffee!" James said in his gruff voice.

In a good mood, Ben replied in a W.C. Fields voice, "Don't mind if I do!"

James explained the different areas of the ranch. "I have a trout pond over there, and a staging area for observing UFOs over there and sacred gardens located around the property. I'm building two large structures to use for conferences that'll be finished in a couple of weeks."

"What is that pyramid shaped building on the top of one of the cottages?" asked Ben.

"Oh, that's a meditation room for the ranch. It's not usable right now, but I'm going to fix it up soon," said James.

"That's too bad," said Ben, "I love meditating in a pyramid, the energy inside is really high. In fact, Christopher Hills says that there are several different types of energy inside the pyramid: positive taction energy, energy that moves faster than the speed of light, and a negative ray he calls a pi ray. Ben had pyramidal shapes he had used to make cottage cheese, purify water, grow seeds bigger and even mummify a piece of fish that he had for 10 years. "The meditation potential is great," Ben continued, "because you can astral project easier with taction energy vortexes. The downside to the pyramid is that the negative pi ray that will affect you emotionally if you stay inside too long." Meditating in a pyramid was known to make people feel emotionally down and irritated. Ben had never experienced that himself, but he had never had the opportunity to sit in a human-sized pyramid for any length time.

"I hear there's a large pyramid near Mount Shasta that's available for meditators – for a price," Steve said.

"Yes, I've heard of that," James replied. "Actually that reminds me of an experience I had in the backcountry near there. I saw a Bigfoot. I was camping with my girlfriend one night, and I heard a loud wailing noise in the distance. I said to my girlfriend, I bet you that's a Sasquatch. I'm going to try and find out. She was horrified and hid in the car. I came upon a large female Bigfoot sitting on a log, crying, next to a lake. She rose, startled, but calmed down when she saw my arms outstretched and felt my loving energy projection. She walked past me, about 50 feet, giving me an expression and communication that there was nothing I could do. She had lost her baby. As she walked past me, she disappeared into thin air."

"Did she morph into the background or just disappear?" Ben asked.

"She just disappeared," he said.

Shape shifters tend to morph into the background, thought Ben.

"There was another time when a friend of mine was playing a swivel whistle out in nature, and a Bigfoot came out of nowhere, took his whistle, broke it in half and briskly walked off" James added.

At that, they all broke into laughter.

"Well, do you guys want a tour of the grounds?" asked James.

James showed them his living space first. It was a large two-story room, with an open space upstairs where his bed was and his books lined the walls. There were deity sculptures, posters and a large tapestry that hung from one of the walls. James told them to have a seat downstairs then brought out some of his photo albums. He shared pictures of his sanctuary area and his Mother Mary statue garden. He also showed them pictures of light ships and a photo of a light beam that caught Ben's eye.

"What is the light beam coming down to the Earth?"

James said, "It's a beam from a ship. I think it's extraterrestrials that were beaming down."

"Wow," said Ben, "you were lucky to get a shot of that."

Tilley said, "Let's take some pictures of ourselves." Using a digital camera, they took shots of everyone, and when they looked at them, they noticed James and Tilly had ethic orbs on their bodies.

James told them, "That happens a lot up here. I think they're spirit entities."

"Like nature spirits?" Ben asked.

"Oh, maybe," said James. "Let me show you the rest of the ranch."

They went outside to see a large open area with a couple of large platforms set up.

James said, "The staging area is where we look for UFOs in the evening. We will come back here tonight." Pointing to another area of the grounds, he said, "Here is my sanctuary for mother Mary, with a statue of the Buddha as well. I've had some interesting meditative experiences here. It is a vortex center. I have several on the property." He also showed them the pond where he raised catfish for food. "There are poles in the cottage if you want to do some fishing," he said. Finally, they looked at the two-story buildings James was constructing for conferences. Ben thought to himself,

God he's building them by himself. They must be at least 8 feet wide and 80 feet long. They took some more photos then left them at their cottage, reminding them to meet him at the staging area just after dark.

At the cottage, they decided John, Gary and Tilly would go to town and get supplies for dinner. Meanwhile, Steven and Ben decided to do a short meditation before trying their hand at fishing at the pond.

Ben said, "I did a lot of fishing with my dad up on the Sacramento River when I was a kid."

"Really? I don't have much experience fishing myself," said Steve,

"It's easy. Let's see if we can find some worms, because catfish love worms," Ben said.

"OK," said Steve. "How do we do that?"

"We need to find some fertile soil around the pond and dig into it for worms. They won't be too far down." Using a knife, Ben dug up some soil. "There be worms!" said Ben. He grabbed several out of the ground and showed Steve how to thread them on his hook. Next, he helped Steve cast his line before casting his own. It wasn't long before Ben got a bite on his line and, giving his line a good yank, reeled in a ten-pound catfish.

"All right!" said Steve.

"Now, we'll need to gut it."

Grimacing Steve said, "I'll leave that up to you." Suddenly, Steve got a hit on his line.

"Yank it, and real it in! You know how to do that don't ya?" said Ben humorously.

Steve followed Ben's prompt and started too real in the fish after a hearty yank. *He's a natural*, thought Ben. Steve tried to grab the flopping fish, but it slipped out of his hand several times. Ben came to the rescue, grabbing the line and whacking the fish over the head. Taking the hook out of its mouth, Ben held it up by the gills."Nice one Steve. It must be about ten inches and seven pounds. You'll be a fisherman in no time."

Ben cast his line again, and it wasn't long before he got a hefty strike that almost knocked him off balance. It was another 10 pounder. "That should be more than enough for dinner tonight," he said.

Ben was showing Steven how to gut the fish in the backyard sink as the others returned from the store. They were excited that they would have catfish for dinner. Tilly, who was from Europe, said,"I love fish. I used to go fishing in my country all the time." Turning to Steven, she said, "I didn't know you fished."

"I don't really. It was Ben's idea. He's the fisherman."

They started preparing the dinner. Ben parpared the fish and the others got to work preparing a healthy salad and baked potatoes. They all sat down to a lovely dinner.

"Would you like me to show you how to eat fresh fish?" Tilly.

Of course, Tilly knew exactly how to eat a fish. But for the benefit of the others Ben launched into the steps to follow when consuming a whole fish. "The main thing you need to do is debone the fish. You don't want to swallow a bone. Cut the head off and spread open the fish. One side will have the backbone. Grab it with your fingers and pull it out all the way along the fish. It should come out easily. Check for other smaller bones, and that's it, you're done. The white meat of the catfish is delicious with salt and pepper, but try not to eat the skin its nasty."

Steven and John tried the deboning, and to their amazement, it came out easily. They were impressed because they had only ever eaten fish deboned by cooks at restaurants. They ate and talked about UFOs and fringe topics, hence the name of the group, "Shift." The conversation continued until shortly after dark.

Meeting James just after dark at the staging area, they all greeted each other and remarked how clear the night sky was. "It should be a good night to call in and look for UFOs," said James.

Ben was debating whether he should tell everyone about the ISETI protocol method that Steven Bear had developed to call in ships – the Mind Sequencing process. He decided to ask James if he knew of the protocol that Bear developed for his groups.

"Yes, I heard about it from friends of mine who went on Bear's retreats."

"How about close encounters of the fifth kind?" Ben asked.

"Yes, we respond to the craft by flashing a laser at them once when we see them in the night sky. We also do mental projection at the sky as well. If they respond by powering up or flashing us, we signal back. We also use infrared goggles to look for them. Setting up a communication with them and signaling back is a close encounter of the fifth kind."

Ben sat down and went into a meditation, going through the ISETI protocol to pull in any ships that might be in the vicinity.

Of course, James was contacting his personal sources as they stood looking at the night sky, and it wasn't long before they heard James say, "There is one in the southwest sky."

They all looked to the southwest and saw a tiny rounded light moving through the sky. John pointed a green laser at the moving ship, and James tracked it using infrared goggles. Then it started getting closer, and at one point powered up to twice its size with a greenish round corona. Everyone cheered and said, "Do it again," and the ship powered up once again, this time to three times its original size.

"Boy," said Ben, "that expansion is spectacular."

"Yeah," said James, "they do that all the time. We saw a golden mothership one time that was amazing." Shifting his attention to the bottom part of Mount Adams, James shouted, "Look! There's a portal opening. Here, Ben, look through these infrared goggles."

Ben took the goggles and looked at Mount Adams. There was a light on the lower part of the mountain, and pretty soon he saw a lighted craft emerged from that same light and shot up in the sky at supersonic speeds heading for outer space.

"Boy they're fast," said Steve. "You don't need goggles to see the ship accelerate through the night sky, either."

After a while, the clouds rolled in and James announced that the sky viewing activities were over for the night.

"That was really great," said Ben, "I haven't seen a ship power up in a long time. I wish we could stay another night, but we're heading for the Columbia Gorge and maybe Mount Saint Helena tomorrow."

"Well thanks for coming by," said James."I enjoyed having you here. I hope you come back again sometime."

As Ben headed back to the cottage with the others, he thought that James's reputation as the most spiritually focused Light Worker/Star Seed in the UFO community might just be deserved.

They awoke early to head for the Columbia Gorge. Moving up the main highway, with Oregon on one side and Washington on the other, the Columbia Gorge appeared with its fantastic waterfall looming 100 feet in the air. Ben thought that view by itself made the detour to the Gorge worth the extra miles of driving. In the parking lot, Ben realized there was a suspension bridge across the waterfall about 50 feet in the air. He suggested they cross it, and the group agreed. As they ascended the stairs to the bridge they could see this scenic view of the tiled in plaza below. They arrived at the bridge and slowly made their way across, stopping to focus on the magnificent view of the top of the falls and the grandeur of the cascading water in the pool below. Ben took out his camera and took a few pictures of the falls and spied a sculptural shaped rock at the very bottom of the cascade. Ben, being a sculpture major in college, appreciated the square and rounded features and the symmetry of the three-foot rock. It was perched at an unusual angle that defied gravity. That by itself made it an interesting photographic subject for Ben.

Ben thought to himself *I'm going to have to photograph that rock when I get to the bottom.* The functional shape would be a nice contrast to the waterfall behind it. *Oh, the lines, the lines,* he thought, pursing his lips and kissing his fingers in the manner of an Italian chef appreciating a splendid meal. The bridge was bigger than he thought from the plaza, making it possible for pedestrians to walk both ways and not interfere with someone next to them. Ben went to take his photographs of the waterfall and magnificent rock sculpture, thinking, *there's something about waterfalls that uplifts the spirit.*

When they got back, they checked out the gift shop then Steve suggested visiting the historical museum not far up the road. At the museum parking lot, Ben spied a huge wooden sculpture of a naked woman in a lovely pose carved out of a redwood tree. It was around fifteen-feet high, and made for a great photograph. The museum was an interesting experience. An old Chinese rickshaw loomed in one corner, and a ten-foot sacred scroll tapestry hung from the opposite wall. There were Indian artifacts throughout the museum, including hand-carved totem poles with animals and symbols of the local lore of the ancient culture that lived in that area. Ben couldn't forget the full-size boat used to transverse the waters and rapids in the area.

There was a photograph of an ancient petroglyphs sitting between two rocks. The caption for the photo read, "The Watcher." Ben really appreciated this ancient work of art. Being an empath, Ben had the ability to interface with the energy coming from the image. It was similar to what was originally termed, in dowsing circles, psychometry – the ability to read energy from an inanimate object. In those cases, you had to touch the object, but this photograph was up on the wall, so Ben projected a light wave from his middle eye and a light beam from his heart that intersected at the photograph. This was a good technique if you couldn't get close to the object. The petroglyph figure felt like a female energy signature.

The two figures flanking each side of her were some kind of animals that were very masculine. It was almost as if they were guarding a powerful princess doing her work of overlooking the valley for any kind of menace that could harm the people living there. It might have been a tribal shaman who had carved the fantastic manifestation in the stone. Ben decided right there that he was going to make an 11 x 14 image of this photograph and put the framed picture on his wall.

After that, they headed in the direction of Mount Saint Helena. Passing signs to the lower falls, Ben suggested they visit them when on the way back from the top of the mountain, and everyone agreed. For some reason Ben felt the falls would be interesting.

Mount St. Helena was famous because she had blown her top not too long before. Ben remembered seeing the news of a reporter making his way down the mountain, barely being able to breathe with all the fallout of dust particles that filled the air. As they drove, they could see some of the devastation, including fallen trees that were topped as Helena blew. The vegetation was just starting to grow back. They made it almost to the top, but decided to stop at the visitor's center since the clouds had set in and visibility was so bad even the mountain was obscured. They listened to the ranger talk about the mountain's recovery a reforestation. Ben thought about the time that Gertrude gave him an Indian clay relief made from the dust from Mount St. Helena.

When they left for the lower falls, Ben decided he would take a turn at driving. As he approached the lower falls, Ben started feeling sick to his stomach. "I need to pull over. I'm feeling too sick to drive. Does anyone else feel that strange energy?"

Steve said, "I can feel it too."

So, someone else was feeling this energy as well, thought Ben. *It's not just me.*

They parked near falls and went to the edge of the cliffs. Ben was still feeling the uncomfortable energy, but the longer he was there, the less the energy affected him for some reason. Ben turned to the trees on the other side of the river and focused on the strong magnetic energy coming from that area. He closed his eyes and tried to see what was behind the trees. He started seeing, with his All-Seeing Eye, a huge bolder. *That's interesting*, Ben thought, *is the bolder the source of this strange energy*? Somehow it came to Ben that this bolder was more than it seemed. He probed the image for more details and realized that this object was an ET ship and not a boulder at all. He tried to communicate with any possible beings inside but got no response. *I wish I could get across the river so I could check it out*, he thought, but the cliffs were too steep and the river was too rapid to make a crossing.

Looking at the sandbar on the bank, he noticed that the sand had coalesced into a heart shape. He knew that the heart found in nature is an expression of the energy of love. Heart shapes sometimes appeared in his photographs and artwork though he didn't intentionally put them. The energy of the area was very powerful and Ben wondered if the energy of the craft expressed this heart energy. He recalled how certain frequencies of sound vibrations focused on metal plates could cause sand to organize itself into specific geometric forms. They have even determined that if you put certain words on a jar of water, "love," for example, the vibration will filter into the water. Water is an excellent conductor of vibrations. In the Bible was a passage – and there was first the word, God – Ben contemplated.

Turning to the others, he told them of his discovery. "I picked up a magnetic vibration over there across the water behind trees."

"That's interesting," said Tilly. "You picked up an image of ship. Boy, I wish we could go over there. We should try and come back sometime and see if we can find a way across."

"Yeah," Ben said, "I wish I had my Natural EM meter with me. We could track down the energy focal points and track the forms of energy. The meter can detect ET ships' magnetic signature, even in the sky."

"I'd like to see that," said Steve.

"I do have my hand-held magnometer with me," said Ben. He pulled it out of his pocket and pointed it in the direction of the energy across the river. As he did, the needle swung all away over to the other side of the scale. "It's powerful," said Ben. At that point everyone looked at the meter, impressed by the intensity of the power the reading indicated.

"Well," said Steve, "we definitely have to come back now."

"You know, I don't feel sick anymore from the energy," said Ben.

"Yeah, me neither," said Steve.

"I don't feel it either," said Tilly. "I didn't say anything before, but I felt it too."

"I thought you did," said Ben. "You're a very sensitive person."

Gary and John seemed to be oblivious to the power in the area.

"It's interesting." said Ben, "we must have acclimated to the vibrational field. I wonder if the ETs had anything to do with it." With that they headed for the airport.

At the airport, they said their goodbyes.

"Well guys, it's been a memorable trip. I really enjoyed it," Ben said, and the others chimed in that they had enjoyed themselves also.

As they headed for their respective gates, Ben yelled over his shoulder at Tilly, "E-mail me those pictures, would you?"

"Sure, Ben," she said with a wave. "I was planning on doing that anyway. Bye!"

Chapter Fifteen

Ben Changes his life

It was getting harder and harder for Ben to live in San Francisco on a substitute teacher's salary. He had already moved from his Potrero Hill apartment to a two-story townhouse in the Ingleside district of the city, but it wasn't working out for him – living with two other people and sharing one bathroom was not his idea of living. Then he found a tiny place in the Avenues that he was lucky to get. It was a little cottage with a cute backyard at great price. He had made arrangements with a moving company, and on the Saturday of the move, as the truck was being loaded, Ben got a call from the owner of the cottage. He had rented Ben's apartment to someone else who had offered more money. Ben went ballistic at the news. He had to be out of his current place that day and was at his wit's end. "What am I going to do now?" Ben shouted.

As he watched the movers load the truck with his stuff, he wondered where he would tell them to take it. Considering his options, he got a phone call out of the blue.

"Hi Ben. "It's Coral Pioneer from the Shift group. I thought I'd call you to see how you were doing."

Ben told her of his woes and complained about the skyrocketing rents in the city and the fierce competition for apartments.

"Well, it's your lucky day, I just fixed up my garage. I could let you rent it for a while if you wanted."

"Are you kidding Coral?" Ben exclaimed. "That's exactly what I need to hear!"

"But I'm way out in Walnut Creek. Would you be all right living here?" she asked.

Walnut Creek was a suburb at the edge of the East Bay – a forty-minute drive from the city in good traffic.

"You know what?" said Ben, "I'm about finished with San Francisco. It's changed too much in the last twenty years, and I can't deal with the hassle and rising prices anymore. Anyway, I'm starting a new job at a high school teaching art and physical education in the East Bay. I guess it's fate. I can't believe you called me today, of all times. That blows my mind."

"Well OK. We'll be looking for you. By the way, you forgot to ask about the rent!"

"Oops," Ben laughed.

"It'll be reasonable, Just $450 a month."

That was cheap by Bay Area standards. "Fine with me," Ben said."I'll see you in a few hours."

Coral was an interesting person. She was a super master vibration, a UCLA graduate and owned her own furniture moving company. In addition to her participation in the Shift group, she was friends with Robert, the organizer of the Living Life Expo. They had several UFO sightings together. He wrote a book on his experiences of meeting extraterrestrials and his abduction. Unfortunately, Ben would find out later that Robert was a scanner.

Ben arrived at Coral's place in Walnut Creek in the afternoon. It was a nice house on the outskirts of town nestled on a hilltop. As he arrived, he saw Coral at the door and waved.

"Hi Ben. I had a feeling you were here. Let me show you the room." It was a nice green carpeted large space off of one of the bedrooms.

"This is great Coral. I love it."

She also showed him her home. "Here's the kitchen, living room and dining room. You should watch TV with us sometime. We just bought this new 57-inch flat screen."

"OK," said, Ben. "Where is your husband Sky?"

"He's out running errands right now. He'll be back later."

As he helped the movers, Ben thought to himself, *This is going to be nice.* Just as he got all his stuff settled in,he saw Sky return, and went into the kitchen to say hello.

"Hi, Sky.I haven't seen you in a long time."

"Glad to see you, Ben, and happy to have you as part of the household. We need the extra money."

Sky was a straight-laced engineer who looked at the practical side of situations most of the time. His wife was the spiritual person in the family and believed wholeheartedly in UFOs and related phenomena. Sky would only believe in UFOs if he actually experienced one. Ben got the feeling he was on the fence with the whole idea.

Ben corresponded with psychics around the country and Europe. One day, Ben received a couple of letters from psychics saying that he would meet his Twin Flame soon. The following Sunday, Ben attended a new church for the first time, and that was where he saw Morena. She seemed so familiar to him that he kept wondering where he'd met her before. *Could this be my twin flame?* he wondered.

After church, he introduced himself to her. "Hi. I saw you from across the courtyard and you seemed so familiar to me."

"Oh? It's interesting you should say that. You seemed familiar to me also," she replied.

They chatted for a few minutes, introducing who they were and sharing a bit about their lives. Then a tall, handsome young man of about twenty-two approached and Morena introduced him. "This is my son Chad."

"Hi, Chad," said Ben, extending his hand.

"Good to meet you." Turning to his mother, he said, "I have to go, Mom," and kissed her on the cheek.

"He is my guardian angel," she said. "He protects me."

"Well, I'll see you again. I have to meet someone later." Then he leaned in and gave her a hug, saying, "We have some unfinished business." Ben didn't know why he said that and continued on his way in deep thought.

Morena later told Ben, "When you made that comment, a short burst of energy went straight through my heart."

Ben had heard that once you kiss a woman on her lips, she always knows if you are the right one for her. He decided to try it out on Morena after they had gotten to know each other better. One lazy afternoon at his place, he began to give Morena a massage, and he used the opportunity to steal a kiss. She was not pleased.

"Why did you kiss me?" she asked. "Don't kiss me. I'm not kissing anyone right now because I'm engaged."

Ben thought for moment and replied, "I just wanted to find out if you felt anything for me."

"Yes, I do. But what's that got to do with anything? My son said not to kiss you. I respect his psychic intuitive abilities. He's right almost every time."

Ben continued, "I wanted to find out if you thought, - I was the one."

"You are a strange man, Ben, "she said, shutting down the conversation with a look.

Ben thought, *She just doesn't want to admit I'm the special one because of her engagement to someone else.* He felt he was her twin flame.

Morena soon returned to her cheery self – she always had a big smile on her face, which was one of the things that attracted Ben to her. *Her inside light is always shining through, thought Ben.* It was a characteristic of a super master vibration.

At church the next weekend, Ben didn't see Morena, so he spoke with his friend Alice. The subject turned to UFOs and MUFON.

"The Northern California MUFON is meeting for a lecture next week we should go," said Alice.

"OK," said Ben, "I'd like that. I want to invite my friend Morena."

"The more the merrier," she replied. "I'd like to meet your twin flame. I'm also bringing my boyfriend to the lecture. Can you pick me up on Saturday around 12:30?"

"Sure, see you then," said Ben.

Alice was an interesting person. She was a super master vibration 22 and a very old soul. She was a citizen of England and grew up out in the countryside close to the Stonehenge monument. She was a very strong psychic and boasted that she could turn street lights off and on. She was a model and singer when she was younger and had worked with Phil Collins, whom she was singing for royalties on songs she was involved in. Unfortunately, she was bipolar, and this ailment gave her a lot of problems. She had a child but didn't take it well and went into a deep depression that almost took her life. Afterwards, she went on medication, but she and her husband became estranged and split up. The daughter went with the father, though she had visiting rights at times.

Ben slept with Alice once, but she unfortunately tried to drain him of life force. Ben knew that life force could be replenished by doing certain spiritual disciplines such as looking at the sun, but that was the end of his sexual relationship with Alice. He considered her a psychic vampire and he wondered if she hadn't performed certain related duties for the government in England.

She claimed she had worked for Queen Elizabeth, and Ben thought there might have been something to that since he had heard rumors in alternate circles that the Queen was a reptilian extraterrestrial.

Regardless, Ben didn't hold Alice's transgressions against her and stayed friends with her until her eventual move to Nevada. He had fond memories of a time they made music together. She had used a recording device that she had used with Phil Collins, and she used it to record a duet with Ben. His voice had never sounded that good before – ever. Alice was very pleased with how it turned out too.

After church, Ben headed for his favorite park and walked around the lake and fed the turtles. He spent the afternoon reading one of his favorite books there. When he got home, he called Morena and they made plans to attend the MUFON lecture with Alice and her boyfriend.

Ben and the group arrived in the San Jose parking lot about three o'clock. It was a balmy summer day. They all walked into the conference room and sat down among the rows of folding chairs. The meeting was about to start. It wasn't a big crowd but a nice small group, especially good if there were questions afterwards. Ruben, the head of the Northern California MUFON group, was speaking about UFOs sightings in Northern California. There was a recent sighting around Sebastopol that was corroborated by many witnesses, and one person drew a picture of the craft. As Ben was listening, a strange occurrence happened to him. Sitting in his chair comfortably, a large being suddenly dropped into his body. Ben had experienced channeling before and was somewhat comfortable with the new energy, but he was also a little surprised as always. He didn't realize this was going to happen, but how could he. He never knew ahead of time when a being would drop into his body.

Ben relaxed and let the being become comfortable inside him. Then he noticed Morena becoming very excited – she was aware that a being's energy was in his body, and she was staring at his auric field intently with a big smile. She got out her pen and started jotting something down. A few minutes later, the being lifted off and Ben came back to himself again.

"Did you feel that, Morena?" asked Ben.

"Oh yes, I did, and I wrote down what he was saying about you and me."

Ben said, "That was an interesting energy field. It was very intense, a large being that filled up my entire space. I have not had a drop-in channeling in a long time."

They listened to the rest of the lecture and then decided to go to dinner after the Q&A.As they drove to the restaurant, Alice remarked, "That was an interesting energy you channeled."

"You felt that?"

"Oh yeah, of course I did," remarked Alice. "You know I'm very psychic."

Morena piped in, "I wrote down everything he said about Ben and me. I'll read it to you over dinner. The being's name is Telefon."

In the restaurant, Morena pulled out her pad and started reading Telefon's words: "Good evening, Ben. I'm a member of the Galactic Board of Regents, and you have completed much work for us in the higher dimensions. You have a female counterpart alive and well in our outer realms of your galaxy. You often meet and exchange communications. She is known to you as Alexandre and sends welcome and loving life. You are a warm and loving being of the blue light group of Tirates who has volunteered to raise the energy on the Earth plane. Keep holding the light Ben and know that we are with you and well connected. Joy is a catch word if you need to talk with me. Keep a watch for signs in your world of our presence. Call upon me, I am Telefon, your comrade in light. Light is often the craft we use to communicate with your species."

Triad Informmancy of Justinian Forces,

Keeper of peaceful vibrations,

location: Enertin, our ship. *This part of the channeled letter must be the way they sign off after imparting a message,* Ben thought.

Morena explained, "Telefon is a source being to you Ben. You run biologically conforming energetic soul frequencies like matrixes and process similar organization forms."

"I'll send you a typed copy," she added.

Ben was moved. "That's fascinating. I wish I could better understand some of the things he said. I'm going to try to communicate with him when I call on him, if I can. I'm so glad I have a new Galactic friend in the higher consciousness level. I love my ET friends; they watch over me."

"Let me know what you learn when Telefon clarifies some of these things the next time you talk with him," said Morena.

Alice and her boyfriend were beaming with enthusiasm at the prospect of witnessing a channeling. "I'd like to hear that information myself," she said.

As the dinner conversation moved on to new topics, Alice told Ben she was going to send her father in England two copies of his book. He was a retired military person and liked that type of information. Ben thanked her and asked about her condition. "I heard that you passed out in your kitchen for 48 hours, recently."

Alice replied, "Yes it was very strange. I seem to be all right now."

"Well," Ben said, "I'd like to tell you my perspective of what happened to you that night."

"OK," said Alice.

"You know that I did your numerology chart and you are a super master vibration number 22, a very old soul. I have studied the physical characteristics of that vibration as well as other mannerisms. You still have the long wide tall facial features but intuitively I sense you are younger soul now. I think you had a walk-in experience when you passed out in your kitchen. You seem like a different person now."

"It's interesting," said Alice,"I feel younger now... let me think about that and get back to you."

"Walk-ins" was a term coined in the 80s to describe individuals who can't handle their mission and leave their body if they can convince another soul to take on their mission and karma and complete it in that lifetime. "I'm sure you ascended beings understand what walk-ins are," said Ben. Everyone nodded except Alice's boyfriend, who stayed silent.

Ben thought, *this guy must really be a novice.*

"I've read what Gregg Braden said on the subject," said Morena. "There is quite a lot written on walk-ins in general. It's a very difficult task to complete. These are extremely strong and ascended souls to take on another soul's lessons in life. I'm sure they are rewarded handsomely for their service – karmically."

Alice nodded her head and said,"I saw something about that on the Internet and I should look up more details on the subject, but I know in my soul that what you are saying is true."

It was pretty quiet on the drive home. Everyone was in deep contemplation over the day's events. Ben pulled up in front of Morena's house and she said, "I had a channeling last night from one of my guides who told me you and I should go on a retreat to celebrate our love for each other."

"Oh! OK." said Ben, "I would love that!"

"I'll type the channeling up for you and give you a copy. Right now, I want to try and track down a retreat close to us to do an overnighter."

An overnighter! said Ben. "OK, Morena, call me about the date." Ben was ecstatic about this chance to be alone with Morena. Maybe he had a chance to get her away from her boyfriend, who was her soulmate, unfortunately. *Why had Morena scheduled a possible retreat? Did she have second thoughts about her commitment to her boyfriend? I don't know, maybe she wanted to turn over this rock,sort to speak, to realize if this person was the one she wanted to spend the rest of her life.*

A couple of days later, Morena called. "I found a retreat we can go to in Woodside. Gill turned me onto a very nice place. You know Gill, he is a healer and medical practitioner that put on some workshops at church."

"Oh, yeah, I remember I went over to his house for a workshop one time."

"He said it was very nice, and there wouldn't be a lot of people there at this time of year," remarked Morena. "Why don't we go this Saturday overnight? We need to go Dutch, I don't have a lot of money right now."

"That's OK Morena. I look forward to seeing you Saturday morning," said Ben.

Woodside was a beautiful rustic wooded area not far from a large reservoir. On the way down, Ben got to know a little more about Morena's family and she got to learn a little bit more about his history. They weaved their way down the hill towards the retreat. Nestled among the trees was a modern natural wooden building with all the accommodations of a nice health spa retreat. They went inside and got their room. The matron was the only one there and showed them around – there was an indoor pool, an outdoor hot tub, a commercial kitchen, a large living room area with a stone fireplace with a very large crystal and sculptures of Eastern deities dotted around the area. There was also a library of books on holistic health, meditation, Hinduism, Buddhism, Christianity and contemporary spiritual subjects.

Morena said, "Let's take a swim and a hot tub and then go to the sitting room. I will channel Emmera for you again. You remember Emmera, the ET from the future you met at the dowsing conference fifteen years ago," said Morena.

"Sounds great," said Ben with a twinkle in his eye.

As Ben approached the room, he noticed a small stone over the door he hadn't noticed before. It had a saying on it, "Expect a Miracle." He checked to see if the other rooms had similar rocks over their doors, and they all did – spiritual sayings painted on river rocks. Rumi the famous poet would be proud.

They put on their swimsuits and went to the pool. It was the edge of winter, so it was a little bit drizzly outside.

Morena said, "Let's go to the hot tub first."

"OK, said Ben, "I'll go back and get the umbrella and meet you back at the tub."

Carrying the umbrella, he met Morena in the courtyard at the hot tub, popped the canopy and gathered up Morena as they stepped into the hot water. The water felt delicious and Morena in her bikini was really enticing. Ben stood at her back holding her but couldn't bring himself to violate his promise to maintain a nonphysical relationship because of Morena's commitment to her fiancé. They even had separate beds. He wondered why she had laid out her nightgown on her bed for him to see. Her supple body was tantalizing and alluring in this intimate setting. Ben heard a voice in his head say, *"Don't go there."* He replied to the voice, *"You never let me have any fun."*

Ben felt the rain hitting the umbrella harder as he appreciated the curvature of Morena's neckline. "Let's head for the pool inside," he said. "It's getting cold now." He was also concerned that his little friend might raise his head.

As Morena climbed out of the hot tub and walked to the pool, she intuitively knew what Ben was thinking. Ben was right behind her, like a bee on a flower. The water in the pool was warm and inviting. Ben took a lap and noticed that Morena was right on his tail enjoying the sight of his wrestler's body. They waded and swam for only about ten minutes before heading back to the room to get dressed.

Morena said, "Let's take a nap first before we get something to eat in the kitchen." She lay down and Ben snuggled next to her back when suddenly a shot of energy flashed down his spine and he jerked up, sending a wave form through Morena's body.

She jumped up and said, "We're not doing that again."

Ben replied, "I think that just was a ship above us" with a depressed look on his face.

"I'm not sure what it was. Let's get going," she replied sharply.

Ben thought about it later and realized he should have tried to communicate with the beings to see if they had a message. Ben thought the energy was an omen but didn't know what kind. *Or was it something else?*

In the kitchen, they put together a salad and turkey tacos. After dinner, they sat down in front of the huge stone fireplace. They decided it would be too much trouble to start a fire – unfortunately. Morena wanted to channel Emmera and Ben wanted to show her how to raise the Over Soul.

Morena went into trance, then spoke to Ben as Emmera.

"Hi Emmera," said Ben.

"You and Morena have been together for many lifetimes over the long history of your incarnated lives. You truly can't be together until you are at the same consciousness level. Your numerology system gives you some indication of this possibility. Morena is a super master vibration level of consciousness and you Ben, are not. You need to evolve to this level first. You're fortunate now that you can move through as many levels of consciousness as you can handle in one lifetime. In the ancient past, this was not possible. You're an ancient and ascended being, Ben, and it will not be difficult for you to rise to Morena's level of mastery. Even though I'm not one of your guides, I feel close to you, Ben, because of our past interactions. You are as great a spirit as is Morena. You are twin flames and in love to the highest degree. When you come together as one, it will be miraculous. Goodbye for now. Love and light." Morena came out of the channeling trance quickly and they proceeded to move into the raising of the Over Soul.

"Close your eyes," said Ben. "Take a few deep breaths and relax. Go deep now and see a garden with trees, plants and a stream. It is an overcast day and in a foggy area. Now see a being moving through the fog with millions of diamonds reflecting and refracting light rays in all directions. This is your Over Soul. Now, try and interface, go into the light ray, as it reflects your way. As you do so, you will feel a raising upwards sensation, as the Over Soul takes hold and your light body stretches as high as you want to go."

Morena rode the wave upward into consciousness as Ben followed along beside her. When Ben felt that she could no longer go any higher, they slowly descended back into their bodies.

He opened his eyes, and Ben asked, "How do you feel, to Morena?"

"That was great Ben, I feel really light and empowered in my body and my Christ self, my, I'M present." *The I'm Present is a well established religious term Ben had heard on many occasions,* he thought.

"Great, I knew you would catch on to this process easily." Ben felt very ascended now and as close to Morena as he possibly could.

"Let's get some sleep, if we can. We need to get an early start tomorrow," said Morena.

They kind of floated down the hall towards the room. They put on their night clothes and got into their beds.

"Goodnight, Morena. I love you," said Ben.

"Good night, Ben. I love you," said Morena.

Ben thought about the day and evening activities and was feeling more content and warm inside than he had felt in a long time, and he was off to dreamland.

Ben woke slowly, noticing Morena was up and dressed. "You're up already," he said.

"Yes, I awoke about six o'clock, took a bath and walked in the garden for a while," she said.

"You're an early riser. Good for you," Ben stated.

"I was thinking."

She was up early because she was trying to figure out whether she should stay with her fiancé or move in Ben's direction, he contemplated.

Ben got up and showered so he could go out for breakfast at the Embassy Hotel which had an atrium and good food on their trip back up the peninsula. Soon, they were leaving the beautiful retreat location of Woodside behind, vowing to return someday.

When they got to the Embassy Hotel, Ben was shocked to see they were in the process of taking the famous atrium down. "What a bummer! Sorry, Morena, I really wanted to show you the atrium. It would have been nice to hear the birds chirping in the background as we ate lunch."

"Well, I didn't come here for the birds," replied Morena. I really enjoyed our stay at the retreat.

"Yeah, it was great," said Ben. "I only wish we had more time there."

During brunch, they shared stories and talked about their childhood histories.

Suddenly Morena's mood changed and she interjected, "Ben, I need a man who is strong and can take care of me."

"Yeah, I know," Ben said reluctantly, "A very strong person." He got the feeling she thought he couldn't handle himself. He didn't know where she had gotten that idea. It bothered him so much he decided to tell her a couple of stories about his life in San Francisco. He told her how he had worked and taught in some of the city's roughest neighborhoods and had been threaten many times with guns and knives but had always kept his cool."I'm a very strong person when I need to be," he insisted.

He told her about a time when he was visiting a Buddhist friend's apartment in the Haight Ashbury one evening. He and his friend Tony were climbing the stairs in a narrow stairwell when a couple of high school kids came up behind them. One of them pulled out a large butcher knife placed it at Ben's throat. Ben was sure he could disarm the kid and throw him down the stairs, but Tony was right below them and the other assailant had a zip gun at his head. *Crap*, thought Ben, *if I make a move toward this kid Tony will probably be shot.*

"Let me see your eyes," said the kid with the butcher knife.

Ben had no other choice but to comply.

"Now give me your money if you wanna live!" he demanded.

Ben knew it wasn't worth getting his throat cut for a few bucks, so he handed over the ten dollars he had in his pocket. Tony was carrying a trumpet case, and the other guy ripped it out of his hand as they both fled. Ben felt sorry for Tony that was an expensive instrument.

Ben told Morena how scared Tony was and long it took to calm him down. Tony was a student Ben had turned on to Buddhism, and they were visiting a fellow member of their "han" or group, going on Monton was the term used by the Buddhist. He was a typical Ivy League kid from the suburbs, and he could never again summon the courage to go on Monton with Ben. Ben, however, wasn't fazed "Sure, it got my adrenaline pumping," he told Morena, "but that wasn't my first holdup, and I don't scare easily."

Morena looked unimpressed, so Ben recounted another brush with violence he'd handled smoothly. He was subbing at a child development center in Hundreds Point community with a strange assistant teacher. As he directed the assistant to help him cover a table with newspaper for an art project, she suddenly ripped the paper off the table in anger. Surprised by her hostility, Ben stepped back and muttered "bitch" under his breath. She heard, and it didn't sit well with her. A short time later, she came back a with a Phillips screwdriver ready to stab him. "It was surreal," Ben told Morena, "as she approached me, time went into slow motion. A spirit dropped into my body and I could see clairvoyantly that she was going to jab me in the stomach and then rotate the screwdriver and stab me in the jugular vein. It seemed like a trick she might've learned on the street."

Ben explained how he was able to defend himself with the skill of martial arts expert. First, he stepped back, sliding his feet along the ground, and then he raised and crossed his wrists to block her blows under and over. Then, using my hip for leverage, he would have managed to throw her body over his hip into a wall. "That was a 'hip throw.' I used the move many times in my days training to be an Olympic wrestler," Ben told Morena.

"When the other staff members showed up and pulled her off me, my eyes were as big as saucers. I was definitely in a trance. But as soon as the threat was gone, I felt the spirit lift and move back to its ascended position in hyperspace above my head," he said.

"What happened at the school, after that?" Morena asked.

"Well, it wasn't good for either of us. The assistant got fired, and I was told my services were no longer needed there. To tell the truth, I wish I could have diffused the situation differently. As soon as her anger passed, the assistant became sad and remorseful. I think she really needed that job."

"Well, it was her own fault."

"True," said Ben. "Anyway, the point I'm trying to get across is that I'm not soft. I can handle myself when things get tough."

"I know that, Ben. In certain ways, you are very strong person," she replied.

"I'll take that, for now."

Then, looking straight into his eyes, she added a point he'd hoped to avoid. "But financially, you're not very strong. You know that, don't you?"

Ben sighed. "OK. I acknowledge that. And I'm sorry I can't be that person for you. I know your fiancé does very well in finance. I know I can't compete with him in that way."

As Ben's words trailed off, Morena changed the subject. "Listen, I need to get going now. I'm meeting a friend later this afternoon."

"Sure," Ben replied.

"Ben, I know who you are now, and I appreciate you. And I appreciate that you understand me. You're right about my fiancé. He can provide for me better than you can."

Ben saw the writing on the wall, but he didn't want her to leave just yet. "Morena, do you have a minute more?"

"OK," said Morena, "just a minute or two."

"After you told me about your destiny to open light portals in Northern California, I had a vision of you and me. Can I tell it to you?"

"Sure."

Ben told her how, in meditation, he experienced the two of them sitting in the lotus position in a forest, holding hands. Suddenly, a vertical wave form descended between them and expanded outward to encompass them both in a white light, and they were levitated upward toward a spacecraft. The dark metal underside of the craft opened, and they floated into the craft unimpeded. They were sent into a dimly lit bay where there were a number of small gray extraterrestrials and a being that looked like Emmera. "We all exchanged greetings, but you were terrified for some reason, so I held you in my arms to soothe you," he told her.

They walked through a wall into the bay area of the ship and found themselves in a console compartment with an oval shaped window with was a two-inch lip. They peered outside and were surprised to see they were high above the Earth and there were light grids circling its circumference. "I had heard of light grids around the planet before, but this was the first time I had actually seen them," Ben explained.

In fact, Ben remembered a man named Feather at the dowsing conference who wrote a book called *Geomancy* that talked about the planet grid and lay lines that ancient cultures built their stone walls and structures on, because they were power points on the planet. He recalled other book references of lay lines and the Earth grid system.

The beings spoke to Ben and Morena, but they couldn't understand their words. Ben asked if he could have a souvenir of the experience, and one little gray agreed telepathically. "He gave us something, but I don't know what it was. Then it was over, and we were teleported back down to the same spot we had been sitting in. Then I came out of meditation," Ben concluded.

"That was a great vision story, Ben! I'll type it up for you," Morena said. "Actually, I do remember something about that incident in my own meditation, but I can't really remember the details." Seeing the interest in Ben's eyes, she added, "I really do have to get going now."

They drove to Morena's place in silence. As she got out of the car, Ben said, "I'll talk you later."

"Yes, you will," Morena replied, with a twinkle in her eye.

Ben had forgotten that Morena had talked about their experience of being pulled up onto the ship. When he got back to the apartment, he reviewed a tape of Morena channeling Emmera. On it, Emmera explained that the experience had been a precognitive vision. "You were taken up to the ship in your light bodies, but if you want to be taken up in your physical bodies, you need only ask. Look for signs of this vision in the future.

"When can I expect this to happen?" Ben heard his voice ask on the tape.

"It will be up to you to decide, but it will come with communication with yourself or the appropriate timing in your timeline," Emmera replied through Morena's voice.

Turning off the tape, Ben thought about Emmera's words and the light energy he and Morena shared. Suddenly, he recalled a similar energy that had passed between them.

It was when Morena used psychometry to tune into a stone Ben had brought back from an ancient wisdom conference in Berkeley. He bought the stone from David Moonhouse who said it was given to him by Native Americans from the desert backcountry of New Mexico.

He told Ben the stone was actually a piece of a downed craft, and he had taken it to the Colorado Institute of Mines for analysis. When he sold it to Ben, he included a copy of the report.

The report was interesting because it gave a breakdown of the stone's properties. There was a green shiny cylindrical shape with large inclusions in it with gray material inside. It had obviously been a processed stone. The green mineral was light as a feather and looked almost like plastic at first glance. The report from the Institute revealed that it was a combination of volcanic stone, metallic silver balls and a gray substance unknown to this planet. It was a very remarkable stone. Ben believed it could indeed be a piece of an extraterrestrial craft, and if so, it could contain a form of consciousness since some ET cultures created ships to be sentient beings.

Holding the stone in her hand, Morena said she was seeing clairvoyantly and feeling the object's energy. She said she could see a very tall light being, and this being was connected to Ben through an umbilical cord linked to Ben's solar plexus. "I guess, you have some connection with them. I think you also have to do light work on the planet and keep light portals open for them."

"What type of being is it?" asked Ben.

"This one is strange and unknown to me, "said Morena.

The memory jogged more memories floating in Ben's mind, and he began to recall other times Ben and Morena shared a telepathic link. One especially powerful image of Morena, lying Christ like on her bed, entered Ben's mind. He had been teaching her the Christ consciousness visualization when he suddenly found himself hovering above her in his light body, his arms outstretched, perfectly matching her body. Soon, the room disappeared, and they found themselves floating in space with Earth and the universe as their backdrop. Suddenly, a pink laser light shot right through their hearts, facilitating a reverberation of energy up-and-down their bodies. Morena asked Ben telepathically to send her another burst of energy, but Ben replied, telepathically, *"It wasn't from me. I think it was from creation."* They basked in the love energy passing through them for some time. Ben later sent Morena an account of the experience along with a drawing depicting it.

Chapter Sixteen

Psychic Abilities Are In Full Bloom

Still lost in his memories of Morena, Ben heard a knock on his door, and Coral entered his room. She had a pleasant demeanor as always, *super master vibrations are like that most of the time,* thought Ben.

"Ben, I need to talk to you about some changes."

Uh-oh, Ben thought.

"There are a lot of things going on with my family right now, and my relationship with my husband isn't going well. We need to have some space to ourselves, and it's just not a good time to share our home with a tenant. I'm going to have to ask you to move out as soon you can. You've a been a good tenant, and I can recommend you to a friend who's renting out a nice apartment over by Lunardi's shopping center, if you want."

Ben took in the information and then tried to put Coral at ease. "I knew this was only a temporary situation, and you were really nice to take me in on such short notice. And now that I'm teaching full-time in Oakland, I can afford to live in my own again. So, yes, please recommend me to your friend."

Ben called the apartment owner and learned he had one apartment available. Ben went right over to see the apartment and met Bill.

The apartment complex was laid out like a resort, with sidewalks to different areas of and round globe white lights lining the walkways. Bill walked Ben past the pool to the second-story apartment. The apartment was pretty standard but it had a balcony that faced a forest area. Ben sat on the balcony and looked out at a beautiful grove of oak trees and underbrush. Ben,a nature lover and American Indian, was sure he'd see all kinds of animals from this balcony. He turned to Bill. "I'll take it. When can I move in?"

When Ben got back to the house, he told Coral that he'd be moving at the end of the month.

"Coral, you have been a good friend. I'm sure we'll see each other at the Shift meetings. Anyway, I'm just on the other side of town if you want to give me a jingle."

"You've been a good friend too, and it was nice to have you here," she replied."I especially appreciate you teaching me to raise the Over Soul. That was special."

In all the time that Ben lived at Coral's place he'd never mentioned his history of scanner involvement and the mind control issues that had plagued him for years. The topic had never come up, even at the Shift group. Ben had kept it to himself, waiting for the right time to come out with the truth about this secret problem so prominent in his life. It didn't seem appropriate at the time to bring the topic up to Coral.

Ben enjoyed his new apartment. Not long after he moved in, his friend Aldina came down from Ashland Oregon for a visit. Ben told her he'd recently learned at a workshop on natural healing that one of his totem animals was the red-tailed hawk. As they spoke in the living room, a large bird suddenly landed on the balcony. It was gray-white and about 15 inches high, and Ben recognized it immediately as a red-tailed hawk. He stared at the bird for around a full minute before motioning to Aldina to turn her head, but as soon as she did, it lifted off the balcony and was gone in a blur.

Ben hadn't seen a single hawk in Walnut Creek since he moved there, much less one on his balcony, and he considered the appearance of the bird to be an important omen for him. His life was changing drastically with his new job and home, and this spontaneous occurrence of his totem animal told him something wonderful was about to happen in his life.

"I'm being acknowledged by spirit in the physical," Ben told Aldina. "The future is looking bright and I feel great."

Near the end of Aldina's visit, she invited Ben to visit her in Ashland for the Wellness Weekend conference being held in a couple of weeks' time. One of the speakers there would be JamesTwining, a singing troubadour Ben had once met. Twining had found an indigo child at a monastery in Bulgaria and brought it to the states. He chronicled the tale of this child with supernatural abilities in his book.

"I'll definitely call about the conference details later this week," said Ben. "Maybe I'll bring my friend Tom."

"The more the merrier," Aldina replied.

After waving goodbye to Aldina in the parking lot that afternoon, Ben returned to his new apartment and went into a deep trance. He raised the Over Soul and connected with his Christ self on high at the eighth chakra. There, he contacted Morena in consciousness. He did his familiar tuning-in process to ensure it was truly her he was contacting.

Then Ben said to her, "I want to take you to Creation again."

Morena replied "OK, I'd like that."

Ben and Morena ascended above the planet with a background of starry space. As they prepared to start moving towards Creation, something drew Ben's attention to the space between them. It looked like an egg shape, but as Ben reached out and scooped it up in his arms, he realized it was a baby. Ben stared at it with disbelief. Then he said to Morena simply, "Here is a baby," and handed it to her.

Suddenly a voice spoke to them telepathically:"This is Creation. I'm giving you this baby to celebrate your love for each other."

Morena replied, "Thank you. I will try and find out where this baby belongs."

Ben was confused by her reply.

Morena seemed thrilled at the prospect of having an ET baby, as was Ben. But she suddenly flew off on wings of Grace to a destination Ben was not aware of.

Relocating back into his body, Ben was elated that Creation had given him and Morena such an incredible gift. He couldn't believe this was happening. He set to work right away thinking of a name for the baby. Having recently seen the new Superman movie, he had a flash of inspiration, Jarrel! "That's it!" Ben shouted. "I'll name the baby Jarrel after Superman's father." Jarrel the baby had blue eyes with white hair just like Superman's super ET dad.

Looking through the newspaper, Ben noticed an advertisement for the new movie showing a picture of Superman with his son standing in front of him. It was a perfect depiction of what Jarrel would look like at three-years old, he thought and later corroborated.

*All he needed to do was to paint the hair white and color the eyes blue in the photograph,*he thought. I'm going to send a picture to Morena when he gets older.

Over a week passed before he heard from Morena. She entered his mind, and said, "I found his ship."

"I see." Ben was not surprised the baby was connected to an ET spacecraft. "I decided to call our son Jarrel after Superman's father. Is that OK with you Morena?"

"Yes, I like that name. But you should see the ship, it's ten miles around. It also has a forest with trees, a lake and animals." Morena was a gifted psychic and she told Ben she had been astro projecting her spirit up into the ship whenever she got permission from the ET's.

"Do you want to visit the ship Ben?" asked Morena.

"Yes," said Ben, "but I can't astro project like you can."

"That's all right," said Morena, "you can psychically project your spirit up into the ship. The difference is that when you astro project you already are in the fifth dimension/density. Psychically, you have to go through the veil in order to have perfect clarity within the fifth dimension."

Ben knew this was true as he had gone through the veil when he was pulled up around the planet and into the hovercraft where he met Zaln, his Pleajaren persona.

They lifted off in their consciousnesses and, traveling at the speed of thought, arrived on the ship instantaneously. Soon a couple of little grays came floating down the hallway followed by Emmera holding the baby. Emmera who had telepathically realized the baby's name, turned to Morena and said, "You can take care of Jarrel on the ship."

Morena took Jarrel and said to Ben, "Let's go to the forest for a while."

As soon as they thought about it, they were instantly at the forest. They sat on a rock in front of a shimmering silver-purple lake. Morena held the baby on her lap, looking intently into his eyes.Ben decided to walk down the path to explore the environment.

He could see mountains in the background and a beautiful waterfall not far off. The plants were largely similar to those on Earth, except they were more magnificent. For example, there were green plants with enormous pink flowers with vibrant secondary and tertiary colors. Elsewhere, he saw flowers of iridescent fuchsia, red, magenta, indigo, teal, blue and green and seemingly every color combination possible. A few of the flowers would collapse when Ben touched them, while the white button plants on the ground would fly up into tall translucent cylinders when he brushed against them. Unfortunately for Ben, this was a third/fourth dimensional experience, so it had a slight glaze to it compared to the fifth dimension that Ben had experienced before, where objects and environments were crystal clear. Still, he marveled at the beautiful light that shone through the leaves of the forest and the gorgeous periwinkle sky and pink-white clouds.

After exploring about a quarter of a mile down the trail, Ben decided to turn back to see what Morena and Jarrel were doing. He found her holding the baby up, helping him learn to walk. Ben watched Jarrel cling to Morena's fingers as he toddled. His white hair and blue eyes were stunning, and Ben wondered what he would look like through fifth dimensional perception.

Morena told Ben that each time she returned to the ship,Jarrel would be bigger. The more time she let pass, the older he got.

"Sure, that makes sense," said Ben, "Children grow faster here."

"But he's growing really fast," said Morena. "It's been over a week and half, and he is a year and a half now. These children mature much, much faster here."

"That's incredible," said Ben. What we are learning about this ET culture blows my mind.

"I have to go now honey, I have a very important meeting with my boss that I can't miss it,I love you and Jarrel so much I'm having a really hard time pulling myself away from you, as a tear came to his eye, but I'll contact you later about coming back up on the ship or you can contact me when you astro-project again."

"I know you have other pressing things going on in your life, we will have other changes to visit Jarrel on the ship in the near future, we love you",replied Morena.

Ben loved hearing that,"I love you both," he replied.

It was about three weeks to a month later that Morena came to Ben again in her light body. Ben always knew when Morena was out of her body because her energy level was dynamic and very uplifting; he always got a rush from her energy level.

"Meet me on the ship," said Morena.

"I'll see you there soon," said Ben.

With effort, Ben projected himself up onto the ship. He saw Morena, Emmera and Jarrel in the hallway. Ben looked at Jarrel leaning against Emmera. He appeared to be about three years old now. He looked very much like the child in the Superman ad he'd that he had on his wall back in his apartment.

Being an early childhood specialist, Ben recognized the spacy look on his son's face. A lot of three-year-olds occasionally go into trance-like states for unclear reasons. Ben thought they were tuning into frequencies average adults are unaware of – a higher consciousness perception. Ben, who was far from average, was familiar with the feeling.

Ben noted the haze that told him he was still in the third/fourth dimensional state. Turning to Emmera, he said, "I'd like to come through the veil."

Emmera looked at Ben with compassionate eyes, like a mother for a child, and said, "Picture that circle you saw on the ship the first time you were pulled up above the planet and met Zaln."

The white circle that had been the portal onto Zaln's shuttle gradually appeared and Ben stepped through it into the fifth dimension.

"That's all there is to it?"

"That's all," said Emmera.

Ben finally got a clear look at his son. Jarrel was even more beautiful now, and he noticed that he had a silicon-based skin structure. It was semi-translucent with a pretty bluish tinge. It was the skin coloration that Zaln had when he saw him on his ship. *I wonder if he has pleadian genes*, Ben thought. Turning to Emmera he saw that she shimmered in her metallic green emanation and her elongated head. She also floated rather than walked. Then he focused on Morena's auric field. It was a blast of ethic colors with pink, blue and purple predominant. Ben looked down at himself and saw a shimmering burst of fuchsia, blue, purple and gold examinations. A thought came to Ben, *an ancient term from China and also was a term used **in** the order of Melchizedeck for a very fine energy; described it in his first book*. Colors were vibrant in that dimension and Ben felt elated. "This is fun," he said to himself with a big smile.

"Let's go out to the forest," Ben said to Morena."Jarrel hasn't seen it at his current age."

"Yes," Ben replied. "I'm sure he'll love it."

Morena picked up Jarrel, they pictured the forest in their minds, and then they were there. Jarrel seemed unfazed by the journey; he immediately began exploring the plants and rocks, looking right at home in the exotic forest.

As Jarrel busily investigated the surrounding flora, Ben quizzed Morena about her experiences on the ET craft."What do you do while waiting for them to bring Jarrel to meet you?"

Morena responded, "Sometimes I'll just wait in a waiting room, or Jarrel won't be ready for a while, I'll visit the teenagers' classroom. Emmera told me the young ones rarely get the opportunity to meet human females, so they consider my visits an honor."

"Why is it rare for them to meet female humans?"

"Well, the ETs want the babies born to humans to have has much interaction with their biological mothers as possible, so the children realize some of the qualities of the primary species. But most of the time this is done in a dream state – the mothers don't visit the ship like me."

"But I can be totally conscious when I interact with Jarrel because I astro-project up onto the ship. My psychic power, and Jarrel's immaculate conception directly from Creation helped also I'm sure. Emmera said Jarrel and I are special."

"Wow," was all Ben could think to say.

"You too," Morena said, smiling.

Returning her smile, Ben asked about her visits to the teenagers' classroom.

"Well, it's in a strange room that you can enter by touching a warm wall that turns into a permeable membrane. It's filled with beautiful young alien young souls. The instructor is a tall and stunning middle-aged female. She wears a long, shimming, pinkish metallic grown, and she's about 7 feet tall, with a stature and appearance like Emmera's. She's not only beautiful, but she emanates an auric field of pure confidence. The room is circular and multileveled, and the students, who are of various races, are grouped in circles of different levels according to species."

"But do they all communicate in the same language?" Ben asked.

"Well, that's another interesting thing," Morena replied. "When I enter, the instructor will say something to them – incomprehensible to me – and they'll all adjust these devices they wear on silver belts. The teacher told me they're instruments that adjust for various linguistics. I guess that's what allows them all to understand and communicate with me."

"What do they look like?" Ben asked.

"Most of the young ET's are humanoid in the sense that they have two arms, two legs, hands, feet, torsos and heads. All of them, no matter the specie, have huge eye, though they might be in black, green, yellow or blue. Some are hydra children, an integration of species, with human characteristics like Jarrel. Some have opaque structures, and some are transparent. The primary characteristics seem to be a favorite genetic structure reflected in the universe."

"How amazing. What's it like being surrounded by young alien beings of multiple species?" Ben asked.

Morena laughed. "You know I don't mind being the center of attention. They ask all kinds of questions; the kinds curious teenagers might ask anywhere. What's interesting to me is how we're able to communicate, which is via a combination of utterances, context and telepathy. This is because, even with the devices they wore, our native grammatical language structures are too far apart to communicate directly. In fact, the instructor said she would use my visit as a language lesson – she plans to have the class analyze recordings of my speech patterns and grammatical structure."

"Wow," Ben exclaimed.

"Some of the students are brave enough to approach me, and the really strange part of my visits is when they touch me. They're especially interested in my hair – some don't have any hair at all. In fact, I got to listen in on a lecture on the different anatomical features and internal differences in the human species, and it's funny to see how fascinating they find us."

"Really? A lecture just like we have on earth?"

"Yes and no," She replied. "It's more interdisciplinary. Like a science class integrated with psychology, sociology and linguistics all at once."

As Morena spoke, Ben watched Jarrel play. He was so cute at three years old. He knew a few human words, including some big ones like "biological mother" and "biological father." He was clearly very smart. Of course, Ben and Morena couldn't understand his native language – it was beyond their comprehension. Ben stood up and said, "Let's take a walk."

Jarrel took Ben's left hand, Morena took the other, and they walked together towards a pink iridescent waterfall as if they were a normal family. It was a perfect afternoon in the ship's forest. They went into the pool of water at the base of the waterfall, and Ben coached Jarrel on swimming techniques, which he picked up quickly. They picnicked on a green lawn by the falls, the food appearing when they pictured the lunch they wished to eat. They had fun teaching Jarrel English and he enjoyed teaching them some of his own language. "Well," Ben said to Jarrel and Morena,"I have to go now. I have to meet with an employer for a very important job interview. I love you and Jarrel very much and I can barely pull myself away from this great day we are having. I promise we'll go on this picnic again as soon as I can get away. He gave them a big family group hug and kiss, and he was off.

Chapter Seventeen

His spiritual Sister Becomes Apparent

His consciousness back in his Walnut Creek apartment, considered his relationship with Jarrel and Morena. As explained to him by Emmera, he understood that Jarrel's race were silicone-based beings that grow faster than humans do. He recalled that, some years back, a psychic told him he would meet his son one day on a third dimensional plane. Ben continued to pine for the time when he would meet Jarrel in the future. As time passed Ben developed new telepathic skills, and at the time of the psychic reading, he had a well telepathic sense. He tried to tune to the psychic's mind to determine exactly when he would meet his son, and the date he intuitively came up with was the year 2033. Ben could only count off the years anticipating this date to come into his view.

Of course, his links to Morena were strong and quite complex. In addition to their recurring love over multiple past alien lives and their ability to connect psychically in their physical and light bodies, they shared other, more mundane links. For example, Ben could transfer the emotions he felt from music to Morena. They also shared a similar connection in terms of humor and laughter. Whenever Ben told a joke to Morena, she would burst into uncontrollable laughter, causing him to respond in kind. He just had to laugh with her; it was an involuntary response over which he had no control.

In fact, this latter connection had developed sometime after Ben had attended the Living Life Expo, where he had a reading with the akastic record people.

The young psychic looked at Ben and said, "You have a fat Chinese guy above your head."

Taken aback, Ben smiled and said, "OK. That's a bit unusual. Are you sure?"

The young woman clarified: "I believe the Laughing Buddha is with you. And I'm quite accurate. About 95 percent of the time," she added.

Remembering the reading, Ben wondered if the Laughing Buddha had bestowed the connection of humor upon him and Morena. He wasn't sure, but there was an interesting correlation. For instance, Ben had already noted that his sense of humor was becoming more prevalent. He sometimes thought of comedic sketches or premises that he would spontaneously perform for friends during coffee or on a drive. This was a change from his usually sober demeanor. His first guess was that a mischievous ET guide had begun visiting him, but the information that it was the laughing Buddha communicating with him made more sense. *Maybe I'll try standup comedy on stage – open mic to start, of course*, Ben thought. This was no joke– he had seen many live comedy shows back in the stand-up comedy's heyday in San Francisco, and the thought appealed to him.

One day after church he got some friends together and performed a few comedic skits at his apartment. It went over fairly well, with some people laughing and others scratching their heads. Regardless of the reaction, everyone was surprised by this new side of him. Ben was usually a quiet and a somewhat reserved person. After weighing the pros and cons, Ben decided not to pursue his new talent for comedy further. After all he wasn't a young man anymore. The stamina, travel, and money needed were not available to him anymore. At least he had mementos of the comedy scene, like the posters, t-shirts and ticket stubs from the shows he'd seen, plus his memories of meeting Robin Williams and Dana Carvey in the 70's.

At any rate, Ben's relationship with Morena seemed to have settled down. The emotional upheavals Morena and Ben experienced when they had met as *twin flames* seemed to be dissipating now, and Ben hoped they had purged their emotional karma from their past lifetimes. He no longer fell to pieces when he heard their favorite love song or saw a movie depicting lovers smitten with each other. She seems to be doing better also. Ben often wondered if their relationship would be over once they'd purged their past emotions, but deep in Ben's soul he knew they were Twin Flames. *Nothing could keep us apart under this sun or stars*, he thought. Though they lived apart and Ben was not able to share Morena's daily, mundane life, they were still locked in daily, constant telepathic communication, sharing their spiritual love for each other in that way. And, of course, Morena came to Ben's aid whenever he needed her to call on her strong connections to higher spiritual and ET beings to protect him by transforming the noxious energies that inundated his consciousness on a regular basis.

After four years teaching at a high school in Oakland, the job had finally come to an end. He felt he'd done great work there, but it was a dangerous district, and he decided it was time to leave when a student assaulted him by throwing a football at his head, in anger. Still, he was proud of his accomplishments: he'd coached the wrestling team and taken one wrestler to a state meet, he'd worked the California Department of Education to create a curriculum for the school's graphic arts program and he'd taught and inspired hundreds of students. During that period, he kept on with his spiritual quests and had traveled with friends and coworker's to Arizona, Mexico, and Hawaii, to name just a few places. He also enjoyed living in his Walnut Creek apartment, with its balcony overlooking the woods. Money would be tight from here out, however, and he would have to think about cutting his costs in the increasingly expensive San Francisco Bay Area, perhaps even moving out of this nice apartment.

In addition to living frugally, he decided to seek some closure on his spiritual explorations. For example, he set up his camera to take pictures of his headband/halo to have a record of himself wearing the apparatus when he needed extra protection. He also wanted to clarity information regarding Telefon. This was Ben's "source being," the ET who had dropped into his body at the MUFON lecture and had communicated with Morena.

Even though she had typed out and sent Ben everything she could remember about what Telefon had said, Ben had long wished for more clarification. For example, Telefon said Ben was a being of the blue light group of Tirates and had a female counterpart called Alexandre, but what that all meant was somewhat unclear to him.

Ben headed out to the deck, a perfect location for tuning into ET friends, and decided to make one more attempt to communicate with Telefon. He began meditating and tuning himself to his source guide, and very shortly, he felt Telefon drop into his body. Though he had tried unsuccessfully to connect with him several times before, Ben did not feel surprised. Still, he decided to get some answers while he can, and began to ask questions regarding the unclear terminology Morena had used in her transcription of her conversation with Telefon earlier.

"Telefon, what are our soul frequencies?"

"Soul frequencies are those frequencies that make up your soul, frequencies that you have accumulated over centuries from various incarnations. All of your life frequencies are contained in an egg-shaped soul shelf around your human body. You have many, many biological soul frequencies and lifetimes."

"What is a soul matrix?"

"It is a specific structure that conforms to a mold, so to speak. A place where something is developed, as in your soul shelf."

"What is a source being?"

"It is a being, like me, who knows all your incarnated life experiences, the lessons that you have learned and the lessons you are still learning. One lesson for you to learn in this lifetime is to how bring messages through the soul and the basic methods of accessing the eternal being – the soul self. Alexandre, in the outer universe, is helping you with this issue, even today."

"What is the blue light of Tirates?"

"It is the color vibration at which you and Morena resonate and function as galactic cultural beings in the constellation Lyra. This is an ancient culture that goes back thousands of years. You and Morena were in the priest caste; you counseled royalty in spiritual affairs."

"What is a Galactic Board of Regents?"

"They are a body of ascended beings that communicates with the galactic federation about their role in helping Gaia and her ascension as well as the beings from that part of the universe associated with the constellation of Lyra. You worked in higher consciousness to help beings in the ascension process in many star systems in the past, just as you have on Earth."

"Who is the person Alexandre, my counterpart in the outer realms?"

"She is a being you visit on a regular basis in the outer part of the Milky Way galaxy. She is your counterpart because her soul is going through the same ascension process as yours at this time. She belongs to a royal family of ascended third-dimensional beings that call themselves the Titans. They were a warring culture similar to your culture in ancient times on your planet. They are also a technological culture like yours. Earth and their planet are on parallel paths of ascension and consciousness. You have been a warrior in many cultures in the past."

"What is the name of Alexandre's planet?"

"Predomia." It is directly across from your solar system on the opposite side of your galaxy." Ben could see her planet location in his mind's eye.

"What is the Triad of Informany of Justinian Forces?"

"These are the forces that patrol the galaxy as peacekeepers for ascended planetary systems."

"Are you part of the Galactic Federation?"

"Yes," Telefon responded. "We mediate treaties for various cultures and your known galaxy in your known universes. We work with planets trying to evolve into the ascension process with higher dimensional levels, as your planet is doing now and has been doing for centuries."

Ben now had a great deal of new information to consider. "I appreciate your clarifications and insights, Telefon. Thank you for the great service you provide in protecting and guiding souls into the higher ascension processes."

Ben felt Telefon leave his body, and he came out of meditation. It was getting dark, so he went into the kitchen and began preparing dinner, deep in thought. As he ate dinner, he considered that, as his life continued to spiral upwards, he continued to undergo positive and disruptive spiritual experiences along the way. The important thing was to keep discovering and learning. He decided to attend church the next day to see what has happening with his friends in the congregation.

The church service was interesting and uplifting, and afterwards, he went out on the patio to visit with his friends. While talking with Glenn, Marie approached with a woman he hadn't seen before. "Ben and Glenn, I'd like to introduce my good friend Alexandria."

Alexandria, beamed up like an enthusiastic child, "Hi, Ben. Hi Glenn."

"Hi," said Ben beaming back, giving her a big hug. Ben stepped back and observed Alexandria from a psychic/intuitive perspective. He could feel that her energy level was very high, but something in her past affected her emotionally on a really deep level. Appraising her carefully, Ben thought, *she's not really into the church scene.*

Alexandria was a very outgoing young woman who wore low-cut dresses, and, as Ben got to know her in the future, he learned that she could sometimes be loud and aggressive, especially if she perceived that someone was trying to take advantage of her. She would stand up for herself, and she let you know it if you got in her way. This attitude got her into trouble sometimes, but she was also a very smart negotiator with wisdom beyond her years. Ben would also find that Alexandria and he shared a lot of characteristics: she was perseverant; she was a fighter; she was loving; and she was compassionate. She even loved animals as much as Ben did.

He wondered if she was a super master vibration number 22, and he later had a chance to do her numbers and determine that she was a number 11 total name vibration – a spiritual master. It would only take a little rise in consciousness experience for her to reach the super master vibration 22. Eleven was half the super master vibration – the highest number in man's consciousness, according to Pythagorean numerology. At this first meeting, however, Ben simply thought there was something that seemed familiar about her, and he wanted to know what that was all about.

"You know, Alexandria, why don't you and Marie join me for brunch?" asked Ben.

Alexandra found this funny."You want to go out for brunch Marie?" she asked her friend, snickering.

Ben thought, *maybe she isn't used to going out for brunch, or maybe she has some kind of a culture bias where brunch is funny.* Regardless, as Ben continued to peruse her vibration, he found her to be very interesting and kind of cute too.

Marie said, "Sounds good to me, let's go."

"I like this new place called Heavenly – how's that for a spiritual name?" said Ben. Heavenly was a small little restaurant with a French bakery and delightful murals of European landscapes. It was very comfy and light with quaint little tables. They ordered a light-hearted menu of croissants and sandwiches with a variety of toppings."We can't miss the light and fluffy croissants! It's a French bakery for heaven sakes," Marie said.

Ben realized that Marie was worldlier than he had initially thought.

They dug into their sandwiches green salads and settled into a friendly conversation when Alexandria suddenly blurted out, "My sister is in big trouble with my mother" in a nonchalant way. Ben thought nothing of it, but when Marie whispered in his ear, "Her sister killed her mother," Ben nearly jumped a foot off his seat. Ben's heart went out to her. *You poor thing*, he thought, as a tear came to his eye, but he didn't dare ask for elaboration.

Instead, he awkwardly tried to offer indirect condolences and change the subject at the same time. "That's almost as bad as getting a fresh cow pie smashed in your face when you were five years old." He knew it wasn't, but he had to say something to take the focus off Alexandria's painful memory.

Alexandria turned to Ben and said, "That's terrible! How did you handle that?"

"Well, I don't know, I was five years old. I would say that it contributed to me being a shy child for one thing." He found himself getting deeper into the subject of his youth then he'd intended. "Actually, I had a difficult childhood. At six-years-old, I had to go door-to-door selling potholders that my mother made to make extra money. I got a lot of doors slammed in my face because of that. That is not an age you want to start being a salesman, especially by yourself. I don't know what my mother was thinking. Six-year-olds are very sensitive at that age. And thank God for my father's awareness. He worked as a barber when we moved up into the East Bay and made me become a shoeshine boy in the shop, because I was so shy – I'm sure. This helped me come out of my shell. I wonder if that's why I like turtles so much," he joked. Ben actually had a pet turtle named Freddie when he was in elementary school.

After Ben had managed to change the subject, the conversation perked up. Marie filled in some of her own history and likes and dislikes. She said she worked for the government as an investigator working on cases as a child advocate. She surprised Ben by saying, "By the way, Ben is looking for a room to rent to save some money."

"And how do you know that?" asked Ben.

"Oh, I hear things at church. Alexandria owns her own house."

"Yes," said Alexandria."I have a spare room right now for rent. Would you be interested in renting the room?"

"Well, how much is it?" asked Ben.

"Four hundred a month. I think it's a fair price for Benicia."

Ben thought for a minute. "That sounds pretty good. Can I come down and see it next week? Say Tuesday in the afternoon?"

"Yes, that's good. Here's my number. Let's talk on the phone before you come down. There are three bedrooms with a washer and dryer and storage. You should know that I'm a very private person. I also have three dogs."

"Dogs!" said Ben."I love animals. Sounds good to me, I'm paying $1100 a month where I'm at right now. I'm on unemployment, but I have money I saved from working at two high schools."

Ben and Alexandria talked during the week about when he could move into her house; their conversations had an easy, natural flow. She was a cordial person most of the time, and they got along well.

Ben was a dowser and let Alexandria know that he could dowse her house for Ley lines and power spots. She agreed, and he got to work. It was an easy task for him to create the schematic for her home, dowse the diagram and come up with the power spots.

"I found your power spots for the house," said Ben. "Let's go around the house and you can see where they are. Let's start with the living room."

"OK," said Alexandria, "let's check it out."

"There are two in the living room, here and here. There are two in your bedroom and two more and in the guest bedroom. Plus, there's one at the entrance to the guest bathroom. Unfortunately, there aren't any power spots in my bedroom."

"I guess you're going to have to spend a lot of time in the living room," Alexandra winked.

"Alexandria, stand under the power spot and see if you can feel the additional positive energy."

Alexandria stepped under one of the power spots and exclaimed, "You're right I can feel a higher burst of energy here! Great."

"Yes, it is a calm waveform energy vortex that accesses all the dimensional levels at once."

Ben also showed her other node points in her house, explaining, "node points are interesting because you also have them around your body and they exist around the planet too."

"Cool. Hey, why don't we go to the Zen store In Walnut Creek and get some hanging Chinese lanterns? We can put them up where the power spots are."

"OK," said Ben, "that's a great idea." He could tell she was a creative person. "We can go to Chinatown in San Francisco to get lanterns as well if the other places don't have them."

Alexandria and Ben headed for the Zen store. They found a parking space pretty easily, which was no easy task at peak time in downtown Walnut Creek, but they set their condition ahead of time, mentally, to find a space. Ben had learned this almost always worked. Walnut Creek was a rustic little town known for its variety of restaurants and shops. It catered to the arts on all levels, stimulating creativity and art from young children to adults in the community. In fact, Ben had found that Contra Costa County, just over the hills from Oakland and Berkeley, was surprisingly cultured on some levels. Benicia, a rustic town further down the 680 where Alexandria lived, was also home to colorful restaurants and creative arts programs. In fact, they had one of the best arts and crafts fairs around the area, with the exception of Lafayette. Benicia attended to have older, more established places, although.

Ben and Alexandria walked down a cute little alleyway to the Walnut Creek Zen store. As they stepped through the door, they saw colorful lanterns hanging from the ceiling. Alexandria picked some out to hang in her home's power spots then lingered over a Buddhist tapestry. Turning to Ben she asked, "How do you like this tapestry?"

"It's not my style, but it's nice," he replied. "It'll set you back a pretty penny though."

"Not a problem," said Alexandria,"It's beautiful, and I'll love it in my living room. Look at the colors and design quality." Alexandria was an impulse buyer; she would buy anything on the spot if she liked it. She bought the lanterns and tapestry and they headed back to Benicia. They put the lanterns up immediately, and both felt satisfied; they knew that meditating under a power spot could be a very powerful experience.

Alexandria's house had a very serene feeling to it. Ben did the numbers on her address and it turned out to be a number 7. *The serenity makes sense now*, thought Ben, *7s translate to meditation and contemplation.* Alexandria had two very nice yards with beautiful trees and shrubs. She could easily go into a blissful state when meditating in them.

Ben felt a positive connection to Alexandria. They felt a strong vibration every time they got together. They had some very special energy vibration effects that affected them on a fourth dimensional level. Spontaneous powerful energy came through them by just being together. Ben couldn't figure out what happened to them energetically when they were in the same vicinity. It was as if their energies were fortified. They were both clairescence but she was more clairaudience and he was more clairvoyant. They made a good team and filled in some of the areas each were less adapted to, metaphysically speaking.

The house wasn't without problems, however. Not long after he moved in, Ben felt an energy communication from Venetian guides. Over breakfast one morning, Alexandria picked up the energy and said, "Two light beings are here. Their names are Iccladces and Antonomee."

Their communication sense came to a heightened awareness as they moved through time and interfaced with the Venetians. The guides were elders from Venus, and Ben believed them to be brother and sister. Their energy seemed to work to clear noxious energies and dark negative entities as well as to clear the dogs' energy of possessions as they became present, if that was needed.

They let Ben know they were working on his and Alexandria's behalf to counteract some noxious energies coming into their house. Alexandria had become aware of them as well and had started working with biofeedback to maximize her brainpower. Ben told the guides that he and Alexandria were, on a regular basis, clearing any noxious energies in the house using color frequency's.

"There also seems to be a black tar succubus energy in the house that I am trying to dissipate," Ben mentioned."A succubus being is a being without a soul. Can you help me with this?"

"We are aware of this, and we will assist you where we can with this dark energy," the Venetian guides replied.

Ben participated in the dogs' healing by visualizing light energy through to their bodies. Ben also told the guides how he was dissipating the energy of the black tar being he had found in Alexandria's room. He thought it was a Tibetan black magician. It took a number of encounters with the archangels to help him remove it from her consciousness and surroundings. It was not only a spirit, but a physical presence that bothered Alexandria more strongly when she was sleeping. It would hide in the corner of her bedroom and come into her body through her back just before she went to sleep. The experience terrified her.

Ben told her how to deal with noxious energies using a technique he learned while attending the Order of Melchezedeck services. Grace, the English spiritualist, said crossing your arms and legs while lying on your back would block entities from entering your body. This is the reason they cross cadavers' arms and legs when they are put in the casket at death, she had explained. Ben had suffered his own encounters with negative entities on a number of occasions, and this technique usually worked for him. It worked for Alexandria too and soon she regained her confidence and strength and felt happier. Ben compared a picture of her taken when they first met to one taken after his help, and the difference in her demeanor was remarkable. She became a much happier person.

Though they continued to feel the cold emanations of a spirit walking around the house, they were able to get rid of it themselves. Still, they also called upon the white light energy to clear their environment.

Ben thought that was the reason he moved into Alexandra's home – to get rid of this negative entity that, he was sure, had been plaguing her for many incarnations. Other entities started showing up in their environment also – good entities. Once, an entity came down from space and engaged Ben's consciousness. He asked Alexandria who it was, and she replied, "Its Jesus." She was so clairaudience that it was easy for her to determine the identity of energy being. Jesus merged with Ben's body with a light force that was like a hundred suns. Ben went into the light of this being, but quickly backed out because it was so intense.

He said to Ben, "You're almost at your full power now, and you will soon be working with us. And then he said as he shot Alexandria an Anaconda size light beam, "You will meet your significant other soon." Then he lifted off and departed. Ben assumed he had returned to his ship, since he had long known Jesus was an extraterrestrial.

Ben was shopping in Trader Joe's one day. As he was shopping, the Venetian brother and sister couple came through with a message of their own for him. As they were communicating with him, he recognized the young

Venetian sister as a being he had seen 15 years earlier – she was one of the guides he had seen inside a crystal during a healing group session. Ben knew her as the Pink Lady, and she was here to help him with psychological perceptions. She was also a guide to one of Ben's friends who said she was actually an extraterrestrial by the name of F5-F.The Venetian couple told Ben, it's your time now. You should use your knowledge and education to help others learn spiritual lessons about the ascension process. In the meantime, we will remain in your house to help clear the noxious vibrations. This was one of the clearest communications Ben would ever have with these spiritual beings, and in fact, Ben and Alexandria would start a meditation group and put on Crystal and Dowsing workshops in the future and hoped they would be around to help them.

He got back to the apartment, put away his groceries and sat down to meditate on the patio. Within a minute, he felt the presence of other beings and had an incredible sense of elation. He didn't try to communicate with the beings but just felt their energy inundate his body. Then he tuned in more specifically to determine who they were. He felt a vibrational communication from them that expressed itself as the Venusian elders. *Well*, Ben thought, *the Venusian elders. I wonder what my connection with them is. I must have been in their culture in a past lifetime.* They ran energy through his body and an incredible healing occurred in him – he felt wonderful. They expressed to him that they would visit regularly.

Once, in another encounter, they communicated to Ben that he should begin a relationship with Jenny, a fellow churchgoer. They said she was a soulmate, and they could help each other to create a positive destiny. They showed Ben her heart, and the tremendous love coming from her was almost overwhelming.

Ben realized that Jenny had contacted him telepathically on several occasions before the elders' communication, but he was unsure what to make of it at the time. In fact, just the night before, she had contacted Ben again, saying she loved him and wanted to get married. Ben saw Jenny soon after and recounted what his guides had told him. Her reply was that her daughter was getting married in two weeks and she couldn't get together until after the wedding.

Ben told her he was ready for a relationship, if they were compatible. She had told Ben her name was Jenny in their telepathic communication, and Ben worked out her numbers, which he explained the next time he saw her. She had very powerful numbers, especially in her birthday. Having a22 in that category meant that, on the one hand, she would have a turbulent life, and on the other hand, if she could master the lessons of the 22 vibration, she could raise to that super master level that this number signified in consciousness. However, she had an 8 name vibration, making it a tall order to raise her vibration super master level. But Ben knew it was her destiny to live, and anything was possible.

Jenny and Ben interacted telepathically a number of times. She was a beautiful woman, tall and slender as a well-formed dancer. She had that athletic body type that turned Ben on, even from a distance, and they had telepathic sex on several occasions while Ben waited for Jenny to become available. In the end, however, it didn't work out for them. After her daughter's wedding,

Ben approached Jennifer on several occasions, but she rebuffed him with increasing hostility. Considering their shared telepathic experiences, it didn't make sense. Months later, Ben unfortunately picked up from her the familiar noxious vibration that scanners use.

There was one occasion, around that time, when he had a different kind of telepathic interaction with Jenny. She stepped into his auric fields and tried to control him. This felt like such a violation to Ben that he called upon Creation for help. With that, her spirit was forcefully catapulted out of her body, causing her spirit to fly backwards at high speeds. He realized she had gone to the dark side, and he was glad she never tried to contact him telepathically again.

Chapter Eighteen

ET Contact Becomes More Special

Ben thought about his son Jarrel often and looked at his picture on the wall as he did his daily stretching exercises. One morning, he felt his son nearer to his consciousness than usual. That day, he attended church and ran into a man named Tom who did Pranic healing. That sounded good to Ben, so they went to the backyard of the church under some nice redwood trees for a session. It was a perfect place for this type of healing, or any healing really.

Tom was very good at his craft of healing. He came out from Texas with his wife and two children. The boy David, 15 years old, was autistic. Tom and his wife had to keep an eye on him 24/7. He could have been a savant, because he played classical piano almost perfectly, like a super master vibration. Ben often wondered about super master vibrations that incarnate into a lifetime of this kind. He must be here to bring a better understanding of autism into our times. We really don't know much about this level of consciousness. Our communities are plagued with difficult medical problems among children today; he wondered if it was true that the Mercury-laced vaccines given to children was the cause. Tom was trying to make a living doing healing work. *Bless him for his dedication and tenacity*, Ben thought.

Over time, Ben and Tom became friends; Tom helped Ben set up a crystal healing workshop and advertised his numerological readings to his healing clients. He was an excellent spokesman and brought in the largest group of students Ben had seen at his workshops in a long time; he had the gift of persuasion.

On this day, just before the Mayan calendar ended on December 21, 2012, Tom had Ben sit in a chair in the dappled light under the redwoods, took out his crystal and bowl of water and started the healing session. Ben could feel the swooning, controlled energy going to different places in his body. *Now, this is a real healing*, thought Ben.

Suddenly, Ben heard a voice from his son, Jarrel, he told Ben he had recently morphed his ship from the fourth dimension into the third and would be in his galaxy for a short time. Ben saw the ship was 30 to 60 degrees off the horizon in the West. He could see it with his- All Seeing Eye. As Tom continued his healing work, Ben sat up alert and shared personal news with his ET son. Jarrel even offered to help Ben with his back pain from injuries during his wrestling days. "I am in contact with a being on Neptune who will triangulate a healing energy process on your back," said Jarrel "We hope to help heal your back as soon as possible."

"Thanks, son, It's good to know you are there," replied Ben.

Jarrel continued, "Various ET races are visiting Neptune from different galaxies to watch the energy changes to the Earth and the local solar system based on the prophesies from the Mayan calendar. They have been getting ready for this change to occur since ancient times. They are here to witness an evolution on your planet of a new spiritual energy coming from the galactic center that will uplift humanity into a new level of spiritual consciousness. Gaia, mother Earth, is also moving towards her ascension to become a fifth-dimensional planet. Humanity is riding her ascension towards the fifth dimension. This term is a catch word for developing our consciousness to more of a expanded level with Gaia-a senent being.

Ben was not entirely surprised by this news. Not long before, while traveling to Creation in meditation, Ben was passing Neptune and admiring its true color, indigo, when he noted hundreds of ships amassing on the planet.

"You would be wise to consider other ancient prophecies, such as those of the Hopi, to determine what is happening to humanity during these turbulent times," Jarrel added before taking his leave. "Goodbye father, we will talk soon."

Coming back the church backyard, Ben looked at Tom and said, "I just had a most wonderful communication with my ET son."

Tom was unfazed. "Really? I didn't know you had an ET son."

Yes, my twin flame and I, while getting ready to take a trip to creation, we experienced a miraculous thing. Ben told him all about his son during the rest of the healing session.

"Thanks Tom, you're a God Send," Ben said, slapping him on the shoulder.

"No problem. I'm here to serve," said Tom.

One day at Alexandria's house, Ben recognized a waveform passing through the living room. It went to a house two-doors down, and in the other direction, it went out into the community, he thought. Later Ben determined it was coming from the house behind them.

Ben again used his abilities to tune directional vibrations to different locations and pinpointed the waveform in the house. When he stepped into it, he was hit with a terrible, toxic feeling that adversely affected his memory; he could go into another room and forget what he was just thinking about. They learned from experience that it wasn't safe to stand in that type waveform. This was Ben's first indication that Alexandria was being targeted by people in her neighborhood. He started teaching Alexandria visualization techniques to counteract the noxious energies coming through her living room.

These techniques were only partially effective, however. They also found it necessary to seek help from their extraterrestrial friends. Telefon and Zaln were pretty responsive when asked to intervene, but most of the time they turned into Semjase, who was more effective at clearing the noxious energy field. They found out later she was their sister in another incarnation on the Pleiadean planet Alcoyne-Eta.

Semjase started communicating with Alexandria first, and then Ben started being able to tune into her energy and her ship's energy as it rushed through him. Semjase was an important contact with important spiritual figures in history, including Billy Myer, a Plejaran farmer in Sweden who took photographs of her ships, talked with her in person and even traveled with her throughout the galaxy. She was also in contact with Dr. Fred Bell, a physicist and New Age scientist. When Ben and Alexandra started receiving information from Semjase, they were overjoyed to have contact with such a prestigious extraterrestrial friend. Alexandria didn't know who she was when she heard her name in her head until Ben informed who she was.

Despite their shared connection with numerous ETs, past lives and psychic experiences, Ben and Alexandria eventually reached the appropriate time to split up. More and more, they began to clash and get on each other's nerves. This mutual irritation increased rapidly and the sudden rift between them seemed irreconcilable. Soon, Ben started looking for a new place to live. Alexandria was a nice person, but something was off in their communication and living arrangements that he couldn't put his finger on. Ben had been clear with Alexandria that he didn't have sexual feelings for her and was not interested in a romantic relationship. This might have been the reason for Alexandria's sudden coldness – it also made it easier for them to part ways. Soon, Ben found a room in the house of a friend from church, but he intuited that he and Alexandria would meet again under different circumstances.

The room Ben found was in Gertrude Swedenborg's house. She was a friend Ben met on a trip to Hawaii with another teacher from church. Gertrude taught kindergarten and was really good at what she did. She was a robust Swedish super master vibration with a jovial personality. She spent a lot of time at her retreat in Lake Tahoe. She loved swimming, and you could always find her in the water someplace. She had aquatic flotation devices for all occasions –she even had her own kayak.

Gertrude lived in a small quaint suburban rural location bordering a naval base. A couple miles away you could see, especially at night, the local refinery. The lights at night created a colorful imaginary city on the water. The house was nested behind an old oak tree and weeping willow trees giving it a Southern flavor. The raccoons were friendly, for the most part, and big as medium-sized dogs. They weren't afraid to plunder the storage area and garbage cans at night.

Waking up one morning Gertrude encountered Ben in the hallway and said to him "I'm going to get a small fridge to go in your room because there is not enough room in my refrigerator in the kitchen. She went over the rules of the house and schedules and routines. Ben was used to all of these schedules because he had lived with roommates for 20 years in San Francisco; and he was also a teacher; organization was his middle name.

"Okay," replied Ben, "I have a couple of ideas that I think would make our living together easier." Gertrude came from a military family and she meant what she meant, but fortunately she was a teacher used to communicating and problem solving, as was Ben.

"You know," said Ben, "one thing that really worked for me with regards to roommates is that if we have a disagreement we would set up a house meeting to discuss the issue."

"OK, I think that could work," replied Gertrude.

Having my own bathroom is a plus for me, thought Ben, *because I've been in situations where I shared a bathroom with one two or even three people.*

"It was never any fun waiting to go to the bathroom," said Ben.

"Yeah, I know what you mean. I did some roommating myself in college," said Gertrude. "Well, I'll leave you to setting up your room and I'm off to lecture at the church."

"Yes," said Ben, "I go to some of their lectures from time to time myself. I also do the Ions group that Fernando runs for the Integral Studies Institute at JFK and other locations, where they learn about consciousness studies and psychical research and healing modalities taught by a PhD."

Ben settled in quickly. He didn't have a lot of things to move this time. He had put most of his belongings in storage, furniture and other big items. He really missed his pictures that went on the walls. He had collected them over the years from trips; they included his own artwork as well as some college craftsman's artwork. He still had an original batik of a female Indian dancer that he had bought at arts and crafts day at SFSU from an Indian man in 1969. And of course his linoleum prints of Mount Fuji and the Buddhist temple Shohondo in Osaka, Japan, that he had completed in a printmaking class. Or the photographic collage that he bought at the ISETI retreat in Crestone, Colorado. It looked like a space ship coming down through the trees. His artwork was very important to his mental and emotional balance. He couldn't wait to get his own place in the near future. It took Ben about a week to get into the house routine before he felt like it was home.

It didn't take him long to start feeling a strange vibration coming from the house next door, his sensitivity was at full bore now. It was that same old feeling that he had felt many times over the years. It signified a vibration that was toxic to his consciousness. It was hard to describe, but it felt like a numbing sensation, sometimes, giving him a headache or making his skin crawl. He always saw an image associated with the energy that was a dark, sometimes black tar-like energy that crept up on him. At times it would make his arm ache.

Ben used his visualizations that worked to collide noxious energies, giving him a signal that told him that the energy no longer functioned to disrupt his energy field. He soon felt 100% better.

Of course, sometimes he could recognize the technician behind the machine, who would get seriously pissed off that his device had been tampered with energetically. *I bet it sent his meter back to zero*, Ben thought. On this occasion the neighbor called in an Ariel attack from a satellite or airplane that Ben quickly deflected away as he brought his consciousness into alignment with the pulsed electrical photon, microwave, radio or Gamma ray frequency energy; it wasn't hard to do; he'd done it many times before. *That was easy*, he thought. Gertrude's neighbor was between jobs as a machinist with grown boys that had gotten into trouble with the police on many occasions, most likely drugs and drinking, he thought.

Ben had talked with the neighbor, Fred, a few times, and it seemed like he was an intelligent man with problem children. He had mentioned to Ben on occasion that he got more out of his dreams, all in Technicolor, than normal life. Ben thought about his friend David who would say the same thing. The images in the dream were clearer than his waking life. And of course more fun. You could fly and do extraordinary things. *It's funny*, thought Ben, *these people seem like ordinary nice people but underneath they are really scoundrels; they are wolves in sheep's clothing*. Ben didn't ask him if he had a radionics device in this house, but he probably wouldn't have told him if he did anyway. He could have said something to draw him out but didn't think it of it at the time. Ben continued to apply his energy techniques whenever he felt the noxious energy interface with his consciousness. It was very interesting that Ben started feeling the noxious energy coming from other directions as well. *What have I gotten myself into?* he thought. He checked the back of the house, and a house just in front and just to the right of Gertrude's house that had scanning devices also. *Interesting*, Ben thought.

He had been able to sense noxious energies for over 25 years. He had learned to use the dowsless dowsing technique that was specific to him and his psychic abilities while researching and using his divining tools. He could visualize a green vertical band and rotate it 360 degrees around his body and was able to feel a glitch as he went along, signaling him that this was the direction of the incoming energy or feeling of the energy as the energy collided. *The energy on the right was a very powerful electronic wave form belonging to the new people that had just bought the house in the back. The other house had a normal radionics device carrying a normal frequency, not an all-electrical vibration, though Ben wasn't sure what it was*. He checked the front and side of the house, searching the house located just off to the left of the yard diagonally across the street. He was in a semi-conscious state during this process. He came back to beta level consciousness as he heard Gertrude come through the door.

"Hi Gertrude," Ben said as she came into the kitchen. "Are you aware of the psychotronic energy coming from the house next door? You know, Fred's place."

"No," said Gertrude I'm not aware of those things. "And I'll really don't care, that doesn't interest me."

"Okay," said Ben, "you may want to or don't want to know, about two scanners in the front of the house and the one in the back off to the left and right."

"Okay," Gertrude said. "I've gotta be going. I have an appointment at 2 PM."

"Bye, have a nice one," said Ben. *She seems not very interested in knowing anything about this topic for some reason*, thought Ben. His intuitive inklings were signaling him on a subtle level.

Ben only brought up the subject one more time with Gertrude while he lived there. Ben and Gertrude were coming back from a trip to Sonoma.

Ben said, "I'm feeling a noxious energy vibration coming from you right now." Ben was sitting next to Gertrude, who was driving.

"Oh yeah," said Gertrude, in a flat tone. "I do feel a headache on my right side, a little."

"Okay," said Ben, "create a shield-like radar dish to reflect the energy."

As Gertrude tuned the energy form, suddenly the headache went away.

"How's that now," said Ben.

"You're right, the headache went away. That's interesting," said Gertrude. "I'll try that when I have a headache again."

"Yes, it works when you have noxious waveforms coming into your head. If it's an ordinary headache it can also be alleviated by going into the pain and irradiating it with color vibration. Try white light and then pink colors, it's very effective," said Ben. Of course she wouldn't hear anything about scanners and deliberate mind manipulation. This seemed to be a strange position for an inquisitive and learned person like Gertrude.

It was five o'clock when they got home.

"I have to go out to a lecture at the church. I'll be back later," said Gertrude.

"Okay," said Ben. "Have a good time."

Ben fixed dinner and watched his favorite TV programs. At nine o'clock, Ben started feeling pain between his shoulder blades. It was faint at first, which seemed like indigestion, and gradually got more intense. Pretty soon the pain was coming in waves of raising and falling in intensity. Soon the pain started moving around his arm, which went numb. His heart began to throb as well. Ben lay on his back on a stool,because it was the most comfortble place to lie. *What am I going to do now*? he thought. At that moment Gertrude walked through the door. What's going on, Ben?" she exclaimed in horror. Ben was writhing in pain.

"I don't know. I think, maybe, I'm having a heart attack."

"Do you want me to call an ambulance or should I take you to the emergency room in Martinez?" She knew Ben couldn't afford to call an ambulance.

"Take me to the hospital. I don't want to spend 700 bucks, in a disgruntled tone."

Gertrude held Ben up as they made their way up the long walkway up the back of her house and to the car. Ben continued to writhe in pain in the front seat. They were off, racing to Martinez General Hospital. The hospital was about ten minutes from Gertrude's house.

Ben stumbled into the hospital as Gertrude parked the car. He filled out the paperwork and was taken into the ER right away after the nurse yelled at him for not filling out the paperwork fast enough. After running some tests and putting in the IV, Gertrude came in and she learned that Ben would be transferred to John Muir hospital, one of the best cardio hospitals in the state. As we were waiting for the transfer to the hospital Gertrude lay down on some chairs and slept. It was four o'clock in the morning. At five, they came in to take Ben to John Muir.

Gertrude said her goodbyes and that she would see him later in the afternoon at John Muir, and she was off.

Ben was still in immense pain. The doctors came in to go over the issue with him and sign the paperwork to see if he would sign the papers to have the operation at John Muir. The doctor filled Ben in on the details of the surgery. "You'll have to have a triple Bypass procedure and stay in the hospital for at least five days. If you don't get to surgery, with a 90% blockage, you will have another episode and you will die," said the doctor.

Ben thought, *God, they want you to make a major decision about your life when you were just on the verge of having a heart attack – unreal.* Unfortunately Gretchen was not there yet. Ben replied, "I guess you'd better proceed. I don't want to die." They all became very happy at that reply.

"We have to give you an angiogram to see which arteries need replacing," one doctor said.

"Okay," said Ben, "let's get on with it." Ben's symptoms calmed down considerably after the angiogram and an IV medicine drip was administered. He was placed in a room with a young man with a lung problem. Then it started happening again: the pain was back with a vengeance. He heard a nurse ask what she should do and the doctor said, "Take him back to the ER."

The doctors returned. The cardiologist said, "We are scheduling you for surgery tomorrow morning. You can't wait."

Morning came about 5 AM and Ben was whisked off to the operating room. The next thing he knew he was waking up in a private room with a great view. He had wiring going into his abdomen that recorded his heart rate and blood pressure, a wire going into his heart and an IV drip stuck in his arm. He looked like the walking wounded as he had seen on TV. The docs came in and explained that they had replaced three veins. Ben had four staples in his chest that held his sternum in place. They taught him how to cross his arms across his chest and hook his foot under the bed to lift himself out of bed when he needed to go to the bathroom. It was all routine to the docs and nurses, but it was a major step for man who had to learn to get out of bed in the beginning. It was a good thing Ben had strong stomach muscles; he didn't know how weaker people did it.

Ben was up at 5 AM every day for blood tests and shortly afterward, he had breakfast. Then it was more testing and physical therapy to keep up his muscle tone. On the fifth day, he was up walking and climbing a couple of steps. Unbeknownst to Ben, climbing stairs signalled to the doctors that he was strong enough to leave the hospital, making room for someone else to take his bed. They had a long waiting list. Interestingly, Ben never felt depressed—not even when the priest came in to talk to him about God. Ben assured him that he had a good relationship with God and was not leaving the planet anytime soon. For some strange reason Ben was in good spirits most of the time. Depression had not come to visit.

The nurse came in the room one day while Ben was enjoying his marvelous view. There was a structure in the distance.

Ben remarked, "If you look at that building from your right brain, it turns into a castle."

The nurse looked closely out the window and exclaimed, "You're right, it does look like a castle!"

"Yes," said Ben, "I'm an art teacher and I try and teach my students to use their right brains to perceive differently." Ben was voted the best patient on the ward before he left, due to his upbeat attitude and cheerful disposition. *I have become a celebrity in my own time*, thought Ben. The staff gave him a questionnaire before he left. Hospital intake procedures were very efficient. But when it was time to leave, things were handled differently. You had to be out right away, even if you didn't have a place to live. It was a good thing Gertrude was letting him stay at her place due to his heart condition. No one else had stepped up to the plate.

Gertrude would have to help him in and out of the tub and fix food for him and organize his medications, which made it difficult to think after the operation. Another friend, Meryl, came by, and volunteered to help organize his medication for him. She was a big help and she was there the only time Ben broke down, nearly crying. Ben apologized for the emotional outburst and Meryl said, "I get depressed all the time and I didn't go through what you just went through."

Ben read over the discharge papers and noticed they didn't describe a specific symptom of the heart attack. They had left out the pain that had started between the shoulder blades. This omission bothered Ben and would become more of an issue when he would have a second heart attack a couple of years later.

Gertrude came in a little while later and mentioned to Ben, "Ammachi, the hugging guru, is going to be at her ashram in San Ramon in a couple of weeks. Do you want to see her? It might help you heal faster."

"That sounds great," said Ben. "I should be more mobile in a couple of weeks. I had a hug from Ammachi before and it was impressive."

Chapter Nineteen

Miracles Never Cease

They arrived at Ammachi's ashram late in the evening, with apparently great fortune, receiving their tokens right away. They didn't have to wait long to see Ammachi. They were ushered to their handicap section as soon as they learned Ben had had a triple bypass recently. Ben went into meditation as soon as he sat down. He interfaced with Ammachi right away and said, "Do I need to get a healing hug from you to help me heal from my triple bypass?" She replied yes. A short time later they went to receive their hug from Ammachi. Ben asked Ammachi again shortly before the hug and said, "Do I really need a healing hug from you? Her reply was "Absolutely." Ben remembered his first encounter with Ammachi. She was low key with a somber demeanor, but he could see the light behind her eyes. Ben felt a powerful rush of energy through his body as Ammachi vocalized an ancient sound and something locked into Ben energetically. And that was it, it was over. Ben exited the stage.

Ammachi had her primary ashram in India and had hugged more than 10,000 people in her service. Her ashram was a fully-functioning spiritual center that healed the sick, had groups of people meditating around-the-clock for world peace and had outreach programs to educate and feed the poor.

When they had gotten their hugs, Gertrude, Ben and Meryl went off to receive their personal mantras. Ben could not climb the long stairs the way others could, so the ushers let him sit in chairs close to the stage. But first they were led to a table to have their choice of deity that could be included in their mantra. It wasn't long before they were led to the stage, one by one, to receive their mantras from Ammachi. Ben had wanted to include Jesus in his mantra, and was given a slip of paper by Ammachi with his personal mantra on it. Meeting Ammachi a second time that night was a little different, in that she had a big smile on her face during her presentation to Ben.

Later Ben had the thought that she was happy that someone had wanted a mantra that included a Western spiritual sage from a devoted Hindu guru and also to practice the mantra on a daily basis.

Again Ben, felt charged with a mantra energy. Ben's mantra – a universal sound – seed – the Christ – offering -in Sanskrit. You were not supposed to tell your mantra to anyone, otherwise it would lose its power. This became Ben's chant/mantra for nine months as he did his daily 30-minute walk to recover from his heart attack. You had to recite the mantra 120 times a day. Some days he walked longer. He could use his mantra any time to bring enlightened power to his personal journey. He had a lot of time to think over the circumstances of his heart attack and was wondering if any of the psychotronic instruments he had picked up at Gertrude's house had anything to do was his condition. *Only time and synchronicity will tell*, thought Ben. During Ben's long stay at Gertrude's place he found himself thinking about his ET son, Jarrel.

Ben replayed the situation back that transpired while drinking coffee and working on the Internet at Borders bookstore. It was a quiet afternoon in Borders when Ben saw it: his three-year-old son standing off to one side of his table. He had the same entranced expression on his face and was wearing a Superman costume pictured in the magazine photo in the pink page of the Sunday paper. He was still as a statue – frozen in time.

Ben thought, *Wow! How do they do that, creating an image in 3-D on my timeline?* Of course, Ben was referring to his extraterrestrial son, now grown somewhere in 5D space in a his ship, able to create this living hologram right in front of him. *Boy, what we don't know about consciousness we could fill an encyclopedia*, thought Ben. *How could they manifest my vision so precisely in real form, appearing as I remembered him on the ship.* In that next moment a young woman appeared, looking disgruntled. She took the little boy by the hand and led him away, not paying any attention to Ben.

Life is really interesting sometimes, mused Ben. He must've walked away from his mother and she didn't know he was gone. These synchronistic experiences would turn out to be a reoccurring theme in Ben's life.

Ben finally got what he had been waiting and projecting for. It was time to end his stay at Gertrude's place so he could get his life back. He got a call from Las Sentra senior apartments, saying that they had an apartment that had just opened up on the third floor.

"I'll be right over to see it," he said. "I got the call from Los Sentra," said Ben to Gertrude. I'm going over to see the apartment now. If it's what I think it is, it's what I've been waiting for and the price is right."

"Ben, you have been a good roommate."

"Thanks," replied Ben, "we have had our ups and downs but overall I'm really indebted to you for taking me in on such short notice, you were a Godsend."

"I couldn't have lived with myself if I had left you at the hospital."

"I wasn't looking forward to going to the homeless shelter," said Ben.

A couple of weeks later Gertrude called Ben and said, that she was having her retirement party and she wanted Ben to attend.

Ben attended a party with Gertrude's son and wife and other relatives as well as her close friends. It was a festive potluck and Ben sang Gertrude's praises for supporting him and his life during his dire need. Gertrude was beaming from ear to ear, but further, she expressed a spiritual light emanating from the great Central Sun, her Christed being inside of her, in all directions. Ben praised Gertrude for the humanitarian she was.

Ben remarked to Gertrude, "My life is indebted to you for your sacrifice to nurse me back to health. You have created a massive amount of good karma in this lifetime that you will reap the Benefits for in the future."

The day continued on a fun high with games, food and drink. Others also got up and spoke about knowing Gertrude and her service to the district and children was also a 26 years model for her peers; what goes around comes around.

Ben threw in one more gem, getting an intuitive inspiration, about the difficulties happening to everyone on the planet today. But behind the scenes the spiritual forces of light were bringing about major changes; there was hope for the future, finally.

Ben had finally put up all his familiar photographs and artwork as well as posters he had collected over the years. He now felt balanced again and his creative processes were returning to him to support his consciousness and destiny. Sitting in the bathroom, shaving one morning, a powerful energy overtook him and he went into a trance. That old familiar feeling was returning to him again letting him know that some higher entity was communicating with him; it was something like a conscious channeling.

"We want to talk to you about Alexandria," the messenger stated in Ben's head. "We know you don't understand your connection with her at this time. But we're here now to tell you that she is your Sister. You are brother and sister from your incarnation from the Pleaidan planet – Alcone-Eta. Semjase is also your sister from that incarnation."

Ben was surprised and overjoyed to learn that he had a special connection with Alexandria that he had not considered before. He tried to figure out their connection together in hindsight.

Every time we get together strange energectic things happen to us; it's hard to explain, Ben thought.

We have set up this connection with you and her to support each other's growth in your ascension together and make your lives easier moving forward, they continued. This is your next step... Don't overlook the significance of this communication.

Ben asked, "Who are you and where do you come from?"

"Who we are is not important at this time, but know we are a group of elder beings with higher ascended consciousness from the 10th dimension."

"Do you believe in the Law of One?"

"Of course we do."

This was a technique Ben had recently learned, to ask the beings communicating with you to determine if they were coming from the light. Dark forces and lower energies would say *No*. Then you could choose not to communicate with them. And ask them to leave, and they would have to comply.

Of course this wouldn't apply to earth bound egoistic scanner projecting a wave form at you, they would say anything it wouldn't matter to them if they lie. Projecting thoughts into a person's head was prevalence these days.

Ben couldn't wait to communicate with Alexandria. She was still at work right then, and he would have to call her later after work. They had a casual relationship, seeing each other from time to time at church. Later, Semjase had also communicated with Ben that Alexandria was our sister from our incarnation on Alcone-Eta that cooperated with the ascended beings from the 10th dimension.

"Alexandria, this is Ben, on his cell phone, how are you?"

"Oh, hi Ben, I've just been working at Lucky's three days a week. They are running me ragged, flip-flopping my hours all the time, I'm exhausted."

"Some employers think they are still plantation owners with slave workers. Anyway, Alexandria I'm calling because I have something important to tell you."

"Okay, what's on your mind, Ben?"

"Well, this afternoon I was shaving in the bathroom when all of a sudden, a powerful energy came near my consciousness and told me that you are my sister."

"Really," she blurted out, "that's very interesting!"

"Yes, they said we were brother and sister from the Pleaidan culture. They also said they were beings from the 10th dimension and have come to lay out a better life scenario for you and I." Ben could feel and see Alexandria's big smile and twinkle in her eye as she listened.

"I never could figure out what our relationship was for a long time," Ben continued. "I spent an hour in a trance meditation talking with them. We have a promising future if we work together as brother and sister."

"Okay, that sounds great, Ben. I'm looking forward to meeting with you soon, I'm overjoyed, I need to fix dinner now. Bye."

My spiritual sister, imagine that, thought Ben. *No wonder interesting energy things happen when we get together. Alexandria can really channel when she is tuned in. She is much more clairaudience than I am with a acute sense of hearing. She hears the music of the spheres.*

Being retired, Ben had a lot of time on his hands. He called Alexandria during the week and asked her if she wanted to come over for dinner and to watch a movie. She was more than happy to be connecting with Ben because of their new relationship connection. A couple of days later they met for dinner. After dinner Alexandria and Ben settled down on the couch to watch a movie. Ben had picked out a movie he was sure was going to be interesting to Alexandria. He introduced Alexandria to an interview was Randolph Winters and Billy Mier. Randolph was a physicist who broke the story of the famous Pleaidan contactee who lived in Sweden. Billy took photos of Pleaidan beam ships that would show up above his farm. Billy would tell his stories of his contact with the Pleaidans.

In one of these contacts, was Semjase. She would land her ship on his property and sit under a tree and talk with Billy about the universe and things going on our own planet.

She would also give him rides in her craft to different planets and galaxies, as well as planets in our own solar system. Also issues in ancient times and our world history origins were laid out including where we really came from.

Alexander was elated that she was in contact with the famous ET, especially one from her own spiritual history.

After the movie Ben walked Alexandria to her car and Along the Way, Alexandria stopped and said, “I feel a tall light being standing behind me.” She started having a conversation with him about their relationship. He has been with your her entire lifetime and his name was Envelton. They talk about other subjects and finally the being started telling her things about Ben.

"You have a space being around you that you don't know very well," interpreted Alexandria.

"I think I know who he is talking about, somewhat," said Ben.

Ben asked the being, "Was he a blue being?"

Alexander replied, "Yes."

Ben thought back in time, years ago, an experience he had in his bathroom. *He was looking into his mirrors he turned blue. I think he was one of the blue beings that I saw when I was pulled up above the planet in 1982. It could be Maza, the prehistoric beings*, Ben thought. *My bathroom is a spiritual center*, with a big smile.

The being interpreted Ben's thoughts. "You are right, continue your thought along those lines."

They moved to the car and Ben remarked, "That was an interesting contact, to Alexandria. Let me know if he contacts you again."

"Okay," replied Alexandria and she was off for home.

Ben went back into his apartment and settled down to a TV program. Soon he started feeling a noxious vibration coming through the apartment and he went into the bedroom and got his Trifield EM Natural Meter. Pointing it in the Southwest direction he flipped it to electric, electromagnetic, magnetic and finally to radio/microwave settings, getting a strong reading over the microwave frequencies, as the needle swung over there 100% percentile, with the sound gauge going off with a loud squealing noise that accompanied the needle reading. A strong electrical feeling running through Ben's body that seemed like the effect of having a electric wire toughing your leg. Ben tried different thought forms to counteract the disruption and it dissipated in about two or three minutes; which was unusual. Most of the time the disruption, continues for a longer duration. *He must be doing something right*, he thought.

Ben thought, *That was intense. I might have had to call in the higher beings that I work with if this bombardment continued.* Of course, Ben was used to these interruptions in his daily life. They'd been happening for years. The EM natural meter was an interesting device, it could read almost any vibration and cut out all background noise. And now, he had a concrete way of recording the disruptions. This somehow made it more real to Ben, that he was experiencing what he was actually experiencing; but it wasn't really necessary, he instantly knew the truth. Ben pulled out his journal and recorded it just in case he needed it later for his books or some other reason, as he has been doing for years. He thought, *This is one more nail in the scanner's coffin.*

Alexandria came over the next week for dinner again. This time their spiritual connections pulled in beings she wasn't familiar with, namely the Serian ET elders. Ben was familiar with the Serian elders because a couple of weeks earlier he had been over at Bill Pin's house to partake of his wonderful crystal meditation and sound room. Bill had collected hundreds of crystals over a period of time and had built a geometric meditation sound room to house them. While sitting in the chamber room meditating Ben perceived an ET craft above Bill's crystal room.

"You have an ET craft above your room," Ben said to Bill as he was fooling around with some crystal bowls.

"Oh," said Bill, "who are they, I know they were there but I didn't know who they were."

"They are the Ancient Serians," Ben said.

Returning to their dinner, Ben tuned into the Serian ET's again. There energy reply was swift and clear. They pulsed a barb like energy down into Ben's body.

"Back off!" Ben said, "Your energy is too painful."

They responded immediately. They then faded out and they were gone.

"That was intense," said Ben. "Their energy was like pins and needles."

"I think I know what you mean," said Alexandria.

There had been reports by other ET channels that the Serians were related to negative ET's. The Egyptian deity RA, the Sun God, communicated with these Serian beings. But in the last few years Ben had gained more respect for them because of people like Sheldon Regel, who communicated with them and was a past life Serian himself. He had a much more positive image of them now; there were positive ET and negative ET's.

After Alexandria and Ben finished eating, Ben again felt a strong vibration from the Serian elders. Energetically their energy felt like a block of a dark brown crystalline stone with angled corners like a cube, also seeing it in his mind's eye. They wanted to talk to him and laid down a tan strip down the front of his body. He guessed this facilitated communication and was a softer energy that was not as painful as their initial energy. Ben appreciated the gesture. They told Ben a number of things. He tried to focus on the communication stream among the energy in his environment. Ben was doing a pretty good job of interpreting what they were saying using his clairaudience sense, but it's wasn't his strong point.

One of the many things that they communicated to Ben was that being in the presence of Alexandria facilitated a stronger and clearer communication stream. They said he should get back into his artwork to develop his consciousness. A woman would come into his life to help you with your workshops in a different area, where he had to travel. Ben had put on crystal and dowsing workshops in the past. His communication started bogging down now. He was losing the communication stream or, more accurately, he couldn't hold the stream stable. They wanted him to tell Alexandria that they want to communicate through her, because she was much more adept at using her clairaudience sense.

"She accepts your communication," said Ben, and they told her telepathically to put Ben's generator crystal on the coffee table to pull in a Ley line.

Ben remembered dowsing for Ley lines or power points in his apartment. He didn't find any going through his living space. He was, of course disappointed, not finding any Ley lines or power spots, that's the way it was. Then he exclaimed, "I feel an energy form, a Ley line magically appearing moving across the living room." Ben received the energy manifesting in his mind's eye. "That's miraculous," he said.

The energy had somehow changed in Ben's apartment, as he perceived it as a much higher energy frequency than before that the Serians had helped to create this Ley line using his generator crystal. "Fantastic!" said Ben, grinning from ear to ear. "Thanks Serian friends, I'm glad to see you are on our side."

Alexandria broke in. "Their energy is getting too intense for me!"

Ben came to her rescue and said, "Tell them to back off, your energy is too intense. She complied and felt much better when they backed off."

"I know how intense this energy can be," said Ben.

Ben's remembered a giant brown solid square block crystal he had seen at the living life Expo one year. It reminded him of the image he had seen when the Syrian elders contacted him. *It was interesting to make a connection in the 3-D world of a image that you see in your minds eye, thought Ben; that was synchronicity.* The giant crystal was a representation of their consciousness level, but he didn't understand it.

"I should have said something to the owner, but I didn't for some reason," Ben said.

It was a short and interesting communication with the Serians, but very memorable. Ben walked Alexandria down to the car and she said goodbye, and Ben said, "Call me when you get home, Alexandria."

Alexandria nodded and pulled out of parking lot, heading for Benecia again.

Chapter Twenty

Scanner Paradigms Continues manifesting in Real time

Waking up in late morning, Ben noticed a pain between his shoulder blades, and his left arm was somewhat nonfunctional. He became alarmed at these symptom, which had come on with his first heart attack. Ben thought, *Scanners must've been working on me during the night's sleep.* He called on Zaln to protect him with a healing waveform. Then he tuned into the archangels that worked with him: Michael, Ariel and Hencel and his personal angel, Myha, to stand on all sides of him to counteract the incoming noxious energy. Ben's connections weren't working well with these beings so he called on Telefon, his representative from the Galactic Federation, who dropped into his body at the Mufon lecture.

Ben called on his twin flame, Morena, for good measure. Then Ben felt from his other sources that felt he needed additional help and pulled his light body out and ushered him off to Creation, through space, contacting the white ethic planet in it's 5th dimensional space. They merged him into the center of the giant planet for healing. Ben didn't know how long he was there in subject time, but it seemed like an eternity. As he returned to his body semi-consciously he went back to sleep.

Feeling a lot better when he later awoke, he again found himself picturing Zaln ship from the bottom, and felt that he needed additional healing, he moved into the opening bay to the giant slabs of Crystal that were the healing tables in an adjacent room. It was, again, 8 foot long, 4 foot wide and 6 inches deep. Ben crawled between them for a metallic color healing.

The first color was a metallic purple colored substance that dissipated any additional noxious energies in his body and his auric field. In a short period of time ET light beings came out to heal Ben taking out the old ethic crystals and replacing them with clean crystals along his spine. They also did other healing techniques using crystal wands to clear any additional noxious energies in his system. As he came back into his body he remembered Creation had set up the ships healing process with Zaln when he needed healing. He was feeling much better when he came back. He had again overcome the horrific bombardment of scalar energies that plagued him on a daily basis. He thanked his contacts and guides for their fantastic help in his healing process this time; he had again dodged a bullet.

The next day, Alexandria called and wanted to go to the Walnut Creek crystal faire. Ben was always interested in going to the crystal faire. He was on the lookout for interesting crystal to add to his collection. Ben went over the early-morning episode about the scanners energy and their intervention with Alexandria.

Alexandria commented, "You are lucky to have so many beings that will help you when you need them."

"You can say that again," said Ben.

The traveling fair was an interesting venue for healers, psychic readers and New Age products including various crystal venues.

Alexandria said, "I want to have a reading by Joseph because he is one of the best readers here."

"Okay," said Ben," let's go look for him."

"Hi Joseph," said Alexandria.

"You're back," said Joseph. "I was wondering when you would come to see me again."

They got along famously. Alexandria had had a reading with him five times already. He knew about her life. But this was an exceptional reading.

Alexandria had a special question she wanted to ask Joseph. She had reserved a 45-minute session to answer relevant questions. Doing this reading the special question came up: whether her sister was at fault for her mother's demise. Ben was poised on the side of his chair to hear the answer to this very important question.

The answer came back from Joseph with a resounding, "No! Your sister was targeted to go into a rage at the appropriate time. She was a sacrificial lamb and an easy target for psychotronics/scalar waves to her brain, being a schizophrenic. She was a prime candidate with her condition to have her brain manipulated in this way."

This brought Ben into a full focused memory of psychical research done during the Cold War by the Russians.

A book that came out in the 90s called *The Maze* told the story of a Russian medical scientist that did experiments on the criminal insane. They would project a waveform into the subjects halathums in the lower part of the brain and send patients into a rage. It was a specific frequency in the E LF range (extremely low frequencies) piggybacked on another waveform.

After reading this book a few years later Ben was cleaning his bathroom on a clear Sunday afternoon with no cares at all. He was happy and content and doing this mundane chore of cleaning the bathroom. He wasn't thinking any negative thoughts. All of a sudden, *Zap!* he went into a rage and punched his sliding glass door to the shower and cracked it in several places. He ended up replacing the glass door, reluctantly, out of his own pocket. This episode with Alexandria's sister reminded Ben of the story told in *The Maze*; it had an eerie familiarity to his situation. He tried to convince himself that this didn't really happen, but it did, in fact happen.

Ben also flashed on a short blip on the news. They had just put a waveform frequency device around the president's body to protect him; Ben assumed they all had to wear a counteracting energy device now. He couldn't believe his ears. Was this synchronicity or what? Unfortunately there was little detail to the newscast.

Alexandria and Ben finally finished her reading and Alexandria wanted get another reading from another good psychic, Angelina from Mount Shasta. Ben wanted to look at crystals at different booths.

Ben threw out a thought as he was headed for the booths. "We need to talk about what Joseph said about your sister when you finish your next reading."

"OK, Ben, that's a good idea," said Alexandria.

Ben joined Alexandria shortly and overheard the reader say, "You could be a psychic reader yourself and get paid for it."

Alexandria was overjoyed to receive this information.

Ben jumped in at that point and said, "You're right, she's a very accurate empath herself. She has a strong clairaudience ability and we talk to entities all the time."

"I see great things for you Alexandria in the near future. I see your significant other coming into your life next year in the springtime. He will be very successful and balanced in his life and he will have owned his own business and have several properties besides his own house. He will be a super soul that will care for you, very deeply. He will take you away from all these trials and tribulations and create a stable life for you. You will be happy and he will help you promote your empathic gifts and attract clients for your business," said Angelina.

Alexandria was really excited now for her future.

Ben asked, "How do you feel about what Joseph said about your sister?"

"Well, that makes sense based on what you said happened to my sister. I absolutely know she wouldn't hurt a fly, it wasn't in her nature. Attacking my mother never really made sense to me. Hearing Joseph cooperate your findings and your actual observations, seems to me but sadden me. I'm going to go over my memories at some time later to see if these explanations make more sense. Alexandria was in deep in remorseful thought for the rest of the day.

Ben arrived late at his apartment after taking Alexandria home. He brushed his teeth and went to bed. Pretty soon, lying in bed, he felt a nagging subtle pain between his shoulder blades again. This was alarming because it was the remnants of his first heart attack and a recent episode. As he lay there the pain intensified. Ben scanned his environment in all directions to see if he could locate the direction of the waveform coming into his shoulder blades. After all in the Tibetan book of the dead they say that all energy has direction. Finding the waveform Ben perceived an image of what looked like a scorpion tail on its side with a light on the end of it and moving through the universe towards his direction. This was a disturbing image that Ben had never felt at any time before. He did his visualizations to counteract the intense vibration, calling on guides, angels and some help from Creation. He fought for 20 or 30 min. gaining again the high ground and finally overcame the disruptive energy bombardment.

Then Ben was able to go to sleep, not bothered the rest of the night.

Waking about 9:30 in the morning he again notice the pain between his shoulder blades and it got progressively worse and he was feeling a pulsation, between the blades, that raised and fell in intensity. It was so intense he was not able to find the source of the disruption or get any help from his guides. Finally he was not able to fend off the pain. He threw on a his shirt, pants, and shoes fumbled his way down to his car and drove himself to the emergency hospital downtown. He drove with the pain in his back trying to breathe deep at the same time, thinking that if the pain got too strong he could stop and call 911. Pulling into the parking lot he yelled at the attendant, "Emergency!" Ben opened the door because his driver's side window wouldn't roll down, and the attendant moved the cones to let him into the only parking space left. Ben stumbled into the ER and slumping over said, I think I'm having a heart attack!"

The nurse jumped out from behind the desk and grabbed a wheelchair, and stuffing him into it, and they were off to the ER. A battery of doctors lifted Ben onto a gurney and ripping off his shirt, recognized the scar down the front of his chest. They hooked him up to the IV and listened to his heart and drew blood. Ben stayed the night and was scheduled for a stent in a miner vein the next day, according to the doctors.

Alexandria had found out about Ben's heart attack, somehow and was at his side the next morning. Waking Ben came face-to-face with Alexandria. Hi Alexandria, Ben said, a little dourly.

"How long have you been here?" said Ben.

"Oh, about an hour," replied Alexandria. "They called me on your cell phone and I came over as soon as I could. How are you feeling?"

"As best that could be expected," said Ben. "The doctor told me I needed a stent in a miner vein. I told him I had a triple bypass a couple of years ago, so how come I needed stent in a vein around my heart? Of course they didn't have an answer for this question."

Ben continued, "I think I saw an insectoid like creature making its way through the universe towards me last night. I fought it off and went back to sleep. Waking in the morning it became a different story."

"That's terrible," said Alexandria.

"Yeah," said Ben. "These insect races of ET's have been cited, mostly in abduction scenarios and beings looking like praying mantis's and other insects on board a ship. They are one of the negative ET's that have been plaguing humanity for decades. They work with the reptilian races." Of course I have to remember that there are always positive entities in their race or any race.

After Alexandria left, Ben decided to go up on Zaln's ship for extra healing by light beings that would help him heal faster. Three days in the hospital was enough to get Ben ready to leave.

Boy, Ben thought later, *I had to fight to get sponge bath on the third day. In the olden days you were assured of a sponge bath at least once a day, this place sucked.*

After Ben was home for a while from the hospital he again felt and saw the scorpion ET's coming for him while he was in bed. *Oh no*, thought Ben, *they are trying to give me another heart attack... these scumbags are too much.* This time Ben called Semjase, his ET sister, to possibly help him in thwarting these demonic ET's attempting to kill him. Ben could feel the familiar energy of Semjase's ship reverberate over his apartment. She got to work right away, projecting a laser beam at the insectoid ship and slowly it started moving off and Ben's pain in his back started subsiding.

"Thanks Semjase," said Ben, "your a godsend." Semjase was over Alexandria's house a lot also, especially if they called her in, to help them clear the house of noxious energy and thwart the psychotronic bombardment from scanners flanking her house from all sides.

"I'm glad I was able to help. We need you around for a longtime, we love you," said Semjase.

The insectoid ship came by one more time while Ben was watching TV in the living room and calling on Semjase made short work of them, moving them away from his apartment complex to never return again.

"Thanks," said Ben, "You are my sister from the Pleiades that I can count on you to assist me when I need help.

"That's right," said Semjase, "we're here to assist you and Alexandria anytime you call upon us."

Ben thought, *all the guides and beings I know Semjase is the only one that could do anything about this insectoid Menis. Did it have something to do with dimensions/density's and consciousness, he thought. Are other ET consciousness not able to morph into the third dimension closely enough or is it something else to do with frequencies, interesting Ben Mused, what we don't know about consciousness could fill a library.*

Ben was feeling good. He had dodged another bullet the night before with the negative ET's. He went to Starbucks to work on his computer. Starbucks was a good place to do his internet work. Getting coffee and sitting down to drink, he started to work on his computer. He was concentrating on this e-mail when he picked up a noxious waveform. He scanned the room using a dowsless dowsing technique to determine where it was coming. He noticed Daniel Allen looking at him. Ben waved to Daniel, a friendly hi, and went back to working on his computer. Ben didn't think much about the noxious vibration after that. Pretty soon he noticed an energy impingement of his personal space that inundated his auric field. He intuitively and accurately felt that Daniel was tuning into his consciousness with his iPhone.

He had heard that the iPhone was a mini computer that had tremendous microwave energy potential. He also felt others tuning into him as well but Daniel's wave was a stronger signal. Ben tuned into Daniel's auric fields and projected a laser beam at his third eye, the pineal gland, and put a spinning waveform around him and to his surprise the disruptive energy field collided and the energy dissipated immediately. This is the only way Ben could describe the reaction of the noxious energy field – "colliding" because the energy may be imploding. Shortly after this reaction Daniel came over to Ben's table and said, "What's up Ben!"

Ben replied," just reading an interesting article." He glanced up at Daniel's eyes and he recoiled, as Ben drilled into the large black ominous eyes that reminded him of some other consciousness invading a body as he had observed before with others. Ben went back to reading his e-mail.

Daniel continued, "I have just come back from a meeting in San Francisco on BART." With that he whipped around and headed out the door and down the street. It made Ben sad that his previous minster was using scanning techniques to project into his consciousness. But, it did bring to mind a few times that

Ben saw Daniel giving the service at church. Ben being a seasoned channeler recognized when a being dropped into your body. It was hard to describe in words what takes place.

Ben thought, *I know when I see and feel it; and maybe both because you sometimes feel with your eyes as strange as that might sound.* Michael Tabot, the author of *The Halographic Universe*, said the same thing.

The eyes grow larger and change color and you have a feeling of unbalance, not a centeredness in yourself, when a being suddenly drops into your body. Especially if it's consciousness is not in a positive space. But if it was a scalar wave you would also feel a disruption of your energy field but it would not be the same as a channeling phenomena. It would be a frequency vibration rather than a beings consciousness. If you were not used to it, it might jolt your system at first.

I could see Daniel, at times giving his sermon, being very uncomfortable when he felt an energy burst or had another entity drop in his body, I couldn't tell which at the time, Ben thought. It concerned Ben when he felt other members, especially older members, scanning him or if he picked up noxious vibrations that he recognized in them at church. Of course non-members that attend the service had scanned him as well. In these situations he felt an energy crawling up his back or pain starting between his shoulder blades or accessing his solar plexus chakra. This seemed to be the norm lately. It's sad, Ben thought, the karma they're creating that is disrupting their ascension process during these "end of days" on the planet. Of course people involved in this type of disruption were not cognizant of their ascension process that everyone went through, or is it that they don't believe in what is said that's going on the planet at this time, or both?

Ben continued to have feelings at odd times of the night. He remembered at his apartment one night at 3 AM. He was startled and woke to hear a voice and movement in the living room. It seem like he heard a voice whisper. He thought, *I live alone. There couldn't be anyone here but me in the apartment. It must be another ghost coming through my space, as I have perceived before.* He closed his eyes to go back to sleep and felt an almost physical presence in his bedroom. He had felt the sensation once before when he lived at Coral Miner's house when he had moved out from San Francisco. Then, he felt and clairvoyantly saw the small squatty dark ET beings that Whitney Sieber described in his book, *Communion.*

He knew they were not in the third dimension but more than likely the lower fourth dimension, where they are invisible to the naked eye. As before Ben, crossed his arms and legs to keep the entities from entering his body. He could feel several entities around his bed trying to project noxious energy into his body. This continued for about 15 or 20 min while calling in all of his guides and angels.

Ben came back to his current situation perceiving entities in his room again, after dozing off to sleep.

They left as quickly as they arrived. The next day Ben used his I-Ching to determine more about the incident that night. He also used his pendulum and dowsed for ghosts, individual astral projection into his space and

ET's. He received Yes and No answers and decided to ask if he should ask this question at that time and the answer dowsed-swung to NO. This was a technique used by dowsers to clarify their reading.

He got the same message through the I Ching. So he put the divining tools aside and went to take a shower. While showering he received an intuitive message that said, the entities were holographic androids or drones that were projected into your space from a spacecraft above the apartment. After Ben finished his shower, again he dowsed and used the I-Ching to ask if this intuition was correct and the I-Ching revealed, you can rely on your intuition to answer this question. The pendulum said YES. He had been throwing the I-Ching and using his pendulum for over 25 years. Ben had come to rely on these tools to answer difficult questions, but this time the answers came after his intuition responded; or should he say his higher self. The intuition is used by your higher self/over soul to communicate to less dense consciousness.

Maybe he was ready to rely on his intuition totally now. He was accurate enough to rely upon his intuition and less on his divining tools. He also consulted his other soul self about which ET group it was that woke him up that night, and he got the answer – it was the Syrians. His intuitive conduit was getting stronger and stronger every day.

[illegible] rested [illegible] and no [illegible] and decided to ask if he should ask this question at that time and the [illegible] drawings to NO. This was a [illegible] complete [illegible] answers to [illegible] their reading.

He got the [illegible] through the I Ching. So he got the [illegible] and [illegible] were [illegible] taking a lawyer. While shoveling [illegible] work [illegible] that said the [illegible] were not [illegible] and [illegible] comes [illegible] received [illegible] space from [illegible] above the apartment. After he finished [illegible] went again [illegible] used the I Ching [illegible] intuition [illegible] and the I Ching [illegible] can rely on your intuition [illegible] the pendulum said YES. He had been [illegible] with the I Ching and using the pendulum for over 25 years. But [illegible] to rely on these tools [illegible] difficult [illegible] but [illegible] the answers [illegible] of [illegible] The [illegible] his [illegible] to communicate [illegible] consciousness.

Maybe he was ready to rely on his intuition [illegible] now. He was [illegible] enough to rely upon his intuition and less on his divination tools. He also [illegible] PA [illegible] that [illegible] the [illegible] the answer [illegible] and [illegible] even [illegible]

Chapter Twenty-One

Ben Continues To Learn About Higher Consciousness

As the days marched on Ben continued researching psychotronics bombardment and ran across a book by Dr. Bagage: *The History of Mind Control.* This was a real eye-opener about the types of bombardment effects on the body and mind and the latest instruments developed to disrupt individuals and groups. The instruments are being utilized by medicine, law enforcement, armed services and governments. Ben saw Dr. Bagage at a conference one time and tried to get a little more information about ELF frequencies that continue to plague him for two decades. Dr.Bagage was a genuine and caring person that developed and also wrote books on the Harp Program. *Angels Don't Play These Harps* was one of the titles. He had grown up in Alaska and was raised by a political family involved in government politics.

"Hi," said Ben, as he extended his hand to Dr. Bagage. "I'm Ben Chavez."

"Nice to meet you," said Dr. Bagage.

"I read your book the History of Mind Control, Ben said, "and it was fascinating. I particularly liked the section on ELF frequencies. I have personal interactions with this type of disruptive energy. I wonder if you have had any experiences with this type of bombardment."

He thought for a moment, and replied, it depends on your energy level. I have a high energy level and I'm not bothered by a lot of these types of frequencies. Of course as this field progresses in this area, I may find myself being under the gun at some point.

"Well, thanks Dr. Bagage, I appreciate your candor in this matter. Can you sign my copy of your book?"

Glad to. I have a workshop to conduct, so excuse me. I hope you enjoy the information in my other books, as well," he said, heading for the conference room with the wave of his hand.

Great guy, Ben thought. *But thinking about what he said about bombardment, he also thought that higher spiritual levels makes you more sensitive and prone to subtle disruption. But, at these higher levels you are more able to use your consciousness to protect your self from these possibilities.*

Ben sat down and in reflection remembering his personal observations at the apartment dealing with ideas that were cited in Dr. Bagage book. He learned that these devices have the ability to tune into the muscular structure of the body and send out a electrical charge to disrupt the electrical signal of the muscle. One evening Ben was watching TV on his couch and fell asleep. It was funny because he wasn't tired. Waking up in about

30 minutes he felt his right leg tense up hard as a rock. Then he started getting pain in the upper thigh of the leg and the inner thigh of his leg. It felt like an electrical charge had hit his leg.

He perceives the waveform coming from the German lady down the apartment complex where she lived. He tried to use a laser beam, and send the visualization to her middle eye. It didn't work. He didn't feel that familiar colliding of energy he usually felt. He clairvoyantly saw a wave pattern that look like hooks or barbs attached to his leg. He had his guides tune into the energy pattern and disruption to eradicate it. He calls on all his angels, ET guides, Semjase and personal persona – Zaln, and Telefon to come to his assistance; it seemed to help somewhat but not totally. Then Ben called upon Creation, taking his normal visualization trip there to get a healing and laying down for two hours afterwards, he was finally was able to clear the noxious vibrations. Using his Orgone blanket and his Halo headband was a big help in this situation. This cleared his mind and energy levels. *It was just another day in the circus of the illusionary world,* Ben thought.

Shortly afterwards Ben remembered the psychotronics bombardment that Dr. Bear, from CSETI, received. This was a story he told often about experiences with his two friends, that all got skin cancer and he was the only one to come out alive. Humans were just starting to become aware of the possibilities this type of technology held for the human race. If the dark state could weaponize this technology first, they undoubtedly would before we ever saw anything positive come out of our efforts in this field. *I have a sneaking feeling they have already developed the technology and I'm the brunt of the experiment,* Ben thought.

The next day Ben received a call from his sister.

"Hi Ben, can you come over I need some help with repairing the dog door," said Alexandria.

"Sure," said Ben. "I'll be there at three."

"You're such a good brother. I can always depend on you."

"I'll go work on the dog door," said Ben.

After about 30 minutes Ben finished the job and remarked, """That's done," to Alexandra.

"I'm glad you were able to get to the steal strip at the hardware store... that should last a long time before it's needed to be replaced," remarked Ben.

"Oh, good that one thing is done," said Alexandria. "I'm glad you are here because I also wanted to tell you what happened to me with the scanners today. You have been a great help to me tuning into each disruptor, on every side of me, from your apartment in Walnut Creek. Using the visualizations you have taught me, you are able to collide their energy frequencies, from their computers, almost every time. I still don't know how you are able to determine the direction that the disruption is coming from, but it is very accurate."

Alexandria continued, "like I explained to you over the phone recently they are projecting psychotronics/ scalar waves at my head with the emotional trauma attached from my childhood and I can't take that anymore! Some things that you do to counteract the negative energies, I'm not able to do. I'm at the end of my rope! The other day the Galactic Federation came to me and offered to protect me when I needed help. It wasn't that they haven't been protecting me all along, but this was different. I called on them and they were able to disrupt – collide the scalar waves in a matter of minutes. They haven't been able, to counteract the childhood emotional trauma feelings I am getting, although."

Ben tried to console Alexandria by telling her additional stories and personal knowledge he has had dealing with these disruptive energies for a long time.

"I've been calling on other ET sources when Telefon can't drop into my body, when I need help," said Ben.

"By going high up in the sky I can feel the Galactic Federations tremendous energy download into my body. I have isolated several scanners in my building. There's a Polish lady, I call her Owly, across the garden from me, the Catholic lady next to her and the German lady at the end of the row of the apartment. There are at least three others, one being David the engineer, on the other side of my floor along with someone else in that area and the white haired lady around the corner, I'm pretty sure. Running into the white-haired lady one day in the elevator I told her to stop scanning me and she laughed and headed for her apartment." It's interesting Ben Mused, this is a first person I've ever mentioned anything to about scanning too. I think there is more in the building but I haven't isolated them yet. So far I'm holding my own for the last 35 years of my life. This location seems to be a hub for these individuals for some reason.

"Well, sis, I've got to go to a meeting with someone later. Go to your God source and Semjase to see if you can alleviate the emotional bombardment."

"Okay, Ben, I love you, talk to you later tonight."

"I love you, sis, as always," responded Ben.

Ben always enjoyed Alexandria and their trials and tribulations. A few days later Alexandria called Ben, crying.

"I thought the Galactic Federation could help me with these strong emotional memories from my childhood," she sobbed. "I can't go through this again, I've done my work, and I have paid my dues. I have started praying to God every chance I get."

"Oh honey," said Ben, "let me try and contact Semjase to see if she can help. I'll try and talk with you soon also. I'll tune in and send you some good energy to disrupt their field."

Ben got off the phone and went into meditation to talk to Semjase. In a minute Ben could feel her ship's energy above his apartment.

"Hi Semjase." *She always shows up now in a couple of minutes when I call her because of my encounters with noxious ET's that gave me my last heart attack,* thought Ben.

"Hi Ben," Semjase replied telepathically.

"I want to talk to you about Alexandria," said Ben. "She's very emotionally upset about the scanners tuning into her mind and projecting negative emotional memories from her childhood. I think they piggyback thought forms on microwave or radio waves. They have tried to do that to me on occasion but it never worked."

"We will see what we can do. I have an idea that might work."

"Semjase, thanks, talk to you later."

A few days went bye, when Ben noticed Semjase was close by.

"Hi Ben, we have taken care of the problem."

"That's great, Semjase, what had you to decided," said Ben.

"We have approached the prime creator and convinced it that Alexandria has done her work with the her childhood traumas and could not emotionally survived the torment directed at her. It would put her into an emotional depression in the place she is at in her current consciousness level. We were successful partitioning the prime creator. We got confirmation and the scanners won't bother her again."

"Okay, that's great," said Ben, I can't believe it was that easy. I'll have to call her right away, thanks Semjase."

Ben called Alexandria.

"Hi sis, I just talked to Semjase about helping you with what's going on with your emotional trauma."

"Yes, I know," said Alexandria. "I'm feeling better now. For a couple of days I haven't been bothered by the scanners, nothing," she replied. "Semjase contacted me and said she talked to the prime creator about transmuting my trauma from childhood. I can't believe it worked so quickly."

"Yes," Ben replied.

"You know Alexandria, I've been researching the God, or prime creator source for some time now. I wanted to try and understand the concept of God a little better. There are other sources that talk about God, ET's, ancient writings and Internet sources, that site God in a different context. I came across an Internet article about a nine-year-old child from northern Europe. She said she can heal water with Star language. She gives us a lot of information on the connection with her ET guides and the knowledge they are channeling to her on education, science and issues about consciousness."

"I can't believe she is nine years old," said Ben.

"One subject she mentions that she seems to have a lot of knowledge about, is the topic of God. She says about God, that humans don't use the term God correctly... that they miss use it. She goes on to say, that God is a being who resides in the daylight, it is an Over – Terrestrial. We all originate from the light, God is androgynous. It creates the seeds of life and love and finds its home in light with the Angels. The Over – Terrestrial is a description from Ben's guides/persona's Zaln and Telefon. They mention, an Over Terrestrial being that is so large that it fits into our concept of light years in quadrants and sectors of hyperspace.

"We are also in the body of God/Prime Creator. In Carlos Castaneda's books, *Don Juan*, his sorcerer mentor, says that God expands billions of light years out into space and is taken over by a bigger God, and on and on to infinity with different Gods.

"In the Talmud of Jamanual, supposedly scrolls of Jesus true testaments that were found in the area of the dead sea scrolls, that ended up in the hands of Billy Myer the ET contactee. He says that God is a being, a tremendous expansion and the creator of man."

"Wow," said Alexandria, "this information is blowing my mind. The little girl must be an indigo child."

"She fits all the characteristics of these children that first came into the planet in the 80s. I wrote about these children in my first book in more detail," said Ben.

"They came in totally conscious with all memories of past lives and are extremely psychically empathic. Their system busters and can't learn in old ways."

"You're probably right," said Alexandria.

Ben continued, "I recently found a new reference on Galactic Connection website. Alexandra channels information from the prime creator. One of the last posts of a channeling said 'I'm erasing all previous karma that goes out into my domain 350,000 billion quadrillion sectors in my universe, the farthest reaches from the prime source' – ME."

"Well, you have a good start Ben, it is too early to tell if you are right," said Alexandria.

"Yeah, said Ben, I continue to seek out information, I want to know about how consciousness works. I'll talk to you later I got a get some things done around the apartment."

"Keep me informed on new ideas, I feel better now. Bye."

Ben read a little further on G.C. channel from the Prime Creator. He read that the aspects of the triangles – the Trine, connects you to sacred geometry connecting you to nature. The system was set up by the dark gods to control humanity. Love cannot be controlled by sacred geometry of the Trine of three; it has no boundaries.

If you know how to navigate the geometry of the 3 you can us it to your advantage, Ben thought.

Ben signaled Semjase to give her some feedback on this issue.

Semjase commented, "This is true, but also you do not need sacred geometry to communicate with nature or Creation. You can access a love of the Prime Creator through your own I AM present – your Oversoul – your light body/Christ Self."

"Thanks Semjase," said Ben.

These days, Ben has been going to healing night at the church. After laying out his crystals for healing individuals in the meditation group, Ben closed his eyes for a moment and called in the archangel Ariel to help him to do healings while people were signing in. Each healer had his or her own bio and sign up for each practitioner. Ariel the archangel indicated that he was here and would help with healings.

A young woman came over and said, "I am Joan, I'm the first one on your list."

"Okay," said Ben, "sit here facing the stage. I'm going to start with checking your chakras and regulate them to the right function and the right level of energy expression. Then I'll check your aura for any pain you may have and noxious energies. And I'll finish up with bringing in the atomic energy of the Christ from on high, the gold white light to dissipate the first karmic level of your consciousness."

"I learned about the Christ energy from the order of Melchezedeck," said Ben. He started with the brow chakra and proceeded through all of the seven chakras, major energy centers.

"If you are blocking in a chakra help me by visualizing a Lotus flower expanding and opening with the color of that chakra," said Ben.

A few minutes later Ben finished checking the chakras. "You are all tuned up now. How do you feel, Joan?"

"I feel great, light and airy," Joan replied. "I can't put it into words, but it is as if a weight had just been lifted from my shoulders."

That sounds like karma lifting to me,said Ben.

"Okay," said Ben, "let me check your auric field."

Ben tuned in and asked Ariel to help him do healing if this person needed it.

"I feel some dark energy in your auric field here," he said as he touched her arm.

"Yes, I have an old injury from playing softball as a teenager," said Joan.

Ben went into Joan's muscle with white light and pink light. He also projected energy into the noxious energy that Joan was still holding on to in her aura. Ben felt Ariel move closer to his auric field to assist with the healing.

"How's that," said Ben.

"Oh, that feels much better now," she said, moving her arm around in a circle.

Joan was becoming happier and he perceived more of the personal light emanating out through her auric field.

"Let me bring in the Christ energy," said Ben. "I use a tuning process I learned from a world renowned Crystalologist named Marcel Vogel. I'll tune the ametitine purple crystal between your shoulder blades, looking for the key to the lock, as Marcel used to say.

In a couple of minutes Ben replied, "There it is."

He felt the sensation more forcefully now as he tuned the atomic energy of the Christ above, at the eights chakra, as a beam of golden energy shot through his body at instantaneous speed. He arched his back and projected the download of energy into Joan's back, seeing and feeling its pulse down through her body using his clairvoyant sense.

A couple of more downloads and she was finished accepting the energy.

"The atomic energy will stay with you for about two days, doing its healing work," said Ben. Ben came around the side of the chair and observed Joan in a deep trance meditation. She wore a peaceful expression.

"Come back into the room at your own pace," said Ben.

"Ground yourself," mentioned Ben, "if you are feeling a little flighty. I can teach you a grounding exercise if you want me to."

Joan thought for a minute and said, "Okay, I'm feeling a little flighty as you describe it."

"Visualize a green translucent pole going down the middle of your body and bring your energy to the center and bring it down the green pole into mother Earth – Gaia."[1] "How you feel now?"

"Thanks I feel more grounded now."

"Oh good, I would hate to have you running into the furniture, with a big smile. You look like you're feeling better," said Ben.

"I feel wonderful, and I feel so light, with a little twinkle in her eye.

"Some times you can reach up and grab your light body and just pull it back into your body…to ground your self," said Ben.

"I'll see you next healing night," Joan said, and moved towards the door as she seemed to float.

The archangel Ariel was one of the archangels that had helped Ben do healings for many years. He had learned about the archangels more clearly while in the Order of Melchezedeck. He had contacted them on a number of occasions to cleanout negative spirits from people's homes and use them for protection when a negative entity inundated his living space. Michael used his sword to dismantle the entity and Ariel and another archangel Hensel used huge nets to carry away the spirit and deposit them into the outer universe or the sun.

One of Ben's first contacts with Ariel was celebrating his birthday at a restaurant with friends and a Los Angeles psychic that tried to help him with finding another name to use. The name he had chosen was a name that Ben wasn't satisfied with but at the same time an energy pierced his consciousness and he heard a voice say, "Ariel."

Later that evening, Ben was attending Sanaya Raymond's trance channeling group session in Oakland. She mentioned to Ben that he had a winged being in his auric field. He later confirmed on the Ouija board that had a colored auric field of silver purple. Ben had been healing for many years by then.

The next recollection he had of spiritual healing was when he used to do healings at Ameron metaphysical church years before in San Francisco.

His deaf friend,Tommy, was at one of his healing nights. Ben started healing Tommy and the energy of Ariel came in to assist his process. As the energy flowed through Ben, Tommy went almost into elation with this energy and started pawing and climbing all over Ben. It was a uncomfortable interaction with Tommy and Ben had Ariel back off so he could recover.

"Are you all right?" Ben asked Tommy.

"I flipped out feeling that energy! Sorry," I got overheated," scribbling on his note pad.

Deaf people were really tuned into subtle energy vibrations. One time Ben had attended a deaf party and was drinking a glass of wine standing in silence as a group of friends communicated in sign language and read lips. In the silence Ben became aware of the space between each person in the group. The feeling in the space was overwhelming. The space was filled with an energy that was thick and energetic. It filled up the space entirely. It was almost like they were in communication with each other on a different level of consciousness. The manifestation of subtle energies in different forms never seemed to surprise Ben.

Ben was reflecting on his life in a quasi-meditative state with all the trials and tribulations with people he had met and the torment he had endured over the years. People needed to wake up and become aware of all the ways we were manipulated by lame news, the violence in movies, the GMOs in food, pharmaceuticals and medicine. Still, little was known about the subtle manipulation of our minds and bodies by ELF frequencies and other energies used to disrupt our consciousness. Everyday Ben's mind was impinged upon by mind control experts. He didn't regret the challenges that he had to endure, as he knew he had come into the planet this time to overcome the frequency manipulation rampant in the world. There were groups trying to alert others of manipulation and processes that will continue to take away individual solvency, like Controlled America.com. Ben became aware of this group some years ago. He started to try and understand these latter days on mother Earth and the depravity that plagues all of humanity. Ben and others alerted people to mind manipulation and the control that the unseen were trying to impose.

Mother Earth/Gaia was going through many changes in her own ascension process, as sentient groups like Galactic Harp and Galactic Connection were telling people on their websites. Ben particularly liked Belden's blog from various enlightened individuals who channeled various ascended Masters that gave him the latest info about the many transformations going on in the planet from a spiritual perspective.

Ben came out of his contemplation shortly after returning home, which seemed like an extended period of time, and decided to call his sister Alexandria.

"Hi Ben, what's up?"

"Well, I wanted to tell you about the wonderful website I recently I came across. Sheldon's-Galactic Harp and Alexandria's – Galactic connection are connecting us with ascended beings and masters and the real news in our country and issues going on in the world. They are also giving us tips on how to manage our ascension processes. On Sheldon's website the ascended Masters are really great explaining the details in the process of moving the prosperity funds into place so that it can be distributed in the near future with the help of the light forces surrounding the planet, in hyperspace.

"I told you about the prosperity funds coming soon after NASARA is integrated into our society, right Alexandria?"

"Yes, I remember you saying something about the funds. This is a complicated subject and I don't remember all the details but everyone on the planet will be receiving funds to make a better life for themselves when a certain number of people start working on their ascension process. We also need to clean out the dark forces, the deep state, before any changes will come into play."

"I would be remiss if I didn't mention Bridget Nealson also," said Ben. "She channels ET children and draws examples for people that are interested. She's an uplifting Star Seed on the planet that is enlightening the young affluent people in her circles. Her website has some great teachings and lessons about our consciousness development in contemporary language and takes people to different spiritual location on the planet. I can tell she is a super master vibration #22."

Of course Ben considered himself Star Seed as well, incarnating into the planet this time to uplift the consciousness of individual sovereignty.

"I'll look it up when I come back from work tonight," said Alexandria.

"How is your connection with God, the Prime Creator," said Ben.

"Oh, great, I haven't been plagued by the scanners at all anymore."

"I guess the reprieve worked," said Ben.

"It did, and the Prime Creator came to me last night. It was a tremendous light energy of love that filled my body."

"God said I'm a special person and I have a different destiny to fulfill in this lifetime. It wouldn't tell me what my destiny was but said, you should continue working on your ascension processes. I will be with you always. Call upon me when you want to talk, was its total message."

"That's great," said Ben, "you are a very lucky person and the ascended being I always thought you were. I remember doing your numerology chart a couple years ago. I knew that you were destined for something great. There is more in your heaven and earth than you know, sweetie."

"You know there is a man named Bill Wilsh that has written three books on his communication with God. I read the third book and it was very interesting," said Ben.

"Well, okay," said Alexandria, "there is a lot for me to check out but you know how hard it is for me to sit down and read a book these days."

"Yeah, I know, it was just a thought. You may be interested in reading it at some other point in your life," said Ben.

"I'm glad I'm still connected with Semjase. I miss my sister," said Alexandria.

"Well, you know she will be in our lives from now on," replied Ben. "I wonder if spiritual blood is thicker than water, applies here. Anyway, she is our precious sister from the Pleiades and I don't think that will ever change. She is with us in our ascension process from now on."

"I hope so," said Alexandria, "I love her."

"One more thing, Alex. I read some new information about replicators, from Sheldon's website, that we all are going to inherit from the Andromedans when they land. They are great healers in the universe and designers of the replicators as well as being part of the Galactic Federation.

"Anyway, I learned recently, how these devices work. They interface with our consciousness, our telepathic and psychokenesis abilities in order for the machine to work."

"Oh yeah," said Alexandria. "We can make anything in the third dimensional space just by our mental images interjected into the device?"

"That's right sweetie, you can make whatever you want or need with a replicator, according to our extraterrestrial friends." They also said we won't need agriculture or manufacturing. We can make all the things we need."

"Well, what about all the people that work in those industries?"

"They will be free to work on themselves and their personal dreams and destinies," said Ben. "They won't need to work after the prosperity funds are distributed to everyone on the planet; everyone will all be on the same level, finally; Sheldon's webinars explained these new ideas. Money will become irrelevant in the future, ET's don't use it. Of course everyone has free will and can toil on things they're interested in pursuing, of course."

"Well it sounds great, but I won't believe it until it happens," said Alexandria.

"I can't wait either," said Ben, "but it's going to be a while before the landing happens and the NASARA governance system comes in."

"Okay," said Alexandria, "I'm going to have to go to the website to see what Galactic Harp and Galactic Connection have to say."

"I can't believe channeling has picked up again, since it somewhat died out in the 80s or did it," said Ben.

"Maybe it's because the new channelers are very clear conscience channels now." The energy on the planet has risen to a level where the veil between the dimensions is thinner making it easier for consciousness to step up to a higher level; communication is always higher faster and clearer than the lower dimensions and densities."

"I have to go to work now, I'll talk to you later tonight."

"Bye sis," replied Ben.

Chapter Twenty-Two

The Truth Shall You Free

Ben went out on his balcony to finish his juice and contemplate his continued destiny. *They have continued their surveillance of me to this day, in the middle days of the 21st century, as they had told me in the early days,* Ben thought.

He continued to develop his skills for protection and call in his guides and light beings to work with him to shed more light on the unfolding of his destiny. Shedding light on the subtle vibrations that individuals that are not aware of directed energy weapons that impede their spiritual truths and development, continues to be a focus in his life. With his super skills, that all possess, he would return to his rightful place as an ascended spiritual master.

This would make him more capable of living in harmony and love with other ascended beings in the

Universe. He would become the master of his own destiny, free as a sovereign being, to finally realize the Divine and Sacred consciousness beings with individual rights, in and out of time, on the planet and off.

The slave mentality would be a thing of the past as humanity continues its ascension into a higher consciousness.

Ben had just learned that our individual divine sovereignty under universal law continues to be declared by the Prime Creator. He finally understood why he had directed his studies and research on an individual focus, rather than on a group focus, on many occasions, even in his professional life. He had realized the monad, the one, in numerology but did not realize that we had the sovereignty of one. It was all becoming clear to him that our freedom was at stake here in our bodies. Our Christed selves that have lead us all towards breaking the bonds of the illusionary matrix that locks us into our 3rd dimensional selves will also transform us into higher conscious spiritual beings.

What was in store for humanity in its ascension state of being was that we would remember again that we are members of the Galactic off-world civilizations and who we were as ascended beings. Humanity would again have our 12 strands of DNA as it was in our early history.

The new technologies that awaited would end poverty, war, and create a society of cooperation, the key to communication struggled for in these End of Days. Ben had been on many other worlds before, helping oppressed societies with their ascension processes. Healing had been a key process for teaching others about the sovereign beings in the fight for sovereign rights in many cultures as well.

The dark side was not interested in individual sovereign but collective slave cultures to assure their deprived agenda.

Ben did not want to be a being that continued to reincarnate into the Karmic wheel of life. He'd done with this level of consciousness and wants to fly on the wings of his ascended self to his rightful place in the universe. It was possible to do that, when he sees the light at the end of the tunnel, now with the real possibilities showing up every day. It was no longer a dream but a true reality. The prime Creator had assured him that the dark forces no longer have power and they will wane slowly and surely as the energy of love comes from the Galactic center to uplift humanity in these times of trials and tribulations.

Hold on to your butts, as Morgan Freeman would say, we are on the ride of our lives, Ben muses. *Thank you, Prime Creator.*

Ben came out of contemplation with a big smile on his face. He knew that the end was near and the possibilities were endless. This did not mean the struggle was over but a renewed sense of personal power had made its home in Ben's heart and consciousness.

Now, Ben thinking of his destiny, had been preparing to shed light on these obscure subtle manipulations in its relationships of man's consciousness for over 30 years. He continued to be followed and subjected to low frequency radiation in his car or sitting in coffee shops. The computer had made it somewhat easier to tune into a person's brain wave frequencies, personal energy signature or nervous system using this device. Targeting the energy center of the solar plexus seemed to be a new approach in the scanning group. They had adapted the ancient knowledge of the energy systems, the chakras, to tune their disrupting waveforms. Algorithms seem to be the wave of the future with computer technology these days as well. There were some that still use noxious energies projected into them as a natural process of disrupting another's consciousness, but that seemed to be a rarity in these days of advanced technology. They still tune into the age-old sneeze response to focus on individual consciousness when all else failed. But Ben had learned to deflect the wave form to break the chain of repercussion.

Sitting in a café Ben, felt a light wave hit his solar plexus chakra. He quickly cut the light cord and sent it back to its source. His crystals helped do some of the work for him, sucking in noxious light energy into their matrix. When this energy was determined, he perused the ambient field to ascertain the direction of the disruption. Ah, yes he felt the energy coming from the young man on his computer in the corner. He also detected an energy coming from two other directions as well. He mused, *Maybe they are triangling their efforts.*

This had been a technique used for years by the military as far back as World War II. Nick Norseno, a metaphysican, had alerted Ben and others to this possibility years ago in his Crystal skull workshops. He had used it in the military police after the war. Being a Wiccan, he was experienced in using his psychic abilities to achieve the mind reading process. But, this was just speculation at this point. Tuning into someone using different frequencies may have been closer to the mark in the 21st century. There were many levels to turning different frequencies Ben had learned in his studies of radionics and psychotronic many years ago. Tuning into a person's consciousness is not as easy as you might think. The computer had revolutionized this whole field of frequency manipulation and it would never be the same. The genie is out of the bottle and you couldn't put it back in.

Ben felt another waveform inundate his head, causing it to go slightly numb. He projected a spinning light cone around himself and dissipated some of the energy. He called upon Telefon to drop into his body and feels the manifestation of his energy, with a subtle thud.

"Okay, I'm in," said Telefon.

"Thanks Telefon, I think the disruption is coming from that person over there, and the one in the black shirt," said Ben.

"I'll work it."

"She is also projecting at my solar plexus," said Ben.

Sometimes Telefon wanted to take care of the disruption himself, and would call in more of his Galactic people if he needed them, and sometimes he didn't mind if Ben assisted him using the techniques he had learned over the years of disruptive practice.

Ben continued his line of thought. *They, the proverbial they, think they are collecting information on him with these sessions, but he is collecting his own data observations during these episodes and the information is of course uploaded to his Galactic connections surveilling each situation, as is Telefon.*

I'll be glad when this incarnation comes to a close and we have finally ascended to our rightful place as enlightened beings on the planet.

Until then, Ben continued his plight to perform his role as a Star Seed, watching the planet transform as the love energy from the Galactic center energies continued to rise the vibration of Gaia towards her ascension and humanity's. Ben prolonged working on his computer and, with the help of his friends, transmuted the disruptive energies coming into his system in a short period of time. This was not the last time he'd have to deal with this disruption but he continued to get the upper hand on their sinister ways; where there is a will there is a way.

Ben had a metaphysical encounter up on Lime Ridge searching for a new labyrinth that he heard about with a couple friends one day at church. They had send him a Christmas card with the labyrinth printed on it that sparked Ben's interest in going with Vincent and Jill to Mt. Diablo to walk the new labyrinth. Ben called Vincent wondering if he wanted to hike up the labyrinth this Saturday.

Vincent said, "Sure, you have good timing. Jill and I were thinking about going up there this weekend. I'll pick you up Saturday about 9:00 am."

"Oh, great," said Ben. "I'll be looking for you."

They hiked up the hill and Vincent said, "I think I know where it is now, I've been there three times. It took a while for us to locate it, but we finally found the trail."

Ben thought, *Good, I didn't relish being a nomad searching around the foothills all over the mountain.*

Up, up they went following the switch back towards their destination. Ben kept his pad in his hand making a small map of their quest so he could get back to the labyrinth himself at a latter date.

He thought to himself, *don't forget the natural landmarks, trees and rocks that blazed the trail.* By that time they were going into their 3 hour. This was a difficult feat for Ben as he had a bad back. It was a good thing he brought his cane chair to sit down when he needed to,as well as his pain pills.

As they came around the hill Vincent finally pointed out the large labyrinth overgrown with weeds.

"I guess no one has walked this one for the sometime," said Ben.

Vincent also directed our attention to the direction of the other labyrinth the one on his Christmas card, just around the corner. Vincent had a subtle way of not responding to your questions.

Ben thought, *For a super master vibration, he wasn't very aware of what was going on around him, maybe it was a deliberate ploy to through someone off there game. On the other hand maybe he was a space cadet, spacing out a lot, not hearing what people were saying.*

Ben explained to Vincent and Jill that, "spiritually, walking a labyrinth was a natural process of purging noxious energy from your body, and when you reach the center stop to meditate a few minutes before following the labyrinth back out, this time breeze in the positive energy, and recharge your system as you move towards the exit."

Vincent really appreciated the insights moving through the labyrinth, as he didn't have much of a spiritual bent... but was eager to learn. Ben led off moving into the entrance of the labyrinth and made his way to the center, in about 5 minutes, it was a big labyrinth.

Labyrinths are loosely constructed with four switchbacks on each side before you arrive at the center making it a long trek. As Ben arrived at the center he set down on the collapsible chair he had brought with him. Focusing on bringing down the atomic energy of Christ, on high, he felt a surge of energy moves through his body instantaneously... grounding it into the center of Gaia. He also asked if the great spirit would also come into the circle. As he did a young Indian male spirit dropped into the Ben body.

"*How rude, Jar-Jar Binks would say*," said Ben.

Ben felt an unfamiliar energy come into his frame and he asked the spirit, "*do you believe in the sovereignty of one.*"

"*Yes,*" *was the reply.* "*We are the Hiwaska tribe from your ancient times.*"

Ben remarked, "*I'm from the Cherokee tribe.*" Ben thought, *This was not the Great Spirit, The Great Spirit was the Native American Indians name for God.*

"Oh, *welcome brother to our sacred land, you are welcome to partake of the energy's here,*" the young Indian replied.

Ben continued telepathically, "I hope you don't expect to stay in my body, I won't allow that. I will catapult you out or you can leave on your own."

There was no reply. His noxious energy continued to inundate Ben as he spoke to the young Indian. The energy was pretty toxic and Ben really didn't want to continue communicating with him with his lower energy consciousness. At that point Ben rose and started to make his way out of the labyrinth. He did his deep breathing and brought in the positive energy as he moved out. They all finished in about 5 minutes or so. Ben felt a little bit more energy in his body as we return to the beginning of the Labyrinth.

The young Indian man was no where to found in my consciousness,I guess he took my advice and left my body of his own accord,thought Ben.

"How do you feel?" Ben asked Vincent.

"Oh, I feel a little different but I'm not sure what I'm feeling," Vincent said.

"Ok, that's fine said Ben, you'll understand it eventually, give yourself time for it to filter through your consciousness."

"The other labyrinth is just around the hill... let's go," said Vincent.

As they rounded the Hill, Ben could see the pathway lined with rock totems on both sides going down the hill. The labyrinth, as they approached it was unfortunately underwater; it wasn't visible at all.

Jill exclaimed, "Where did it go! There must be an underground fisher to have this much water here."

Ben remarked, "Well we just had a dynamic rainstorm come through recently."

Jill was really disappointed, as they all were.

Vince interjected, "Let's follow the trail up above and see if we can see the labyrinth from up there. We walked back up the trail and then posed for a picture next to another rock totem.

This is a great totem, remarked Ben, it's in perfect balance.

"Yeah," said Vincent, "I try and build one every time I visit."

Making their way around the ridge in about 10 minutes they arrived and peered over the edge of the cliff into the water below.

"Boy it's dark," said Ben, "you can't see anything. I was looking forward to walking this labyrinth."

"I hope it comes back when the water recedes," said Vincent. "Let's hit the road, there's nothing here to see anymore."

"I wonder who built the other totems," said Ben, "they're really nice."

Jill and Vincent made no reply as they made their way down the hill.

I think I'm talking to myself some times, thought Ben.

It took them about 50 minutes more to descend down the hills and along the way they could see the trails that kids used on their bikes to go up and down the cliffs and hillsides. The trip took about four hours from beginning to end. Ben didn't realize he had been hiking that long, specially because he had a bad back with two pancake disks. *I continued to take my pain pills when the pain got bad but this track was not that taxing on my frame*, he thought. Maybe because he had taken himself out of time and didn't feel the strain on his lower lumbar. *Cortisone shot seems to be holding also*, thought Ben.

Ben went into a kind of a trance state as he walked, and thought, *I haven't taken myself out of time for along time and didn't feel the strain of my body muscles and fatigue.*

He had done this on one occasion when Gertrude and he went to San Francisco for fourth of July. They had missed their bus after the fireworks and ended up walking to Bart and seeing it was closed, walked downtown and finally caught a bus to Berkeley at four o'clock in the morning. Then taking a cab to the Pleasant Hill BART where the car was. By that time was five o'clock in the morning.

Ben had taken himself out of time for the 20 blocks they had to walk to fine the bus. Meeting drug addicts at the bus stop, stepping over the homeless sleeping on the side walk on the way to the bus station and finding it closed was a harrowing experience. Moving spirit out of your body was something that Ben had naturally learned to do when he was under tremendous stress, during the years he was held up by gun point in San Francisco. When you know as much about your light body, as Ben did, it wasn't difficult to raise it up out of the physical body creating a barrier from pain; time has no relevance in that consciousness, it was suspended from 3-D time. Higher consciousness functions on many levels at a time and can be utilized when you are in dire stress and in a life-threatening situation. We are higher consciousness beings and we can function on these higher levels when we consciously "know" we can do what we perceive. As Yoda would say, either do or do not. The indigo children already have this ability... They come into the planet as fully conscious beings.

Back at the car Ben remarked, "well, I have my notes to find my way back when I want to walk labyrinth again."

Jill said," I'll runoffs a map for you and give it to you next Sunday."

Ben replied, "Thanks Jill. I appreciate that. I look forward to seeing if the Labyrinth comes back in the spring time."

And with that they took off for home.

Chapter Twenty-Three

The Purging

Ben thought, when he arrived home to his apartment, *This is been a very interesting day. I need to record my personal observations of the labyrinth in my journal, so I can refer back to it. Another thought came into his head, a long forgotten thought, one pertaining to his spiritual name. My spiritual name. I haven't thought about that in years. Is spirit communicating with me?*

Years ago while using the Ouija board Ben heard also telepathically, "You have the spiritual name Amijim." He didn't think much of this thought, but one of his guides remarked, "Your consciousness can be located anywhere in the universe using this name, it has a history. It was like" a code in a universal computer that instantly references you as an individual sovereign being anywhere in time or space or out of time, even. Ben really didn't understand why he needed this information but there it was. Maybe more understanding would come through in the future.

As Ben continued to contemplate his destiny he knew he would have to continue his vigilance in protecting himself from the barrage of scanners for the rest of his days, until the great change happened as our planet ascened into the fifth dimension. He often wondered if he would be here to see this occurrence happen.

Ben was also reflecting on new unfolding evidence of scanner influence in the world he recently ran across on the Internet.

Could this be synchronicity? he mused.

The focus was on the Polish people, an open letter from the European commission in Belgian to the Polish defense minister, visiting the University of Father Tadeusz Rydzwk discussing problems of politics, armed conflict and knowledge about signals that conducts electrons. He was very interested in a field that he learned about from his people that impinged on their consciousness. Specifically, ions that stimulate the nerve cells to fire in the nervous system controlled by Neurons/axons that send a signal throughout the nervous system. Microwave energy is also projected into the brain, with specific frequencies, to stimulate the hypothalamus, which controls emotional reactions in the body to disrupt an individual's physiology. The minister was just starting to create a commission to study these allegations focusing on the European Union. Everything seems to be coming out and revealing itself in these latter days on the planet. *I'm really getting to like this term, transparency,* thought Ben.

Ben also included in his journal the challenges we will face with our ascension process and the opportunities that will open up, so he can continue to enlighten people to the subtleties that face mankind both positive and negative. We are learning more about transmuting noxious energies from the dark forces on the planet. The computer is becoming that golden messenger that continues to enlighten all of us to the subtleties of the illusions that frame us at every turn. Of course it has its draw back... Certain corporations are taking advantage of at this time of individual information, ie. tracking everyone's personal information on their sites.

As we are going through our ascension now, purging all the karma that we possess in these latter days of Gaia and her ascension, as well, the dark forces are losing their footing on the planet.

The benefits of meditation were becoming more apparent to Ben. Visualizations were becoming much more real now and making Ben aware for some time that life can be revealed on a deeper and more personal level, as one interface with the divine energy inside of oneself. He became aware that we are not separated from any level of consciousness including species in different dimensions/densities with degrees of consciousness. The joy, inspiration, love and the beings that came through, is a testament to the energetic fabric that connects all of us in the universe and universes.

After service, Ben met with their brunch group at the Butter Nups restaurant. The Polish woman, Owly as he called her, his neighbor at his apartment complex was there along with a few other friends from his church. Owly started telling us about her dream or rather a dream vision that she was having about something like a tribunal that was asking questions about her life. Was she satisfied with her life and other subjects. She went on to describe that she awoke around 3 am to use the bathroom... And a voice spoke to her, telepathically, to look out the window, and complying she saw a ball of plasma as bright as the sun over Ben's building, directly across the garden on the third floor of the apartment complex from Owly. She didn't realize the connection in the dream with the beings in the craft until Meryl told her to make that connection. Ben agreed with Meryl on this issue. Ben went on to tell Owly about ascension and transmuting the darker lower energies as well as old paradigms. Ben deliberately was explaining the dark – negative energies because he knew Owly had been scanning him for about a year with psychotronics ELF energies frequency's from her apartment.

He could counteract the energies using techniques he had learned over the years and also in coordination with the Galactic Federation to transmute the lower vibrations in his apartment when he calls upon them. Now, he was seeing a light ship with a horizontal line through it on Owly's iPhone, as she passed it around the table, that corroborated his experience calling in the Federation in real time, in physical form, to help him transmute noxious energies in his individual living space. More than likely they morph into and out of the third dimension when they came close, revealing themselves; they de-cloaked sort to speak. It was also interesting because Ben had asked Galactic Federation if they could manifest themselves in the physical time so that he could see them.

They replied, they could but it depends on the individual's consciousness level i.e. Super Master vibrations see more materializations because of their lifetimes of knowledge and their personal consciousness development. We have manifested an experience for you to realize that your projection is being received by us in real time.

Owly was a Super Master vibration alright, even through Ben hadn't worked out her numbers, he recognized the facial structure and persona. At any rate, she became quiet as the others talked, contemplating her dream and its deeper meaning. Ben thought, *I hope Owly got the message, to change her ways, for her own personal ascension.*

She had just had a heart attack. I hope she can make it, I forgive her for trying to affect my heart health and consciousness in negative ways.

But unfortunately she continued to try and disrupt him, as Ben found out later. There were two others in the group that Ben had picked up disruptive energies from. He could always tell because the noxious vibration that emanated from their auric field would repulse him when he communicated with them. It was like a pungent smell that would make you recoil. He also prayed for their recovery from the influences of the dark forces. Their health would only go downhill as long as they continued to participate in their own destruction, as ancient texts had stated.

Ben was back at his apartment and noticed a disruptive energy coming from the roof of his apartment again. He called on his friend Semjase and Galactic Federation to disrupt electronics in the devices that he felt were placed on the roof of his personal living space. He was able to collide the some of the noxious energies himself,to a point, but not totally. Ben felt Semjase come in with their ship just about the apartment to check out the devices that he made reference to on the roof. They were able to affect the devices somewhat but were not able to totally dismantle the noxious vibrations. Semjase and friends lifted off and said they will be back later to finish the job and check on the progress of their work. In the meantime Ben checked to see if the noxious vibrations still were being generated from the devices – they were almost gone.

Ben thought, *I live in a senior center who could be setting up devices on the roof to disrupt him. It really didn't make sense until a light bulb went of in his head; it could be the technicians that come out to check the solar panels.* That made more sense.

Ben went out for coffee and worked on this e-mail and blogs for his book the next day. He came across a blog by Barbara M., who channels the Pleaidian ET's.

One time, recently, Ben had asked Semjase if Barbara was accurate in her channeling of the Pleaidan culture and she assured him that she was very accurate and had up-to-date information. Barbara was talking about the state of affairs on the planet today and coached us that nothing is reality, as far as consciousness is concerned, at this time on the planet. The illusion was the only thing that existed but they, extraterrestrials, were coming up with creative ideas to show us the illusion more clearly, so the truth could shine through as the energy raises on the planet and indeed in the universe.

This was a time of upheaval on all levels of your consciousness reality, it was the change – the purging. There would be a great catastrophe soon, in a year's time.

Semjase had told him that this relates to what Ben had mentioned in their previous channeling at his sister's house, that this event was related to the great exodus that he would participate in. Of course, Ben didn't understand what she was referring to, and maybe he would understand these ideas more in the future.

Ben went back to his apartment and after finishing his blogs and noticed that the devices on the roof were functioning again, spewing noxious energies as before. Semjase had done a great job in coming down the electronics on the roof before but he decided he would try contacting the Galactic Federation this time, to see if they could have some results shutting down the devices. Ben wondered if that's why he hadn't been able to sleep last night. He had forgotten to check the roof.

He continued to validate this energy disruption and his quest to disrupt this impingement on his sovereign self whenever he could. Briefly tuning the devices with the help of the G.F. Ben felt a colliding of the energy from the main device on the roof. *This was always an indication of the disruptive energy that was shut down and I have disrupted the electron flow*, he thought.

They would have to come back and recalibrate later, Ben thought with a big smile.

Earlier that week Ben had been contacted by the Educational Wing of the Adjusting Forces, Telefon's group, about helping him develop his ascension skills.

It was partially, he thought, *in regards to how he understands how prosperity works and how to tune into the flow of energy.*

As it turns out, from galactic's message, pulling in prosperity energy had a color component in the rose hues, that he should reject out into the universe and magnifies the flow of energy and pull it towards him. Ben was happy that the Educational Wing was confirming a previous channeling that was accurate pertaining to color and his consciousness and continued to show him other ways of developing his prosperity issue.

Consider the recent dream Ben had? This dream when something like –Ben saw very clearly, a movie in Technicolor.

The image was a broken door in his apartment complex and he went to the apartment manager to let him know that the door was off its hinges. When Ben came back to the apartment the door opening had changed to a white double glass window door and his dream symbolism dictionary said you learned the doors meaning. The definition was expressed – your dream of the old paradigm of prosperity door had changed to a new vision of prosperity door reflecting that prosperity was coming to you soon.

Yahoo, thought Ben. *Dreams are perfect way to understand our questions about our life on a subtler level. And if you can create a lucid dreaming scenario you will better take control of your life and make major changes, is an additional approach to changing your dreams to work for you.*

The Educational Justine Forces wing also told Ben that Vishnu, the Indian god, was a personas of his and a guide also. Ben had a hard time believing Vishnu was one of his incarnations in the past. But, when he received this information he felt a twinge of joy from what he thought was the Vishnu persona. He recently realized that Vishnu's color signature was silver. Colors always made it easier for Ben to tune into different energies.

Ben found out through talking with Telefon that he was in connection with the 10th dimension and that they said Vishnu was never a persona of his, although he is a guide of yours.

Well, Ben thought, *It's hard to know the truth about some areas of consciousness,* as he fiddled with his lip. *At least Vishnu was a guide, that he needed to get better acquainted with.*

I'm going to have to contact the tenth dimensional group to get more information about this issue, Ben thought.

As Ben sat at his computer looking over his e-mails at the apartment a call came in from Alexandria, his sister.

"Hi Ben," she said, "How's things going today?"

"Oh, you know, the same old same old, I continue to get bombarded from scanners around me. I'm glad I have my Halo and Orgone blankets and crystals, they have been a godsend for 30 years, the psychotronics research really paid off in the end."

"Yeah," said Alexandria, "the headband we made really helped me also until I got a reprieve from God, of course."

"Say, did I tell you Tessie bear got sick. He ate some stuffing from one of my blankets and it stopped up his is digestive track. I had to take him to the vet and he had to have an operation on his intestines. I was so worried for him and I cried. The big guy is always chewing up my blankets, but I love him."

"Oh, I'm sorry to hear that, Alex. I'm very fond of that silly black lab. Is he going to be okay?"

"Yes, he is recovering slowly, but he still hasn't taken his first dump yet."

"That sucks," said Ben, "do you think he is going to be all right?"

"Well, it's nip and tuck right now. I would be really devastated if he didn't make it. I don't mind paying the $2000 for the operation. I couldn't let him die."

Ben shed a tear and blew his nose and said, "it will be all right, sis, he will get better soon.

"Semjase told me something about Tess, that he was going to be fine, but I didn't understand what she was talking about at the time."

"That was spot on," Ben replied. "I can't believe she was so accurate; she called it right, again."

"Anyway, I'm somewhat over it now," said Alexandria. Semjase, told me the some things about Tess also."

"Our connection with our guides is getting much clearer now compared to five or six years ago," said Ben. "I think it has something to do with the raise of energy coming into the planet from the galactic center. That's one of the things that I really feel is happening with the energy change so far with the ascension."

"I know what you're saying," said Alexandria. "My communication is much clearer now."

"I have picked up a new player/scanner in the apartment complex, just down the road from me," mentioned Ben. "I feel her disruption impinging on the space between my shoulder blades; the first symptoms of my heart attack. I'm holding my own, as I raise the oversoul and bring down the atomic energy of the Christ from on high with help from the Galactic Federation. I found out that she comes from a police family, I wonder if she's connected with the cop's two doors down from me."

"Of course there are other new players in my apartment complex that I have picked up projecting their noxious energy towards me on a regular basis, but I have the necessary knowledge and help to protect myself from there encroachments, as you have experienced Alexandria many times when you were over at my apartment. It has been treacherous at times but I have learned to adjust myself to circumstances."

Ben had picked up the energy yesterday and also as he walked by the cop's house on his normal daily walk in the neighborhood. He could feel the horrendous noxious energy being emitted from their house in his auric field. *Keep it up boys,* Ben thought, *your time is coming as the energy raises on the planet.*

"Well, I'm glad you have it under control," said Alexandria, "I'm glad I don't have to deal with that stuff anymore."

"Okay, sis, I'm going to take off now. I'll speak to you later tonight."

"Okay Ben, I hope you are feeling better. Semjase told me she is keeping a special eye on you, because they are trying to kill you, you know."

"I've known about that for a long time, since my heart attacks. She has told me the same thing and that she is not going to let them take me out again. I intend to stay on the planet for many more years; I have a lot to do before I leave, by sis."

Ben went across the street and sat down to work on this computer outside the coffee shop. It was a normal day, sunny and warm. As Ben was reading he heard a loud voice coming from a man walking down the street. As he approached Ben he heard what the man was saying, "get off me" several times as he walked by him. Ben looked up wanting to determine the source and demeanor of this very disturbed soul fighting the images in his head. His pitch raised and lowered as he tried to ward off the demonic energy impinging his consciousness. Ben had encountered this type of individual in his own past, especially in San Francisco. But this incident seemed different as he felt the energy expression. Most people he had encountered on the street in the city where individuals with psychological and emotional problem and delusions, common occurrences with street people in the mental health system. Ben was not a psychologist but he had had various classes in early childhood and adolescent psychology classes to learn about the nomenclature. The guy seemed lucid and functional, at least to a point, enough to go to Sprouts and get himself a sandwich and sit down at the table not far from Ben.

Ben thought, *it's strange to run into a tormented person in a quiet suburban town like Walnut Creek.* The man took out a cigarette and asked Ben if he had a light. Ben replied, "I don't smoke," with a glare, as the guy quickly retreated to his table again. As he puffed on a cigarette he seemed to become agitated again and moves away from the table sitting on the nearby stairs, and started yelling again, "get off me," "get off me," in a lower tone, thinking it would help his position in warding off the demons in his head. He continues to rant for a short time and finally ambles off down the street fighting with the images in his mind.

Ben contemplated what had just happened and interfacing with his intuition, realizing that this person was not just a individual with a mental problem. He was experiencing a torment from some voice or energy or entity that would not leave him alone. This was very familiar to Ben as he had felt mental and energetic torment for years; he knew the symptoms, although he had never succumbed to them.

This person was more than likely a casualty of a mind control program that had started to take him over because of his involvement in this type of program or was a target for some unknown reason. He might have had himself in to deep and was rebelling against his handlers and they were retaliating against him for knowing what he knew and who he might talk to, in fact, spilling the beans or pulling back the curtain, sort to speak, on their program.

They are, most likely, using the frequencies that they have been using on me for years, and worse. Unfortunately this person doesn't have the knowledge and skills to construct devices to protect himself and doesn't have a strong spiritual base of knowledge that would protect him. He seemed intelligent to Ben but didn't seem very spiritually evolved. Ben felt compassionate towards this person but decided there was nothing he could do to help this individual out of his situation. He needed to seek some spiritual and maybe professional help to shed some light on his dilemma.

This was a good chance that Ben saw, firsthand, to witness what the ascension energies were doing to some people trying to swim upstream, so to speak, and the problems that these people were having to cope with these love energies coming into the planet that were revealing or transmuting the lower energies on the planet.

Is this cosmic synchronicity expressing itself again? Ben mused.

For people living an ordinary, normal life, these energies brought out personal stuff that had to be transmuted before they could bring in the new energies and become ascended beings; no one was exempt from this process on the planet. Purging seemed to be the call word for the times.

Ben had a renewed sense of competence, out of conflict, knowing that the collective consciousness was taking those steps to ascend to a higher level of consciousness for the total transformation of humanity. It wasn't very long ago that Ben had contemplated leaving the planet because he feared that we would not see through the illusion that we all felt trapped in or the way out of the whole deceptive situation. We had drugged and numbed ourselves with our addictions to cope with our daily lives. As the Hopi said in a prophecy, we will as a species take the high road or we will take the lower. On the face it seemed that humanity took the low road and there was no way out. But the ascended Masters, including ET Masters, assured us that we were choosing the higher road, collectively, towards breaking all barriers, accumulated over centuries and dissolving the illusion of being a slave race, and become the truly divine beings that was our God-given right.

Most people didn't recognize humanity's relationship with their ET brothers and sisters. In some ways, we were them they were us. They had been with us since the beginning of time, guiding humanity towards the light through ancient civilizations, helping us have experiences that develop our consciousness towards realizing our true purpose and divinity. Ben thought, *Science tells us that we are made up of the substance of the stars. In the end we will recognize our true history when ET shows itself and communicates to us that we have never been alone in the universe and we are WHO we are looking for. I for one*, Ben mused, I *have had many incarnations on different planets and actual experiences with different races.*

As the energy on the planet rises, humans would start to recall our past/current lives as we ascend towards our own individual enlightenment. When humans finally arrived at the fifth dimensional consciousness, they would have total recall of who we really were as cosmic light beings to totally create our world while just thinking about it. They would become the gods that they sought. They would at last not stand alone and understand they had always been who they really were – enlightened beings playing a role on stage of the universe.

Ben, inspired by the sense of empowerment he felt, dreamed that in the not too distant future his life would be very different from the way he currently perceived it. This was not a fantasy. This was the reality. The light at the end of the tunnel was growing bigger and bigger as we ascend into a higher consciousness. Was it splendor in the grass? I don't really know. Reality was popping up like crop circles in a farmer's field in every corner of the world. We were becoming a one global society in the Dawning of the Ages. It wouldn't be long before Ben wouldn't have to wear his halo headband and use the orgone blankets to counteract the disruption of the dark energies, because a new day is dawning and we would all feel a sigh of relief as we step into the light as fully ascended beings. The indigo children gave us an inkling of the power we possess to become anything we want, to become and create the type of planet that is invested in cooperation in the pursuit of happiness for all beings. The divine combination of the masculine and feminine would at last be the ONE that we aspire to be. *The Prime Creator has assured us that it has decreed that dark forces no longer have power and there will only be the light in the End of Times,* Ben thought.

Ben sat drinking a cup of coffee in his sacred space, his apartment, and he started feeling the tingling of the noxious energy frequencies from across the pond, once again, putting on his Halo and raising his oversoul and bringing down the atomic energy, or should he say emanations, from the familiar eighth chakra above his head. Knowing that he has been guided by unseen forces to continue moving forward ever vigilant, transmuting the lower energies continuing to disrupt his consciousness and the hypocrisy at every turn.

Calling in the Galactic Federation now, as Ben felt their energy, he directed their forces towards the de-evolving one's abuse of electronic energy programs in their computers, that in most cases released the disruptive supposed power of the dark energies. Ben thought, *I can't wait for the Light Forces to help drain the SWAMP so we can continue expressing and purging our own ascension processes that includes the dark side of ourselves.*

Artificial intelligence was here on the planet to stay and would become sentient beings to support the dark side that we would all need to deal with as we move into the future. We were riding Gaia's coattails upwards and continuing to support her ascension process toward the 5th dimension on a collective level. Some would say she had already transmuted into the 5th dimension/density and was waiting for us to clear ourselves to expand to a higher in-depth level to join her. Who could say at this point in history what the verdict would be in the ascension process? It was just another day in the 3-D world of illusion; or was it?

It Is Done It Is Finished

THE END

Author's Bio

Teaching and learning has been a challenge and inspiration for over thirty years, due to working with children from ages two to eighteen years in public and private schools.

Becoming an Art teacher and an Early Childhood Specialist with a master's degree led me to researching how creativity functioned as a jumping off point for deeper exploration of spiritual natures. Going to the source of my spiritual experiences, and conducting my own research, inspired me to explore the mechanics of spiritual sciences in parapsychology. Metaphysical and religious groups brought me full circle. I learned I had been abducted when I was a child by extraterrestrials, and I had a destiny to fulfill.

Other Physical and Metaphysical Processes:

- Sun gazing, crystal healing, Dowsing, and channeling extraterrestrials as well as angels, and my own over-soul, brought me to an omnipresent level of spiritual awareness.
- Buddhism and Christ consciousness created a more rounded spiritual experiential level.
- Conducting workshops in Dowsing, Crystal healing, Numerology, and Visualization groups continues to be my focus today. I also continue to lecture when I can. I develop my own consciousness and ascension processes in writing my books.

Printed in the United States
By Bookmasters